MONSTER SQUAD

BOOK 3

SPECTERS

HEATH STALLCUP

Specters

A Monster Squad Novel

Heath Stallcup

MS8 Specters; A Monster Squad Novel

ISBN-13:978-1519223968

ISBN-10:151922396X

ACKNOWLEDGMENTS

There are so many people that I've thanked and tried to recognize since starting this path. The hardest part is getting them all. People like Mark and Tracy, John, Shawn, Armand, Joe…people who I've looked up to and admired for so long who became friends along the way. I've tried to thank them but words simply can't do justice to what I owe them.

There are also those who go above and beyond…Jess, Linda, Sheila, Vix, Steve…so many others who step up and keep me honest. Most of all, the readers. None of this is possible without you. So pat yourself on the back, take a bow and give yourself a big round of applause. Go ahead, you deserve it.

-Heath

DEDICATION

To all of those who think that Halloween is the best holiday out there and that it should be a 'real' holiday…where school is let out and people are let off work. That it should be celebrated as a weeklong event. You know who you are…Holly.

Specters

A Monster Squad Novel

by

Heath Stallcup

1

Mick fought the urge to scream and then his eyes fell on the shackles around his ankles. He almost began laughing as he stared at them. He slipped his shoes off and allowed his body to begin shifting. He watched as his feet elongated and narrowed. The shackles slipped and fell from his legs, clattering onto the floor of the helicopter. He quickly shifted back to human form and slipped his shoes back on. He slid forward and watched the two pilots as they controlled the rotary wing craft.

He wrapped one clawed hand around the throat of the pilot on the right and gripped tightly. "Turn us around! Now!"

"I can't. We have orders." The man struggled against his grip, and Mick ripped a jagged hole in his throat.

He quickly jumped forward and caught the other pilot's hand before he could bring the pistol to bear. "Naughty, naughty, mate. Your chum here didn't want to play nice. How about you?" He twisted the pistol from the other pilot's grip and pressed it to the man's temple. "Let's turn the craft around nice and gentle."

The pilot sneered at him. "Go ahead and kill me. Who would fly this thing?"

Mick smiled back. "I'm a pilot, mate. I only have about thirty hours in a rotary, but I think I could pull it off." He pulled the hammer back on the pistol and pressed the 9MM Beretta to the side of the man's head again. "Your choice."

The pilot cursed and began turning the craft around. "Good choice, mate." Mick dragged the other pilot to the rear of the craft and dumped him over the shackles. Taking his position in the front seat, he pulled on the headphones. "Let's be sure and land this thing far enough away from the hangar that they won't know we're back."

"And then you kill me, right?"

Mick gave him a sideways stare. "Nobody else has to die tonight, mate. Your buddy there? Well, I had to make my point. I knew that saying please wasn't going to work."

*****

Jack flipped the switch on the detonator and the warehouse was nearly leveled by the concussive blow of the C4 exploding in two different directions. The directed blasts had no place else to go but up, destroying much of the ceiling above what was once the office. Each of Jack's crew took shelter behind the heavy concrete columns.

As the shock wave passed, they stepped out and wielded their angelic weapons. They watched in silent fascination as hundreds of demons departed their broken human shells, yellow beams of light shooting upward and into the night sky.

Thorn and Viktor pushed past the debris of the office and began to dig for the remains of the demon queen. She had to be dismembered before she could revive herself.

Samael picked himself from the broken machinery he had been blown into and shook his mighty head, trying to regain his bearings.

"What happened?" He glanced around what was once their safe haven. His eyes fell upon where he knew Lilith was and they shot wide with fear.

"Lilith!" He clambered and fought to free himself from the twisted metal just as the Nephilim appeared before him.

"Demon spawn," the Guardian sneered as he lifted his mighty hammer.

"A Nephilim?" Samael's eyes widened and he lifted his arm to block the crushing blow just as Phil brought the great hammer down. The hammer glanced across Samael's arm and smashed into the metal remains of the machinery.

"I am the son of Rafael, you Fallen abomination!" Phil swung the sword, intending to decapitate the Fallen angel, but Samael fell back into the twisted metal and lifted his free foot. He caught the Nephilim in the midsection and kicked him back and away. Samael pulled himself free and jumped from the metal, his hand pulling up a twisted beam to use as a weapon.

Phil swung both the hammer and the sword as he came back to finish the angel. Samael ducked, blocked and dove, knowing that without an angelic weapon of his own, he had little chance of defending himself from the Halfling for long. He leapt back and took to the sky, his great leathery wings beating rapidly, scooping large pockets of air and lifting him higher. "It will take more than you to defeat me, Nephilim."

A spine-shattering blow knocked the wind from Samael and sent him spiraling to the concrete floor below. He rolled to his side and saw the light-skinned gargoyle flying above him, an angelic sword and shield in his hands. Samael groaned as he rolled to his hands and knees and he felt the blood roll down his back and sides, splattering upon the broken concrete below. He lifted his mighty head and saw the Nephilim charging, hammer and sword pumping as he ran across the once grand warehouse.

Samael reached out and grabbed the broken body of one of his demons and hurled it at the Nephilim. He then leapt to the side and, with a mighty jump, landed in the middle of the wreckage of the office. Both Viktor and Thorn fell back with surprise as the Fallen one landed amidst the rubble.

"She is *mine!*" he growled at the pair as he thrust both hands into the rubble and scooped her broken body from the ruins.

Kalen and Brooke paused in their battles with the demons that survived the blast and watched as the bloody demon creature jumped into the air and with a mighty push of his wings, shot through a broken skylight and into the night air.

Jack looked to Azrael and pointed upward. "Stop him!"

The gargoyle clenched his jaw and made for the skylight himself. He tucked his wings and lowered his weapons to shoot through the jagged opening.

Kalen turned his attention back to the demons. "Kill them all!" He raised his bow and watched as each demon suddenly fell to the ground, a yellow beam of light shooting from the host's body as the demon escaped into the night.

Thorn turned a slow circle staring at the destruction. "*Sacre bleu*, we almost had them."

Viktor placed a reassuring hand on his shoulder. "We live to fight another day."

Thorn shrugged his hand away. "Do we? We will never have another chance such as this." He kicked at a piece of the rubble and stormed from the remains of the office.

Jack motioned for his people to converge on him. "There's still a chance that Azrael will catch them."

Phil shook his head. "He cannot stop the Fallen abomination." He hung his head. "Even with the weapons he has, he does not have the power to stop him."

"He put a hurt on him," Jack added. "If it can bleed, it can die."

"True. But it can also heal."

*****

Laura squirmed as her father stared at her. "Spill it, Punkin. I want to know everything."

"I think I pretty much told you everything." She picked at her fingernails as she chewed at her lower lip.

"I don't think you did. You mentioned that monsters were real. You said that you were dating a vampire. But you said nothing about the men you're working with actually being infected with this stuff like I am."

"Well, how else did you think I'd know it was safe?" She shrugged as if he should have simply connected the dots.

Jim inhaled deeply and sighed. "Tell me, how many are there?"

"Enough to do the job. Dad, I'm not really supposed to talk about it."

"Just like I'm sure you aren't supposed to smuggle that stuff out and shoot me up with it, yet, here we are." He narrowed his stare and watched her squirm.

"Daddy, really…it's classified, and I could get into a lot of trouble for just mentioning them."

Jim nodded. "Fine, I can understand that, I suppose." He pursed his lips as a multitude of thoughts ran through his mind. "Can you at least tell me *why* they volunteered for this?"

She nodded. "To better fight the real monsters out there. So that they could keep up."

"In order to fight the monsters, they had to *become* a monster? Fight fire with fire."

"In a manner of speaking."

"And that's why you were so…adamant about me knowing the rules you expect me to live by? Because if I don't live by those rules…"

She nodded, tears starting to form in her eyes. "Then they would definitely come and hunt you down."

"And then somebody would put two and two together and realize what you did."

She shook her head and finally met his gaze, her tears falling freely. "I don't care if they find out. Hell, I'll probably end up spilling my guts as soon as I get back anyway. I just don't want anything to happen to you. If it did it would be..." Her voice cracked and she trailed off, burying her face.

"What?"

She lifted her face and wiped the tears from her cheeks. "It would be *my* fault. They would hunt you down and they would kill you and it would be my fault. Don't you see?"

Jim shook his head. "No, Punk, I don't. It isn't your fault if I do something I shouldn't. It's called personal responsibility." He pulled her tight and squeezed her. "I know I taught you better than that."

"I'm sorry, Daddy. I should have told you everything." She sniffed as he stroked her arm.

"You told me enough, Punk." Jim stared off into nothingness.

"What's wrong, Daddy?" Laura pulled back slightly and stared at him. "I know when you're not telling me something."

Jim inhaled sharply and let the breath out slowly. He leaned over and picked up something that she couldn't quite make out. He lifted it in the low light and held it out to her. She wrapped her hand around it and recognition hit her like a truck. It was the vial that held the wolf virus she had infected him with. It was empty.

She pulled back and stared at him with shock. "Daddy? What did you do with the rest of it?"

*****

"You got a death wish I don't know about?"

Spalding chuckled. "Buddy, that sounds like simunition to me. They aren't putting any holes in that plywood."

Sullivan's brows knitted and he took a quick glance. "Good eye, boss. I've been listening to them run drills all this time and wishing they'd run out." He checked the safety on his rifle and nodded. "Let's do this."

Spalding keyed his coms, "We're heading for the mockup. Advance and engage. Delta Three and Four, you have the bingo."

The pair scooted across the stack of crates and came to the rear of the mockup. Spalding glanced down the length of the warehouse and could just make out Delta Two and Delta Five making their way down the length of the structure. Sullivan pushed through the flimsy back door and brought his rifle to his shoulder. Spalding slipped in behind him and followed suit.

The pair worked their way from the back to the front, taking turns spitting suppressed rounds through their rifles, watching as wolves reacted violently to the silver jacketed rounds. As they worked their way closer to the front, they waited for the next wave to enter. "Anybody got eyes on the mockup?"

"You may come out now. We have your people," a heavily accented voice spoke directly in his ear.

Spalding froze and glanced at Little John who visibly stiffened. John tightened his grip on his rifle and took a half step forward, but Spalding reached out and grabbed the man by his massive bicep. "Don't." Little John glanced back the way they had come and Spalding shook his head. He keyed his coms. "To whom am I speaking?"

"Chief Warrant Officer Martinez. We have your people. You may come out now or they will die." Spalding slowly lowered his rifle and sighed.

"You ain't giving up, are you?"

"The only way he can come across our coms is if he has one of our guys." He looked up at the low ceiling and shook his head. "And they probably have a signal blocker in place or Major Tufo would be screaming in our ears right now."

"You have five seconds."

Spalding keyed his coms. "Okay. We're coming out."

John grabbed his arm and shook his head. "We don't surrender."

"We're blind in here, and they have our people. As long as we're breathing, we have a fighting chance."

Spalding stepped to the front of the mockup and pushed open the door. He was greeted with multiple rifle barrels in the face.

*****

Director Jameson waited for Ingram to pick up the phone. He wasn't surprised that the man's voice wasn't groggy when he answered. "What is it?"

"You were right. I'm watching a video of someone rifling through my office now."

"Is it him?"

Jameson sighed into the phone. "I can't be certain. I want to say yes." He paused the video and stared at the low-light image. Whoever it was had a penlight in their mouth that cast them into silhouette. Even when they got on his computer, the screen blocked his face from view. "I just can't tell."

"I would say it's safe to assume it's him."

"As would I. The question is, what are his intentions?"

"Only he can tell you that." Ingram shifted the phone and he jotted a few notes. "Do you want me to send a team to pick him up?"

Jameson considered it for a moment. "No. Let me handle him. If he has the balls to break into my office then I may have misjudged him." He leaned back and stared at the assuredness of the man in his office. "He may well be the man for the job."

"How do you want to play him? Let him in on the plan or keep dropping crumbs and see if he goes running to them?"

Jameson pinched the bridge of his nose and shook his head.

8

"I'm not sure. I want to test him a bit more first."

"Did he get anything?"

Jameson chuckled into the phone. "There's nothing *to* get. All of my files are hard-copied and locked tight in my safe. Without my palm print, retina scan and the combination, nobody is getting into it. You should have seen his reaction when he realized that."

"Are you absolutely sure? The little shit can be pretty creative."

"Oh, I'm sure." Jameson closed the video file and closed the lid on his computer. "There's nothing out there for anybody to tie us to the program except what we tell them."

"You'd better be right. We're not just talking about a slap on the wrist here." Ingram shifted the phone again and Jameson got the paranoid thought that perhaps he was recording the conversation. "They could put us both away for a very long time."

"Oh, I'm very aware of the ramifications." He sat back in his chair and spun it to stare out his home office window. "When will they be ready for a field trial?"

"Very soon. They're finishing the medical tests now." Ingram's voice dropped to a near whisper. "You won't believe what these guys can do."

"They'd better be good. These monster hunters aren't to be trifled with."

"Oh, they're good. Good enough to get the job done." Ingram chuckled into the phone. "And for the amount of money we're being paid, they'll do everything we promised and then some."

"If the Council finds out we intend to double-cross them after all of the monsters have been eradicated…they'll send somebody after us."

"That's why we save them for last. There won't be anybody *left* for them to send after us." Ingram laughed as he hung up the phone.

*****

Mitchell stuck his head into the secondary command center and saw it aflutter with activity. "Get me those goddamn coms back now!" Major Tufo was practically standing in the command chair, barking orders.

"Problem?" Matt pulled the door shut behind him.

"They went dark as soon as they entered the damned warehouse. We can't see, we can't hear, we can't…" He blew his breath out hard and turned an evil stare toward the communications tech. "I'm told we're being jammed. We can't even get a good heat signature from all of the activity in the building."

"The drones have been rerouted. They're on their way back. Maybe you can direct them to do a flyby? Buzz the building and get you a microwave—"

"I need something *now*." Mark sat back in his chair and ground his teeth, his eyes scanning the satellite view of the building. He turned to Matt and quickly came up out of his chair. "I have an idea. It's a crazy one, but it's all I have."

"Hit me with it."

Mark pulled him aside and lowered his voice to a whisper. "Take command here. Let me go there and see what I can—"

"Negative!" Mitchell's brows knitted together as he stared the man down. "You're the XO, not an operator."

"It wasn't that long ago I was in the field with Jack's team and held my own…without being augmented. Now I'm…" He shrugged. "I heal faster than the men do."

Mitchell was still shaking his head. "Negative. It ain't happening."

"Matt, Doc can't tell us what exactly I am, but I'm faster, stronger, and heal quicker than anything we have. And I'm not looking to engage. I just want to see what the hell is up. If all is clear, I back off. If it's not, I give the men a diversion. That's all."

Mitchell was still shaking his head. "I don't like the idea at all. You're the Executive Officer. If anything happened to you…"

"It won't." His eyes widened. "I'll take numbnuts with me."

Mitchell turned on him, his face questioning. "Who the hell is numbnuts?"

"McKenzie. Dom sidelined him. He's still qualified. He's the only operator we have on site. I'll drag his sorry ass with me. He can report directly back to you and tell on me if I step out of line."

Mitchell glanced at the boards and then back at Mark. "Reconnoiter. That's all."

"That's all." Mark nodded.

"Go." He slapped the man on the back. Mitchell squared his shoulders and announced, "I have the command center."

Mark pulled his two-way and called the duty officer. "Get McKenzie suited up and tell him to get his ass topside. Now."

Mitchell watched the man leave, the door pulling shut behind him. He offered up a silent prayer not only for his XO, but for himself should anything happen to him.

*****

"Your people will need you." The Wyldwood walked with the griffin through the wide rocky passageways.

"They are not my people." Allister enjoyed correcting her. "I am doing this as a favor to you. And to enact revenge."

"Regardless of your motivation, they are your people now. They will be looking to you for guidance, direction…insight."

Allister paused, his mighty head turning to face her. "Insight? From me? What are they looking for? How to be turned into a mythical creature and lose everything you ever held dear?"

Loren's mouth pulled into a tight line below her hood. "They need your knowledge and wisdom, my friend. Not your self-loathing."

"My loathing is not for self. I loathe the she-witch that did this to me. I have spent thousands of years hidden. Locked away lest I be hunted and killed by man, monster, or beast." He growled low in his throat then turned to continue walking. "The depths of my loathing cannot be fathomed by the likes of you."

She watched the massive being walk gracefully through the fallen piles of rock and contemplated his words. How difficult had it been for him since his transformation? He had chosen not to interact with any other griffins until the race died out. As far as she knew, he was the last. Had he embraced his fate, who knows what he could have accomplished.

Having once been the crown prince of a great and powerful nation, he had the misfortune of running afoul of the demon queen. Her beauty beguiled him and he tried his best to woo her with promises of riches and a nation to rule. He couldn't possibly have understood her true desires, or where her heart lay.

He blamed Lilith for his transformation, but to Loren's knowledge, witchcraft was beyond her ability. She feared that the true source of his curse came from another; one whose ability came from a much darker source. Loren opened her mouth to say as much but quickly thought better of it. Regardless of her suspicions, he wouldn't be easily swayed. After spending multiple thousands of years blaming someone, she doubted that she could sway him.

Allister stopped near a large boulder and sat down. "This is the one."

Loren walked past the griffin and began to open a portal. Once the portal was stabilized she stepped aside. Allister stood and stepped forward. He glanced through the portal then turned back to her. "This isn't the Anywhere."

"No. This leads to your people. The large building you see is where they call home for now."

Allister sat back down and gave her a menacing glare. "I will not reside in the world of men."

She sighed heavily and stepped toward him. "You must. They reside in the world of men. Your people need you."

He shook his mighty head and ruffled the feathers on his wings. "I've not had good luck with...*man*. They tend to be...unreasonable."

"Their leader is a man." She gave him a soft smile and stroked his mighty shoulder. "He is reasonable."

"I thought you said he was a wolf?" Allister gave her a distrusting stare.

"He is. He is also a man." She urged him through the portal. "If I came with you?" She watched him stiffen, and then shake his head.

"I need no woman to escort me." He stepped forward slightly then turned back. "But if I end up dead, I will not be happy with you."

"You will not. Approach them slowly and state your intentions."

"My intentions?" he grunted. "My intentions are to kill Lilith. But something tells me that they will not care."

Allister stared at the building as he slowly walked through the portal. His clawed feet crunched on the gravel as he stepped into the world of man. He walked slowly toward the arched building ahead of him when he heard a low growl and the sound of something digging in the loose gravel. He saw two red lights as it departed and left in a hurry. "A horseless carriage, I presume."

"Actually, it's called a Humvee."

Allister turned his mighty head to see a man slowly approaching him, something in his hands pointed at him. "And you are?"

"Sentry. State your business...sir?"

Allister did his best to appear less menacing. "Mr. Sentry, my name is Allister. I have been sent by the Wyldwood to assist your people. I am supposed to ask for Chief Jack."

The sentry slowed his approach and stared at the large winged creature. "You're kidding, right?"

"I do not kid, Mr. Sentry. If you could show me where to find this Chief Jack, I would be in your debt." He tried to smile, but found it nearly impossible with a beak.

The sentry watched the creature for a moment then lowered his rifle. "Call me nuts but that story is too crazy not to be true." He shrugged and waved the griffin forward. "Follow me, sir. I'll show you the way." Allister fell into step behind him as the two approached the hangar. The sentry pulled a black box from his belt and spoke into it. "Duty Officer, this is Sergeant Davis. I have a…a…well, a *visitor* here to see Chief Thompson."

Allister's eyes widened when the box spoke back. "Escort to the west entrance and hold for clearance."

"Copy that." He gave the griffin a quick smile. "This way."

"The box gives you permission to act?"

The sentry gave him a questioning glance. "You mean the radio? I had to call the duty officer to alert them to your presence. Otherwise they might treat you as a hostile."

"A hostile what?"

"A hostile…uh…person?" He shrugged. "Just trust me, it's in both of our best interest if I get permission first."

"Curiouser and curiouser."

*****

Dom finished writing his field notes and leaned back against the tree. He glanced to the east and nodded. "Sun will be up shortly. Shouldn't your people be heading out?"

Reginald looked to the horizon and sighed. "You're right. I can feel it. But no, we don't have time to get back to the structure we stayed at yesterday. We'll have to go to ground again."

"Again?"

"Yes. During our exodus, we have had to go to ground many times. We've actually become used to it." He bent and scooped up a handful of the rich, dark earth. "There's something energizing about being so close to the ground. I wish I knew the tie."

14

Dom reflected back to the Sicarii and the soil from his homeland. "I think I understand." He shuddered slightly and turned away. "There's no putting it into words. It's just a…feeling."

"Yes." Reginald dropped the soil and gave Dom a curious stare. "You speak as though you have firsthand knowledge. Did you know a vampire who preferred going to ground?"

Dom shook his head. "Not exactly." He cleared his throat nervously. "The Sicarii…he used to keep a box full of dirt from his homeland. Just having it close increased his power."

Reginald nodded knowingly. "You wouldn't think that a vampire that powerful would need a tie like that."

"You wouldn't think, wouldja. But if there's one thing I've learned, when it comes to power, it doesn't matter if you're a vampire, human or…whatever. Once you get power hungry, you'll fight tooth and nail for every ounce you can get."

"True enough." Reginald's voice wavered for a moment as he considered the ramifications of Dom's words. He stiffened slightly and redirected his attention to the man. "Is there anything else we can help you with?"

Dom checked his notes then shook his head. "I think I have everything I need. If anything new comes up, we'll get in contact."

"Very well. Thank you. Sincerely…thank you." Reginald offered his hand and Dom hesitated for the slightest moment before taking it.

"Sorry, it's not every mission I end up shaking hands with the person I was sent to kill."

"Understood." Reginald gave a slight bow and turned back to his people. "To ground. Before the sun rises."

Dom watched them walk into the woods and disappear into the shadows. Marshall slipped in next to him and muttered, "Do you get the uneasy feeling we're going to regret letting them leave?"

Dom continued to watch the woods for a moment then shook his head. "Not this time I don't."

Heath Stallcup

2

Mitchell sat in the command chair and manually switched from one feed to another. He wished that whatever was blocking their coms would stop interfering. He knew that it had to be a signal jammer from within the abandoned warehouse. Nothing else made sense. "Is there a way to override that jammer from here?"

"Negative, sir. It's locally controlled, and whatever it is, it's essentially put a bubble around that building."

Mitchell sighed heavily and leaned back in the chair. He checked his watch again and wished that Mark would hurry and get his ass on scene. He knew it was just across town, but it was still far enough away to make it nearly a half hour drive. Even in the wee hours, without traffic, the best he could hope for was to shave a few minutes from the arrival time.

"ETA on the drones?"

"At least another half hour, sir, and they won't have fuel to stay on site for very long."

Mitchell leaned forward and glared. "Well then I guess it's a good goddamn thing that we're so close, isn't it?"

The drone pilot gave him a stunned look and simply nodded. "Yes, sir."

Mitchell groaned and ran a hand through his close cropped hair. "Sorry about that, son. I'm just a bit on edge here."

"Understood, sir."

The communications tech turned with a smile. "Sir, Captain Jones has reported that they've increased speed to return home. They have the first drone. We did use about a third of its munitions, but it will available sooner."

"Well it's about time something went our way. Tell Jericho to get that bird in the air as soon as he can and take up a high helical orbit. I want eyes and ears on that facility."

"Roger that, sir."

Mitchell glanced at this watch again and cursed under his breath. "Where are you, Mark?"

*****

Jack watched as Azrael fell back through the skylight and landed deftly next to him. "I couldn't catch him. He is much faster than he appears." He shook his head and his shoulders slumped. "I'm sorry, Chief Jack."

"You did your best. That's all anybody can ask."

"Be grateful you didn't catch him, gargoyle. He would have killed you," the Guardian spoke softly, but his voice expressed his belief.

Azrael stiffened slightly and cocked his head. "Do not be so quick to discount—"

"He is an angel, my large friend," the Guardian they all called Phil interrupted. "I mean no disrespect to you. I only speak truly."

"It's going to be daylight soon. We need to wrap this up and get my team back home." Jack cut them both off. He turned to Viktor.

18

"Are you coming back to the base with us?"

Viktor looked to Thorn who gave him a surprised look. "I think…" he paused and turned to Foster who shook his head slightly. "I think that we shall retire to the island. I have much planning to do in order to coordinate our next attack against Lilith."

"As do we." Jack approached him slowly. "The Wyldwood assembled this team for the express purpose of defeating her and sending her back to hell." He lowered his voice and turned away from the others, "If you're serious about fighting her, then come with us. Help us come up with a proper plan of attack."

Thorn inhaled deeply and squared his shoulders. "And what of your intent to enact revenge for my supposed betrayal?"

Jack lowered his eyes and shook his head. "You know, it wasn't that long ago that if you were this close, I'd have just ripped your damned head off and been done with it." He raised his eyes and met Thorn's gaze. "But I've come to realize that everybody makes mistakes. Even you. That doesn't mean I have to like it. It doesn't mean I have to accept it. And it damn sure doesn't mean I have to come back to work for you."

Thorn nodded slowly. "But…"

"But it does mean that I realize that even good people can screw up once in a while. Especially if they think they're doing it for the right reasons."

Thorn gave a crooked smile. "I won't hope for forgiveness. I will accept *understanding*."

"Good. Because you aren't getting the other." He turned and motioned to Kalen. "Find us a portal out of here. I'm ready to go home." He turned to Rufus. "You can come with us and help us figure out a way to kick this bitch's ass, or you can go and do your own thing. The choice is yours."

*****

"Answer me, Dad. What did you do with the rest of it?" Laura shook the empty vial at him. "You didn't inject Crystal with it, did you?" Her face paled at the very thought.

Jim shook his head. "No, Punkin. I can't believe you'd even think such a thing."

"What am I supposed to think? I find this thing empty and…" She stared at him and her eyes shot wider. "You didn't…"

He nodded slightly. "I thought if a little would help, then more…" He gave her a sheepish grin.

"Oh no!" She fumbled in her bag and dug out her cell phone. "I can't believe you'd do that." She flipped open her phone and began punching through her call list.

"What are you doing, Punk?" He reached for her phone and she jerked it clear of his grasp.

"I have to call Evan. I need to know what that can do to you." She found his number and punched the call button.

"Like hell!" Jim snatched the phone and pushed the top closed, hanging up mid-call. "It's none of his business."

"Daddy, you don't understand. He told me to give you a specific dose. No more than 15CCs per dose. You took the *whole* vial. I need to know what sort of side effects that could have."

He held the phone away from her when it vibrated in his hand. He stared at the device and threw it against the wall. It simply bounced away and clattered to the floor. Laura gave him a smug smile and bent to retrieve it. "It's a ruggedized military-grade cell phone, Dad. You could run it over with a Humvee and it would be fine." She flipped it open and saw a missed call from Evan.

"Don't do it, Punk. I'm telling you, I'm fine." He glared at her as he spoke.

"You aren't acting fine." She punched the redial button and stepped away from him. "Besides, if you're lucky, there won't be any side effects. But if there are, we need to know what they are."

"Laura?" Evan's voice sounded tinny over the tiny speaker.

"Evan, sweetie, I need to ask you something."

"Okay. Is something wrong?"

"No, no, nothing's wrong. I mean…maybe not." She bit at her lower lip then blurted out the question. "What would happen if I accidentally gave him too much?"

"Too much? Like, how much too much? If you mean just a few CCs then not much. There's always a margin of error in—"

"No, Evan. Like, if he got hold of the red vial and took the whole thing?"

"Oh no…"

*****

Mark was out the door of the Humvee before McKenzie rolled to a stop. He hit the ground at a trot and brought his carbine up to his eye, both eyes scanning the darkness. It still surprised him that he was able to so easily adjust to near total darkness without the aid of night vision. He paused and held a fist in the air, halting Mac mid-step.

Without turning he keyed his coms and whispered, "There are sentries at the gate."

"Then we go around." Mac began to advance again, cutting to the left when Mark held him.

"They've got guards at each side of the compound."

"How the hell can you know that?" Mac shot him a questioning glare.

"I can smell them." Mark advanced slowly, his body sinking into the grass until Mac couldn't tell where he went. With a silent curse he tried to follow the Marine's movements. Mark popped up next to a thicket and held a casing up. "They staged here."

Mac slipped in behind a large oak tree and hugged the trunk. "Do we take out the sentries?"

"Negative." He brought a pair of field glasses to his eyes and studied the western fence. "There's only one on the western side. One on the roof. If we remove them at the same time, we should have at least a few moments."

Mitchell's voice cut through his earpiece, "For recon."

Mark sighed and nodded. "Copy that, OPCOM. Recon only." He switched off his coms and looked to Mac. "Unless we find out our people are neck deep. Then all bets are off."

"Copy that." Mac shot him an evil grin. "Westward ho."

The two branched to the left and eased up on the clearing facing the western fence. Mark motioned to Mac to take the guard on the roof while he took out the fence patrol. He held up three fingers and the two operators counted down.

Almost simultaneously, both carbines belched silver plated death through suppressed barrels, their receiver actions making more noise than the bullets. The two commandos slid into the fence and Mark grabbed the bottom of the chain link fabric ripping it from its ground anchors, allowing Mac to roll under. Mac propped the fabric with his knees while Mark slid under and the two made for the nearest lit building.

As Mac came to rest alongside the building he keyed his coms. "OPCOM, signal check." He waited only a moment before looking to his XO. He shook his head and stepped to the side of the door, stacking along the north side of the entrance. "Should we switch to First Squad's frequency?"

"Already have. It's silent." Mark nodded toward the door and Mac pulled it open slightly, checking for booby traps. Convinced it was clear, he pulled it open further and the two men slid along the shadows. At the far end of the warehouse they could see a plywood mockup of some kind with a small crowd of men surrounding the north side. "Looks like we're late for a party." He motioned Mac along the southern wall, behind crates of equipment and supplies.

The two worked their way closer, pausing only long enough to try to make out what held the rapt attention of the crowd. Mac grabbed Mark's arm and pulled him back behind a crate. "They have them."

"Who did you see?"

"Spanky and John. There was somebody else, but there's too many of them between us. I couldn't see who."

Mark nodded. "They have at least three. That doesn't mean they have them all. Eyes and ears open for any they may have missed."

Mac was about to acknowledge when something fell onto his head. He swiped at it and looked upward into the rafters of the building. Lamb gave a subtle wave from the shadows. He pointed further down, and Jacobs gave a mock salute. "I think that answers your question, Major."

Mark pointed to his ear bud and Lamb shook his head. He pointed to the group below. Mark nodded and held up two fingers. *Go to alternate frequency.*

Lamb adjusted his radio and Mark's earpiece buzzed. "Delta Three and Four standing by for orders, Major."

"What's their strength, Three?"

"I'm counting nineteen, sir. Most are armed."

"Flashbangs?" Mark shrugged.

Lamb nodded. "As soon as you're in position, sir."

"You heard the man." Mark patted Mac's shoulder. "Take up position behind those crates. We'll catch them in a crossfire." He watched as Mac worked his way further down and got set up. Mark took a deep breath and prayed that he wasn't about to get his men killed.

*****

"Son of a bitch!" Bigby kicked a chair over in his office before shoving the laptop into its bag. He began throwing his papers into a satchel and rapidly going through the drawers of the desk that he called his to ensure anything that could be used against him wasn't there when the shit hit the fan.

"What are you doing?" Martinez stared at him as he hurriedly threw things into a duffel.

"I'm getting the fuck out of here." He jabbed a finger at the man. "You'd be wise to do the same, mate."

"Why? We have them. Don't you see? We can order them to send us Ms. Simmons in trade. We can ensure her safety, and they'll never know that we were about to attack."

"Are you daft?" Bigby tossed the computer bag and satchel into the duffel and zipped it tight. "Those blokes aren't exactly stupid. I'd bet your left nut that others are already on their way." He glanced through the window of the office leading to the back of the facility. "If they're not already here."

"Don't be absurd." Martinez leaned against the counter and chuckled at him. "We have their communications blocked. They can neither send nor receive any—"

"And what would you assume if you lost coms with your team in the field, eh?" Bigby tossed the duffle over his shoulder and made for the window. "I can't believe you're a warrant officer and you're that stupid."

He fought with the painted over lock and pulled his knife to pry the latch. "I'm getting the fuck out of here now."

"I knew you were a coward." The venom in Martinez' voice was unmistakable.

Bigby paused and turned, the knife glistening in the low lit room. "I'm many things, mate. But a coward isn't one of them." He pointed out the door with the tantō blade. "You have no idea what you've done out there, do you? Each of those men are worth twenty of yours. And how many do you have left?"

Martinez squared his shoulders. "I'll show you what they're worth. I only need one of them alive to trade for Senorita Simmons."

"Ha. I hate to break it to ya, mate, but she's mated now. I believe she's Señora Mitchell, yeah?" He turned back and jammed the knife blade into the frame of the window.

"I do not care who she is mated to. I only care that she is unharmed." He turned and threw open the door then turned back to Bigby as he fought with the stuck window. "You can run like a woman. I will deliver Mister Simmons his daughter. And I will be sure to tell him of your behavior this night when we were on the verge of our victory."

The window thrust open, and Bigby grunted a sigh of relief. "You do that, mate. I'll send someone to slice onions at your funeral so that folks will cry." He gave him a sarcastic wink before hefting his duffle up and out.

Martinez stepped out into the crowd and lifted his hand to get their attention. "We only need one of them alive to trade for Miss Jennifer. Choose the ones to die."

*****

Brooke stepped through the portal and sighed with relief. The sun wasn't up yet. She didn't know why, but she felt like they had been gone for days rather than hours. She practically dragged her feet as the group trudged back to the hangar. A familiar scent wafted near and she knew he was close before he spoke.

"I'm going to see if I can run the shower out of hot water. How about you?" Kalen gave her his best brilliant smile.

Brooke smiled back out of habit. She couldn't help herself. The white haired, golden skinned fellow was starting to grow on her. She chuckled to herself as she thought, *like athlete's foot*. She shook her head. "I think I'm just going to collapse in bed and sleep the day away."

"An excellent idea." Azrael strode past her, his long legs carrying him further with each step. Kalen noted Gnat riding the gargoyles shoulder, his eyelids heavy.

"So, um, you want to get something to eat before..." Kalen

paused realizing his *faux paus*. "I mean…" he sighed. "I'm sorry. I just thought maybe…"

She held him back by his arm and gave him a soft smile. "It's okay. I know what you meant." She glanced ahead to Chief Jack and the others, ensuring they were out of hearing distance. "I meant what I said before, Kalen, we can't pursue this."

"And I meant what I said. I fully intend to." He gave her a crooked grin and a shrug. "I can't help myself."

Her brows knitted together with frustration. "Why, Kalen? Why can't you just drop it?"

"Have you ever had anybody enter your dreams before? I haven't. And yes, I admit it frightened me at first. But once I realized it was a first for you as well, I knew it meant something."

"Yes, it was a warning. It was telling us to stay away." She pushed away from him and began marching toward the hangar with renewed vigor.

"Wait, Brooke."

"Raven!" She spun on him, her finger in his face.

Kalen slid to a stop and stared at her wide-eyed. Her anger shocked him, but his reaction shocked them both even more. Without realizing what he was doing, he reached up and took her hand, pulled it to his face and kissed the tip of her finger.

Brooke stepped back, her mouth hanging open as she stared at him. He held her hand gently and slowly kissed her fingertip once more, his eyes probing hers as he did so. He smiled to himself as her fangs descended as though spring loaded.

She pulled her hand away and covered her mouth, her eyes wide. "Just stay away, Kalen. I mean it!" She turned and ran toward the hangar as fast as she could without raising too much suspicion.

Kalen watched her, his breath caught in his throat.

*****

Samael touched down on a wooded mountain top, the boulders and outcroppings acting as a wind block as he laid his queen on the ground. His great arms shook as he took in the extent of damage her body had taken.

She lolled like a ragdoll as he stepped back and checked for signs of life. He knew she must still live or he would not be on this plane of existence. He watched her chest rise and fall as she took a shallow breath. "Glory be," he whispered.

Samael summoned what little strength he had left and ran his hands over her broken body. He concentrated on her broken bones and internal injuries, the green glow lighting the early morning like a neon sign. "Please come back to me."

"She will live."

He spun and stared at his brother standing above him on the rock outcropping. "Why are you here, Azazel?"

"Why do you think?" He squatted upon the rock and cocked his head to the side, studying his brother clothed in dead flesh. "Michael has sent me yet again."

Samael grunted and waved him away. "I'll not hear any more of his prophetic proselytizing."

Azazel laughed and sat upon the rock, his feet swinging below him. "He's not trying to convert you, brother. He simply wants you to see what will be." He stared down at the broken body of Lilith and noted the drying blood across Samael's back. "You both are a mess." He hopped from the rock and slapped his hand to Samael's back, eliciting a hiss from him as his hand emitted a bright green glow.

"What are you doing?" His voice was a low, deep growl.

"What do you think? I'm healing you. You don't have the strength to heal yourself much less your wench." He pulled his hand back and placed it upon Lilith's forehead. Her entire body began to glow a bright emerald green as Samael staggered to his feet.

"Do not call her that." He steadied himself against the rock that

Azazel had appeared upon. "She is…more."

"I'm fully aware of what she is, brother." He stood and studied his handiwork. "As I said, she'll live."

"Does Michael expect me to bow and scrape to him now?"

Azazel sighed and leaned against another boulder. "Your hatred has closed your heart and your mind, brother."

"I refuse to believe that all we have worked for is for naught." He leaned back and screamed to the heavens. "You'll not stop me, Michael! She shall reign over this speck of dust as queen!"

Azazel shook his head and drug a sandaled foot through the dust and pine needles. "Are you finished?" He pushed off the boulder and walked past Samael. "Michael wanted you to know that the ass whooping you took earlier is just the first step. Very soon the hunters will be joined by one who hates Lilith more than you care for her."

"Impossible."

Azazel turned and gave him sad eyes. "You don't remember all of the evil the two of you did before, do you?"

"I remember every glorious moment," Samael stated proudly. He thrust out his chin defiantly. "I wouldn't change a single thing about what we did." He averted his eyes then hung his head. "Except…maybe…the end."

Azazel sighed. "Remember one named Allister? You cursed him at her behest."

Samael's brows knitted in thought. "No, the name escapes me."

"The two of you never escaped his thoughts. He's spent millennia planning revenge. And now he's about to join forces with the hunters." Azazel placed a comforting hand on his brother's shoulder. "If you truly care for her, depart from this plane, never return. Allow her to rule some other planet…some other dimension. Never return here, Samael. It brings only death, destruction and heartache."

Samael pushed his hand off and stepped back. "Tell Michael I won't be swayed. We follow through with our plans. She *will* rule this world."

Azazel shrugged and loosed a heavy sigh. "You were warned, brother." He stepped away and shook his head. "More than once. There's nothing else I can do."

Samael opened his mouth to utter a string of epithets when Azazel disappeared in a green beam of light. He stepped forward to where he once stood and felt the ozone in the air. He turned his head to the heavens once more and narrowed his gaze. "We won't be deterred."

*****

"Bob, Director Jameson wants to see you." The intern dropped a stack of folders on his desk and Bob looked up to watch the man walk away.

"That's Agent Stevens to you," he muttered under his breath as he collected his briefcase and shut down his computer. He glanced at his watch and knew that the director couldn't have been in the office more than a few minutes. He had surely discovered that his office was left open. Had he somehow known that it was him? No…security would have come for him. Did he want Bob to try to discover what the intruder wanted? He found it difficult to put away the things on his desk as his hands began to shake.

Bob stood and looked about the small cubical. He knew he was supposed to go out in the field with the NSA group that afternoon, but to be called to the director's office so early? It had to be tied to the break in. He silently cursed himself for leaving the door unlocked. How stupid could he have been to be so blatant?

He stepped off the elevator and nearly tripped over his shadow as he made his way to the corner office. The receptionist barely glanced up to see him before buzzing him in. "He's waiting for you."

"Th-thank you." Bob cleared his throat, silently kicking himself for allowing his voice to crack to someone as unimportant as the receptionist. He pushed the door open and stepped inside.

Closing the door behind him, he walked to the director's desk and stood in front, waiting to be acknowledged. The director was reading something in a file and didn't look up. "Have a seat, Stevens."

"Thank you, sir." Bob quickly sat and found that his hands were trying to outdo each other in fidgeting.

Eventually, Director Jameson dropped the file on his desk and stared at him. "Do you know why I called you up here?"

"I assume it's because I'm going out with the NSA group this afternoon, sir."

Jameson leaned back in his chair, his eyes probing the smaller man. "Try again."

"Uhh…was something missing from my report, sir?" Bob shook his head, doing his best to act confused.

"Nope. Strike two."

"Strike…uh…I'm not following you, sir." Bob gave a sheepish grin. "Is there something specific you wanted?"

"I'm going to ask you one more time. Do you know why I called you up here?" Jameson leveled his gaze on the man and expected him to crack at any moment.

Bob swallowed hard and shook his head. "No, sir, I don't."

Jameson rocked back and forth slightly, waiting for Bob to blurt out something, *anything* that verified his culpability. The room was completely silent as Director Jameson continued to stare at him. Bob sat silently, waiting for the man to speak again.

Jameson inhaled deeply and leaned forward. "Stevens, somebody broke into my office last night."

"Oh my…I hadn't heard." He found himself having difficulty breathing.

"Whoever it was went through my desk, tried to access my wall safe, and went through my computer."

Bob nodded. "I see. And you...what? Do you want me to see if they got anything from your computer, sir?"

Jameson shook his head. "No. There's nothing on my computer for anybody to get." He nodded toward the wall. "Anything of any use would be in my safe."

Bob glanced in the direction he indicated and nodded. "I see." He swallowed hard. "So...if they didn't get anything of value, why did you want to see me, sir?"

Jameson cracked a slight smile. "Well, Stevens, *whoever* it was that broke in here, didn't realize that I have a camera hidden in my office that is set to a motion sensor. After I leave and shut down my computer, if anybody enters the office, it sets off that camera."

Bob nodded, instantly sweating in places he shouldn't. "Okay..."

"The only problem is, whoever it was...I can't see his face."

"And you want me to clean up the video so you can?"

Jameson leaned back and shook his head. "No, I have people who can do that for me." He pulled a file from his desk and tossed it across to him. "Those are stills pulled from the video. I have a pretty good idea who it is."

Bob nodded slowly as he reached for the folder. "And, uh...who is that, sir?"

"You tell me." He smiled and Bob noted that his eyes appeared cold as he did it.

He opened the folder and picked through the images. They were dark and fuzzy, the person impossible to identify. "I can't tell who it is, sir."

"You can't?"

Bob shook his head. "No, sir." He handed the folder back and set it gently on his desk.

"Well, that's okay. I have some of the best visual guys in the business working on it. I should have an answer sometime today."

Bob gave him a weak smile. "Excellent, sir." Jameson continued to stare at him and Bob felt an uncomfortable awkwardness. "Is there anything else, sir?"

"Yes, Stevens. Get out of my office." Jameson spun in his chair and propped his feet on the corner of his desk. "Don't you have a surveillance team to report to?"

"Yes, sir." Bob stood up so suddenly that he threatened to knock over his chair. He turned quickly and exited, pulling the door shut behind him, breaking into a cold sweat as he made his way to the elevator.

Jameson watched him walk past the receptionist then picked up his phone. He dialed the number and waited for Ingram to answer. "The trap is set. Let's see if he trips it."

"What did you do?"

"I showed him some stills pulled from the video. Poor guy was about to shit his pants," Jameson chuckled. "I'll give him props though. He never broke. Never even broke into a sweat. He just kept playing dumb."

Ingram grunted on the phone. "I guess we'll see what he does next."

"I'll lay five-to-one odds what he does."

"No thank you. When you start laying odds, that usually means you know more than you're telling. But I do want to ask you…what if you're wrong? What if it wasn't him that broke into your office?"

Jameson pulled the file closer and looked at the person in the blurry image. "Oh, it was him."

"How can you be so sure?"

"Because it just so happens that he and I had a little heart to heart that very afternoon about something he wasn't supposed to see."

"Don't tell me…"

"Don't worry. It's taken care of. And even if he talks, he doesn't know enough to hurt anybody."

Ingram lowered his voice as he shuffled the phone closer. "What could he do with the info he has?"

Jameson chuckled as he propped his feet back on the corner of his desk. "The only thing he can do, trip the trap. He'll either play along and we find somebody else, or he'll go running to the monsters and try to warn them. Either way, they're about to face a reckoning like they never knew existed."

3

Mitchell sat nervously at the edge of his seat and stared at the screens above him. "What the hell happened? Where did they go? What happened to their coms?"

The communications officer turned to him and shrugged. "Colonel, Major Tufo was fully aware of the coms issue. I can't believe he'd get so close as to lose communications." He paled as he considered the possibilities.

Mitchell ground his teeth as he leaned back in his seat. "Get me a thermal on that place. I want to know where he went." He punched up the command to place the satellite overview directly onto the big screen and sneered at the lack of heat signatures outside the building. "He went in." Mitchell cursed and came to his feet.

"Sir, the drone is closing on the location."

"Low elliptical orbit. See if it can pick up their coms. Relay to us." Mitchell stood on the command platform, his hands planted firmly on his hips as he glared at the screen, wishing he could *will* each of his men from the building.

"Sir, we're getting nothing." The tech shrugged as the drone made for a second pass.

"What I wouldn't give for an EMP right now. Put 'em in the dark, kill their jammer..."

"It would kill our coms as well, sir."

Mitchell turned and glared at the tech. "At least we'd both be blind and deaf."

"Copy that, sir."

"What I wouldn't give for an operator that will follow fucking orders." Mitchell plopped back into his chair and shook his head.

*****

Jack stood in shock when Loren stepped from the shadows. She was the last person he expected to be waiting for him when they returned. If he were completely honest with himself, her beauty still struck him with awe. The few times he spoke with her through the stone, he always left with a feeling of admiration towards her, but seeing her now, in person, he was reminded once more of the aura she had about her.

After the initial shock, he almost expected a dressing down for their failure to stop Lilith. She didn't seem to pay his attempt at an explanation any mind, brushing it off. He could only assume that it wasn't 'the right time' yet. He could never really tell with her or any of the elven people.

He was still recovering from her dazzling radiance when she took him by the arm. "I need to introduce you to someone."

Jack did his best to remain professional as she wrapped her hands around his arm. "Of course. Who do I have the honor of..." Jack's voice trailed off as he came face to face with the first griffin he had ever seen.

"I am Allister." The beast's head cocked side to side, measuring up the human as he stood next to the elven leader.

"I'm…holy shit. You're huge." Jack had to snap back to the present. "I'm sorry. I'm Jack Thompson." He held his hand out without thinking.

Allister raised his clawed hand and displayed the talons. "I wouldn't recommend it, Mr. Thompson." His features twisted somewhat in what Jack could only guess was an attempt at a smile.

"Yeah, I see that." He turned to Loren. "I take it you got tired of waiting on us to hunt him down."

She gave a curt nod. "The elders implored me to locate Allister and convince him to assist us in…our endeavor."

"In killing the she-devil Lilith," Allister's voice hissed with obvious disdain.

"I take it you're not the president of her fan club." Jack smirked.

"Chief Jack, Allister has been…out of touch for quite some time. Many of your colloquialisms may be lost on him." Loren glanced over Jack's shoulder. "If I may excuse myself, I'd like to speak to Kalen before I leave. Perhaps the two of you can acquaint yourselves better." She gave the two a slight bow and stepped away.

Jack watched her leave and had to shake his head. "She's not much for words, is she?"

"She says what it is necessary." Allister sat and watched Jack closely. "You have feelings for her."

Jack chuckled. "I'm married, pal."

"It was not a question."

He gave the griffin a confused look and shook his head. "I'm a wolf. I can't…I mean, I can only…" Jack groaned. "I can't have feelings for anybody but my wife."

"Not so." Allister stood and walked past Jack. "For a wolf, you have much to learn about yourself." He slowed as he stepped closer to the brighter lit area of the hangar. "Where will we be working? I prefer darkness."

Jack chuckled again, thinking of Azrael and Brooke. "Another one, huh? We haven't really set up a spot yet. We pretty much just got here when we got a lead on Lilith."

Allister spun on him quickly. "Where is she?"

"Gone now." Jack threw his hands up. "We went in with a plan and it all went to hell. We were so close but…that damned angel."

"What angel? Samael?" Allister bristled, his wings fluttering.

"I guess, yeah. He looked like a demon. Leathery wings, shredded ends…big sucker." Jack sighed and ran a hand over his stubbled face. "He scooped her up before we could finish the job and flew off."

Allister growled low in his throat and Jack actually felt the hair on the back of his neck stand on end. "And nobody followed?"

"We have a gargoyle who tried, but the angel flew east into the rising sun. Azrael had to return before he turned to rock."

"Azrael?" Allister stiffened. "A gargoyle you say?"

"Yeah. He's part of our team. Along with a Nephilim. The son of Rafael. We also have an elf, a gnome, and a vampire."

The griffin gave him a shocked stare. "Surely you jest."

"Nope." Jack hooked a thumb toward Loren. "It was the Wyldwood's idea. I can't think of a more ragtag team to have, but they do work well together."

Allister narrowed his gaze toward the crowd of young warriors as they milled about, waiting for Jack to return to them. "And why a hybrid?"

"A…what?"

"The Nephilim. Why?"

"Oh," Jack inhaled deeply as he glanced toward the Guardian, "He was put here to guard a horde of angelic weapons. We were told that they were the only things that would kill Lilith. He agreed to allow us to use them if he came with us."

The griffin stiffened. "Who told you that only angelic weapons would do the job?"

Jack scratched at the back of his neck as he thought back. "I think it was Loren. She's the one who told us where to find them."

Allister turned and cocked his head to the side. "And millennia ago when Lilith was first defeated, did they use angelic weapons?"

Jack shrugged. "I have no idea. But if Loren tells me to use them, I use them." Jack turned to the griffin and squared his shoulders. "I don't know if they're a requirement or not, but if it makes our job easier, I'm all for it."

Allister nodded almost imperceptibly. "Perhaps they would."

"If it's all the same to you, I'm tired, and my team is tired. We're all hungry, and we have demon splatter all over us. There's nothing I'd like better than to stand here and have my every move second-guessed by you, but I need a hot shower, a meal, and a bed." He pointed to the group of warriors and Kalen off to the side speaking with Loren. "And I know they need it even more than I do."

"Very well." Allister gave him a slight bow. "I am here only to assist."

Jack sighed and pointed to the stairwell. "If you'll go down a flight of stairs, you'll come across an open area with a lab in the middle. There's a vampire there named Doctor Peters. He's our go-to guy for most things. Talk to him and I bet he can get us set up with a spot to use as a…I don't know, a command center or central planning area or batcave…whatever you want to call it."

Allister watched him walk away. The young warriors seemed to perk up at his approach and they only spoke for a moment before they broke up and exited. Allister considered the probability of this 'team' being able to defeat the she-witch and he shuddered again. He was going to have to dig deep into his bag of ancient magic if they stood a chance of pulling this off.

*****

Doc hung up the phone and began nervously digging around his lab. He had to find his notes. He had no idea what to expect when someone overdosed on the serum. On a healthy soldier…maybe, but someone who was ill and barely hanging onto life? He tried to think of the possibilities.

Evan forced himself to stop before he went into full panic mode. "Infection is infection," he tried to reason with himself. "What difference would it make?" He began calculating in his mind. "If the serum were actually an infection, then…but wait, it's not. It's genetic engineering. One has to control the rate of conversion and meter it in small, regular intervals or…" He sat back down and pulled his empty notebook toward him. Pencil in hand he began to calculate the conversion rate, the cellular transformation, the rate of transpiration…all of which would be offset by the cancer. How sick was the subject?

He sighed heavily and stretched his neck. "Too many unknowns."

"Doctor Peters?"

Evan spun at the unknown voice and nearly jumped from his seat. He heard a squeaky squeal and it took him a moment to realize the sound had come from himself. "Oh my…you…you're a…"

"A griffin, yes. My name is Allister and Mr. Thompson sent me to find you." Allister's head seemed to almost twitch from side to side as he took in the lab in its entirety.

"Thompson? Oh, Phoenix. Yes…I…" Evan trailed off, his eyes darting about. He quickly closed his notebook and stood. "Um, how can I assist you…uh…did you say, Allister?"

"Yes. I am hoping you might assist in finding a place that we can utilize as a 'command center' as Mr. Thompson put it," Allister sighed. "We need a place that we can plan and coordinate our attack against the demon Lilith."

Evan sat back down, his imagination at work. "And what limitations do we have?"

"Some of the members, such as myself, prefer darker environs.

I've spent a better part of my existence underground. We also have a vampire and a gargoyle to consider."

Evan nodded. "Yes, I gave them physicals when they arrived." He suddenly brightened. "I don't suppose you would allow me to give you one as well? I've never examined a griffin and would love to study you." His excitement was not well contained.

Allister stared at him blankly. "If I must."

Evan's face dropped. "Well, no. It's not exactly *required*. It would just be…" his voice trailed off.

"It would bring you academic pleasure."

Evan nodded. "Yes."

Allister inhaled deeply and let it out slowly. "Very well." He stepped up and into the lab, being careful not to damage anything within the cramped space. "Being an avid academic myself, I understand your desires."

Evan turned to him wide eyed. "Truly?" A large smile crossed his features. "Thank you, sir."

"Perhaps we can assist each other." The griffin studied the vampire as he collected his examination tools.

"How so?"

"I will be your test subject for your studies, and you can bring me to the present."

Evan paused and stared at him. "I'm afraid I do not understand."

Allister averted his gaze and lowered his voice. "When I stated that I have spent the greater portion of my life underground, I should have said, I have spent the last few millennia underground. Reading ancient texts."

Evan fell into his chair. "Millennia?" He swallowed hard. "You've been reading the same ancient texts for…millennia?"

Allister nodded. "I acquired the Library of Alexandria prior to sequestering myself to the caverns of…"

"Wait!" Evan interrupted excitedly. "The Library of Alexandria was supposedly lost in a great fire."

Allister nodded. "Supposedly. As were the ancient texts locked away under the Sphinx. I acquired both collections prior to locking myself away."

Evan collapsed in his chair and stared at him, a goofy smile crossing his face. "I could spend a hundred lifetimes just asking you questions about the contents of both."

"And I will gladly share whatever you would like to know. But I would ask that you catch me up on what has happened in the world since."

Evan shook his head. "Since…when?"

"Since I sealed myself under the mountain." He stared at the vampire. "From one academic to another."

Evan smiled and nodded. "Oh, yes. Yes, yes, yes."

*****

Laura pushed the door open to find her dad pulling on his shirt. He had removed the IV's feeding fluids into his arms and already had his pants and shoes on. He finished buttoning his shirt and began tucking it into his pants when she quickly shot into the room and pushed the door shut behind her. "What the hell are you doing?"

"There's no sense in me staying here. You and I both know it."

"Dad, they need to…I don't know, run some tests or something. They need to say, 'well…gee, Jim, your tests came back clear. Go home and wait to see if it comes back.' You can't just unplug yourself and leave!"

Jim Youngblood turned and gave his daughter a hurtful glare. "Watch me."

"But, Dad, they think you're going to die. You need to let them figure out that you aren't."

Jim pulled his jacket from the wardrobe and slipped it on. "Punk, it doesn't matter what they test or don't test. I'm not a prisoner here. If I want to go home, I'll go home. If they don't like it, then they can kiss my ass."

Laura threw her hands into the air and cursed. "Dammit, Dad, why don't you just paint a huge target on your head while you're at it? No. Why don't you paint a target on *me*? Just go out there and flag down the next doctor you see and tell him that I brought you the 'cure' and it makes you turn hairy in the full moon?" Tears started to form in her eyes as she considered all of the real ramifications.

He paused and turned to her. "Punkin, it don't matter to them if I go home to die or if I die here. They don't care if I live or die. Their job is to make me comfortable until the end." He pulled her to him and stared down into her eyes. "As far as they're concerned, if I feel good enough to go home to die, then so be it. Now, if I go home and I *don't* die, I'll give them all the credit and they can sprain their arms patting themselves on the back. I really don't give two shits what they do."

"Dad, I still don't know the possible side effects from your taking that whole vial. Evan didn't know. The only thing he could say was 'oh shit' and that didn't sound too promising to me, does it to you?"

Jim hung his head. "Okay, I'll admit, I may have screwed the pooch. And if I ended up giving myself parvo or rabies by doing it, then it's my own fault." He kissed her lightly on the forehead and let her go, turning back to collect the rest of his belongings. "But it was my mistake and I made it. It's my responsibility."

"And if it ends up causing you to do something you can't control? If you end up…" She paused and stared toward the door, lowering her voice, "If you end up shifting at the full moon? If the bane doesn't work?"

Jim sighed. "Then it's my own fault. I'll make arrangements to chain myself up during the moon."

Laura groaned. "Dad, that may not be enough. What if you end up biting Crystal or scratching her or…one of the boys? Or one of your grandkids?"

Jim paused, his eyes glossing over as he considered the possibilities. He shook his head. "I'll be careful. I won't let that happen."

Laura tried to hold back her emotions but a sob escaped her throat as she tried to swallow it down. "Daddy, please, let me call in help."

He spun on her, his finger jabbing toward her, "I told you I can handle this, and I will."

She watched him shove the rest of his belongings into the plastic bag and brush past her as he left the room. She collapsed into the chair and shook as the door shut behind him.

*****

Mark signaled McKenzie to advance just as someone walked outside the office. He watched as the man raised his hands, quieting the crowd. "We only need one of them alive to trade for Miss Jennifer. Choose the ones to die."

"Screw that. Deploy flash bangs." Each of the four operators tossed their grenades then turned their eyes away from the area, covering their ears. Once the reports of the grenades sounded, each man turned back to the task at hand.

Mark and Chad advanced, dropping targets closest to them, carefully picking those with weapons first. Lamb and Jacobs worked from the overhead dropping the armed targets at the rear of the group. Spalding and Little John didn't allow the diversion to be wasted. They had heard the clang of the M84's metal canister hit the concrete floor and dropped to the ground, eyes clenched shut, hands covering their ears. Both men recovered and came to their feet looking for weapons.

Donovan and Tracy weren't so lucky. Deafened by the hundred and eighty decibel blast, both men were disoriented. Knowing what had occurred, neither man panicked, but instead dropped to the ground to avoid being caught in crossfire.

Little John sprang forward and caught Martinez in a chokehold, pulling him to the ground and twisting his neck until the vertebrae gave an audible crunch and the man twitched once before going limp. He pulled the sidearm from Martinez' holster and slid it to Spalding who began taking headshots of the men closest to him.

Little John knew that they had to act quickly. These wolves would recover quicker than your average human from the effects of the stun grenade. He snatched a rifle from the hands of a dead wolf and took aim at the closest man standing near him. He opened fire and watched as the man stumbled and fell, the simunition splattering the side of his head with colored paint balls. John's eyes widened as he remembered that the wolves weren't using live ammunition.

He quickly turned the rifle around and beat the man upside the head with the stock, shattering the plastic and splitting his skull open. He stood holding the weapon like a club as the other four operators leveled the small army around him. He glanced around the falling bodies and saw Donovan and Tracy slowly coming to their feet, shaking their heads as they fought off the effects of the M84.

"Clear!" McKenzie yelled.

"Clear!" Tufo called.

"Clear!" Lamb echoed.

"Clear!" Jacobs repeated.

Spalding pulled Gus Tracy to his feet while Little John helped Donnie up. "You hit?"

"Negative, but I can't hear for shit." Donnie stuffed a finger into his ear and wiggled it around.

Mark stepped forward and kicked over a body. "I need an ID on a Brit named Bigby." He pulled a photo from his pocket and handed it to McKenzie. "Chief Thompson thinks he's Apollo's shooter."

Spalding stiffened and began walking from body to body, flipping them over to see the faces. It didn't take long to check them all. "He's not here."

Lamb asked the obvious question. "What are the odds he wasn't the shooter?"

Spalding ground his teeth and shook his head. "I suppose it's possible." He pointed to Martinez. "I'm pretty sure he was in charge."

Mark sighed as he stared at the carnage. "Maybe we should have left one of them alive." He caught Spalding's glare. "You know…for questioning."

"They can't lie to us if they're dead."

*****

Bigby sat just outside the perimeter of the facility and lay low in the brush. He listened to the stun grenades then the whispered coughs of the rifles as the Yanks cleaned house. He squeezed his eyes shut and shook with rage as he imagined all of the soldiers being decimated. "Fuckin' Yanks."

He snatched his duffle from the ground and turned, pushing through the brush and making his way out and away from the carnage.

As he travelled on foot he debated the odds of Simmons sending him more men to do the deed. He still had the photos and the plans that his inside man had sent. He fought with himself as he considered the possibility of raising his own army.

Bigby froze mid-step and stared back toward the warehouse. "Who needs an army?" he chuckled to himself as he turned back and continued on his path.

An army was just more people to have to watch over. More people to have to feed. More people to have screw things up. But one man? One man could slip in and recon the squads. One man could find out for sure if they had really moved. If they did, so be it. Plan from there. If they didn't…he could stick to his original idea.

Poison gas in the air inlet. And with nobody from camp Simmons to stop him, he could act regardless of where the little prat was. What did he care about the old man's little girl? He couldn't give two shits about her, especially if she mated with the leader of the squads. Piss on her. She's as much a traitor as her mate.

Bigby chuckled to himself again as he began making his own plans. He didn't need an army to do this. He only needed to be careful. And he still had some of Sheridan's guns stuffed away in case of emergency. He could do this on his own. He didn't need anybody else to tell him it was okay. He was his own man. He was a major now…and majors didn't take orders from nobody.

*****

Kalen skipped the meal and went for the showers first. The others tried to convince him to come and eat with them, but he was simply too tired. And after his altercation with Brooke…and the talk with Loren, he wanted to wash away the grit and sleep away the failure.

He slipped off his robe and turned the water on as hot as he could stand it. Stepping under the steaming stream, his mind drifted back to Loren's visit. She wanted to know why he had covered the viewing stone. He tried to claim that he hadn't realized he had…but it was obvious. The rag he had tied to intentionally blind her was still in place. He explained that he felt like he was lying to everyone by giving her the ability to see their every action, but she didn't agree. How could she help and direct their actions if she couldn't see? She had cut the cloth from his wrist and ordered him not to replace it.

His mind drifted further back to Brooke. Raven. She was so insistent that they couldn't pursue their feelings and it made his chest hurt. He didn't understand why. He understood that they were different, but were they really *so* different? He sighed heavily as he thought of her. The biggest part of him ached for her and he couldn't explain why. She made him feel things that he had never felt before.

Kalen slowly turned and leaned against the tile wall, the water beating against his pale skin, reddening it. He pushed off the wall and reached for the soap. His hand closed on nothing. He opened his eyes and saw that the soap wasn't where he thought he had placed it. He hung his head and shook it slowly. He was so tired and distracted that he was losing his mind.

He felt long slender hands wrap around his middle and begin to rub a bar of soap against his chest. He immediately stiffened and his eyes shot wide. He spun and faced Brooke standing behind him; her dark hair soaked by the hot water and her dark eyes staring upward, her arms still wrapped around him.

Kalen swallowed hard as he stared at her wet, nude form. She slowly pulled her arms from around him and began to lather his chest. "Why are you here?" He tried to control his voice, but it cracked as he spoke.

"Don't you want me here? With you?" Her face looked so innocent as she spoke but he could see the mischievous glimmer in her eyes.

He swallowed hard and nodded slightly. "Yes. Now and forever."

She smiled and pulled closer, her lips barely brushing his as she leaned to his ear. "Forever."

He shivered even with the steaming water beating his bare skin and he felt his body reacting to her nearness. He wrapped his arms around her and pulled her to him, feeling her body pressed to his own. Her skin felt cold next to his, but it only served to excite him that much more. He lifted her chin and he kissed her, his tongue probing her mouth and he felt her fangs extend as her own excitement grew.

His hands slid down her wet back and cupped her bottom, squeezing each cheek in his strong hands and lifting her from the ground. She wrapped her arms around his neck and he felt her press her breasts to him as she deepened their kiss.

She released one hand and slipped it between them to grab his excitement and guide him. He could feel her trying to lower herself in his grip so he loosened his hold on her, lowering her gently onto him.

He sucked in a stuttered breath as he lowered her further still, her velvety wetness gripping him tight. His arms clenched and his hands squeezed her bottom tighter as he raised her gently then lowered her again. She thrust against him harder and he quickened the pace, driving himself more forcefully with each thrust.

Without breaking their kiss, she pierced his lip and sucked at his elven blood, tightening her grip around his neck and bucking against him wildly. Kalen spun and planted her to the tile wall, his legs tense and his arms shaking as he continued to raise her and lower her, meeting her thrust for thrust.

She sucked at his tongue, her teeth scraping his flesh until she threw her head back and screamed, "Forever!"

Kalen leaned forward and bit her neck just as his body released…but she wasn't there.

He staggered and fell against the tile wall, spinning and looking around the shower. Where had she gone? Where had she…was she… had it all been a dream? He looked to where he had placed the soap and it was still in the tray. He placed one hand against the tile wall and lowered his head, tears threatening to come. He reached up blindly and shut the water off.

Without drying, he wrapped himself in his robe and half staggered to the door. He stepped into the hall and crossed to his room. He opened the door just as the door to the other shower opened and Brooke staggered out, her hair wet and her eyes glazed. She leaned against the wall and ran a finger lazily across her lips. She glanced down the hall drunkenly and their eyes met. Her face paled and her eyes widened suddenly. He couldn't be sure, but he could almost swear that she blushed before she darted back into the shower.

Kalen stepped toward the shower but caught himself. If she experienced the same thing he did, she definitely wouldn't want to 'talk about it'. He turned slowly and pushed open the door to his room. He pushed the door shut and ran the towel over his head quickly. He pulled it away and noticed…blood?

Stepping to the mirror, he noted a smear of blood near his mouth. Kalen opened his mouth and inspected the area. A perfect piercing of his lower lip bled out onto his chin. He dabbed at it and noticed it wasn't sore. He touched it with his tongue and flashes of memory shot through his mind.

He sat down on his bed and closed his eyes. "We are destined to be, Brooke."

4

Mitchell sagged in the command chair, playing with the controls to the screens, his eyes absently scanning the different views. Static suddenly filled the air from the overhead speakers and Delta One's voice boomed, "OPCOM, Delta Actual. All clear. Jammer located and FUBAR'd. Standing by for cleanup crews."

Colonel Mitchell sat up and keyed the coms. "Casualties?"

"Negative, sir."

Mitchell released the breath he had been holding and sagged in the chair again. He motioned to the logistics tech, "Notify the cleanup crews. Get 'em onsite ASAP."

"Roger that, sir."

Mitchell keyed his coms again, "By chance is Major Tufo with you?"

"That's affirmative, sir."

"Put him on the line." Mitchell spoke through clenched teeth.

"Go for me." Mark's voice sounded a bit too flippant.

"Major, switch to a private channel." Mitchell switched the

coms and waited for the green light. When Mark came back on he forced himself not to light into him right away. "Care to tell me why you entered a communications dead zone?"

"Well...uh, they sort of had a gun to Spanky and Little John's heads and were counting down. It was a 'shit or get off the pot' situation."

Mitchell dragged a hand over his face and pinched the brow of his nose while mentally counting to calm his blood pressure. He keyed the coms again, "Tell me you didn't have to engage."

"Don't make me lie to you, Matt. But you can rest easy, it was a by-the-book hostage situation. Two snipers high, to shooters low. Bad guys are all feasting in Valhalla."

"Oh, for the love of..." Mitchell bit off the epithet he was about to let loose. "You and I are going to have a long talk when you return."

"Copy that." Mark pulled out his earpiece and turned off his radio.

Mitchell noted the coms go dead and sighed. He wasn't sure if his best friend was going to be problematic or if he just needed one last hurrah before riding the desk again. He sincerely prayed that this wasn't a sign of things to come.

*****

Allister walked about the third level and eyed the empty space that Evan offered. "This should be adequate." He turned and nodded to the vampire academic who escorted him through the maze to find the place.

"There is a freight elevator that you and the larger members of the team should be able to use. It goes from here to topside. No other stops, otherwise we could have brought it down." Evan lifted the gate and Allister poked his head inside.

"This will hold our combined weight?"

"It should. It's a commercial freight elevator." He pulled the door shut and turned back to the room. "We can have furnishings brought down here shortly. A conference table and chairs for those who can use them. Computers, couches, whatever you like."

Allister shook his head. "I defer to your expertise. I have not had to deal with human desires in a very long time." He marched past the vampire and stared at the narrow doorways leading out to the hallway and stairs.

"I will see to their needs then." Evan watched the griffin carefully. "Are there any special needs that you will require?"

Allister shook his head. "I ate a deer before I came here. I will be good for at least a few more weeks."

Evan swallowed hard and nodded. "Very well, I have a side project that I must address and then I will make arrangements to get furnishings provided. After that, you and I can start with your lessons."

Allister turned to him and nodded. "Thank you, Doctor. I look forward to it."

Evan waited for him to turn and follow him, but Allister simply sat in a corner and watched him. "Will you be staying here then?"

"Until your return."

Evan gave a slight bow and exited. His mind instantly switched to Laura's problem and he began trying to calculate the effects that an overdose of the serum would have. Would it do any good to follow up with the secondary serum? Even if she gave larger doses? His mind couldn't wrap around the possibility as he hurried to his lab. He simply couldn't find an analogy worthy of the situation.

At 15CCs per dose, the subjects would be genetically altered to the point of being the equivalent to a natural born wolf. At 250CCs... he had no idea what a dose like that would do to a human body. Especially one battling a life-threatening illness.

Evan pushed the smaller items from his desk and pulled his computer keyboard closer. He quickly filled out the requisition form for the furniture and hardware he thought Jack's team might need, then hit send. He switched to a modeling program that he hadn't used in nearly a decade. Shortly after they revamped the augmentation program he had developed the program to predict the outcomes of the new serum and its results were nearly spot on. It was what gave him the 15CC dosage levels that proved reliable in the test subjects.

He started with new subject parameters, inputting a sick human, near death, cancer-ridden. He then allowed for a single dose of 250CC and watched the results calculate. His eyes widened as he saw the predictors range from rapid, near manic-depressive mood swings to uncontrollable shifts without triggers to possibly even having the ability to control other animals with nothing more than their mind. The worst case scenario was a total takeover by the wolf.

"No, this won't do." He began changing the serum parameters. With a secondary dose of the primary, it only became worse. No matter the dosage levels, the subject would eventually lose their mind and shift into a wolf, never to regain their humanity.

Evan fought back the panic rising within and switched to the secondary serum. He adjusted the different dosage levels and read the projected results. He felt his hands shaking as he read the projections. Without a full dose of the secondary, within twenty-four hours of the primary, the subject would be lost to the wolf. If she could get a full dose of the secondary serum into him in time…

He snatched up the phone and dialed Laura. He tapped his nails against the stainless steel countertop as he listened to the phone ring. When she answered, he nearly shouted into the phone, "Tell me you still have the secondary serum!"

"Uh…yeah. I still have it. Evan, what's wrong?" Her voice switched to one of concern from the panic in his tone.

"Laura, listen to me. You don't have much time. You have to give him the *full* vial. The full dose. All 250CCs of it, within twenty-four hours of when he took the first protocol, do you understand me? That's the only thing that can save him."

"What do you mean 'that can save him'? Is he going to die?"

"Worse," Evan sighed into the phone and gripped the receiver tighter. "He could be lost forever if you don't. Look for massive mood swings. I'm talking like bi-polar type swings. He could lose the ability to control the shifts, even with bane in his system. He wouldn't even need a trigger." Evan ground his teeth as he fought with himself. Should he tell her? He had to... "Sweetheart, listen to me. If he doesn't get the full dose right away, he could be lost to the wolf forever. The feral part of the wolf could take over and he might never switch back. If he did shift back, his *mind* would still be that of a wolf's." Evan sighed and shifted the phone. "There's something else. Even if he gets the full dose and it's in time...there's only a fifty-fifty chance it will work. I know that sounds horrible, but it's all I have. And as bad as it sounds, it's better than nothing."

"Oh, my God. What have I done? And he just..." she trailed off as she jumped for the window to see if she could see her father outside. "Evan, he stormed out of here earlier. He said he was going home, but I really thought he would return. He has no ride home and...I have to find him!"

"Hurry, love, you don't have a lot of time. The longer you wait, the more effect the serum will have and the harder it will be to convince him."

"Wish me luck, Evan. I love you." She hung up before he could reply.

Evan stared at the phone a moment before slowly hanging it up. "I love you, too."

*****

"Boss is pissed." Mark leaned against a concrete pillar and crossed his arms. "Apparently I was supposed to sit outside and just report as you boys got your brains splattered across the floor."

"Well, I for one am glad you didn't." Donovan gave the major a mock salute. "I'd rather you run in and pull my bacon out of the fire, thank you very much."

"Copy that." Spalding patted Mark on the shoulder. "I dunno if my talking to him will do any good or not, but I'd be more than happy to let the old man know we probably wouldn't be here if you hadn't breached."

McKenzie snorted. "What am I? Chopped liver?"

"Were you here, too? Sheesh, Mac, in all the fun, I didn't see you," Little John teased. He punched him playfully in the shoulder. "Thanks for covering our six, buddy."

"So now we're buddies?" Mac raised a questioning brow at him.

"You save my life, I'll call you buddy." Little John shrugged. "If you don't like it, I can go back to calling you an asshole."

The other men watched the pair as they spoke, each waiting to see what was about to happen. Mac bristled for just a moment then turned to Sullivan. His features slowly softened into a smile. "As much as I enjoy being called an asshole by you...I think I can stomach 'buddy'. Just don't let anybody else hear you. They'll think you went soft."

Spalding chuckled as he clapped John across the shoulders. "Of course he's soft. In the head. He followed me out here, didn't he?"

Lamb stepped out of the office holding a small handful of papers. "Didn't you say you were looking for a fellow named Bigby?"

Spalding stiffened, and Tufo took the three steps up into the office quickly. "Let me see that."

"Tell me the son of a bitch is dead." Spalding pushed through the small crowd of operators and stood beside Tufo.

Mark shook his head. "He was here." He handed the papers off to Spalding. "Spread out. Search every corner of this place." He pointed to Donovan and Mac. "Search the perimeter. Look for prints leading away, probably in a hurry."

Lamb pointed back into the office. "Outer window is open. He might have hauled ass when he heard the shit hit the fan out here."

Spalding pushed past him and ran to the window. He sniffed the air hard and shook his head. "I don't know why I thought that might work." He strained his eyes in the early morning light and could just make out where feet had landed outside the window. The packed ground gave little clue as to what direction the person may have went. "Son of a bitch."

Little John appeared by his side. "Come on, I'll go with you. We'll help do an outside sweep."

"He's long gone." Spalding shook his head.

"You can't be certain."

Spanky turned and looked up at the large man. "It's what I'd do."

"Let's hope this joker isn't as smart as you then." John pulled him from the window and handed him his rifle. "Come on."

*****

Laura ran to the front of the hospital and pushed through the large double doors leading to the parking lot. She trotted out toward her Jeep and paused, her eyes scanning the surrounding area. "Where are you, Daddy?"

She dug her keys from her pocket and climbed into the Wrangler, starting the engine and popping the clutch, chirping the tires as she pulled out of her parking space. She drove slowly, her eyes scanning the surrounding area as she headed the only direction she could think to go: Home.

She pulled off the main road and hit the smaller side streets. "If I were on foot and walking home, I'd want the shortest route." She drove slowly through the mini-mall, through the edge of a residential area, and finally she came back to the main road leading back to her father's house. She goosed the gas pedal and shifted up, her eyes still scanning the surrounding area.

She merged onto the highway and set the cruise on her Jeep. If he walked this way, she might see him on the side of the road. She pulled her cell phone and called Derek. He finally answered and she all but yelled at him, "Have you seen dad?"

"Isn't he in his room with you?"

"No, D. He took off. He got dressed and said he was going home. I…" She paused as she realized she left her brother at the hospital. "You're still there, aren't you?"

"Well, duh, Einstein. We went down to the cafeteria and got coffee. I thought you were calling to tell us to come back up." She heard him cover the phone and when he uncovered it, Crystal was near hysterics.

"Great. Listen, Derek, I'm making my way toward the house. I'm looking for him. I really—"

"How could you just let him walk out, Punk? Jesus, he's a sick man!"

Laura ground her teeth and squeezed the steering wheel. "He's not *that* sick anymore, remember, Derek? And do you think either of us could stop Dad once he made up his mind to do something?" She slowed the Jeep and stared down the side of a steep embankment as cars whizzed by on her right. "Besides, I really thought he would come back…that he was just blowing off steam."

It took him a moment to reply but when he spoke, his voice was softer. "You're right, Laura. Once Dad makes up his mind, he's gonna do it come hell or high water. Okay, you keep heading toward the house. Me and Crystal are gonna look around the hospital here just to make sure he didn't get part way, maybe get winded and just sit down to rest or something, okay? If either of us finds out something, we call the other, okay?"

"Agreed. Thanks, D." Laura snapped her phone shut and slipped it back into her pocket. She continued to drive, panic rising in her heart as she considered the possibilities. If her father lost his mind because of the drug she brought him. Wait, did she just call it a 'drug'? She laughed mockingly at herself. "I'm losing it." It was no drug. Evan was right. It's a curse. And she brought it upon her family herself. She snuck it out of the supply, sealed it in the case, and drove all the way here to give it to her father herself.

Laura slowed the Jeep as tears stung her eyes, trails running down her cheeks. How could she have allowed herself to do such a thing? She *loved* her father. She was a daddy's girl...and she felt like she'd turned on him. He was ready to give up. He was ready to pass on. To be with her mother in whatever afterlife there was, and she had swooped in with promises of a better way. Live forever, take little black pills to stave off the side-effects. Be strong again. Be healthy. Stay alive so that we can have you around, so that we don't have to feel guilty for not spending as much time together as we could have when you were alive and healthy.

She swiped at her eyes and had to slow the Jeep even more. The tears were pouring now and she was angry with herself. She brought the curse to her family home. Told her brother secrets that she swore she would never burden any of her family with. She did things that she had sworn she would never do. Had she crossed some unseen line in the sand between good and evil? Had the line between the two always been so blurred?

She took her exit and turned toward her father's house. She sniffed back the tears and tried to get a hold on herself as she closed the distance. She was a CIA operative at one time. She was the executive officer for the Monster Squad. Now she felt like a lost child trying to deal with the end of the world. Fear was her enemy, and it was winning.

She hit the driveway to her family home and pulled the Jeep slowly up, her eyes looking for any sign that her dad had been through there. Surely he couldn't have gotten this far? He had to still be back at the hospital somewhere. Maybe he stopped for a soda or something? She glanced in the rear view mirror and cringed. While she was here, she could at least try to freshen up. She didn't want to look like this when she finally did find him.

She parked the Jeep and went inside. She hit the bathroom first and splashed cold water on her face, praying the coolness would reduce the redness and swelling around her eyes. She looked up into the mirror and shook her head. "You look like shit, Youngblood."

She dried her face and stepped out of the bathroom, intent on grabbing a juice before hitting the road again. As she stepped into the kitchen her father stood in front of the sink sipping a cup of coffee. "About time you got home."

Laura froze, her mouth open. "How did you get here so fast?"

He gave her a questioning look. "I took a cab. How else?" He held out a mug to her. "Coffee?"

Laura all but collapsed in the chair at the counter. "Dad, we need to talk."

*****

Kalen sat in the darkness, his eyes watching the light under his door. He watched a shadow pass by and pause. It appeared to him that it came closer to his door for just a moment then disappear entirely. He strained his ears and heard Brooke's door close. He let out the breath he was holding and lay back on his bunk. His mind tried not to think of her, of what happened in the shower. He tried not to think of the 'experience' that he had.

He tried not to wonder if she may have experienced the same thing. He couldn't explain it. It wasn't a dream this time. Both of them had been awake. Tired, battle worn, and possibly exhausted, but not asleep. How could they share a dream if they weren't sleeping?

He turned and faced the wall they shared. His hand rose instinctively and he pressed his palm flat to the wall. "I wish I could feel you," his voice a whisper in the dark, but his heart stretched out, through the cinder block wall and touched her. She could feel his presence near her.

Raven lay on her cot, her face toward the block wall they shared, her palm pressed flat against the cold cement. "What is this hold you have over me, elf?" She pressed harder and wished she could feel his touch when *something* washed over her. She closed her eyes and felt his warmth envelope her. She groaned in the darkness and felt a familiar ache in her chest.

Her mind screamed 'no' but her body and her heart screamed 'YES'! She lowered her head and chewed at her lower lip. How could anybody have such a hold on her? It wasn't possible. Her heart was dead…she knew it was. She'd sworn that she'd never feel anything for anybody ever again.

When her brother suddenly appeared again and wanted back in her life, the part of her that wanted to wrap her arms around him and smother him in hugs was quickly quelled by the part that swore she'd never allow herself to feel again. Neither man nor beast would win her emotions again, ever. Like the Raven, she would go from here to there and think of nobody but herself. A black clad messenger of death.

But now, here she sat, her heart and body rebelling against her over a blue eyed, white haired, golden skinned warrior. She sighed again as she thought of him lying on just the other side of the wall. She smiled as she recalled the… 'vision' she'd had in the shower. His taught abs and strong chest more than caught her attention. She remembered how they *felt* under her wet, soapy hands. She caught herself moaning slightly as she remembered his kiss. The taste of his blood when she bit his lip. How he grabbed her ass and squeezed it so—

She sat up suddenly, her breath caught in her throat, her eyes wide in the darkness. "What am I doing?" She stood and paced the tiny room that she called her own. "This is insane. That couldn't have happened. It couldn't have. It was a…a…a dream." She swallowed hard and turned to the door.

Before she realized what she was doing, she was pounding on Kalen's door. "Open up, you pointy eared devil!"

Kalen pulled the door open and shielded his eyes from the bright lights of the hallway. "Is something wrong?"

Brooke pushed her way into his room and began jabbing him in the chest with her finger. "How *dare* you! You used some kind of elf magic to…to…mess with my head again, didn't you?"

Kalen was pressed back against the far wall, her finger continuing to jab into his flesh. "I didn't. I swear."

"Yes, you did. I know you did." Her features suddenly changed in the low light of his room. Her eyes began to tear as her voice quivered. "Please tell me you did something to me."

Kalen shook his head slowly. "I'm sorry. I didn't." He slowly reached up and took her hand from his chest. He raised it to his mouth and she watched with anticipation as he kissed her fingertip. "I would do nothing without your consent."

He watched as her lower lip began to quiver and a tear flowed from her eye. "This can't be happening…"

He pulled her into a soft embrace and rubbed her back through the silk gown she wore. "Whatever is happening, it's happening to us both." He leaned his face close to her ear and whispered, "But I'm glad that if it must happen, it is you."

She raised her face to stare at him. "Why me?"

Kalen smiled and she felt something stir inside that could only be described as two puppies fighting over a feather pillow. "Why not you? You are the most beautiful, most intriguing woman I've ever met. You are a ferocious warrior and a master thief."

She felt something melt inside and she slowly smiled at him. "Wait…master thief?"

Kalen nodded. "You stole my heart." He leaned in and ever so gently kissed the corner of her mouth. He felt her fangs flick down into place and her eyes shot wide. Her hand came up to cover her mouth but he held it back. "Don't, they suit you."

He kissed her again, harder than the first time and ran his tongue across her fangs. He felt her shudder and she leaned into him. When finally they parted her eyes were as glazed as they were when she stepped out of the shower. She looked up to him and Kalen felt as though his heart would rip from his chest. "Shall we make the vision a reality?"

Kalen nodded. "I thought you'd never ask."

*****

Samael kept constant vigil over Lilith as she slept. Even though Azazel healed her body, her mind still needed rest. The angel took flight twice to find a suitable place for the pair to respite. He found a hunting cabin deep within the woods that he felt was far enough away from others that it was unlikely they would be discovered. He took her there and got her settled on the old bed, covered her in handmade quilts and worked diligently at preparing food for her once she awoke.

Now he sat in the shadows, the light from the fire casting strange orange glows across the cabin as she slumbered. He tried to think of anything else, but the glow of the fire reminded him of the torture pits of Hell. He remembered the numerous ways that the Fallen and the demons had dreamt up to torture the lost souls sent there. Of all of the tortures, he felt the total loss of hope was more torture than any should have to endure. To be anywhere where God's presence wasn't…was intolerable to most souls. It made them go mad. Some eventually became so twisted that they searched out the torture. They helped to dream up new and even more inventive ways to inflict pain.

Samael shook his head forlornly and stared at her form on the bed, breathing softly in the corner of the cabin. He had paid a hefty price once for her. He would gladly do it again. He would do whatever it took to keep her away from his brothers. If it meant surrendering himself to them to take her place, so be it.

Lilith stirred and groaned. Samael was on his feet and by her side before she could open her eyes. "Tell me how you are." His hand grasped hers and squeezed gently.

Her eyes fluttered open and she glanced about the room. "Where are we?"

"Safe. For now. How do you feel?"

She sat up and placed her feet on the floor. "I'm okay. A little shaky." She touched her head with her hand and tried to replay the last memories she had. "The room…" She turned questioning eyes to him.

Samael growled and turned his gaze from her. "The vampire turned against us. His people attacked. They brought explosives."

Lilith stood suddenly and glanced about. "My demons!"

Samael patted her hand, calming her. "They are fine. They are collecting new bodies as we speak."

"And the devices?" She sat slowly, her eyes searching his features.

"We lost a good portion, I do not know exactly how many yet." He groaned as he sat beside the bed. "Not all of the shipments were sent out before they struck."

Lilith ground her teeth in frustration. "How many shipments were sent out safely?"

"Two." He lowered his head, avoiding her gaze. "One was headed for Europe."

"Oh no, no, no…" She stood and began pacing. "We have barely a third of what we started with. Can we make more?"

"I do not think there is time. Nor do we have the supplies." He stood and had to bend his head to keep from brushing it across the ceiling.

"The vampire's people took them?" She scowled as she stared

out the window.

"Yes, my queen. The ones not destroyed or damaged were taken by them, I am certain."

She squared her shoulders and an evil smile crossed her features. "Then we will just have to take them back."

*****

Agent Bob Stevens rushed through his small apartment scooping up anything that he thought may be of value to him. He shoved it into duffle bags and set them by the door. He fell into the chair behind his computer and began copying files to a thumb drive. When he was done, he pulled the USB and slipped it into his pocket. He then started a worm and put his computer to sleep. If anybody other than him tried to access his computer either locally or remotely, the worm would be deployed. Once deployed, the worm would physically destroy his hard drive, and if activated remotely, it would infect the user's computer and destroy it as well. Heaven forbid that person be connected to a network when he tried to hack his computer. The whole thing would go down before anybody could isolate and stop it.

Bob stepped toward the door and took one last look at his place. Odds were good that he'd never be returning here. He glanced through the shades of his window and once he was satisfied that nobody was watching him, he grabbed his duffle bags and slipped out the door.

Bob shoved both bags into the back of his car and shut the trunk. He went around to the front of the non-descript sedan and climbed in. He started the car and pulled it from the parking garage of his apartment building. He glanced down the street and headed for the interstate. It was a long drive from Virginia to Oklahoma, but he intended to load up on coffee and energy drinks and make it a non-stop journey. Other than filling the Crown Vic's tank and emptying his bladder, he hoped to be at Tinker Air Force Base about the same time he was supposed to report to Ingram's surveillance team.

They would have their own transit time once they realized he wasn't coming. Bob could only pray that there would be enough time for him to make his journey and make contact with the targets before things got way out of hand.

5

The helicopter touched down just north of the hangar and Mick raised his arms to remove his headgear. He paused and turned back to the pilot. "I meant what I said. Nobody else needs to die this day. Don't be a hero."

The pilot raised his hands in defeat. "You know I can't be quiet about this. You killed a good man. They will come for you."

Mick nodded as he pulled the headgear off. He patted the pilot's shoulder. "Tell them good luck."

He jumped from the helo and stood back as it lifted again, making a quick hop across the base and to the hangar where he knew that Laura was. Mick pulled the wallet and ID he had taken from the dead pilot and began to jog across the base toward the Base Exchange. He'd have a little time, he assumed, before anybody could be gathered and sent to find him. He also knew from previous experience that the BX offered a barbershop and a uniform shop. Losing his facial hair and getting a military haircut might help him to blend in. A set of camo BDUs would help even more.

As he approached the BX he noted the numerous soldiers coming and going, nobody seemed to really look at their face. "This should be easy enough."

He entered the barbershop and reached for a number. "No need son. I have a chair ready." The older gentleman slapped the hair crumbs from the leather seat and Mick stepped up onto the chair. "What'll it be?"

"Shave and a haircut, my good man." Mick flashed his best smile.

"I was going to say you weren't sporting a regulation cut." The old man wrapped the cotton drape over him and began to lift the chair. "You Special Forces or something?"

Mick raised a brow and had to fight back a laugh. "Me? No way. I was just...on extended leave. Had a death in the family."

"You ain't from around these parts, are ya?" The old man pulled out an old-fashioned lather cup and began swirling his brush in it. He placed a hot towel across Mick's face to soften his beard.

"You got me there, pops. Definitely not from around here."

"I'd have to guess the Northeast or something. Funny accent."

"My mum was Aussie." Mick smiled under the towel as the old man continued to make lather. When he lifted the towel and began brushing the lather across his face, Mick sighed. It had been many years since he'd had a professional shave.

"We'll get you all proper like in no time, son." The old man was definitely skilled and knew his craft. Mick felt completely relaxed as he pulled the straight-edge razor over his face. He made quick work of the stubbly growth and the trimmed goatee. He knew he was done when he wiped away the excess lather and placed a fresh towel on his face.

Minutes later, he was spritzed with aftershave and sitting upright, having his curls trimmed off into a nice high and tight taper. When the old man was finished, Mick reached into the stolen wallet and withdrew a handful of bills. He handed it to the barber and winked at him. "Keep the change, mate."

He whistled a tune as he stepped out of the barbershop and made a hard right. He glanced about to see if anybody was going through the area checking people. Satisfied, he stepped into the uniform shop. "It would seem that my bags were misplaced on the flight home. Can I pick up a spare uniform?"

"With proper ID, we can get you suited up."

Mick reached for the stolen wallet and flashed the ID at her. "I just need one set of BDUs until my stuff arrives."

The lady pointed toward the back. "It's all back there, sorted by size. Get what you need and I'll get you checked out."

Mick whistled another little tune as he went from shelf to shelf pulling out what he wanted.

*****

Mitchell cursed and threw his coffee cup when he got the news about Mick. "Why the hell didn't you find a way to get word to us?"

The pilot squared his shoulders and stared straight ahead. "Colonel, the man is a pilot. After he killed Lieutenant Davis, he assumed his spot at the stick. He watched everything I did. I had no way of sneaking off a message."

Mitchell hung his head and nodded. "Very well, Captain. Dismissed." He picked up the phone and dialed security. "Pull any images that you can of that pilot that came here with Laura and Jenny and get it out to the security forces on the base. Tell them to assume that he's armed and extremely dangerous. Do *not* engage. They are to contact us for response immediately."

Mitchell leaned across his desk and shook his head. "It's all just going to hell at once." He glanced at the secret hiding place where he once kept his scotch. He really wanted to pull the bottle and suck down about a third of it, but he had to keep reminding himself that he didn't have it anymore. He had donated it to the effort to save

Mark.

He collapsed in his chair and reached for his coffee pot. "What the…" He noted the broken coffee cup on the floor. "Great." He pulled out the ugly Boston Red Sox coffee mug that Mark had given to him just to get under his skin. "Gonna make my coffee taste like crap, but oh well."

He sat back and tried to put things into perspective. The vampire council is apparently on the warpath. Laura has left. Mark is playing cowboy. There's some new big bad threat on the horizon that he's being left out of the loop on. His wife's childhood bestie just killed one of his pilots and escaped after trying to help her dad kill them off. And it seemed like so long ago, but it was really just a matter of days since Mark lay on Evan's operating table fighting for his life. Matt took a sip of his coffee and tried to wrap his mind around it all.

"I picked a hell of a time to quit drinking."

*****

Allister sat stoically as crate after crate was brought into the area that the vampire said they could utilize as their work center. Furniture was brought in, computer stations, a large table and chairs. Couches were brought in and placed along two walls. He watched as two men came in carrying a flat, black rectangle. The man approached where he was sitting then paused. "Uh…I think we can mount this over here." They quickly turned and bolted the thing near the ceiling on a nearby wall.

After the deliveries had been made and the men left, Allister caught the scent of something he hadn't smelled in a long time. Sulfur permeated the wooden crates. He approached cautiously and pulled the top from one of the boxes. Layered within were white vests with white balls inside, bathed in a light blue liquid. Multiple strings ran from every side of them and he dared not pick them up lest they be poisoned. "Demon witchcraft."

He placed the lid back on the box and resumed his position in the corner, waiting for whoever should return first. He had the distinct impression that he was not going to enjoy his tenure with the humans as much as the Wyldwood may have suggested.

*****

"Do you still have sway with the Vatican, *mon ami*?"

Viktor shrugged. "I do not know. After I returned the unused relics, they didn't seem much pleased with me."

Rufus sighed and ran a hand along his chin. "We must at least try, *non*? See if we can convince them of the threat."

"The Roman Catholic Church does not officially recognize Lilith. She is a…Jewish myth, at best." Viktor sat and his shoulders slumped. "They recognize that the word 'lullaby' may have come from '*Lilith abi*', or 'Lilith, go away', but they refuse to acknowledge her as a true historic being."

Rufus shot him a look of amazement. "Even when she is threatening to send suicide bombers into all of their largest cathedrals? You would think they would care more for their parishioners than the one making the threat."

Viktor shrugged again. "They may. They may listen, I simply do not know."

"You must try." Rufus took him by the shoulders. "I implore you, *mon ami*. You must go to them and make them see the light. Take them one of the vests. Show them. Make them see that the threat is real."

Viktor nodded. "Very well. I can try. I do not think that I can get one of the vests into Vatican City though. I will have to see if Cardinal Sardelli can meet me on neutral territory."

"He can still be trusted?"

Viktor nodded. "He risked all to allow us access to the relics. I believe he can still be reasoned with."

"Very well. Take my jet. Go and be quick. Tell him that the lives of many thousands may be in jeopardy."

Viktor stood and turned for the door. "And if he can be reached, but he cannot convince those higher than himself?"

Rufus averted his eyes and shuddered. "Then woe be unto any who cross paths with the demons of Lilith."

*****

"What are you trying to tell me, Punk?" Jim stared at her sternly as she tried to reason with him.

"You heard me, Daddy. I told you everything that Evan told me. You overdosed on the serum. If we don't give you the full dose of the second stage…" She averted her eyes as they threatened her again.

"I call poppycock on that." Jim swallowed the last of his coffee and grimaced. "I used to love this stuff, but now it tastes…off."

"That's just a side effect of the drug, Dad. And he wouldn't lie to me about this. He knows how important you are to me. He said there could be mood swings, that you could shift without a trigger, that—"

"And that!" Jim interrupted her. "What the hell is a trigger?"

She blew out a breath and tried to explain to him. "It can be anything from a stressful situation to…to the full moon."

"Yeah, right. Look, Punk, other than not sleeping too well, I feel fine."

"Then just take the second dose so we can ensure…"

"I don't need another dose. I can feel it pumping through my veins, Punk. Would you really want to take that away from me?"

"Daddy, if we don't, you could shift into the wolf and never shift back. Or if you did shift back, your mind would remain as a feral wolf. You don't want that, do you?"

Jim shrugged. "I don't know. I might." He gave her a crooked smile. "Sounds like it could be fun."

"Daddy! This is no time for jokes." She reached for her bag and he stopped her.

"And I'm serious, Punk. I don't need that second shot. The first one cured me. That's what you wanted, wasn't it?"

She shook with frustration as she tried to think of a way to reach him. "Dad, the longer we wait, the less of a chance it will even work. At best, we're looking at fifty-fifty." She pulled her hand away from him. "I'd like to keep you around and *healthy* for your grandkids. And for Crystal."

Jim leaned back on the counter and crossed his arms over his broad chest. "For Crystal, eh? Who do you think you're kidding, Punk. You can't stand her."

Laura groaned and reached into the bag. She withdrew the syringe and was reaching for the other vial when he stepped away from her. "No, I mean it. I don't want it."

"Dad, don't make me call the boys here to hold you down to take your medicine." She gave him a childish smile. "You're as bad as a little kid who doesn't like the cough syrup—"

"I said 'NO'!" he yelled at her just before he turned and darted through the back door.

Laura watched him make for the woods and her heart fell. "Oh, shit."

*****

Mark stepped from the old Humvee and walked into the hangar as McKenzie parked the beast. He noted Second Squad cleaning their gear and reloading their ready sections. Dom glanced up and saw the XO as he crossed the hangar. "Yo, boss, I hear you went cowboy in the field. Hoo-yah."

Mark slowed his walk and turned toward the team, still grab-assing as they finished their chore. "Yeah, Spalding got his tit caught in the wringer, and I had to pull it out."

Hammer tossed his gear bag up onto the peg then turned to face Tufo. "I hear the colonel ain't too happy about it."

Mark stiffened slightly then shrugged it off. "He'll get over it. It all works out in the end."

McKenzie came up behind Mark carrying his gear. "Hey, XO, you gonna stow this crap or you want me to do it?"

"I'm admin. You get to." Mark shot him a wink then turned for the elevator.

Dom stiffened when he saw Mac enter the hangar. "What the hell are you doing, Chad? I sidelined you."

McKenzie froze and glanced toward Tufo. Mark spun back and approached Dominic slowly. "He was the only operator still on base and I needed support. I wasn't necessarily trying to go over your head, Dom, but it was an emergency situation."

Dom's features softened somewhat and he nodded to Mark. "Very well, Major. I guess I'm glad he was here to assist."

"He did more than just assist. We probably couldn't have done what we did without him." Mark shrugged. "I may be wrong, but you may want to reconsider his being sidelined."

Dom gave him a confused stare but simply nodded. "I'll take it under advisement."

Mark spun about and headed for the elevator again. Dom and the rest of Second Squad watched until he got clear then he turned to Mac. "What gives?"

Chad sighed heavily and shrugged. "Let's just say I had a bit of an epiphany. You were right." He tossed the gear bags up onto the table and began going through them. "I won't argue with you sidelining me, but I owe you an apology." He turned to the rest of Second Squad. "I owe *all* of you one. And when the time comes that you're ready to let me train with the squad again, I look forward to it."

Donnie chuckled and nudged the newbie. "Who are you and what did you do to our McKenzie?"

Mac took the ribbing in stride. "Yeah, yeah. I know I was being a prick." He stowed the major's gear and turned to his own bag. "I just had a bit of a wakeup call, that's all."

Dom approached him from behind. "So what did it take to wake you up?"

Chad stiffened slightly and he gently lay the spare magazines on the table. "I think seeing how quickly things can fall apart out there…how much we're needed to operate as a *team* for this to work." He nodded as he spoke. "I think that woke me up more than anything."

"So what happened out there, Mac?"

Chad dumped the rest of the gear out while he tried to find the words. "I know I've been busting on Sullivan pretty hard. But seeing him on his knees with a pistol to his head? Yeah, that woke me up."

Dom clasped him on the shoulder. "I hate that it took that to snap you back to it, but I'm glad you're back. We hit the trainer first thing tomorrow. Be there." Dom turned and headed for the rear stairwell.

Chad watched him for just a moment before turning back to his chore. All the while, he kept thinking, *If anybody is going to hold a gun to that bastard's head, it will be me.*

*****

Bigby backed the stolen pickup to the smaller storage locker. He knew there wasn't near as much hardware inside this one as the larger one, but it gave him something to work with. America might be overflowing with firearms, but you simply can't walk into any gun store, plop down money and buy fully automatic, military grade weapons.

He kicked open the door to the storage locker and loaded the two crates. He lifted the lid on one and shook his head. "More fuckin' Sigs. What is it with these South Americans and their Sigs?" He slid the box further into the truck then pulled the door shut on the locker. Barely enough ammo to run through half the hardware he had, he sat behind the wheel and tapped at his jaw. Regular rounds will hurt like hell and take a while to heal, but silver kills. What to do, what to do?

He put the truck into gear and eased out of the storage rental. He hated the idea of trying to trade weapons for ammunition, and where would he find silver ammo? He pulled out and followed the main road to the interstate onramp. He wasn't sure where he was going just yet, but he knew he wanted to get away from the city.

He took I44 and headed south of town. Why it wasn't called south, he couldn't say…but that was the direction the compass stated.

About twenty minutes outside of the city, he saw an exit for Newcastle and Tuttle. "Newcastle? Here in the middle of nowhere?" he chuckled to himself and took the exit. It was nothing like he had hoped. Little more than a double row of storefronts and businesses, residential areas packed in behind it all.

He cruised through the town slowly and found a cheap looking hotel near the southern edge. "This is as good a place as any."

He pulled the truck in and did a quick once over in the mirror. With a shrug he hopped from the cab and entered the small place. He had stripped a wad of hundreds from Sheridan's stashed money and shoved it into his pocket. He arranged to rent a room for two weeks and paid in advance. A few inquiries told him where the best diners were and that he'd have to drive a bit to find any place that sold ammunition. At least there was a small drug store nearby. He could pick up what he needed to make the chlorine gas there.

Big backed the truck to the room door and entered slowly. The room wasn't much, but it would provide shelter from the weather, had cold and slightly less cold running water and a sink.

He unpacked the two crates on the spare bed and locked the door behind him. Taking one more glance out the window, he shut the curtains and laid down on the bed. It wasn't the most comfortable he'd ever slept in, but it wasn't the worst either, by far.

He sighed heavily as he closed his eyes and drifted off to sleep, visions of the Monster Squad choking on poison gas dancing in his head.

*****

"You need to regain your strength."

"I'll have plenty of time to rest when I'm dead. Do you think that being the queen of this world will allow me much time for rest?" Lilith pushed away from Samael and tried to head for the door. Her legs gave out and she began to fall. He was there to catch her before she ever got close.

"You nearly died in the attack. If it had not been for angelic healing, you would be dead."

She turned her eyes to stare into his. "You healed me?"

Samael lowered his eyes, a slight shake of his head as he carried her back to her bed. "I was too weak." He laid her down carefully and pulled the blanket up over her. "Azazel appeared to me once again while we rested in the mountains. He had to heal me as well."

She tried to sit up, concern painted across her features. "You were injured?"

"They had angelic weapons." Samael sat on the floor next to her, his head still well above hers. "They also had a Nephilim in their midst."

"Impossible. The Nephilim all died in the great flood."

"Apparently Rafael decided he needed one of his own seed set to guard the cache of weapons left here on earth."

Lilith stared at him, her eyes wide. "Angelic weapons left here were guarded by a Nephilim?" Her anger rose as the realization set in. "We wouldn't have needed the hunters or the elves. We could have honed in on the Nephilim."

"Had I known he was here…perhaps." Samael shook his massive head. "But he was right there in our midst, and I could not sense him."

"He was warded!" Her eyes were large as she smiled at him. "Another of your kind has been practicing the craft!" she cackled as she laughed which soon led to a coughing fit.

"Calm yourself my love." Samael stroked her long, dark hair. "You need to rest. The day of reckoning is coming for the Nephilim and his human hunters."

She raised her hand and grasped his arm. "What did he want?"

The Fallen one gave her a confused look. "The Nephilim? He wanted my head, of course."

"No, not him. Azazel. What did he want?"

Samael sighed heavily as he continued to stroke her hair. "He came to implore…that we drop our crusade. He warned that many would die and that it was foreseen that we would not succeed."

She stiffened slightly under the blanket, her body shivering uncontrollably. "What did you tell him?"

"I told him that I did not believe his lies. That we would not be deterred." His eyes met hers and she was not happy.

"Why did you tell him that? You could have lied to him and told him that we would quit. It would get heaven off our trail until our task was completed."

Samael gave her a soft smile. "They would see through the lie. They know the future. They would know that we were not giving up."

Her grip on his arm tightened. "They know the future?"

He nodded. "Of course they do."

She paled and gave him a worried look. "Then we are destined to fail?"

He patted her hand. "No, of course not. They just want us to stop because their love for the humans is so strong. They do not wish you to rule over them."

"How can you be certain?" She fought to sit up and stared at him. "I cannot take another eternity as a phantom. Without my body and soul together, I am lost."

He shushed her and gently pushed her back down into the bed. "We will not fail." He tucked the blanket back under her chin and gave her a smile. "We cannot fail. Remember? The light bearer has condoned our actions."

"I do not trust your brother." The fear was evident in her eyes. "He was the one who allowed me to be tortured, drawn and quartered, the pieces sent to the four corners of the—"

"Shh." He cut her off. "That was then. Now we have a purpose to serve." He lifted her hand and kissed it gently. "He would not have us do this if it were not foreseen."

She nodded slightly, but even Samael could tell that she was not convinced. And if he were honest with her, neither was he.

*****

Ingram sat across from Director Jameson's desk. "Where is he now?"

Jameson smiled. "Oh, he's on his way. Just like you said he'd do, he's headed straight to them."

Ingram leaned back and steepled his fingers under his chin. "Are you sure this is such a good idea?"

Jameson gave him a creepy smile. "Of course I am. I wouldn't have baited him into it if I weren't."

Ingram considered the possibilities. "The gladiators haven't even been field tested yet."

Jameson nodded, the creepy smile broadening. "Ah...but, Robert, if everything goes as planned, they will be in just a few days. Then it won't matter if these monstrosities come looking for them. They won't like what they find."

Ingram swiveled back and forth nervously in the chair. "I'd feel a lot better about this if they were tested and proven battle ready."

"They'll be fine." Jameson reached for a remote and clicked it. A small white screen dropped from the ceiling and imagery from a satellite came up. "You do realize I've had other techs and analysts besides Stevens watching them, right? They intercepted a group of fangers just last night. Met up with them right about here." He pointed to a spot on the satellite map with a laser pointer. "They said they were 'good guys' just heading north to escape the vampire council." He chuckled as he spoke.

"Let me guess, they allowed them to go?"

"Oh yeah. They convinced these Dudley Do-Gooders that they weren't a threat and voila! Instant free pass."

"How do you know all this? Do you have a man on the inside?" Ingram gave him a questioning glare.

"Of course not. No, they're using standard military encryptions. Every word of their transmissions were scrambled, but of course, we have the code to unscramble it. I had just finished reading the transcript before you arrived." He tossed a stapled bundle of papers to him. "Your copy."

Ingram gave him a dirty look. "This might have been nice to know before you started your dog-and-pony show."

Jameson chuckled. "Maybe, but it certainly takes away from the 'wow' factor when I show how the trick is done, first."

Ingram flipped through the pages. "Okay, so they gave a free pass to a bunch of fangers. And this means what to us?"

Jameson punched up the satellite images and focused in. Numerous freshly dug graves could be seen in between the trees. "The fangers had no place to go, so they went to ground. I have my analysts keeping a watchful eye on this group." He pointed to the sheer numbers of dirt piles. "I would think that big a fanger party would be a pretty good field test for the gladiators, don't you?"

Ingram sat back and studied the image on the screen. "There's got to be over a hundred earth piles."

"Those are the ones we can see." Jameson's creepy grin was returning.

"So, after we do our final checks, you want to send them straight out into...this?"

Jameson leaned back in his chair and crossed his hands behind his head. "I see no reason why not. I think it would be the perfect test."

"Over a hundred fangers against our gladiator corps." Ingram was shaking his head. "You're nuts."

"You don't think they can handle it?" He leaned forward and gave him a curious stare.

"Possibly, but right off the bat? There's only twelve of them." Ingram stood and stepped closer to the satellite image. "I understand wanting to put them into real world situations, but this isn't a test by fire, this is...this is suicide."

"So, you don't think they can handle it?" Jameson was nodding his head. "Perhaps I was wrong about your program."

Ingram spun on him. "This program is in its infancy. You're wanting to send it off to college on the first day. I think you're expecting them to bite off a hell of a lot more than they can chew."

Jameson stood and pointed to the lighter spots scattered around the area. "Do you see all of these lighter areas, here, here, here...all of them?"

"Yeah, so?"

"Those were attacking fangers. A six-man team of monsters, *without armor*, killed all of these. They had new recruits in their ranks as well."

Jameson stepped aside while Ingram stepped closer and counted the number of ash piles. "Are you sure these are dead fangers?"

"I'm certain. Go back to the first pages of the transcript." Jameson turned and took his seat again. "Now, it is true that they could have been over run, but with the armor your boys have, those animals could chew on them for a week and never get through that silver reinforced Kevlar." He tapped his desk with the laser pointer. "And you also need to remember how allergic these sons of bitches are to silver. As long as the supplier in Italy can still get us the silver ammo, your boys should be good. It will literally be like shooting fish in a barrel."

Ingram sat back down and rubbed at his neck. "I'm not a fan of this idea."

"Nor am I, but these are the only monsters that we know exactly where they are and in what kind of numbers. Setting up that infrastructure will take a bit more time."

Ingram nodded. "I can see that being problematic."

"Besides, do you really want your boys going up against the 'monster squad' without dirt under their nails?"

"Well, no, but I expect to ease them into it."

"Do we ease our new troops into it when we send them into battle? Hell no, we dump them out of a transport, hand 'em a box of shells and tell them to not shoot anybody wearing the same uniform they are. How is this any different?"

"For one thing, we don't spend thirty million dollars and two years transforming them into the next generation of super humans." Ingram tried not to put as much bite into his words but he found it increasingly difficult. "But, I can see where you definitely have a point. If they can't handle something like this, then how the hell are they going to handle battle hardened monsters like the squads." Ingram sat back and pulled his tie loose.

"Relax, Robert. They'll do fine. They'll have air support as well."

Ingram stared at the screen and nodded. "Out of the frying pan and into the fire."

6

Mitchell tossed the daily reports aside and glared at the door as it opened. His face softened with surprise when Jenny stepped into his office. "Do you ever rest?"

He pushed his chair from his desk and gave her a soft smile. "Not when I when I have teams out."

She straddled him in his leather chair and planted a soft kiss on his chin. "I waited for you. Then I fell asleep alone."

He sighed and lowered his head, his nose inhaling her scent as he buried his face in her chest. "I'm afraid that may become a common occurrence around here."

She wrapped her arms around his thick neck and pulled him closer. "I was afraid you'd say that." Her fingers ran up into his short cropped hair and she squeezed, pulling his head back to meet her gaze. "I might get tired of sleeping alone you know."

He fought back the smile. "Want I should get you a puppy?"

She jerked his head back further and nipped at his chin. "Wrong answer, cowboy."

He growled low in his throat and tried to nip back at her, but she held his head tight in her grip. "A cat then?"

"I want you, you mangy mutt." She kissed him hard and he felt himself being dominated. He enjoyed it. For the briefest of moments he could imagine her decked out in black leather and stilettos.

He liked the image.

"What are your thoughts on leather and lace?"

"What are yours on whips and chains?" Her eyes twinkled and he knew he was about to be in trouble.

"I don't suppose you believe in safe words?"

"Never use them," she growled as she bit his ear, sending shivers up his back.

"Okay Jen." He lifted her from his lap and set her aside as he would a small child. "As much as I hate to do this, I have to nip this in the bud. You're about to drive me crazy and I still have work to do."

She gave him a wild grin and reached into his lap to squeeze his crotch. "Something tells me you don't really want me to leave."

"You're right. I don't. But I really do have…"

The door to his office opened and Mark stepped in. "I figured I'd go ahead and get my ass chewing over with-" He paused, his eyes wide as he stared at his boss sitting in his chair, his new bride holding him by the cojones. "Bad timing?"

"No!" Mitchell shifted uncomfortably and rolled his chair back behind his desk and out of Jenny's reach. "She was just…you were just…"

Jen stood up and smiled. "I was just leaving." She walked seductively past the two and stopped at the door, hugging it as though it were a new lover. "I'll be going to breakfast in an hour. You had better join me." She spun and disappeared down the hallway.

Mark's eyes stared after her for just a moment before he turned back to his CO. "Did she give them back before she left or do I need to wait 'til later?"

"Give what back?" Mitchell tried in vain to straighten his uniform from a sitting position.

"Your balls." Mark smirked at him as he plopped into the chair. "Looked like she was either ripping them off or reattaching them when I walked in." He kicked his feet up on the desk and crossed them, the grin growing broader as Mitchell's face reddened.

"She was just...I was..." He cleared his throat and took a large gulp of coffee. "I'm glad you came in. We definitely need to talk."

"You bet we do. You need to get that girl to a chiropractor and quick. If she keeps swinging her hips like that every time she has her tail in your face, she's gonna throw her back out something terrible."

"That's *not* what we need to discuss." Mitchell took a deep cleansing breath then turned and filled his coffee cup. "Your behavior in the field..."

Mark nodded. "Yeah, if I hadn't broken orders, we'd have a dead squad and those asshats would've probably found me and Mac, too." He tsk'd and shook his head. "That would have been a crying damn shame if you ask me."

"You know what I'm talking about. Going off coms without so much as letting us know? Engaging the enemy? That was outside the scope of the mission."

Mark simply nodded. "Agreed. But you have to admit, if the situation were reversed and you were the one in the field, you would have done the same thing." He pulled his feet off the corner of the desk and leveled his gaze at Mitchell. "Look, Matt, it's not like I went there to pick a fight. We had to know what was going on with the squad. Once we did—"

"You mean, once *you* knew. We had no clue what was going on." He leaned back and crossed his arms.

Mark studied him a moment then nodded knowingly. "Is this really because I had to play it by ear or is it because I was in the field and you weren't?"

"No, this is because you went against the mission parameters."

"Well, okay then. I can live with that, Matt." Mark stood and walked to the coffee pot. He glanced around for the spare coffee cup.

"Mine got broke. I'm using the spare."

Mark shrugged and picked up the pot. He took a long pull from it and noted Matt's eyes widen. "Oh yeah. Did I forget to tell you? I'm pretty much impervious to pain and heal instantly." He took another long pull from the coffee then set the pot back on the burner.

"When did…how…"

"The other day. I talked to Doc about it. I think it has something to do with the whole vampire gene thing." Mark shrugged. "I can still feel pain, but only if it's truly life threatening."

Mitchell shook his head. "This isn't good. That sort of neurological deficit can't be a positive thing."

Mark sat back down and stretched. "Doc didn't seem too concerned."

"How could he not be concerned? You're impervious to pain and you said you heal instantly?"

Mark nodded slowly as he pulled his knife and made a slice across his hand. He felt the cold steel enter his flesh and felt his skin stitch up behind it. Barely a thin line of blood was left behind as evidence of what he had done. "Not even a scar."

"We need to do some testing or something." Mitchell slowly came to his feet, his eyes studying his best friend.

"Matt, if those guys had shot me, I doubt they could have done any real damage. Unless they shot me in the head and even then, I'm not so sure." He wiped his hand on a tissue and tossed it into the trash. "As of now, I'm as close as you have to a real live immortal."

*****

Jack walked into the new command center and looked around. Between Doc and Allister, the place had been set up while the crew rested and it looked to him as though it had always been there. He noted the stacks of crates in the corner. "Is that what I think it is?"

"It stinks of sulfur." Allister stepped back from the stack and shook his head. "I believe it was all handled by demons."

"Good guess." Jack pried a lid off and stared at the suicide bomber vests within. "I need to get these checked out." He lifted the device and held it to the artificial light.

"It smells."

Jack smiled to himself as he laid it gently on the table. "You wouldn't know it by looking it at it, but it's extremely dangerous. One of these devices could kill hundreds, if not thousands of people in the blink of an eye."

"If it is demonic in nature, I believe it." Allister sat back and eyed the vests warily. "What manner of witchcraft is it?"

Jack held a vest toward him. "It's not witchcraft. It's explosives. These ceramic balls inside act as shrapnel."

"I do not know what you speak of, but will take your word for it." Allister leaned further from the foul smelling thing and stared at Jack through narrowed eyes. "You should remove it from these enclosed spaces. The stench is overpowering."

Jack raised a brow and held the vest closer to his nose. He could barely make out the smell of sulfur and plastic from the vest. "A bit touchy, aren't we?"

"If you had a natural aversion to demons, you would want it gone as well."

The door pushed open and Azrael stepped in, Gnat following closely. The Nephilim followed the pair and paused just inside the doorway. "I smell demons."

"So I gathered." Jack tossed him a vest and the angel spawn let it hit him then fall to the ground. "You were, uh, supposed to catch that."

Kalen bent and retrieved the vest. "Is it safe to have these here, Chief Jack? They are explosives, yes? Couldn't Lilith trigger them?"

"We have a signal jammer here at the hangar, kid." Jack packed the vests back into the crate and replaced the lid. "And even if we didn't, we're far enough underground that I doubt she could do much without a satellite uplink."

Brooke slid across the table and took a seat across from the griffin. "Shouldn't we be having those demil'd? You know, just in case?"

"We will, but first, we need to know what exactly we're up against." Jack reached for his two way radio just as Doctor Peters came in.

"Apologies for my tardiness." He dropped a stack of folders onto the table and turned his attention to Jack. "I had a chance to pull the signature files of known bomb makers from the FBI's database. I had no idea there were so many."

"Did you find a match to the vests?" Jack hopped onto the crates and studied the vampire's face.

"No, sir." Evan pulled the top three files and handed them to him. "These are the closest, but they're too dissimilar."

Jack thumbed through the files, unsure of what he was really looking at. "Dissimilar how?"

"Well, Chief, a suicide vest is used by most Middle Eastern terrorist groups, but this one is unlike any of them. If you'll note the fiber optic rather than wire? I can't find any reference to that. Anywhere."

Jack flipped the folder closed and chewed at his lower lip. "Metal detectors."

"Excuse me?"

"They're trying to avoid metal detectors." He hopped from the cases and marched to the white board at the front of the room.

Popping the top on a marker, he began noting the differences on the board. "Lack of metal in the vests allow them to pass through metal detectors. Like they use at train stations and other mass transits."

"Airports?" Evan raised a brow, his stomach sinking.

Jack shook his head. "You can't fly public anymore without some guy with hairy knuckles checking your prostate." He turned back to the board, "Trains and busses would be the most likely scenario."

"We already know they are targeting Catholic churches." Azrael shrugged. "Who cares how they get there?"

"That was their original targets. They could just as easily change that now that we've thrown a monkey wrench into their works." He capped the marker and stared at the board. "Besides, they have to get their people there somehow."

Allister stepped from the shadows. "Is there infrastructure in place to search these demons out at your train and bus...places?"

Jack shook his head slowly. "No."

Gnat spun his hammer by the handle, seemingly ignoring the conversation. "Then we are right back where we started. They intend to cause mayhem and we are left in the dark."

*****

Laura paced the kitchen while she waited for Derek to show up. She practically ran to the front of the house when the door opened. Derek looked frantic and Crystal was still climbing out of the truck as Laura pushed the door shut. She quickly dragged him to the rear of the house, doing her best to explain as she did.

"Wait, hold on, sis. What do you mean, he *has* to have another injection or he'll die?"

She pointed out the kitchen window toward the woods. "He went out there and we have to get him back. He has to have another injection or...it's complicated. Just know that I know what I'm talking about. And he isn't in his right mind. He refuses to take it."

"Just explain it to him that he needs it. I'm sure he'll—"

She grabbed his shoulders and spun him around, cutting him off midsentence. "You think I didn't try? He told me he felt fine. Then he said he was willing to risk whatever consequences, and he took off!"

She heard the front door close and she pushed Derek toward the back door. "What are you doing?"

She lowered her voice to nearly a whisper, "Find him!" She pushed him out the door and shut it.

"What the heck is going on in here?" Crystal stood at the kitchen entrance with her hands on her hips, her eyes boring a hole into Laura.

Laura tried to smile and shrug. "Oh, you know. Dad being dad. He's taken off into the woods and I sent Derek to get him."

"He what?" Crystal leaned across the kitchen sink and stared out the window. "Why on earth would he leave the hospital like that, Laura?" She turned an accusing eye on his only daughter. "First he throws everyone out of his room so he can speak to you, then he just takes off? What the hell is going on?"

Laura collapsed into the chair at the breakfast bar and shook her head. "I wish I knew what was going on inside his head, Crystal. I really do. He went from his deathbed to claiming he felt better and wanted to go home." She shook her head, her eyes unfocused as she stared at nothing. "I told him I wouldn't take him so he just…left. Took a cab. Left me sitting there."

"That doesn't sound like James at all."

Laura nodded. "Actually it sounds just like him. The old him." She glanced at Crystal and shook her head, a wan smile crossing her features. "Before mom passed, he used to do stupid shit all the time."

Crystal swallowed hard and cleared her throat. Laura looked up and started to apologize but simply didn't have it in her. She sighed heavily and looked away again. Crystal stepped cautiously closer and placed a wary hand on her shoulder. "I'm sure he'll come to his senses."

"He'd better." Laura ground her teeth together and glanced out the kitchen window. "It's not like he has forever."

"No, honey, he doesn't."

*****

"What's the plan, boss?" Little John studied Spalding as the two unpacked their gear.

"Right now, there is no plan." Spalding's voice sounded dejected as he stowed his gear.

John cracked a grin and nudged the smaller man. "You mean to tell me that you aren't cooking up some great master plan to get us both ass-deep in alligators?"

Spalding shook his head. "Nope."

John's features fell as he watched his team leader unpack. "Surely you got some idea what we should do next?"

Spalding paused and leaned across the metal table, the wind blowing out of him as he tried to think. "Sully, the trail went cold. Bigby could be anywhere. He's literally in the wind. The last time I went off on my own without authorization, I nearly got the whole team killed. We didn't have the time to plan or..."

"Hey, boss, that wasn't your fault."

Spalding turned sad eyes on him and nodded. "Yes, it was. It was entirely my fault." He tossed his bag aside and leaned against the table. "With the title team leader, not only am I responsible for the team, I'm responsible for my own actions, and this time, my blind anger nearly got my team killed."

"I don't see it that way." John finished unpacking and hung his own ruck up. "The way I see it, you had a hunch, played it out, and we were able to shut down another attacking army before they had the chance to form up against the entire team." He poked a meaty finger in Spalding's direction. "The way I see it, you saved a lot of lives."

Spalding snorted a laugh. "Every cloud has a silver lining, eh?"

"Why not?"

"You're such a freakin' optimist." Spalding pushed off from the table and started toward the elevators. John fell into step behind him.

"Tell me I'm wrong. Tell me that your hunch didn't stop an invading force and I'll drop it."

"You're wrong. It was pure dumb luck." Spalding hit the stairwell and took the stairs two at a time.

"Yeah, well fine. I hope the next time you have a bout of pure dumb luck that I'm around to see it. Maybe some of it will rub off on me." He pushed him lightly on the shoulder and Spalding nearly lost his balance.

"Easy there, big guy." Spalding spun around the landing and started for the next level. "I'm going to grab a quick bite before writing up my reports. Want to join me?"

"Nah, I'm gonna jot the basics down first so I don't forget the whole 'pure dumb luck' part." He shot him a wink as he headed toward his room. "Wouldn't want to leave out the important stuff."

"Smart ass." John watched him disappear down the stairwell and turned to almost run over Brooke.

"What's the hurry, bro?"

Little John stared open mouthed for a moment before he finally shook his head and stammered, "Nothing. I mean…I, uh, after-action reports."

She nodded and glanced around to ensure they were alone. "I wanted to…" she trailed off, finding the lump in her throat hard to talk around.

"Yeah? What's wrong?" John seemed to grow in stature, his protective nature taking over as he prepared to destroy whatever may have threatened his 'little' sister.

She gave him a sad smile and jumped into his arms, her hands wrapping around his neck in a desperate hug. "I'm sorry," She sobbed through the words as she clung to him.

John dropped to one knee to bring himself to her eye level and wrapped his own arms around her tiny body. "For what, Brooke? What happened?"

"I'm just...so sorry." She sniffed back tears and buried her face into the shoulder of his uniform.

"You have nothing to be sorry for. I know this can't be easy for you."

"I mean I'm sorry for leaving you for so long ago. You were so little." She pulled back and stared at him through swollen eyes. She swiped at her eyes with the back of her arm and shook her head. "And then now, when we finally find each other, I pushed you away."

He smiled at her warmly, his hand cupping her face. "Hey, kiddo, I understand."

"Kiddo?" she laughed. "You realize I'm old enough to be your...well, your older sister, right?"

Little John shrugged. "You still look eighteen to me." He pointed to himself. "Me? Not so much."

"Oh, my God, don't I know it. You look so much like Dad." She ran a hand over his stubbled cheek. "I miss them so much." He watched her face quiver and a fresh round of tears flooded her cheeks.

"Me too, Brooke. Me too." He pulled her close and tried not to squeeze too hard. He glanced at the concrete ceiling above them and whispered a silent 'thank you' to God for bringing his sister back to him.

*****

Bigby sat in the cheap hotel south of Oklahoma City once more.

The small crates stacked on the bed as he went through the familiar task of cleaning and preparing the arms. The thought of returning to the same shops for ammunition didn't set well with him.

He knew better than to use the free Wi-Fi that came with the room to search for easier ways to make the deadly gas he hoped to create. Such searches had a way of catching the attention of the federal authorities and while he was familiar with creating everything from chlorine gas to homemade explosives using over the counter goods from back home, that was using goods he could readily purchase overseas. He had no idea their equivalent here in the states. The concentration, the amounts he would need, the measurements…it would all be off. Damned Yanks had a propensity for avoiding the metric system like the plague. How hard is it to use a base ten?

He scrubbed at the firearms and concluded that the best he could hope for was one of two options. He could either wing it and pray that he got it right, or he could risk looking it up online and hope to be gone before any powers that be came looking for him.

He stared at the gallon bottle of ammonia and saw the metric conversion at the bottom. How accurate was that? What's the concentration? Could he look *that* up online and not trigger the NSA? He tossed the carbine aside and glared at the ammonia.

"Does it matter?"

He finally decided that his best WAG (wild assed guess) was better than most anarchists' best guesses online. He would simply wing it and if it was stronger than he was used to preparing, all the better for it. If it was weaker, the Yanks would just have to die slower. He chuckled to himself as the vision of them suffering a wee bit longer danced in his mind.

"Serves them right, I suppose. Just so long as Jack Thompson is there, I'll be happy."

He picked up the next carbine and the towel from the shower. He had a lot of Cosmoline to remove from the stored weapons. He silently cursed the inventor of the nastiness that he was dealing with as he began to strip the weapon. "Soon. Very soon…"

*****

"We must make arrangements with the Legion." Lilith sat on the edge of the bed, her energy fading.

"We must find you nourishment." Samael pushed her back and pulled the covers back over her body. "Do you prefer human food or human?"

Lilith waved him off. "Neither. I am fine. I need to address my Legion."

"To what end? You can barely stand." Samael crossed his mighty arms and glared at her. "You must regain your strength, then you can lead the Legion."

"We must reclaim what was taken. If we only strike a small number of the churches, they will prepare for our attacks. It must be simultaneous."

Samael groaned and slumped his shoulders. "Very well. First we regain your strength, then we shall gather the Legion unto us. Agreed?"

She glared at him from the bed but eventually capitulated. "Agreed."

He stepped to the door and pushed out into the chill air. He sniffed at the air then took flight. He knew that somewhere in these mountains he could find either a deer or a bear or something large enough to sustain her. He didn't want to enter the human village and reveal himself. Not yet.

He flew high into the air, his eyes keenly scanning the ground below. He spotted movement in the shadows and reduced his altitude to get a better view. As the potential prey came into view, his heart rose with glee. He spotted the blaze orange of a hunter's vest as the man scooted between trees.

Samael sailed into a better position, doing his best to keep the man directly below him so as not to give up his own position. When he was certain he could drop in and pluck him from his spot, he folded his wings and dove.

The hunter had sat between the two large pines all morning with nothing in sight. He would bring the high powered rifle to his shoulder and peer through the scope only to lower it again in frustration. Where had all the game gone?

Moments before all went black, he could have sworn he heard the wind swoosh by his ears, but his mind didn't have time to register the sound before his rifle was plucked from his hands and the world went dark. He feared he actually loosed a scream, but he was lost in the ether before the thought formally formed in his mind.

Samael carried the man by the talons of his feet back down the mountain to the lonely cabin and dropped him unceremoniously on the ground outside the main door. He landed deftly beside the prize and dragged him by the collar into the cabin. "I brought human…" he glanced around the cabin and cursed under his breath.

Lilith was gone.

*****

"Tracker has him right on course," Jameson leaned back in his chair and reported with a smile. "It won't be long now and he'll be spilling his guts to them."

Ingram wrung his hands nervously. "I still don't like this. I'd rather them simply not know about our project. Surprise is a much more effective tool than you could imagine."

Jameson shrugged. "Does the pig going to slaughter have any advantage knowing it's about to become bacon?" He chuckled at his own joke. "There's nothing they can do about it anyway."

"You do realize that they're military personnel, right? We're basically declaring war on our own military."

"Negative, Mr. Ingram. We're destroying monsters. Monsters that live and breathe and kill and destroy on United States soil." Jameson poked the top of his desk for emphasis.

"It's still outside our purview. We have no Constitutional authority to—"

"Don't you start preaching the Constitution to me, sir!" He was on his feet now, his face turning red. "The framers had no idea of the types of monsters we have to face today. And when I say monsters, I mean actual, honest to God *monsters.*"

"I know what you mean, Director." Ingram's voice dropped to a quiet whisper. "Preaching to the choir, remember? I'm just saying that it's going to look, to an outsider, like we have declared war on our own military."

Jameson shook his head. "To traitors. That's all, Ingram. Any man that could allow himself to be turned into…" He shook his head as he paced behind his desk. "They're traitors to the human race."

"And what are we?" Ingram stood, his eyes imploring. "We've taken good men and turned them into automatons."

"They're soldiers!" Jameson pounded his desk. "They still eat and drink and piss and fuck and think!"

"Do they?" Ingram sat back down, a slow smile crossing his face. "Do they really? When they're not training or in the field, where are they? Plugged into the neural net. Software updates, training protocols, tweaks to their hardware."

"All necessary to create the best soldier possible." Jameson crossed his arms and glared at the smaller man. "Don't tell me you're having second thoughts about this now?"

"No, of course not. The Gladiator Project is a necessary evil."

"Evil?" Jameson sat down, his eyes glaring at Ingram. "Evil, you say?"

"Well, yeah. I mean, what we've done to those men…"

"They volunteered for this program."

"They had no idea what they were volunteering for."

Jameson leaned back again and shook his head. "No? To be made faster, stronger, smarter, more adept at killing the enemy? To be made *better*. Isn't that what we've done?"

"We ripped out their soul!"

"Soldiers don't have that luxury!" Jameson pounded his desk again. "Besides, they can have that back when they're dead!"

"We deserve worse than jail, Jameson. We're going to burn in Hell. You know that, right?"

Jameson smiled and it didn't reach his eyes, sending a cold chill up Ingram's spine. "That's fine with me, old boy. As long as we can rid the world of monsters before we do it."

7

"Immortal my ass!" Mitchell stormed to his door and quickly turned the lock, barring any further interruption. "When did all this nonsense start?"

Mark stared at him with wide eyes. "When do you think? Shortly after I was infected by both the vampire and the wolf viruses." He shrugged as if it should make perfect sense. "Hey, I didn't exactly see it coming, but it's here. It is what it is and there's no sense in getting bent about it."

"No sense in getting bent about it?" Matt crossed his arms and glared at the man. "You can't feel pain and you heal faster than a vampire on a blood binge, and you don't find that the slightest bit out of sorts?"

"Oh, hell yeah." Mark was on his feet, his hands moving as he spoke. "I find it all kinds of *out of sorts*, but there isn't much that can be done about it, now is there?"

"We can do some testing and see if—"

"And see what?" Mark interrupted. "Matt, even Doc isn't

weirded out by this. There simply isn't anything to go by, nothing to compare it to. We have *no idea* what should or shouldn't be happening right now because it's never happened before in history." He fell back into his chair and sighed heavily. "At least, not that we know of."

"What does that mean? Are you saying it could have happened before?" Mitchell worked his way slowly back behind his desk and eyed his friend carefully.

Mark shrugged. "I have no idea. I can only give you the canned answers that everybody else has been telling me. When those canned answers all proved to be wrong…hell, I don't know. It just seems to me that history covers a pretty long time. For someone to tell me that it ain't never happened before? I have trouble swallowing it."

Mitchell leaned back in his chair and studied him. "Who would know?"

Mark shrugged again. "Beats me. I doubt that even the Sicarii would know. I'm sure if he got wind of something like me, he'd call it an abomination and have it destroyed."

Mitchell snapped his fingers. "The griffin might. He's been around for a long time. He's supposed to be a bookworm geek or some such."

Mark gave him a cautious stare. "I guess it couldn't hurt to go talk to the bird brain."

"I'd be a bit nicer if you do."

"Hey, tact is my middle name." Mark was on his feet and headed to the door. "Any idea where lion butt is calling home?"

Mitchell shook his head. "He and Doc set up a staging area for Jack's team. Doc can show you."

Mark scratched at his chin. "I wonder if I'd do better to bring bird seed or kitty chow?" He slipped through the door and pulled it shut before Mitchell could yell at him again.

*****

Jack pulled the trolley cart out of the staging area with the two crates of suicide vests firmly strapped to it. Doc had ensured that each vest was made safe before they were repackaged into the crates and samples of the two part explosives were taken for analysis. Doc swore that they could be incinerated as they sat since the explosives hadn't been combined yet, but he truly doubted that any of the techs would want to volunteer to toss them into the incinerator. He'd have to make a call to the EOD unit and have them take care of it when they could.

As the doors to the freight elevator opened, Jack was nearly run over by Major Tufo. "Major, you seem to be in a bit of a hurry."

"Where's your team, Chief?"

"Pretty much scattered right now. We're taking a break and I'm hauling off..."

"Where's the griffin?" Mark interrupted.

Jack gave him a questioning look. "Allister? He's still down below last I saw. He was going over everything we had collected at Lilith's hideout."

"I need to speak with him." Mark pushed past him and squeezed past the crates. "It's sort of important."

"Is something wrong?" Jack held the door to the elevator as Mark reached for the button.

"What? No, I'm just hoping he can help me with a...a personal issue." Mark pressed the button again and watched as the doors shut.

When the freight elevator stopped, Mark was facing the wrong direction. He turned and stepped into what appeared to be an oversized conference room. The lights were dim, but he could easily make out every detail. As Jack had stated, the griffin was seated next to the table going over a stack of crumpled and burnt papers.

The large creature shifted one of its dark eyes toward him as he slowly entered the room then turned his feathered face to meet his gaze. "You smell...different. What are you?"

Mark paused and gave him a curious smile. "I'm Major Tufo. I'm the Executive Officer here."

"Very well. But *what* are you?" Allister cocked his head as he stared at the man.

Mark sighed and his shoulders slumped. "I was actually hoping you might be able to help me with that."

Allister stepped away from the table and slowly approached him. His head cocked side to side as he assessed the man before him. "You smell of both wolf and vampire, yet you are neither."

"Or I'm both." Mark shrugged. "That's what we're trying to decide."

"Curious." Allister sat directly in front of Mark and for the first time, the sheer mass of the griffin struck him.

"You're huge." Tufo hadn't realized he had spoken aloud as he stared at the large lion body before him.

"Yes, my mass increased considerably once I was transformed." Allister raised a front leg and carefully took Tufo's arm. "You are warm and your heart beats, yet, your eyes betray your vampire roots."

"My eyes?"

"I see in spectrums that you cannot. You can see in the dark, can't you?"

Mark nodded. "But wolves can see well in the dark, too."

"Not as well as vampires. They are truly creatures of the night." Allister pulled his arm closer and held out one of his claws. "This may hurt." He punctured Mark's arm, but he didn't wince.

"Yeah…no. Not really. Doc says unless it's really life threatening, I won't feel pain." He watched as the puncture healed, leaving a small point of blood.

Allister held the blood covered claw to his nose and inhaled deeply. "Smells of wolf," he snorted and wiped the claw clean. "And vampire."

"So, I guess you've never heard of anybody being infected by both before, huh?" Mark leaned against the table and squeezed his eyes shut.

"Heard of? Yes. Met? No." Allister walked slowly back to where he was sitting when Mark first came in. "There was a reference to a man attacked by a wolf and a vampire on the same night. He reportedly became as you are now."

Mark's head snapped up. "Who? When? What happened to him?"

Allister shook his beaked head. "It was a story written many centuries ago. A young Romanian man...I don't recall his name ever being mentioned. Reportedly, he recovered from his attacks very quickly and the people of his village feared him. They banished him."

"What happened to him?" Mark stared at the griffin as he waited for an answer.

"He was attacked by a vampire and left for dead. A wolf supposedly interrupted the kill and came in to finish him off—"

"No! I mean *after* he was banished."

Allister stared at him with wide eyes. "There is no record. This was all part of the verbal history of the village that was written down centuries later once writing became available to them. I'm afraid the rest is lost to history."

Mark sighed and leaned against the table again. "I was just hoping for some kind of answers."

"Be happy that you were infected by both and still live. Had it been simply a vampire, you would have died first and..." he trailed off.

"And what?"

"And living without a soul is not truly living."

*****

Derek broke through the edge of the woods and began marching back towards the house. Laura saw him from the kitchen and slipped out the back door while Crystal was laying down, doing her best to rest from the lack of sleep the night before. She rushed to meet her brother and could tell from the look on his face that his hunt was unsuccessful. "Nothing?"

"Not even a hint of a trail. Are you sure he went this way?"

"Yes, I watched him. He went right through there and just..." Laura's shoulders slumped as she realized that, if her father didn't want to be found, he wouldn't be.

"Look, Punk, I was thinking. If Dad doesn't want to take that other shot, there's only one thing we can do."

"Don't say to let him skip it." She squared her shoulders and glared at him.

"No, of course not." Derek rubbed at the back of his neck as he tried to think of a nice way to say what he had in mind. "I'm thinking a tranq gun. We could borrow one from the vet. It should hold 250CCs. We load it up, and we hunt him down. Bring in dogs if we need to. Track him down, shoot him up, let nature take its course."

Laura felt her breath catch in her throat as she considered his idea. "If you miss, there's no second chance. There's only 250CCs in the bottle."

"You think I don't know that? It's a one-and-done type of thing, right?" Derek sighed heavily and glanced back at the woods. "But as it stands, Dad's not going to come back and say, 'hey, I've had a chance to think about it. Go ahead and give me the shot' now is he?"

Laura shook her head. "No. Not in this mindset he isn't." She pulled Derek to her and hugged him tightly. "Be quick, though, we don't have much time."

Derek took off toward the house then turned to her, "If I'm not back by dark, call Jimmy and have him bring his Redbone hounds."

"You just be back by dark." She watched him jog toward the house and, moments later, heard her father's truck start and pull out of the garage. She turned toward the woods and stared into the darkening shadows. "Daddy...where are you?"

*****

Doctor Peters turned at the light knocking and froze in place. His eyes narrowed on Rufus standing on the steps leading up to the acrylic walled laboratory. "I didn't realize you were back."

"Apologies, Doctor. I didn't mean to startle you."

Evan hurriedly stacked his notebooks and placed them in a far corner. "You'll forgive me if I don't exactly trust you again, Monsieur Thorn."

Rufus exhaled hard and nodded. "I understand completely, and it is exactly why I wished to speak with you in hopes of explaining my actions. I could never expect forgiveness for such a betrayal, but if you could be made to understand why I did such a thing..."

Evan held his hands up, cutting him off. "No need to explain megalomania to me. I work with souped-up commandos on a daily basis."

Rufus allowed the jab and gave him a curt nod. "It may appear as a form of megalomania to the uninformed, but I assure you, it was necessary. In my day-to-day to life I encounter many who would just as soon kill or destroy not just myself, but any who get in their way."

"And you think that gives you the right to create a Doomsday Weapon?" Evan nearly screamed as he stepped toward the other vampire. "You have no idea the totality of that kind of destruction."

"Which is why I had it re-engineered by some of the best."

"You *what*?!" Evan's eyes widened with shock. "You allowed others to study that weapon?" He began to hyperventilate and stumbled to a chair.

"I assure you, doctor, they are most trustworthy." Rufus stepped forward, and Evan held his hand out, holding him back.

"No. You have no idea." He gulped air and turned his ashen face toward him. "If that technology ever gets out, there could be no stopping someone hell-bent on destroying any natural born creature. Be it elf, wolf, vampire…any of them!"

"Doctor, it will not happen." Rufus paused and leaned against the doorway. "Besides, the miniaturized version was nothing more than a bomb. It nearly killed me when I tried to use it."

Evan turned hate filled eyes toward him and shook his head. "The very fact that you would even attempt such a thing…knowing the possibilities." He felt his fangs descend despite the fact that he knew he was no match for Thorn. "Get out! If I ever see you again…I'll…I'll…I still have the Holy relics and I *will* use them!"

Rufus stared after him for a moment longer then gave him a curt nod. "As you wish." He turned to leave and then paused. He barely turned his head as he spoke to Evan. "It was never my intent to use the weapon against a natural born creature. I wished only to use it upon the demon witch Lilith. Had I not been backed into a cor—"

"Get out!" Evan threw a stapler at his general direction, watching it break against the door frame.

Rufus stepped down from the lab, his shoulders slumped. Evan watched as the vampire disappeared into the shadows and wished that he actually had the nerve to stand against the monster that had just darkened his door. He knew that, if he tried, one wave of his power could knock him to his feet. He shook with rage as the feeling of being powerless overtook him.

*****

Kalen paused outside of Brooke's room and raised his hand to knock lightly on her door. A reflection caught his eye and he quickly lowered his arm, his hand covering the bracelet on his wrist. He felt his face flush with embarrassment as he raised his hand and saw the stone glowing. The Wyldwood beckoned.

Kalen slipped into his room and lowered the lights. He gazed into the stone and Loren's face came into view. "You called, Wyldwood?"

"Have you found signs of the demon queen?"

Kalen shook his head. "No, she has disappeared. There is the possibility that she was injured greatly in the explosion and may not be able to continue her…"

"No." Loren interrupted. "The elders have seen her attempts to finish what she has started. She will also attempt to attack the capitol building of the United States. You need to warn Chief Jack so that he can prepare for her."

"It shall be done." He turned to rise then looked back to the stone. "Is there more, Wyldwood?"

He watched her glance both directions before lowering her voice. "Yes. Be careful, Kalen. A wound in battle may heal, but a broken heart sometimes never mends."

Kalen felt a lump in his throat as he stared at her image. "I-I'm afraid I do not understand, Wyldwood."

Her face softened slightly, and she gave him a smile. "I believe that you do. It is one thing to trust your heart. It is another to give in completely. Just, be careful, young one. Some loves simply cannot be."

Kalen knew then that his secret was known. "You have been watching me?"

She chuckled slightly and shook her head. "No, my sweet one, I have seen it in my visions." She sighed, and he could see the sadness in her eyes. "Just know that the one you give your heart to can never be a part of our world. She can never enter the Anywhere. As long as the two of you are together, you cannot return home."

Kalen felt a knot grow in his stomach and he felt his head shaking in protest. "But I do not understand, Wyldwood. If she becomes my mate, then surely—"

"She is of the undead, Kalen. She can never enter our world.

Vampires cannot be allowed to exist here. They are forbidden." Her face hardened slightly and she squared her shoulders. "Remember your history, my child."

Kalen gave her a slight nod. "I remember it. But she is different. She doesn't feed on—"

"She is what she is. If this continues, you will be forced to choose." Her face grew larger as she came in closer to the stone and lowered her voice. "Just make sure that whatever you choose, you are *certain*."

*****

Mick walked slowly around the familiar hangar. He could only see the two guards on duty at the outside shacks and they didn't seem to pay him any attention as he walked past. The uniform and haircut went a long way toward hiding him in the crowd. He slipped into an office building that was opposite the hangar and noted that it sat empty. Whatever had occurred here in the past was long since discontinued.

Working his way upstairs and finding a location that he felt comfortable keeping watch on the hangar, he made himself a small campsite. Nothing more than a few discarded sofa cushions and a barricade made from desks left behind by the previous occupants, he settled in for what he hoped would be a long and uneventful watch.

He just wanted to make sure that Jen was okay. He needed to see her with his own eyes. He needed to know that she was indeed happy and not under some sort of spell cast by the Fates. He had tried on so many occasions to put himself in a wolf's shoes. To be fated to one mate forever? He couldn't wrap his mind around it. To be fated to somebody who tried to kill you? That just wasn't right. The Fates were a bunch of messed up psychos in his book.

He wished he had Walter Simmons' phone. He could call him and tell him that the intel was bad, that Jen was still inside. He could let him know that he was forced to give them bad info and that his men were going to be set up. He could let him know that the man he intended to hunt down and kill would end up killing his daughter. He could tell him that it was too late.

Mick tried to think how Simmons would react. He knew the man was twisted in the noodle. Could he be reached? Could anybody make him understand that his daughter's life would be endangered no matter what he did? Would he care at this point? So much money had been spent and the attack was thwarted. How many of his wolves died in that attack? Where were the others at? Could Mick catch up with them before they tried anything?

He sat and watched the hangar, knowing that if he had any chance of reaching Walter Simmons, it would be through his wolves when they came back to finish the job. Once they realized the intel was bad, they *would* return to the hangar to finish the job. If he could just intercept them first.

*****

Bigby shoved the weapons into his duffle bag and tossed it onto the bed. He pulled the night vision goggles and checked them then slipped them into the side pocket. A little late night recon wouldn't hurt anything. Better to get a lay of the land before planning his attack. He didn't really get a chance to study the hangar drawings much before it all went to hell last time and he wasn't given a chance to recon much while under fire.

He hefted the duffle up onto his shoulder and reached for the door when the phone in his pocket buzzed. He paused and dropped the duffel. He knew who it was before he ever pulled the sat phone and looked at the incoming number.

Clicking the phone on, he heard Simmons' voice, "Where's Martinez? He isn't answering."

"Your boy Martinez and his mates are all dead." Big took a

certain degree of satisfaction in saying those words.

"What do you mean they're all dead? What the hell happened?"

"He wouldn't listen to me and it got him dead. That's what happened. The old boy said he had everything handled, and instead of bugging out when I told him to, he tried to make a stand and it cost him." Bigby chuckled into the phone as he sat at the foot of the bed. "Actually, it cost you, didn't it?"

"What the hell am I paying you for if you can't keep my men alive?" Simmons' voice bellowed over the phone. Bigby had to hold it away from his ear as the old man screeched. "You're supposed to be a professional."

"I *am* a professional, mate. I can't help it if your boys don't know how to take orders. Maybe next time you'll send real soldiers instead of these puffed up Boy Scouts."

"I don't have to take this from you. You work for me!"

Bigby chuckled into the phone. "You think so, do ya? Well, not any more. I'm a free agent, mate. From now on, I'm doing things my way."

"What does that mean?" Fear crept into Simmons' voice as he spoke to the deranged man.

"Exactly what I said. I don't need your wolves to act as cannon fodder. I can creep in, do what needs doing, and sneak back out before anyone's the wiser."

"What are you planning, Major? What about my daughter?"

"For cavorting with the enemy, she's collateral damage as far as I'm concerned. If she's in there, she's a casualty of war."

"Now see here! I'll not have you—"

Bigby clicked the end call button and tossed the phone into his bag. "The old windbag doesn't know who he's dealing with. If those blokes were the best he had to offer, he's no threat." He picked up the bag and shut the door behind him.

*****

Samael stormed out the cabin and absently tossed the limp body through the door as he stood on the porch. His eyes scanned the woods surrounding the cabin but he couldn't see Lilith anywhere. "Where could she have gotten to?"

He stormed to the rear of the cabin and stared down the slope, hoping to see her trail in the dead pine needles. "Damn that woman and all that she stands for." He stepped away from the rustic structure and took to the air, making slow circles outward from the cabin and hoping to find her or her trail.

He let the wind carry him in a lazy arc, the rustling of his leathery wings flapping in the breeze as he dipped through the air currents to gain speed. He felt his jaw clenching as his eyes cut through the gloom of the trees, constantly searching for her lithe form as she apparently made her attempt at escaping the mountain to meet with her Legion.

He fought the urge to call to her as he knew that there were hunters in the area. He doubted that their bullets could kill his physical form, but he had just been healed by Azazel, he didn't need to add any more injuries to the body he had.

Cursing to himself as he widened the arc once more, he thought he saw a figure cutting through the trees. He banked to the side and swooped low, his eyes piercing the gloom below. There! He caught a whisper of light blue darting between the trees. It had to be her gown. He rose into the air and found a break in the canopy. Folding his wings, he shot downward and landed with a thump just yards ahead of her. He rose to his full height and noticed the startled look on her face as she slid to a stop before him.

"What do you think you are doing?" he growled.

"Going to my Legion. I told you, they need their queen." She pushed past him and tried to go around his huge form.

Samael reached out and took her by the arm. "You need to regain your strength first."

"Once my Legion is reformed, I will rest." She tried once more to go around him, and he scooped her up into his arms.

"And I said, once your strength is regained, we will gather your Legion to you." He leapt into the air and, with a beat of his wings, was airborne once more. He soared higher until he could spot the roof of the cabin then began a gentle glide toward the structure. "I found you a hunter to feed upon."

He placed her on the ground beside the front of the cabin and she punched at his massive chest. "You fool! I don't need to eat to regain my strength." She pushed away from him and stormed into the cabin. "I've got my old body back. I feed it through sex."

"And blood." He lifted the prone body of the hunter and waved it in front of her. "I'm offering you both."

She glared at him and shook her head. "I'm not in the mood for either. I want my Legion! I want them now! We have work to do!"

Samael dropped the hunter on the floor of the cabin and glared at her. "And what would you do with them once you have them. You'd start making plans to storm the human hunters to regain your lost devices. You can't even think straight when you are weak, how do you intend to lead?"

Her eyes narrowed on him as she stepped forward and grabbed the hunter by the arm. "Fine! First I'll feed, but then you had better get my Legion to me."

He grabbed her by the shoulder and tugged her gown from her shoulders, exposing her breasts. "They're already on their way." He spun her around and bent her over the unmade bed and lifted her gown. "Now eat!"

He watched as she bit into the hunter's wrist and began sucking the lifeblood from his body. He grabbed her by the hips and took her from behind as she fed.

*****

Analyst Robert Stevens sucked the last of the coffee from the cup as he turned off the interstate and to the main gate at Tinker Air Force Base. He had a rough idea where the hunters based their operation, but he wasn't completely sure where to go. He knew that asking at the front gate would just get him stared at as if he were crazy.

The gate guard checked his ID and allowed him to pass. He maneuvered through the concrete barriers and drove slowly past the different buildings. He drove past the base exchange, the commissary, a few operational buildings, and began to make a slow circle through the base.

This would take forever. Clandestine groups don't hang a sign outside their workspace advertising that this is where they operate from. Well, except the CIA. They didn't care who knew. Their main building was well advertised.

Robert pulled the car over into a parking area and began sifting through his notes. He knew that there had to be something in the paperwork that would give him a clue to their location. He sorted through emails, phone records, purchase records…something would point him in the right direction.

Wait…purchase records. He went back through the records and noted a peculiar purchase. He smiled to himself as recognition hit him. "I know where you are now."

He pulled the car out of the parking space and began looking at building numbers. He followed them through the base until he came to a dilapidated looking hangar on the southern end of the base.

From the outside, it didn't look like much. Yes, there were quite a few vehicles parked outside, so it was obviously still in use. There were two guard shacks; both manned. But what he saw parked by the main doors is what made him smile. "Bingo."

Robert pulled the Crown Vic into the gravel parking lot and stepped out. He stretched his tired body and went to the trunk. Popping it open, he retrieved the rest of his files and started toward the door. He only made it a few steps before he found himself staring down the barrel of a pistol. "State your purpose."

Robert froze in place and stammered as he stared at the man holding him at gunpoint. "M-my name is Robert Stevens. I'm an analyst with the Central Intelligence Agency."

The man holding the pistol cocked it and leaned slightly forward. "I said, state your purpose."

Robert swallowed hard and nodded. "I need to see your leader. I mean, uh…Colonel Mitchell, right? I need to see him. I have information that he needs to know. It's life or death." Robert knew that the color had drained from his face. He felt it happen.

The guard stepped back and spoke into a radio. A moment later he holstered his weapon and two other men appeared from nowhere. He was handcuffed and his papers were taken and sifted through in the parking lot before he was escorted into the lion's den.

8

"Wait out here and observe. Don't think for a moment that we're done discussing your... 'problem'." Mitchell stared at the slight framed man through the two way mirror. "If you get a read from his body language that I miss, key the two-way."

"Roger dodger, *mi capitain*." Tufo gave a mock salute as Mitchell pushed the door open and walked behind the man cuffed to the interrogation table.

"Mr. Stevens, I'm having difficulty verifying your credentials. Care to enlighten me on why that might be?" He slapped the folder down on the table for effect.

"Colonel, I work for a branch of the Central Intelligence Agency that..." He glanced over his shoulder then lowered his voice. "Sir, they're targeting your people."

Mitchell sat down and crossed his arms, his face stoic. "Why on earth would an intelligence agency attempt to target a little black operation like us. We fly under the radar, Mr. Stevens."

Robert lowered his face and cleared his throat. "Because,

Colonel, they know what you are. Rather, what your *men* are." He raised his eyes to meet the man's gaze. "They discovered that monsters were real and they stumbled upon your operation here. They've sworn to eradicate all monsters. Including those who work for the United States, defending her interests."

Mitchell's face remained stoic. "Assuming that anything you say is true, we've dealt with threats before."

Stevens began to shake, his head nearly convulsing. "Not like this, sir. I'm talking about super soldiers. They have battle uniforms specially made to combat nearly any threat conceivable. They—"

"They're still human. Humans bleed, Stevens."

"Look at the notes I brought you, Colonel. Their battle uniforms are made to repel most small arms fire. If they're punctured, they're self-sealing with clotting foam dispensers built in. They have pneumatic rings built into the limbs that can be activated to act as a tourniquet if need be. They've brainwashed these men until they simply will not stop until the mission is completed!"

Mitchell leaned back and thumbed through the stacks of folders taken off the man when he was detained. He pulled diagrams and schematics of technology that only Doc could understand. "Let's play devil's advocate for a moment and assume that what you're saying is true."

"It is true, Colonel. Every word. I came here to warn you."

Mitchell held up a hand to stop him. "Let's assume that you're telling the truth. How did you find us? We're off the grid."

Stevens shook his head again. "Your telecommunications aren't. For the most part, they're still land lines. And the internet you do use? You use a standard military algorithm to mask it. Any high school hacker could defeat it." Stevens smiled impishly. "I actually used your procurement records to locate the physical location of your operation here."

"Procurement records?"

"You recently purchased three black Ford Raptors as rapid

response vehicles?"

Mitchell turned his head slowly toward the mirror and glared at where he assumed Tufo would be. "Yes, we did." He turned back to Stevens. "And you used that purchase record to locate us?"

"Yes, sir. It was actually pretty easy."

"And that's how your people located us also?"

Stevens shook his head. "No, sir. I don't know how they got wind of you. I swear. I was called in by the director of the agency and ordered to intercept any and all communications, gather all intel that I could, in essence, build a dossier on your people. It was when he accused me of being incomplete in my data mining for not digging through other agencies information that I stumbled upon the Titans and Project Gladiator."

Mitchell nodded. "Tell me about this Project Gladiator."

"Sure. What do you want to know?"

"Everything."

*****

Viktor stepped from the private jet and walked to the limousine waiting for him. The driver opened the door and he stepped inside. Sitting in the rear of the car he smiled to his old friend, Cardinal Sardelli. "Thank you for meeting me on such short notice."

"Do you any idea how difficult it is for me to get away from the city these days?" The cardinal offered his hand, and Viktor quickly kissed his ring.

"I apologize, my friend, but this is of most importance."

"You said life and death." The Cardinal sat back in the limo and eyed Viktor suspiciously.

"It very well could be." Viktor stared out the window as the ground crew prepared to fuel the jet for the return trip. "You have heard the stories of Lilith, yes?"

"Wives tales. Stories told by ancient Jews to keep children in line, that is all."

"No, my friend. She is very real, and she has reared her ugly head once more." Viktor shifted in his seat and gave the cardinal his full attention. "What I am about to tell you will be difficult to believe, but what you do with the information…"

Cardinal Sardelli reached forward and took Viktor by the hand. "I am listening Viktor. I listened when you told me of the Sicarii, did I not?"

Viktor took a deep breath and began his tale. He told of the history of Lilith and her resurrection. He told of their attempt at stopping her and her escape. He was hesitant to mention the winged demon looking angel who spirited her away, but he felt that his friend should know everything. Then he broke the news of her plans to attack the Roman Catholic Church. As many as she could at once…and the suicide bombers. When he finished his tale, he studied his friend's face. "What can the church do to help us thwart her plans?"

Cardinal Sardelli shook his head. "What can we do? It sounds totally implausible. Thousands of suicide bombers, striking all at once? How could she have that much sway over people?"

"No, my friend, the bombers are demons. They have stolen the bodies of humans. As each blast destroys the host, the demon is free to take another."

Sardelli rubbed at the bridge of his nose. "I cannot fathom such an attack. We cannot possibly order the churches closed. They do too much in the communities. People depend on the works and the charity of the church."

"Is there nothing they can do? Even for a short time? If we can determine her timeline and can notify you first, can you order the churches emptied?"

Sardelli shook his head. "That is not for me to say. I will notify my superiors, and it will have to be taken to a much higher authority."

Viktor groaned as he leaned back in the supple leather seat. "The pope will not believe that the Demon Queen Lilith has returned."

"No, but he might can be convinced that another is at work here. Perhaps a terrorist group? One that cannot abide infidels?"

Viktor turned curious eyes to his friend. "You would set up another to take the blame?"

"If it can save the lives of our followers, I would blame the priests themselves." Sardelli opened the door for Viktor, indicating their conversation was over. "Tell me when she plans her attacks. I'll do what I can to convince the pope to order the churches abandoned."

*****

Jack finished his reports to update the powers that be about Lilith and her suicide bombers. He hated leaving the report open ended, with no resolution code. He submitted the report and prayed that whatever power that be higher up didn't bring the hammer down on his team. No matter how he many times he went through it in his head, he couldn't see how even having another team present could have prevented her escape. There were just too many of her demons present.

Jack knew that the Oversight Committee had the authority to notify others within the Pentagon, but he doubted that it would come to that. With Kalen's report from the Wyldwood that the capitol was threatened, he did his part by running it up the chain. It would be up to the Secret Service to beef up security at the White House and the rest of D.C. He sat back and waited for his copy to print then slipped it into his box. He knew that once Colonel Mitchell and Major Tufo read the final report, they wouldn't be happy either. They technically had nothing to go on. No leads meant down time, and down time meant that the clock was ticking between Lilith's taking action and the team being able to *re*act.

He cursed under his breath as he made his way to the simulators. He watched as his team went through the motions of taking down mock threats and knew that the simulator was the wrong kind of trainer for what they would be seeing. They needed something more 'real world' and this simply wasn't it.

He watched a moment longer and then did something he rarely had in the past. He prayed. He prayed that they could get a lead on the demon bitch before she could act again and hurt any innocents. He prayed that his team would be prepared for whatever the ancient monstrous bitch could throw at them and come out of it unharmed. He lowered his eyes and prayed that the Wyldwood was right and that this team she assembled was the right way to go.

He raised his head again and watched as they flawlessly ran the gambit once more. He had to admit, until he was told that they were all 'young', he never would have thought it. They handled themselves like veteran warriors. He watched them as they fluidly worked their way through the CQB trainer and a smile crossed his features. His fears for them being able to handle themselves in battle faded and he found himself only worried about whether they could locate their target in time.

*****

Laura paced by the edge of the tree line and stared cautiously into the darkening shadows. She kept stealing glances at her watch and huffed when another minute ticked by without Derek's return. She had flipped open her phone three separate times to call Jimmy and ask him to bring the dogs, but she couldn't bring herself to do it. How could she explain it was to track down their father?

She stared toward the house and strained to see headlights that weren't there. She fretted and glanced at her watch again in the dwindling light. "Do you really think the two of you could track me if I didn't want to be found, Punk?"

She nearly jumped out of her skin and spun so fast that it took her eyes a moment to focus on the silhouette of her father standing behind her. "You *have* to have that second shot, Dad. The longer we wait, the less chance of it working." She fumbled in her bag for the vial and Jim reached out to gently take her hand.

"Wait a minute, sweetheart." He pulled her hand away and held her loosely by the shoulders. She looked frantically to him and read the sadness in his eyes. "Let me explain before you go doing something that we may both regret."

"We don't have time for—"

"Laura." His voice turned stern and she started again. "Let me explain so you know I'm not crazy, okay?"

She relaxed her shoulders a moment and found her head nodding. Perhaps if she played along long enough, Derek could return and they could hold him down and give him the shot. "Sure, Daddy, I'll listen."

"I mean it. Actually listen to what I tell you. Don't just hear me, but listen."

She nodded again, her brows knitting as she studied him. "Okay. I'm listening."

He leaned against the fence post and gave her a soft smile. "You know, I thought it was kind of odd when you brought me the cure and the side effect was becoming a 'wolf'. Did I ever tell you that when I was younger, the wolf was supposed to be my spirit animal?"

She shook her head. "No. But I know you have a lot of native artwork depicting wolves."

"That's your mother's handiwork. She knew that the wolf and I were bound together." He stared over her shoulder at the rising moon and smiled as he thought back to simpler times. "A lot of people never forgave me for stepping away from office."

"You were dealing with Mom's death. Surely they couldn't expect you to—"

"I was the governor. The tribe is a nation, and they expected me to continue my job after a period of mourning." He squeezed her shoulder and shook his head. "My heart just wasn't in it any longer. It was more your mother's dream than my own."

"Daddy, I don't see what any of that has to do with your not taking the shot." She didn't mean for panic to rise in her voice, but it crept in and she couldn't stop it.

"I'm getting to it, Punkin." Jim stood next to his daughter and continued to stare at the moon. "That first night, I had a vision. I *was* the wolf. I felt so free. I could feel it calling me. It was the wolf who told me to take the rest of the medicine you brought. It told me that I could become what I always desired."

"Daddy...no..."

"I'm not joking, Punk. I felt my spirit leave my body and enter a wild wolf. We hunted together and it felt so...pure. I was free. Free to be what I was meant to be." He turned and gave her a heartfelt smile. "I have no regrets, Punk. This is what I want. I *want* to become the wolf. I want to run free in the mountains, hunt, and become part of a pack. I want to become one with my spirit animal."

"Daddy, you don't believe in any of that stuff anymore. You told me so yourself." She tried to pull away, but he held her in place.

"But I do, Punk. I think I always did. And now you've brought me the greatest gift I could have ever asked for." He reached for her bag and pulled the second vial out. He raised it into the night air and let the moonlight reflect off of it. "I could break this right now and then we'd have no choice."

"Daddy, no!" She reached for the vial, and he held it up and away from her. "Please no..."

Jim Youngblood stared at his daughter for just a moment before he lowered his hand and dropped the vial into her palm. "It's what I want, Punk. I want to become what I was always meant to be."

"But...what if you don't become a *wolf*? What if you become the Halfling?" She felt the hot tears running down her cheeks as she cried.

He shook his head. "I won't. I'll be the wolf. It told me so."

"Daddy, I don't think I can do this. At least with the serum, there's a chance you can stay human."

"Don't you get it, Punk? Since losing your mother, there's no reason to stay human. Crystal cares for me, and bless her for being there when I needed someone. But you were right, she's not your mother and she'll never be her. I'm incomplete without her. But this? This would be my final transformation before moving on to the great spirit world."

Laura inhaled deeply and shook her head. "I'm not ready to let you go."

"My time was up. You've only given me a chance to live a dream, Punk." He kissed her lightly on her forehead. "I can't thank you enough for that."

"What could I possibly tell the others? They'll never believe that you left to become a wolf."

Jim smiled at his only daughter and pulled her closer. "Tell them that I left on my final spirit walk. At least it's true. If they press you, lie to them. Tell them that I know an ancient burial ground on the res and I went there to die in peace."

"You know they'll come looking for you." She sniffed back the tears that were free flowing now.

"You can stop them. I have faith in you. You're more like her than you know." He wrapped his arms around his daughter and gave her a squeeze. "She was the only woman in the world who could tell me what to do and make me feel like it was my own idea."

Laura chuckled despite herself. "I'm not ready. I can't lose you like this."

"You're not losing me, Punk. You're setting me free." He leaned down to kiss her once more and noted the headlights coming up the driveway. "Looks like your brother is home."

Laura glanced at the pickup pulling up the driveway and buried her face in her father's chest. "Please don't go."

"I need to, Punk. Just know that I will always love you. Even as a wolf, I'll never stop loving you."

She felt his strong arms slip from her and he melted into the shadows of the trees. She never heard his footfalls on the dry leaves as he disappeared into the woods once more. She raised her hand to him and whispered, "I love you, Daddy."

*****

Brooke waited until they had all finished their training, had eaten and hit the showers. She made her way to her room and paused outside Kalen's door. She placed her hand to the grey metal and tried to sense if he was inside. She couldn't tell by simply touching the door, so she checked the hallway and knocked lightly.

Kalen answered the door and his breath caught in his throat. "Brooke. I mean…Raven."

"Brooke is fine." She pushed him into his room and wrapped her arms around his neck. Her lips met his and soon her tongue was probing his warm, sweet mouth.

Kalen felt himself reacting, his hand working up her back, sliding into her wet hair, the other squeezing her bottom. He returned her kiss and fought the smile tugging at his mouth as her fangs descended. He ran his tongue across the point of them and sucked her tongue into his mouth.

As he pulled her back further into his room, the Wyldwood's words came back to haunt him. He stiffened visibly and he pushed her back slightly. "We…um, we can't be doing this."

Brooke smiled up at him, her tongue flicking at the points of her fangs as she gave him a seductive smile. "Don't worry, sugar cookie, I won't make you scream."

Kalen stepped back further and held his hands up. "No, Brooke, that's not what I meant. I mean, we can't be doing *this*."

124

Brooke tilted her head as she tried to read his body language. She smiled again and stepped forward. "Looks to me like part of you wants to continue." She gripped his manhood and caused his throat to tighten as she gently squeezed.

"Brooke, please." Kalen pushed her hand away and turned from her. "The Wyldwood knows."

Brooke paused for just a moment then shrugged. "Okay. One less person to eventually have to tell." She stepped forward and wrapped her arms around his chest from behind. She playfully bit his ear and whispered, "That is assuming that this lasts, whatever it is."

"You know that it would. We're connected somehow." Kalen stepped further away and found himself nearly to the rear wall of his room. "She told me that we cannot be. That you can never enter the Anywhere. That I cannot return home if you and I are…"

Brooke stared at him, her eyes slowly widening. "So? What are you telling me? That you're dumping me?" She stepped back and closed her robe, suddenly feeling underdressed.

"I'm saying that we simply cannot be." Kalen averted his eyes. "You were right when you said that we could not be together. I simply did not understand how right you were."

Brooke stiffened, her heart hardening as she felt him closing himself off from her. She clenched her jaw and fought the mocking smile that was trying to form. "I should have known better." She tugged at the belt on her robe and tied it roughly around her middle. "As soon as I allow myself to care for somebody, I knew it would come back to bite me in the ass."

Kalen turned to try to alleviate her pain but watched as she spun and reached for the door. She jerked it open and paused in the light of the hallway. "Stay the hell out of my dreams, sugar cookie. You've lost the right to even think about me as anything other than a teammate."

Kalen opened his mouth to say something, but no words would

form. He watched her march the short distance to her own room and stood silently as his own door slowly pulled shut. He sat down on his narrow bed and held his head in his hands. "What have I done?"

*****

Samael lay stretched upon the cabin floor, a smile plastered to his face. Lilith curled next to him, her hand drawing lazy circles across his chest as he tried to slow his breathing. "You must have been truly famished."

"I didn't realize how long it had been." She let her hand slowly slide down his abdomen and draw a pentagram across his navel. "I'm not sure which hit the spot more, the hunter or the desert." She gave him a wicked smile and giggled as he growled at her.

"I know which you had better say." He pulled her closer and slid her across him, straddling his middle once more.

"Surely you aren't ready for another so soon?"

"I'm an angel. I'm always ready." He leaned up and nipped at her chin just as a noise outside the cabin caught their ear. He scooped her up protectively and placed her back on the bed then stood and worked his way to the front porch.

"My queen! Do you reside within?"

Samael pushed the door open and noted the man dressed in hunter garb, the blaze orange vest dangling from his shoulders. "She does."

The man smiled and nodded to the Fallen one. "Then I read you correctly. More are working their way up the mountain as we speak. We shall set a guard until you are ready to relocate."

"And the others?" Lilith poked her head from behind Samael, pushing to get past him.

"They are on their way to the nearest town, my queen. They should be here soon."

Lilith smiled and patted Samael's arm. "We can begin making

plans to attack the human hunters and reclaim that which is ours."

The hunter cocked his head to the side and gave her a quizzical look. "My queen? You would have us reclaim the devices? Why not simply create more?"

"We do not have the resources. The components are of a finite amount." She held her head high as she spoke. "Have transportation made available and have the others procure us a location from which to operate."

"As you will, my queen." The hunter bowed before marching into woods once more.

"Are you sure this is the wisest course of action?" Samael kept his voice low. "Perhaps if we sent one or two waves of bombers first and allowed the humans to respond to the attacks, then we could thin their ranks?"

"No, I want all of what is ours. There is no other way that we can strike at the heart of Christendom and remove the largest parts of it with one fail swoop." She shook her head. "Otherwise, they will have time to prepare and possibly thwart our attacks. We can't have that, can we?"

"No, my queen, we cannot."

Samael watched her walk back into the cabin with purpose. He stood on the porch of the cabin and stared up the mountain to the rocky outcropping where Azazel had given him the warning of Michael. For the first time, he truly feared that they would fail. He feared that Michael's warnings were true and that they would be lead to their own destruction by a woman blinded by her own rage.

*****

Jameson stood within the bunker and donned the night vision goggles. He couldn't understand why the final tests couldn't be performed during daylight hours. He hated the green tint that the goggles gave everything and they destroyed his depth perception.

Ingram stood beside him and listened in over the communications. Director Jameson had opted not to listen to the chatter as he often found it confusing. He would find himself trying to determine which call sign went to which operator and the distraction caused him to miss the little things.

Jameson had been thoroughly impressed with the Titan warriors. They truly were 'titans' in size. At nearly seven foot tall and pushing more than three hundred pounds each, the men reminded him of oversized professional football players. Yet when they moved, he noted the grace and agility of a large predatory cat rather than the bumbling of an oversized man stuffed into interactive armor.

They watched as the twelve man team set up and camouflaged themselves. They were nearly invisible even with the night vision. Jameson made a note to ask how they were able to blend so easily with the background when the action began. A series of pop-up targets rose and fell, and tracer rounds lit the night sky as the Titans moved forward, advancing on the positions and destroying the targets as they moved.

Drones came in from different angles, firing simunition as they made their pass and the rear most operators removed them from play almost as soon as they arrived. Ingram tapped Jameson and announced a little too loudly that their heads up displays within the helmets displayed the radar feeds from a base location, allowing them to postulate the trajectory and target the incoming drones. Jameson merely nodded as he kept his eyes on the team on the ground.

"Now comes the fun part." The smile on Ingram's face belied the seriousness of the test. "Release the captured subjects." He released the key on the coms then turned to Jameson. "A little surprise just for you. We captured a small band of vamps and kept them handy just for this test."

"Where did you keep them?"

"We had a detention center revamped just for monsters. You know, in case we need to study them."

Jameson turned and scowled at the man through the goggles. "Study them for what?"

"Better ways to kill them, of course." He pointed through the bunker window. "There they are."

Jameson turned and watched as a line of people came rushing up the hillside; the wild look in their eyes evident that they weren't human if their unnatural speed wasn't enough of an indicator. "What if some of them escape?"

Ingram shook his head. "I suppose that's the real test then, isn't it?" He nodded back toward the battle outside.

The first of the vampires hit the front line of Titans. The camouflage came down as the oversized operators engaged the incensed monsters. Fangs and claws sprung to life and flames flew as flesh met the silver embedded in the Kevlar armor. One unfortunate bastard bit into the forearm of a Titan only to scream as his body burst into flames, the operator simply shook the ashes loose from his arm then continued on to engage another target.

Tracers interspersed with silver rounds made quick work of the main body of the attackers. The few who tried to bolt and run past the flanks of the operators soon found themselves being run down, silver coated blades sunk deep into their bodies. Ingram chuckled as he leaned in close to Jameson, "No sense in wasting ammo when a sharp blade will do the trick, eh?"

"I suppose not." Jameson studied the movements of the Titans and nodded his approval. The fluidity of the large men as they engaged the monsters gave him high hopes that when they attacked and removed the hated Monster Squad, none would be left.

"They seem to adapt quite well in the field, wouldn't you say?"

Jameson nodded. "Against fangers. What about wolves? Any chance you collected some of them to test them with?"

"Sorry, but wolves are a bit harder to come by." Ingram hit a few keystrokes and finished the recording of the encounter as the Titans mopped up the last of the vampires. "All in all, I'd say it was a good test."

"It was too easy." Jameson pulled his goggles off and tossed them on the table. "We need to see how they react in an uncontrolled environment."

Ingram paused and turned to the older man. "What are you saying?"

"I'm saying, we need to sic them after that band of fangers that we're tracking. The ones headed north. Let them earn a few stripes on a real hunt. If everything goes as well with that operation, we can send them after the Squads."

Ingram nodded his head slowly. "Are they still moving on foot?"

"Yes, and they're not making very good time. They've hit a bit of weather. It doesn't affect the fangers much, but their human livestock can't take the cold as well as they do."

Ingram shuddered. "Just the thought of humans volunteering themselves to be food for those...*things*, makes me sick."

Jameson patted the man's shoulder. "Make sure the Titans know that we don't give quarter to traitors."

Ingram watched the man walk out of the bunker as the realization struck him. Not only were they going to kill the fangers, but they were going after the humans as well.

When would it stop?

9

Mitchell pulled the door shut and handed the stack of files to Lieutenant Gregory. "Get these to Doc. I want a detailed report of just what in the hell this means."

"Right away, sir." Gregory hefted the files and turned for the stairwell.

Mitchell watched him go, his eyes avoiding Tufo. "What was your take?"

Mark continued to study the man behind the glass. "Whether it's true or not, he believes it." He crossed his arms and turned to his CO. "I just don't get why the Agency would decide to target us."

"Me either. According to this wisenheimer, they've buddied up with the NSA as well. They're both overstepping their Constitutional authority."

"I thought the NSA was aware of our mission?"

Mitchell shook his head. "They're aware that we handle certain threats on American soil. They just weren't aware of what kind." He cast a furtive glance at his XO. "I hate to say it, but I think it's time we notify the Oversight Committee."

"Joy." Mark fell into step behind Mitchell as the two worked their way back to the CO's office. "Any chance that rancid pile of politicians can actually do something about this?"

"Probably not, but they need to be made aware that there may yet be another threat against our operation. This one coming from within."

"I thought we were done with this sort of crap when Franklin bit the big one."

Mitchell paused in the hallway outside his door at the mention of Senator Franklin's name. "I always suspected that would come back to bite me in the ass."

"What do you mean? This has nothing to do with him, does it?"

"Karma's a bitch, Mark." Mitchell pushed open his door and took his chair. "Find a holding cell for Stevens until we can either verify his story or debunk it. It's either for his own safety or…"

"Or he's gonna pay for sending us on a wild goose chase. Gotcha." Mark turned and headed back out of Mitchell's office leaving the man alone to think.

Matt jotted a few notes then picked up the phone. "Get me the OC. Whoever might actually be at work today. Tell them it's important."

*****

Jack walked into the conference room and paused. He saw Allister standing in the middle of the large room, his wings spread wide and a low grumbling growl reverberating through the room. "What's going on in here?"

"It would seem we have an intruder." Allister slowly lowered his wings and Jack saw a man with dark hair standing in the rear of the room, his demeanor one of mild annoyance.

"Explain yourself before I let my Second in Charge eat you for lunch." Jack slowly approached, wishing he had a weapon on hand.

The man held up his hand and Jack watched as Allister slowly lowered and tucked his wings then sat down. "I mean no harm." The man stepped around the griffin that now seemed catatonic. "I come bearing news."

"That's far enough." Jack pointed at the man, his hand reaching for the angelic dagger. "You still haven't told me who you are or what your business is here."

The man stopped and flashed a soft smile. "I mean you no harm, Chief Jack Thompson of the human hunters. My name is Azazel and I bring you word of Lilith."

Jack drew the dagger and took a defensive posture. "How the hell do you know we're looking for her?"

Azazel held his hands up and indicated that he had no weapons. "I come in peace, Chief Jack Thompson."

"Just call me Jack. But you better explain faster."

"Michael sent me to try to stop Samael and Lilith." He shook his head, and Jack could read true sorrow in his face. "They won't be stopped by words. So I have been sent to you. You are destined to lead the force that will stop her." He waved his hand up and around the room. "You, and your people here."

"Michael *who*?"

Azazel cocked his head to the side and shot him a questioning look. "Why, the Archangel Michael. Who else?"

Jack slowly lowered the dagger and stepped closer. "You're telling me that an angel sent you…here?"

"Yes. Precisely."

"And you? You're…an…"

"An angel. Yes." Azazel stepped closer and continued to hold his hands out empty. "I'm no Archangel. I'm simply a messenger."

"And does Michael know that Phil is helping us?" Azazel gave him the same confused look. "The Nephilim that was guarding the angelic weapons, he's joined the resistance so to speak."

"Ah, yes, he is aware."

Jack sighed and tucked the dagger back into the sheath. "Tell me something. Why the hell don't you guys just come down here and kick her fat ass back to Purgatory or Hell or wherever it is she's supposed to be? Why do we have to do it?"

Azazel shook his head solemnly. "We are barred from interfering. Technically, we are not supposed to even appear to you to tell you what shall transpire." He glanced up toward the ceiling and nodded, smiling. "Let's just say that your prayers were heard and an exception was made."

"My...huh?"

"You prayed for your people. You prayed for guidance. You prayed for assistance in finding Lilith." Azazel held his hands out then brought them together. "I was sent to answer that prayer."

Jack felt his shoulders slump with a modicum of relief. "You've got to be shitting me. Well halleluiah and what's her address?"

"It is not that simple, Jack." Azazel indicated the maps at the table. "I can show you where she will be and when. But I can also tell you that she plans to come here. You took something that she wants. She does not know that you now know. You could prepare for her."

"Wait...what? She's planning to attack us? Here?" Jack felt his heart rate speed up then took a deep cleansing breath. "When and how?"

"You have a choice, Jack. You can meet her on her own grounds or wait for her here. Both choices have merits."

Jack nodded. "If I go to her, it's unfamiliar territory. All the satellite data and blue prints aren't the same as knowing the grounds."

"True."

"If I let her attack us, I risk not only my own people, but the rest of the people who work here and on the base."

"Also true." Azazel pulled a chair out for him. "Neither are the best choice, but you should choose one."

Jack walked to the table and pulled the chair out further. He pulled the map closer and watched as Azazel scanned them. "She is currently here. Very soon, they will all be meeting here, in this town." He tapped the map. "There is an old saw mill there. It has been shut down for some time and they have a large empty building where they will stage prior to attacking."

"How do you know this?" Jack turned a skeptical eye to the angel.

Azazel turned and stared him in the eye. "Some angels have the gift of sight. I am not one of them, but Michael is. He told me."

"Did he tell you which would be the best place to attack?"

The angel shook his head. "He can see futures that are set and he can see possibilities. These two scenarios are still 'possibilities' since you have not chosen either one yet."

"Great." Jack leaned against the table and ran a hand through his close cropped hair. "All I know to do is take it to my people. Let the Wyldwood weigh in on it as well."

Azazel stepped back and eyed him. "That does not sound like the leader that Michael described to me. He said that you were a hard man. A warrior. One whose word was set in stone."

Jack snorted and shook his head. "I'm starting to doubt Mikey's ability to see anything now." He pulled the map off the table and pinned it to the wall next to the white board. "I learned a long time ago to listen to my people. Sometimes they can see things that I can't. Besides, they're not really *my* people. They're on loan. I refuse to put any more risk on their heads than I have to."

Azazel nodded. "I understand. Perhaps if more leaders thought as you do…" He paused and stared up at the ceiling again. Turning back to Jack he gave him a curt nod. "I must take my leave now. You have the information that was to be delivered. Good luck, Jack."

Jack opened his mouth to ask another question but the green

flash of light blinded him. When he opened his eyes again and could see, the man was gone. He noted Allister beginning to stir and he glanced up at the ceiling where Azazel kept staring.

"Thank you. I think."

*****

Derek practically ran through the yard, the large rifle strapped to his back. "It took some serious talking, but I got the…what's wrong?"

"I spoke with him." Laura sniffed back the tears that refused to stop running down her cheeks. "He's not coming back."

Derek unslung the rifle and stared at her, confusion and disbelief painted across his features. "What do you mean, he's not coming back?"

"Just what I said, D. He claims he knows what he's doing. He wants to be a wolf, and he refuses to take the shot." She slumped to the ground, her energy drained as her emotions ran wild.

"No. I don't accept that. He's just running off the delirium from the first shot. Didn't your boyfriend say that could happen?"

"He isn't delirious, Derek. He sounded as clearheaded as I've ever heard him." She looked up from the ground at her brother and shook her head. "This is what he wants."

"I call bullshit, sis. Give me that second dose stuff." He reached for her bag and pulled out the vial. As he began to fill the dart Laura reached for his hands.

"Don't, D. You'll never find him out there. He's seen to it."

"Did you call Jimmy and have him bring the dogs?" She shook her head slowly in the moonlight. "Why the hell not?"

"What would I tell him, Derek? That Dad ran off into the woods and refuses to have anything to do with us? Or…or maybe I tell him everything like I told you? That I injected him with a damned werewolf virus, and now he's overdosed on it so he can become a wolf and never have to come home again? Or maybe I tell him that the crap in the dart is some miracle cure, but it's only a fifty-fifty chance at a cure and Dad might *still* end up a wolf for the rest of his life, except he wouldn't really be a wolf, he'd be a Halfling. Stuck as a half man, half wolf for now on? Which one do you think would go over better at Sunday dinners?" Her voice had risen almost to a screech and Derek found himself slowly backing away from her.

"I think you're losing it now, sis." He finished filling the dart and tossed the vial aside. "I'll go out there, and I'll find him. And when I do, I'll fill his ass with this stuff and we can rest easy for a while."

"Derek...don't." She pulled herself to her feet and stepped between him and the gate. "Every moment that goes by, the chances drop that it will even work. And dad is convinced that this is what he wants."

"Jesus Laura, you drank the Kool-Aid that Dad served up, and now you're ready to give up on him." He pushed past her and threw the narrow gate open. "I don't give up that easy."

"You'll never find him, D. He knows those woods better than any man alive!" she called to his rapidly retreating figure.

"He taught me these woods, sis. If anybody can find him, it's me."

She watched until he disappeared into the darkness, the trees swallowing him in their shadow. Laura leaned against the fence post and sighed. She knew that he'd come back empty handed. She just hoped that he'd find a way to forgive her one day for allowing all of this to happen.

*****

Mark made his way back from the holding cells and paused on the floor where Doc's lab was. He knew that it was early, but he wanted to see if Evan had any insight on the documents that the colonel had sent to him. He approached the lab and knocked lightly on the doorjamb. "Got a second?"

Dr. Peters jumped; his hand flying to a silver-coated knife by his side. He visibly relaxed once he saw who was at his door. "Forgive me, Major. I'm a bit jumpy."

"I noticed." Mark stepped up and into the lab. "What's going on?"

Evan released the blade and gave him a wan smile. "I'm afraid that I had a slight run-in with Mister Thorn earlier. I'm still a bit jumpy from it."

"Did he threaten you?" Mark's defensive posture became obvious, and Evan felt the need to defuse the situation quickly.

"No, not at all. In fact, he came to apologize. Supposedly." He stood from his chair and wiped at his eyes. "I'm afraid that just the sight of the man set me off. I yelled at him to leave, and he tried to insist on telling me why he did what he did. I suppose he thought it would make a difference."

Mark leaned against the counter and listened. "And? Did he refuse to leave or…"

"What? No, nothing like that. He was actually quite the gentleman. I just…" He turned his eyes away and tried to think of the right words. "I just couldn't stand the sight of him after he abused my trust the way he did."

"Understandable. To be honest, I'm not too keen on his being here either. But he's our guest for now, so we just have to tolerate him."

"If you say so, sir." Evan took his seat again and crossed his hands in his lap. "What can I do for you, Major?"

"I was just curious if you got a chance to look at the stuff Matt sent you."

"Yes, I did have a chance to glance through them. I haven't given them a thorough going over yet. I was just making preliminary notes from what I saw." He turned and pulled his notebook to his side. "If the armor that is in these schematics is real, it is quite high tech."

"Talk to me."

"Well, they're a special blend of Kevlar and carbon fibers with silver strands woven into the material. Quite ingenious if I may say so. I'm surprised I didn't think of this, to be completely honest."

"What else?"

"Well, besides the microprocessor-controlled damage control units mounted throughout the system, it's still quite remarkable. The helmets have heads-up display, the communications are satellite uplink capable. Oh, and this is truly remarkable. Tiny CO_2 cartridges mounted for each piece of armor. They're deployed in the event of a bleeding injury. They charge concentric rings that are built into the interior of the suits."

"What does that mean, Doc? English, please."

Evan cleared his throat. "Major, if a soldier is shot...say in the leg. The suit can assess where the man is bleeding, route the CO_2 charge to inflate an elastic ring that is built within the suit itself. It acts as a tourniquet to stanch the flow of blood. Then, that section is filled with an antibacterial foam that also has a clotting agent. It basically seals the wound and enables the soldier to keep fighting."

Mark nodded. "Like 'Fix-A-Flat' but for a person?"

"More or less, yes. And the entire thing is controlled by this back mounted mini-computer. The entire thing is encased in a magnesium housing. Anything short of a direct shot to the casing would just glance off. It's actually quite ingenious."

"Yeah, you said that." Mark stared at the drawings. "Looks like something from a damned video game."

"Agreed. Numerous video games use something similar in their main character's graphics to..."

Mark cut him off. "So how do we stop these things?"

Evan stared at him, open mouthed. "Stop them? Oh...I...I have no idea. I thought you were looking to procure them for the squads."

"Sorry Doc. It's not like I can drop by our local Sears or Home Depot and order this. This is top shelf military-spy shit. Space age stuff that we're supposed to believe doesn't exist. But now there's some kind of super soldier out there that has these, and word has it that they're gunning for us."

Evan blanched and slowly sat back down. "You're serious? Another clandestine group has outfitted their people with these and they are targeting our boys?"

"That's the word. So how do we stop them?"

Evan shook his head. "I don't know. Yet." He turned and pulled the stack of files back to him. "Let me get back to you."

*****

Bigby pulled the truck past the now closed Base Exchange and dimmed the lights. He knew these roads from memory, having drilled the procedure through his mind a dozen times. He drove the slightly twisting road, his eyes constantly scanning for military police, private security or the odd passerby and turned left to pass in front of the hangar. The empty building on his left cast a shadow over the truck as he drove the speed limit past the front of the hangar, his eyes scanning the guard shack out front.

He slowed for the stop sign and rolled through it like most normally do then turned left again, intending to pull around and park behind the empty office complex across from the hangar. He pulled the truck into the empty parking lot and killed the engine. He sat in the cab and strained his ears for the longest time, listening for any odd sounds through the open window. If anything at all felt the slightest bit off, he would quickly determine whether to continue with his plan or abandon it and try again later.

After twenty minutes he quietly opened the door of the truck and slipped from the cab. He stood outside and scanned the area, his eyes taking in everything. He checked both entrances to the parking area and quickly scanned the windows of the building. Convinced the area was clear, Bigby approached the rear entrance of the empty office and tried the door. Locked.

Slipping around to a bottom floor window, he began lifting each until he found one that was unlocked. Within moments he was inside and the window was slid back into place. Bigby quickly found the stairs and silently made his way to the third floor. He wanted a bird's eye view from where he could observe the squads for a while. If he could determine that they were still operating from the hangar and discern any notable pattern, his job would be all the easier.

Big entered what appeared to have been a cube farm in a former life. Most of the equipment and furniture had been removed at some point in the past. He slowly made his way toward the window when he heard a rustling noise in the corner that froze him in his steps. Slowly he backed away and crept around to flank the source of the noise.

Bigby peered over a stack of old chairs to see what looked like a soldier stretched out on a bed of couch cushions under the bank of windows. "Are we hiding or are we AWOL?"

The man nearly jumped out of his skin as Big spoke to him. "Who's that? I-I'm not a…I'm not a soldier!" Mick threw his hands into the air, his head on a swivel, unable to see the source of the voice.

"If you're not a soldier, then why the uniform, mate?" Bigby stepped out from behind the chairs, a .45 leveled at his chest.

"To blend in," Mick admitted, his jaw ticking. "I'm…" He let his voice trail off, unwilling to admit that he was on the run.

"Spill it, boy-o, or I'll poke holes in you for fun."

Mick squinted in the dim light of the cluttered office and cocked his head. "You're not Air Force."

"Says who?"

"You're a limey. And you have no uniform."

"Yeah. And you sound Aussie. But you do have a uniform, so that sends up a red flag, now don't it?"

Mick lowered his hands slowly and planted them on his hips. "Let me guess. You're one of Simmons' men? You come here to spy on them, too"

Big felt a crooked smile cross his features. "The fact that you even know that name makes me wonder who the hell you are, mate."

"I'm Mick. I flew his daughter up here." He shook his head and glanced out the window. "The old man told me to play along, keep his daughter safe, blah, blah, blah. How the hell was I to know that she would find 'her one true love' and get herself mixed up in all this mess?"

"So you're the inside man that fed his wolves all that phony intel?"

Mick held his hands up. "Oy! Now they caught on to what the hell was going on and made me do that. Then they were gonna ship me off to some deserted island. I ripped the throat out of one of their pilots and forced the other to bring me back here. I knew they'd be looking for me so I got a haircut, a shave, and bought me this uniform so I could blend in." He pointed to the hangar below. "I've been camping out here ever since. Eating take out and farting like a freight train."

Bigby considered the man's story and holstered his pistol. "So, what am I supposed to do with you? It's not like you're gonna go running off to the squad and tell them I'm up here, now are you?"

"My only interest is in keeping Jennifer safe."

Bigby snorted. "And my only interest is in killing every last one of them. And to be honest, kid, I don't give two shits if the little bitch gets caught up in it or not."

Mick's eyed widened. "No, you can't."

"I can. And I will." He turned and stared out the window toward the hangar. "And I'll do you too if you try to get in my way."

*****

Brooke lay in her bed and pulled her blanket up to her chin to stifle her crying. She couldn't believe that she had allowed herself to lower her defenses and allow someone inside. For so long she had kept the wall up, keeping everyone and everything at arm's length, not allowing any feelings to penetrate. She couldn't let feelings enter into the equation. Feelings can get you killed. Feelings for others can be used as leverage. Feelings are bad.

But the dreams...they had to mean something, didn't they? They felt so real. They warmed her from within. They broke through the hardened façade and made her realize that without feelings life wasn't worth living. They caused her to weaken and accept another in a way that she never thought she could again. She hadn't wanted to, but she did. Was it his doing or hers? Was it meant to be or was it a cruel trick of another? Were they destined to be together or not? How could dreams feel so real?

Then when they acted upon them, it was even better than the dreams ever hoped of being. Her heart had swelled with emotion that she hadn't realized she was missing in her life. A river, overflowing its bank as it swept her out of her comfort zone and into a whole new world of newness...new feelings that she wasn't acquainted with. It wasn't that it was unwelcome, just unfamiliar.

She pulled the blanket tighter as she remembered the look in John's eyes when she reconciled with him. If she withdrew back into her shell, could he ever forgive her? She had just rekindled that sibling relationship and she could tell that it was something he needed every bit as much as she needed that damned elf.

She suddenly sat up, her breath caught in her throat. She *needed* that elf? The realization struck her as odd and frightening at the same time. She didn't *need* anybody. She never had and she never would. How could she have even thought such a thing?

A light knock at her door brought her out of her reverie and she quickly glanced at the shadow under her doorway. "Go away!"

Kalen's soft voice spoke through the seam along the doorjamb, "Brooke, please. I must speak with you."

"No. You said what you needed to say. Now leave."

She heard the knob twist and refuse to give against the lock. "Please, Brooke."

"I said no." She pulled the blanket up tighter and fell back onto her bed. "Just leave me alone," her voice was muffled under the wool blanket.

"I don't ever want to leave you again," his voice cracked in the echo of the hallway. "I was wrong. The Wyldwood may ban me from ever returning home for being with you, but...how can I ever return home if I'm incomplete?"

She reluctantly pulled the blanket down and listened to him. "What are you saying?"

"I'm saying that you complete me. I'm nothing without you. I'd rather be banished to this world *with* you than to live in the Anywhere without you. I'd rather be any place there is...even to be felled in battle as long as you are in my heart."

Brooke sat up and stared at the shadow under her door. "You don't mean it."

"I do." Kalen pressed his forehead to her door. "I'll surrender the Gatekeeper to Chief Jack. I'll never return to my people...if you'll still have me."

Kalen stared at the grey metal door and was about to give up when he heard the lock turn. Slowly the door opened and he stared at her. Her swollen eyes, her mussed hair and her unkempt gown. She was the most beautiful creature he had ever laid eyes on. "I love you, Brooke."

She threw her arms around him and pulled him inside.

*****

"Damage assessment."

Ingram stared at the printout and smiled inwardly. "Minimal. Barely more than a few scratches."

"Chances of infection?"

"Nil. They have enough colloidal silver running through them that I'm surprised their skin isn't blue." Ingram set the printouts in front of Jameson and turned to the viewscreen to check the edited films of the testing. "You realize that is where the term 'blue bloods' originated from, don't you?"

"Yes, I know. The wealthy in Elizabethan times ate acidic foods from silver platters and goblets that caused the silver to leach into their blood. You've told me this story numerous times."

Ingram scowled at the man behind his back. "I just find it funny that the very thing that turned their pallor grey-blue prevented them from becoming ill, that's all."

"So you've said." Jameson dropped the printout and eyed the smaller man. "You're certain that the colloidal silver is sufficient to prevent infection?"

"Between the silver in their armor and the silver in their system, they should be protected." He turned and gave him a crooked smile. "We can give them injections of infused garlic if you'd like."

"Ha-ha-ha. I'm sure the men would enjoy smelling like a cheap Italian restaurant."

Ingram snorted. "They're so brainwashed, they wouldn't care. If you told them to march off a cliff, they would."

"They're not lemmings, Robert." Jameson stepped over to the viewscreen and glanced at the video. "They're still soldiers with minds of their own."

"Now that is funny." Ingram adjusted the brightness of the image and sat back to stare at the CRT. "You've got them so doped up that they couldn't create an original thought if they had to. I guess it's for the best though. With that much HGH and steroids running through their systems, if they were allowed to run unchecked, they'd probably fall into a hormone induced rage and kill each other."

"You're not amusing." Jameson reached past him and clicked the button to eject the video disc.

"Hey, I was still watching that." He reached for the disc as Jameson slipped it into his jacket pocket.

"Burn another one for your own records." He stretched his neck and squared his shoulders. "Notify me once they're rearmed and rested. I want to be there when they're field tested against the fangers moving north."

Ingram stared at him as though he had just slapped him. "Remind me again who put you in charge? I thought we were partners in this little venture."

"The mere fact that I'm the *Director* of the Agency and you're the Assistant Director for the NSA means I have seniority.'

"And let me guess. Since you're older you get to sit in the front seat on long trips and you get to pick which cereal Mom buys when she goes shopping?" Ingram gave him a sardonic glare.

"Don't be a smart ass, Robert. We have far too much work left ahead of us." Jameson reached for his hat and stepped to the door. "To be honest, with how you've been talking about the way these soldiers have been treated, I'm beginning to wonder if you were the right man for this project."

"Hey, I came to you with this, remember?"

"Yes, I remember." Jameson paused, his hand on the door. "Which causes me to wonder why you're suddenly getting cold feet at this early stage. You read the project reports prior to us implementing them. You knew what would happen. You were on board before you ever presented it to me. But suddenly I'm the bad guy for approving the project and making it a reality?" He pulled the door open and stepped through. "I think you need to get your priorities straight, Robert."

10

Mitchell hung up the phone and rubbed at his eyes. "What a clusterfuck."

"I take it you won't be joining me for food?"

He glanced up to see Jenny standing at his door, a disappointed look on her face. "I'm sorry, love. Things have gone from bad to worse."

She pulled the door shut behind her and walked slowly into his office. "Are things always so stressful?" She slipped in behind his chair and began kneading at his neck and shoulders, attempting to work the knots out.

Mitchell groaned as his eyes closed to slits and the tension worked itself from his body. "Believe it or not, not always, but lately it seems like if it's not one thing, it's another. We're either under attack by a group of crazed wolves or there's some power hungry lunatic trying to take over the world. Now we find out that another government agency has some kind of super soldier in the making and they're targeting us."

"What? Can they do that? Don't you work for the government?"

He shrugged slightly under her grip. "Yes and no. Technically we do, but also, we're military and we're a black op. We're under the radar by most standards." He groaned as she hit a particularly stiff knot.

"So can't the government people you work for tell the other government people to go to hell?"

He chuckled lightly at her over simplification. "I actually just got off the phone with one of those government people."

"And? What did they say?"

"Off the record, they said that if it came down to us versus them, they'll disavow us. They can't risk having their names attached to a group of operators whose purpose is hunting monsters. On the record, he's going to do what he can, but he seriously doubted he would have much pull."

"Why's that? Government is government, isn't it?" She stopped massaging and stared at him. "Can't they tell the others to just stop what they're wanting to do before they do it?"

"That's part of the problem. The other group is a pretty secretive club. Nearly everything they do is hush-hush. Just getting info on them is nearly impossible. Trying to find out exactly who, what, when and why?" He shook his head as he let the statement hang in the air.

"That doesn't seem right, Matt. No group should be so big that one part doesn't know what the other part is doing."

"I agree, but then, I'm not the head honcho in charge either." He reached up and took her hand. Pulling her to him, he cradled her in his lap. "I wouldn't worry too much if I were you. We've had worse problems crop up before."

She stared into his eyes and he could see them tear up. "I know this sounds silly, but I just found you. I'm not ready for us to be over yet."

"I thought we were both in it for the long haul?"

She kissed him lightly and laid her head gently on his shoulder. "We are, I'd just like the long haul to be a bit longer than a few days."

*****

Jack scribbled notes in his pad while his team shuffled into the conference room. Allister appeared almost angry as he glared at the man standing at the front by the white board. Azrael stepped near the griffin and patted his thick shoulder. "You look troubled, friend."

"That is stating things mildly." Allister turned his feathered head toward the gargoyle. "We had a visitor while you were out, and it left me...disheveled."

Jack looked up from his notes and raised his voice. "Everybody grab a seat. We have a lot to go over and little time to do it." He noted the sly grins that Kalen and Brooke shot at each other and how she made sure she found a seat next to the lean warrior. His curiosity piqued, but he kept his thoughts to himself as he finished scribbling in his notes. "As Allister stated, we did have a visitor. An angelic visitor."

A light murmuring went up in the small crowd and Phil's brows hiked as he looked up at Jack. "Did he give his name?"

"Azazel. Ring any bells?"

The Nephilim shook his head, his brow furrowing. "No, but that doesn't necessarily mean much. I've only met a handful."

"He claimed that the archangel Michael sent him with a message." Jack cleared his throat and watched while the crowd gave him their unfettered attention. "He gave us Lilith's location. He also said that, if we wait, she'll come to us."

Kalen glanced about at the crowd. "Why would she come here?"

Gnat grunted as he thumped his hammer down on the table. "We took something she wants back." He glanced to Chief Jack and nodded. "Didn't we?"

"According to the angel, she wants her suicide vests back. But seeing as how I sent them out for demil, she can't reclaim them." Jack slipped the cap back on his pen and made short paths in the carpet as he paced. "I was only able to discuss the details for a short time with Azazel, but there are bad points to both choices. If we go to her, we're in unfamiliar territory. If she comes to us, we put a lot of other lives at risk that don't necessarily need to be."

"Which do you choose?" Phil asked, his eyes narrowing at the human leader.

"I haven't. I decided to leave it to the team to decide." Jack looked each of them in the eye as he spoke. "If you were my team, assigned to me by my superior officer, I'd either make the decision or accept the orders of my commanding officer. But this time, you are all on loan. Yes, I am supposed to train and lead you, but you aren't truly mine to do with as I please. I'm not willing to risk your lives on what I'd like to see done."

Brooke leaned closer to the table and shook her head. "So what? Is this a democracy now? We're all supposed to…what? Vote on it?"

"Exactly." Jack nodded his head. He pointed to the map on the wall. "She and her horde are located here, near this small town. According to the angel, she's holed up inside an abandoned sawmill."

Azazel stood and stepped closer to the map. "This green all indicates forest, yes?"

"Yup. Hence the sawmill."

Azazel turned and smiled to Gnat. "Your kind of territory, is it not?"

Gnat smiled and tugged at his beard. "Mine and the Greaters. You *are* a forest elf, are you not?"

"I am." Kalen nodded. "Most definitely."

Jack stepped forward and caught Azazel's attention. "The tree canopy will be a hindrance to your taking to the air."

"Won't be the first time." He pointed to the concrete ceiling. "And this structure is not conducive to flying either. Unless we met her outside. And at night." he shrugged.

"Let's see a show of hands for taking the fight to her." Jack watched as all of them raised their hands. His mouth slowly curved into a smile until he reached Allister. "You disagree?"

"I have no 'hands'. But yes. My vote is to take the fight to the demon bitch."

"Alright then, everybody gear up and meet me topside in one hour. I'll notify the colonel of what's going on and maybe we can get some communications gear."

The crowd quickly took to their feet and worked their way to the exits. Jack tried not to notice Brooke as she sidled in next to Kalen. "I'll only need a few minutes to get ready. How about you?"

"I'm ready now."

She flashed him a wicked smile. "Imagine that. We have a whole hour to kill."

Jack could almost swear her eyes flashed as she smiled at him. He watched the pair exit and shook his head. "Be careful, sugar cookie. She has one hell of a bite."

*****

Laura paced by the edge of the woods, her eyes trying to focus on the deepening shades of darkness between the pasture and the treeline. She continually glanced back toward the house to ensure that Crystal wasn't coming out to check on their progress in finding Jim.

Laura turned suddenly when she heard the stumbling steps of someone working their way out of the brush. She ran toward the noise and watched as Derek stumbled out of the woods and collapsed on the ground. He panted for breath and shook his head. "Don't say it."

"Don't say what?" She probed his face for some hint at what he meant.

"Don't say, 'I told ya so'." He rolled to his side and coughed, his breathing becoming more labored.

"What happened, D?" She reached for him and he gently pushed her hand away.

"The old bastard jumped me." Derek pulled himself to a sitting position and coughed into his hand. He pulled his hand away and stared at it in the moonlight. "He's definitely got his strength back."

"Oh, my God. Derek, are you okay?" She grabbed his shoulders and lifted him to a better sitting position.

"I think so. I thought maybe I'd punctured a lung or something." He held his hand closer to his face and studied it. "No blood though. I think I'm good."

Laura blanched. "Did he scratch you or bite you?"

Derek shook his head. "No." Another coughing fit caught him off guard. "But he tackled me and sent me into a tree trunk." He looked up at her and gave her a pained smile. "They don't give, ya know?"

Laura chuckled with relief and sat down next to him. "I guess you didn't get a shot at him?"

Derek grunted. "He knew what I was doing. He pulled the dart and crushed it." He slowly shook his head, his eyes betraying him and allowing the tears to flow. "He knew exactly what he was doing and…"

"What happened?"

Derek sniffed back the tears that caused his nose to run. "He told me…quit. Go home. Know that this is what he wanted."

"So, he still had his mind about him?"

Derek nodded. "Yeah, but I don't think he knew his own strength. He looked shocked when he hit me and I went flying."

"Are you okay?"

Derek shrugged. "Cracked ribs, I think. I'll live." He glanced back toward the trees and shook his head. "Wish I could say the same for pops."

Laura sighed heavily and held her head in her hands. "He'll live, D. Just not like what we had hoped."

The pair sat quietly for a while listening to the sounds of nature. Both wished they could hear a wolf howl so that they could pretend it was their father. Finally Derek turned to her. "What will you do now?"

Laura shrugged. "I guess..." She let her voice trail off as her mind raced. "I guess we should probably have a memorial service for the rest of the family."

"That's actually a good idea. Give them some closure."

"Then I guess I'll go back. Unless reports of a Halfling in the area suddenly crop up, then..." She turned and eyed Derek. He watched her shake her head slowly.

"You said he wouldn't. I mean, he'll turn into the wolf, right? That is what you told me."

"That's what is supposed to happen." She lowered her head again and sniffed back her own tears. "It's just that my luck has been so shitty lately, I don't know if I want to put that much faith into it."

Derek placed a hand on her shoulder and used her as leverage to get to his feet. "Help me to the house. We have to break the bad news to Crystal, then call Jimmy, and..." He sighed heavily. "I am *so* not looking forward to this."

*****

Mark worked his way toward his office when Jericho stopped him in the hall. "We have primaries you need to look over, Major."

Mark scanned the report and shook his head. "Seriously? Can these guys not tell the difference between fireflies and pixies?" He shook his head and slipped the sheet into his folder. "Anything else, Jones?"

"No, sir, but this is the third time this year we've gotten a primary on that 'mothman' type creature. We just can't seem to get a secondary on it before it disappears."

"Maybe we need to look for some kind of pattern to the sightings? If we can find one we can have a squad waiting for it."

Jericho shrugged. "It's just sightings though, Major. To date, it's never harmed anyone."

"Doesn't mean it won't start." Mark opened his door and stepped inside. "Keep me updated."

"Aye, sir." Jericho turned and headed back down the hall as Mark slipped behind his desk and fell into his chair. He pulled the report again and ran through the list once more.

"Possible vamp attack. Possible wolf. Possible…what the hell is a wendigo?" He laid the list down and entered his password into the computer. As his eyes scanned the small amount of info he could find, he sat back and shook his head. "Oh, hell no."

Mark reached for the phone and called Jericho back. "When was the primary turned in on this wendigo thing?"

"Yesterday, Major. We've tried to send a secondary spotter into the area but…" his voice trailed off.

"Spill it, Cap."

"Well, Major, the secondary spotter can't make contact with the first. It's like he dropped off the grid."

Mark closed his eyes and clenched his jaw. "Spin up First Squad. Have them make ready."

"Sir? We don't have a secondary yet."

"I doubt we'll get one either." Mark shook his head as he stared at his computer screen. "As much as I hate to say it, Cap, I think our primary may have become a victim."

*****

Bigby stared out the dust encrusted window overlooking the hangar. He jotted a few notes in his pad and bit a chunk from the protein bar in his pocket.

"Wouldn't you rather have something a little more substantial?" Mick's face twisted as he glanced at the wrapper hanging from Big's pocket.

"If you feel like whipping up a steak and tail, I'd be more than happy to eat it." He lifted the binoculars back to his eyes and scanned the area once more. "You're sure they haven't left this location?"

"Well, no. Not positive. But from the way they talked, they had no intentions of actually leaving. They just wanted to make it sound that way to Walter Simmons." Mick stretched and cracked the knuckles in his hands.

"Other than the guards milling about, I see nothing happening."

Mick shrugged. "They stay pretty much inside unless they're needed." He noted Bigby staring at him suspiciously. "That's what I noticed anyway."

"I've seen one vehicle show up but nobody leaves." He jotted more notes in his pad and then turned his attention back through the window. "Strange lot, aren't they?"

"I've seen stranger."

"I'm sure you have." He bit off another chunk from the protein bar and continued to watch the hangar. "I wish there was a building on the other side. I need to see where their air intakes are."

Mick shot him a curious glance. "Air intakes? Why?"

Big lowered the binoculars and shot him an evil grin. "How else am I going to introduce my favorite gas to them?"

"You…you're going to *gas* them?"

"To start with." Big bit off the last of the protein bar and dropped the wrapper to the carpet below. "Then I'll make sure they can't come back by ensuring there's enough high velocity lead in their diets." He chuckled at his own little joke.

Mick groaned and rolled to his side. "But Jenny's in there."

Big lowered the binoculars and studied him. "What part of 'I don't care' did you not understand?"

Mick inhaled deeply and got to his feet. "You do realize that Mr. Simmons will spare no expense to hunt you down. He won't stop…ever. Not until your head is on a pike."

Big chuckled and lifted the spy glass back to his face. "Like I care. As soon as I destroy the squads, Hell itself could open up and swallow me whole and I'd go happily."

"What in the world could they have done to you that you hold that much hate?"

Bigby looked away from the window and shot Mick a hateful stare. "They took my best mate and commanding officer. They took two armies from me." He slipped the dust caps back onto the binoculars and settled into the chair beside the window. "I walked away from my career for that man. We had plans, ya know. Big plans. And along comes these haphazard dumbasses and take it all away. I've got nothing now, and it's all their fault."

Mick listened to him and slowly nodded. "But Jenny had nothing to do with any of that. She just got here. It's not her fault."

"Casualty of war, kid. Casualty of war."

*****

Brooke rolled away from Kalen and gasped to catch her breath. "How much time do we have left?"

Kalen shrugged and nipped at the tender flesh of her side causing her to jump. "Probably enough time for one more." He ran a fingertip down her spine and watched her stiffen.

"Sorry, love, we're about to go into battle. I need to eat something." She stood up and he watched as the sheet slid from her lithe body.

"My goodness. You truly are a heavenly body." He leaned forward and bit her on the cheek of her bottom, causing her to squeal and swipe at him.

"I mean it. Stop or I won't be held responsible for what happens next." She laughingly pulled her top back on and began to shimmy into her leather pants.

"Oh, wow, I love watching you do that." He sat on the edge of the bed and reached for her again. She quickly hopped aside and laughed as he playfully grabbed at her. "Come to me," he hissed as he stood and pulled her to him. He shoved his face into the crook of her shoulder and nibbled up the side of neck and to her earlobe.

"Please, Kalen, I really have to eat something." She tried to push him away and he held his arm out to her.

"So have a quick snack." He smiled at her mischievously.

Brooke paled and quickly shook her head. "I-I can't." She pushed past him and made for the door.

"But why? I don't mind. Really."

She froze at the door and exhaled slowly. "Kalen...vampires cannot feed from elves." She turned slowly and gave him a sad smile. "It's like giving alcohol to an alcoholic. Once we start...we can't stop. And the effects are...not good."

He lowered his arm and closed the distance between them. "I'm sorry, Brooke. I didn't realize." He pulled her into an embrace and gently kissed her cheek. "Go if you need to. Eat and gather your strength." He pulled back and gave her a broad smile. "I'll wait for you topside."

She gave him a sheepish smile and slipped through his door. He felt her own door shut through the concrete wall, and he placed his hand against the wall and closed his eyes. He tried to 'feel' her on the other side, but all he could feel was the cold of the cinder block. He sighed lightly and began dressing.

As he stood at his door and prepared to leave, he glanced once more at the bed that was still warm from their lovemaking. He smiled to himself and wrapped the bow over his shoulder before pulling the door shut behind him. He may never be able to return home, but it didn't matter. She was his home now.

*****

Lilith stepped out onto the balcony of the warehouse and watched as more of her Legion came to her. They were arriving in groups of three or four at a time and quickly making their new home war ready.

She listened to the steady 'beep-beep' of trucks as they backed up and equipment was unloaded. She smiled to herself when she saw some of the crates that she feared had been intercepted being unloaded. She would see to it that they were rerouted. They would attack the largest churches first and work their way down. Amongst those cathedrals, she intended to send a team to attack the Capitol and the White House.

She felt Samael's hand as it slipped around her waist. "Soon your Legion will be complete."

"And we will go to the human hunters and regain that which is ours."

"Until then, you will be sending out the remaining devices?"

She nodded as she watched her Legion hard at work. "They will be in place or close to it. Then once we have reclaimed what is ours, they too, will be positioned and readied."

Samael watched as the Legion repacked the crates and prepared them for shipment. "At what point will I be making my appearance to the humans?"

She turned and ran her hand across his broad chest. "Soon, my love. Once we have destroyed the churches, you shall step forward and declare yourself the one responsible. While the humans are still trying to ascertain how to deal with a 'devil', I'll position myself to step in and take the reins." She smiled at him and he felt his insides flutter. She was beginning to realize her true potential for evil and it made him love her that much more. "After I show them that only I can control the monstrous, evil, vile creature responsible for all of this death and destruction, I'll simply demand that they bow to me if they want to be saved."

"I've wondered, what will you do if they refuse? They can be quite stubborn."

She laughed, a deep, hearty laugh. "My love, they want to be ruled. It's in their basic makeup. They would rather be ruled than allowed their illusion of freedom." She raked her nails across his chest causing him to shiver. "Just look at the people here. They pretend that they're free, yet they do nothing to stop their own rulers from stealing more of their freedoms with each passing day."

"There is a difference in being governed and being ruled, my love."

She turned and leaned against his abdomen. "Is there? I think not. Not truly. And once they think that the only way they can be saved is to bow to me and call me their queen, they'll stand in line to kiss my feet."

Samael raised a brow at her and shook his head slightly. "I hope that you are right."

"I am. Wait and see. They will cower and cry and beg me to save them." She suddenly spun and gave him a chill smile. "But you have to truly step up and show them your evil side. You need to make them believe that you truly *are* your brother."

Samael smiled at her then lifted her to face him. He planted a kiss on her mouth then dropped her. "If anybody knows how evil my brother can be, it's me."

She quickly smoothed her gown then stared upwards at him.

"It's not me you have to convince, my love. It's the surviving humans. They have to believe that you truly are Satan."

"As I said, have no fears." He stared out through the hundreds of Centurions working below. "I know evil."

*****

Ingram marched into Jameson's office and dropped the report on his desk. "Results are in." He sat in the chair opposite the older man and watched as he scanned the report.

"These reaction times are accurate?"

"To the microsecond." Ingram smiled. "We calibrated their reactions to the recordings and it's spot on."

Jameson smiled as she went through the report more thoroughly. "I've never seen anything like this."

"Look at the measured reaction times for the fangers."

"Oh my…" Jameson trailed off as he double checked the report. "And you're positive that these are accurate?"

"Of course." Ingram leaned back in the chair and hooked his thumbs together behind his head. "The Titans are stronger, faster and have quicker reaction times than the fangers they hunt."

Jameson slowly closed the report and inhaled deeply. "You know what this means, don't you?"

"I know that the intel is true. Older fangers are stronger and faster, but for the most part, unless the Titans are dealing with some seriously *old* bastard, they'll have the advantage. Add in their tactical knowledge and weaponry? They'll have the advantage even then, too."

Jameson shook his head. "That's not what I meant." He slid the report to the side of this desk and smiled broadly. "They're more deadly than the Monster Squads."

"Oh, that." Ingram waved him off. "Yeah, I already had that figured out." He chuckled as he sat up. "But do you realize? Once we clean out the squads and then start eliminating the other monsters...the vampire council won't be an issue at all."

Jameson nodded. "We just make sure we get paid first." He winked at Ingram.

"Oh, of course." Ingram laughed as he stood up and turned for the door. "Once the payment hits our Swiss accounts, they're toast."

"Who'd have thought." Jameson rocked back and forth as he stared off. "The very group that hired us to remove the Monster Squad would get taken out by the same super soldiers." He laughed as he came to his feet.

"I love the irony." Ingram reached for the door and paused. "By the way, they'll be ready to head north this evening."

"Are you planning on going with them?" Jameson sat on the corner of his desk as he watched the smaller man.

"Oh, no, no, no...I'll watch the live feed through the drones. They have some excellent video equipment and the lag time is near nil."

"Where are we staging at?"

Ingram turned back and shot him a knowing smile. "The command center is finished. We'll be observing from there."

Jameson cocked a brow at him. "Finished? That's nearly three months ahead of schedule."

"Funny how monetary incentives can do that to a contractor, isn't it?" Ingram reached for the door. "I'll send a car for you."

"See you tonight." Jameson watched the smaller man leave and then slipped back in behind his desk. He entered his password and pulled up the schematics for the command center.

Located within Langley Air Force Base, the newly constructed command center wasn't huge, but it would house the Titans and their support staff. Jameson scanned the blue prints for the center and tried to get a visual in his mind. He placed himself within the structure and imagined walking the halls, going from location to location. Once he was sure that he was familiar with the layout of the new facility, he quickly shut down his computer and reached for his coat.

He had a long night ahead of him and until then, he had preparations to make. The first would be to ensure that the Council kept their word. Half of the payment would be made once they showed proof that the Titans were battle ready.

Jameson patted his coat and smiled inwardly when he felt the video disc still in his inside pocket. He'd email the video to the Council and once the initial payment was made, he could start planning the demise of the Monster Squads and prepare for his early retirement.

Who said that protecting the citizens of this country couldn't be profitable?

11

Mitchell exited his office to find Major Tufo quickly approaching. "I have something." He waved a report in his hand and Mitchell quickly scanned it.

"Secondaries?" He didn't look up as he read the initial write up.

"There won't be any." Mark stared at the top of the man's head with a grimace etched on his face. "I had no idea what a wendigo was so I looked it up. They've been trying to reach our spotter, and he isn't responding."

Mitchell handed the paper back and shrugged. "Give him time. His cell battery may have died or he may be some place without signal."

"He's a victim." Mark slipped the report back into his folder and watched his CO for his reaction. "After reading what a wendigo was…I just knew. I could feel it."

Mitchell stiffened and cocked his head questioningly. "You want to send a team into an unsubstantiated situation?"

"If it's nothing then no harm, no foul. But if I'm right, the faster we act, the better."

Mitchell considered his logic. "I suppose it wouldn't hurt." He scratched at his chin as he thought. "Where is this located?"

"Ontario area. Not too far from Windigo Lake." He raised a brow as he waited for Mitchell to make the connection.

"So the monster is named for the region? Interesting." He inhaled deeply and let it out slowly. "Okay, get a squad geared up and in the air. Better to be safe than sorry. Just be sure they're brought up to speed on this thing before they hit the muck."

"Roger that, sir." Mark spun and marched toward the OPCOM. Mitchell watched him, his own thoughts reverting back to his XO's health and mental readiness.

He slipped down the stairs and entered the large open area that Evan's lab was contained in. He waved to the doctor as he approached and entered the lab unannounced.

"Colonel, I was just finishing my analysis of the technical drawings you sent me."

"Excellent. Thanks, Doc." He quickly glanced through the acrylic wall to ensure they were alone. "I actually came here to talk to you about Major Tufo."

Evan paused and slowly set down his pen. "What can I help you with, sir?"

"How is he, really?"

Evan stood and turned slowly, his brows furrowed. "I wish I could tell you conclusively, Colonel, but I honestly can only go by what he's told me."

Mitchell tried not to register his shock but failed. "How so?"

"Physically, he's the picture of health. Other than not feeling pain like you or I would, he's great. He has a healthy pulse, his muscle mass has increased, his body fat decreased, his strength is…unreal. His mental awareness is as sharp as ever." Evan sighed and sat back down. "I just have nothing to compare him to. There's never been a…a…*hybrid* before. So really I can only go by what he tells me. He claims that he feels fine so I assume he has no reason to lie."

"Do you have any idea why he can't feel pain like we do?" Mitchell crossed his arms and leaned against the counter.

"I can only assume that it goes back to why we feel pain in the first place. It's to warn us of something that is life threatening. Since Major Tufo heals so quickly and so completely, I can only assume that his brain doesn't register the damage as painful. He doesn't need to avoid the damage because it really isn't damage."

Mitchell nodded as if he understood. "What about his appetites? Have you noticed anything different?"

"You mean is he craving blood? No, not so far as I can tell. He hasn't said anything to me about it." Evan pushed his chair over to his workbench and pulled a notebook. "I've taken the initiative to monitor his caloric intake."

"You watch him eat?"

Evan shrugged. "Not overtly. I went over the security footage from the cafeteria. The only thing of note is that he does ingest very large quantities of food, but rarely. His appetite is voracious, but he only seems to feed every other day. Calorie wise, he eats about the same as the squad members, just that he stores it for longer."

"Like a snake."

Evan shook his head. "No, not really. He isn't cold blooded and he doesn't take weeks to digest large meals." He shook his head as he thumbed through his notes. "He just fills up for longer periods, that's all."

"Remind me not to invite him out for BBQ and beer." Mitchell pushed off the counter and sighed. "I just worry. I have this distinct feeling that something bad is going on with him that we have no idea about."

Evan nodded. "If it is, it isn't manifesting in any measurable way."

"Very well." Mitchell turned to leave. "Keep me updated.

Anything that seems out of the ordinary..." he trailed off. He turned and gave Evan a quirky grin. "Well, you know what I mean. If it seems *off* to you, I want to know about it."

"Understood, sir." Evan reached for his report and handed it to him. "The analysis."

Mitchell grabbed it and thumbed through it. "Is it as bad as that fella made it out to be?"

"Worse."

*****

"I'm telling you, he pointed the damned thing straight at me. He knew exactly what he was doing," Popo kept his voice low as he spoke to Jack. "Just the idea that the son of a bitch is here is enough to make me want to shove a silver spike up his ass."

"I understand. Believe me, I do. And I've got no answers for you, Pedro. Just know that as soon as I can get him out of here, he's gone." Jack placed a reassuring hand on his friend's shoulder. "If I could send him packing now, I would. But it's not up to me."

"Just tell me you're not going back to work for him." Popo's eyes pleaded with him.

"There is no way in hell I'd go back to work for him. Besides, he's already replaced me as his Second. I don't have to worry about his problems anymore. If the Vampire Council wants to come after him, that's his problem, not mine."

"It just pisses me off that we went there to help him deal with those guys and then he turns on us." Popo blew his breath out and looked back to him. "Where will you go when this is over? Are you coming back here full time?"

Jack shook his head. "I have a wife and child on the way. I figure I'll go and live with the pack."

"What the hell will you do there? I'm sorry, but I can't imagine just sitting around in the woods chasing rabbits and deer as the life for you."

Jack laughed and shook his head. "No, buddy, it's not like that at all. They have jobs and homes and...their own community. I'll probably go to work as security. It's what I know best."

"Well, if you want backup on this op, you know I'd be proud to cover your six again. I'd feel bad if you didn't make it back to Nadia."

"If I don't make it back, there *is* no Nadia." Jack shook his hand earnestly. "Trust me, I appreciate the offer. But according to the Wyldwood, it's just supposed to be the mod squad."

"If you change your mind, I'm sure the whole squad would be there in a heartbeat."

"I appreciate it. You fellas hold down the fort here." Jack glanced around then turned serious. "And keep an eye on things. I still don't trust Thorn any further than I can throw him."

"Copy that."

*****

"There's just too much ground to cover." Laura paced the living room, her cell phone pressed to her ear. "Jimmy, Derek already went out and searched. He checked everywhere that Dad has taught him. It's got to be someplace that he kept to himself."

Derek rolled his eyes and groaned as he lay back on the couch, the cold beer pressed to his forehead. "Tell him I didn't even pick up a trail. Maybe that will convince him."

"D said he didn't even pick up dad's trail." Laura stared at the trophies along the wall as she spoke to her oldest brother. "Wherever this ancient burial ground is, only dad knows."

Crystal cleared her throat and Laura spun to stare at her. She noticed that her lower jaw quivered as she spoke. "Maybe somebody with the tribal government knows where it is?" She shrugged, her eyes hopeful that Laura would see merit in at least trying.

Laura nodded. "Jimmy, check with whomever you still have contact with at the tribe. See if anybody there knows of any ancient burial grounds out there." She heard the hope in her brother's voice as he agreed, then hung up. Laura turned slowly to her father's lover and met her gaze. "He's got friends there that...maybe."

Crystal made her way to the recliner and sat down gingerly in it. "I can't believe he'd do this."

"I'm sorry you had to hear it like this. I wanted to tell you in a gentler way." Laura stood beside her and placed a hand on her shoulder.

Crystal patted her hand and nodded. "I appreciate your trying, Laura. To find him, I mean." She looked up at the younger woman and Laura noted the tears forming in her eyes. "I'm glad you got to see him before he...before..." She broke down and began sobbing, her grip on Laura's hand weakening.

"If he can be found, we'll find him." She patted the woman's shoulder and looked to her brother. He clenched his jaw and forced himself to sit up straighter.

"Knowing Dad, he had this planned the whole time." Derek avoided Laura's stare. "He used to be so 'into' the ancient tribal lore, he was probably just waiting for a small bit of his strength to return so he could begin his spirit walk."

Laura fought not to groan as Derek gave a feeble attempt at explaining away their father's actions. She dragged her finger across her throat, hoping he would stop, but Derek continued. "You know, he used to really be into the whole spiritual side of our past, right? He probably marched out there so he could transition to the other side and not have to suffer in a white man's hospital any longer. He probably thought he was taking the burden off us somehow."

Laura rolled her eyes as Crystal sniffed away her tears. "Where would he come up with such a stupid idea?"

Derek swallowed hard. "It was a very old story that he used to tell us when we were kids. A great Native chief knew he was about to die so he went to the woods and prayed for his spirit animal to carry him to the other side. His spirit animal was the eagle and when it came to get him, he showed no fear. When the eagle touched him, he was transformed into an eagle and the two of them flew away together. The eagle allowed him to live another lifetime in the physical plane as a spirit animal for another great warrior."

Crystal sniffled again and wiped at her eyes. "Surely he knew it was just a story."

Derek shrugged. "Probably. But if he was too far gone…you know, in the head? He might have come to believe it."

Crystal stood slowly and wiped at her face again. "I think I'm going to lie down for a bit." She reached for Derek's hand as she passed by. "Let me know if the tribe has any information, okay?"

"Will do." The pair watched her work her way back to their father's room and listened for the door to shut.

"Why would you say those things?" Laura whispered angrily.

Derek waved a dismissive hand at her. "She needed to hear something. Better an old tribal story than the truth. Besides, in a lot of ways, I told her the truth, just with a twist."

"The truth doesn't always set you free, ya know."

Derek gave her a steely glare. "Remember that when you go back to your monster hunting buddies."

*****

Mark waited while First Squad geared up then held a briefing. He explained his fears about their primary spotter and how he was probably already a victim.

"The guy would have tried to keep track of the wendigo so that he could easily point it out to the secondary. If the creature got wind of him, it would have attacked." Mark clicked the button bringing up the etching of the monster. "You'll note that it appears a lot like a normal human. The creature may be slightly larger than a normal man, but it will have the strength of *many* men. Only a direct hit to the brain or heart will drop it, and even then, you'll need to quarter it and burn the remains. These things are tough as nails."

"Where do they originate?" Donnie asked.

"They're indigenous to the area, but their creation is unknown. There are rumors that they were men forced to revert to cannibalism at some point, and the taste for human flesh remained. We really can't be certain. Other origination stories claim that they are men inhabited by demons or spirits. Local Native Americans believe that they are evil spirits that have taken over the bodies of great warriors, destined to live forever but forced to feed off other men. Just know that they are hard as hell to kill and we can't be certain that there's only one. Cover your six out there. These things are silent, mean, and strong."

The team downloaded what little information was available for the creature and studied the sketched drawings. Gus scratched at his chin as he read through the report. "How can we tell what's a wendigo and what's human?"

Lamb ribbed him. "The wendigo will be chewing on your face. Humans will squeal like a little girl and run away."

"Point taken." Gus closed the file on his PDA and turned to Tufo again. "These things are nocturnal?"

Mark shrugged. "Your guess is as good as mine. You may end up facing this thing day or night. Just keep your eyes peeled for any kind of natural cave system." He dismissed the squad and sent them to their waiting chopper. He worked his way toward the OPCOM when Dom and Marshall intercepted him. "Major, we need you to green light an op for us."

Mark stared at the large Italian standing before him. "What op might that be?"

"We want to back up Phoenix when he hits the Devil and Miss Jones. I really think he should have an extra set of operators on the ground if she's supposed to have hundreds of demons with her."

Dom elbowed Marshall who stood taller.

"If nothing else, we can provide support."

Mark lowered his eyes and shook his head slowly. "According to Jack, it's supposed to be the Junior Rangers, only."

"We know that, sir. But maybe you could tell him that you insist?" Dom was reaching and he knew it. "Just...I dunno, tell him that if he's going to be basing his group out of here, we need assets on the ground, too."

Mark stared down the hall toward Mitchell's door. "Clear it with the old man and you have my blessing."

Dom broke into a toothy grin. "Thank you, sir."

"Don't thank me yet. Jack's liable to kick your can all the way back here even if the CO says yes."

*****

Rufus stood near the open door of the hangar, the twilight warning him not to leave the shadows just yet. He listened intently on his satellite phone while it rang. When the voice on the other end answered he turned deeper into the shadow and glanced about to ensure it was safe to speak.

"I got your text. Are you certain it is ready?"

"We tested this one. Twice. After what happened with the last one...I can only apologize Monsieur Thorn. You were adamant about receiving it so soon, it couldn't be tested and..."

"As long as this one works." Rufus held his hand to the phone to prevent his voice from carrying. "It is still selective in its operation?"

"If you mean it will only kill what you aim it at, yes. Of that we are certain."

Rufus shuddered as he tried to imagine how the device had been tested. "I'll take your word for it. I'll be sending my man to pick it up. No need to ship this one. Just make sure that it is properly cased."

"Already taken care of, sir."

Rufus quickly pressed the end call button then dialed Viktor. When the man answered Rufus didn't allow him time to speak. "I need you to pick up a package in Austria."

"They have finished already?"

Rufus fought the smile tugging at the corners of his mouth. "And it has been tested. There will be no repeat *accidents*."

"Might I suggest that we *not* bring it the hunters? If they caught wind…"

Rufus nodded solemnly. "Agreed. Leave it on the plane. Contact me when you are close, and I shall meet you at the airport."

"We'll be taking the fight to her?"

Rufus glanced toward the stairwell leading to where Jack and his team of warriors were set up. "We will be taking the fight to someone, but I am not yet sure to whom."

*****

Little John boarded the transport and strapped in. He tucked his rucksack beneath his seat and kicked it under tightly with the heel of his boot.

"Yo, boss, you ever face a Winnebago before?"

"Wendigo. And no."

"Yeah, well Winnebago rolls off the tongue easier." Little John checked his weapon safe then stowed it beside him. He watched Spalding strap in across from him. "You think this thing is as bad ass as the major thinks it is?"

Spanky shrugged. "I haven't met a monster yet that was warm and cuddly. From what the spotter said, a lot of hikers have gone missing up there."

John glanced about and watched the other hunters prepare for takeoff. Their demeanor seemed relaxed and uncaring for the most part. He hooked his thumb toward them and nudged Spanky. "Just another day at the office for these characters."

"No sense getting twitchy 'til you have to. Learn to relax until you have to tighten the sphincter." Spanky gave him a quick wink.

John blew out a nervous breath and tried to relax his shoulders. "Easier said than done. If this thing is anything like what the XO sent to our PDAs?"

"Every monster has its weakness. If not silver, then it's something else. I haven't met anything yet that a good beheading and a big fire couldn't kill."

John stared at a spot in the wall, his mind elsewhere. "I pray you're right."

"Look, Sullivan, this thing eats so it probably breathes. If it breathes or bleeds, it can be killed. Don't get wound up over it. We'll probably get boots down, run into it and find out it's nothing big. Hell, we may even find the missing spotter and find out his cell was busted. There's no telling."

John nodded absently. "I suppose you're right. I just have this creepy feeling."

"Why's that? Because they think that these things were once human? So were vamps and wolves. Hell, just about everything out there that we hunt was once human." Spanky snorted and shook his head. "Doesn't say much for human nature when we can be turned into a monster so easy, does it?"

"There but by the grace of God go I." His voice was barely a whisper above the engines spinning up.

"Yeah, well, just remember…we're the good guys." Spanky slapped the man on the back of the shoulder then settled back, his eyes closed for the ride.

John stared at his hands, his mind wondering, *Are we? Are we really?*

*****

Bigby watched as the team loaded into a truck then pulled away from the hangar toward the airstrip. He eased around the edge of the window sill and focused tightly on the hangar. The setting sun threw shadows across the different openings and he couldn't make out what was within.

"Looks like some of them are leaving. Probably out to hunt some unsuspecting werewolf." He cast a quick glance toward Mick. "Or werecat."

Mick didn't take the bait. He kept his eyes focused on the tips of his boots. "You going to wait until they return to do your thing or do you plan to gas the other two-thirds while these are away?"

Bigby smiled at the disdain in his voice. "I'm not sure yet. First things first. I need to put eyes on those air inlets."

"They're on the back side of the hangar. You'll have to actually leave here to find them."

"Aye, and I intend to." He put the caps back on the binoculars and set them aside. "I just need to wait for it to get a little bit darker."

Mick snorted. "Just walk up like you own the place. You did it with me, and look at how that worked out."

Bigby squatted next to the man and tilted his head, studying him in the growing darkness. "These men aren't pussies like you are. They actually put up a fight."

Mick turned hateful eyes to him. "So take the fight to them. Face them like a man."

Big smiled and Mick felt a lump form in his throat. It wasn't a happy smile.

"If it were one on one, I'd do just that, mate. But these boys are trained killers. Just like me. Unlike some people, I know when the odds aren't in my favor."

Bigby reached across the man and plucked a protein bar from his stack. He ripped it open and bit off a chunk. "I'll be taking the fight to them, but not until the time is right."

"Gassing a group of people when they aren't expecting it isn't taking the fight to them. It's cowardly and you know it."

Bigby refused to be baited. "Maybe. But I see it as a way to even the odds."

"How is poisoning the whole group evening the odds?" Mick sat up straighter and stared at the man.

Bibgy swallowed the bite he had in his mouth and sat down on the floor across from Mick. "If I had a missile, I'd use it. If I had an army, I'd use it. Since I don't have either of those weapons, I'll use my head. And my head tells me to gas them all and then go through and sink a round into their skulls while they're twitching on the ground." He bit off another chunk of the protein bar then tossed the rest aside. "We came at these buggars with an army once. They sent 'em packing with their tails between their legs. Then they hunted us down and they took out that army. That leaves just me."

"So rather than admit defeat, you're going to poison the whole lot of them?"

Bigby nodded. "Every last one. Right down to the little shits whose only job is to sweep the floors and empty the bins. If they're part of that operation, they die. Plain and simple."

Mick exhaled hard and settled back against the wall. "It's still wrong. I'm no *warrior* like you claim, but even I know that."

"One of these days you'll care about something enough that you'll be willing to put your life on the line for it." He stood and stretched. "When that happens, you'll understand why I'm doing what I'm doing."

Mick watched the man stroll across the empty workspace but his mind was wrapped around Jennifer. She didn't deserve to die because this maniac wanted the rest of them dead.

Care about something enough to put his life on the line for it? He thought of Jennifer again and swallowed hard. He found himself standing, his fists clenched as he watched Bigby stare through the binoculars again.

In his mind he was moving toward the man, his body shifting, preparing to rip him apart. In reality, he sat back down and stared at his hands.

*****

Lilith stood along the upper railing and stared down at her demon army as they began grouping into battalions. She smiled to herself as fully two-thirds of her people had already found their way to her once more.

"Very soon the rest will arrive." Samael hovered nearby, his body hidden in the shadows. "We can arrange transport once they are assembled."

Lilith turned slowly on him, her eyes questioning. "Tell me, lover, why don't the demons simply possess the bodies of the hunters and bring me what is mine?"

Samael sighed and placed a hand on her hip. "The hunters have been warded from possession. I cannot tell if it is a spell or talisman, but your demons cannot physically inhabit their bodies."

"A shame. It would be pleasing if I could retrieve what is mine and simply have my demons cut the hunters throats before departing."

"As soon as we realized who we were facing, the demons attempted. It was…painful to say the least." Lilith gave him a quizzical stare and he continued, "The warding burned them. Much like silver to a vampire. The hunters never even realized what was happening but the demons who volunteered? They will not soon forget."

"Interesting." She turned back to observe her troops once more. "And can we discover the source of the warding?"

"Perhaps once we have attacked and decimated their force. We could leave one or two alive and question them."

"And if they don't know or are unwilling to share this information?"

Samael smiled. "Then we shall bury them alive in the rubble of their stronghold."

Lilith smiled and stepped close enough to kiss her fallen angel. "You're starting to sound more like your brother."

Samael snorted, "You have no idea."

*****

Jameson walked through the newly constructed halls and heard his own footsteps echo off of the walls. The structure appeared nearly abandoned but he knew that was intentional. He strode to the stairwell door and pulled it open just as Ingram stepped out.

"I was just coming to escort you in." He gave Jameson a puzzled look.

"I have a copy of the schematics, remember?" He held the door for Ingram and waited while he slowly turned and began to make his way back down the stairs. "How long until the operation begins?"

"The drone just verified that they are assembling and preparing to move. The Titans will be in place in a matter of moments."

"They won't begin without us?" Jameson waited while Robert punched the codes into the door to the operations room.

"Negative. They are in stand-by mode waiting for the order to go."

Jameson took his seat and waited while the small handful of technicians prepared their consoles. Ingram walked slowly behind each one and pointed to the large flat screen mounted above each station. "Communications. Satellite Imagery. Air Support. Life Support."

Jameson's brow furrowed. "Life Support?"

"They monitor the vitals of the Titans via their interactive armor. If anything goes south, we'll get a report here in real time."

"How do you mean, 'goes south'?"

Ingram shook his head as he sat beside Jameson. "If they incur any battle damage, it's reported here. We monitor their heart rate, adrenaline and cortisol levels, blood pressure…the works."

Jameson hiked a brow. "And it's all read through their armor?"

"Yup. We can even feed their heads-up displays there. Or we can switch to a helmet camera and see things as they do. It's quite remarkable."

Jameson crossed his arms and leaned back in his chair. "I'd say it's time to get the party started."

Ingram smiled and leaned forward to the communications tech. "We're a go."

"Affirmative, sir." The two older men watched as the tech typed commands into his console then hit enter. Almost instantly, the Titans began moving from their camouflaged cover and converging on the moving targets.

Ingram leaned across to Jameson. "This shouldn't take long."

"Let's hope." Jameson watched the screens and could almost imagine it was the mutated hunters that the Titans were engaging. "For their sake."

12

Mitchell eyed the two men standing before him. "You're telling me that Major Tufo gave you his okay for this op?"

Dom shifted uncomfortably. "Well, Colonel, he said he would okay it if you did."

Mitchell leaned back in his chair and studied the pair. "You realize that Jack isn't going to stand still for this. He's convinced that the Wyldwood is some kind of soothsayer. What she says is law, and she told him it was only supposed to be his crew."

"Yes, sir, but I'd feel better knowing he had another set of eyes covering his six." Dom could feel the man's eyes piercing him. "I know it sounds like 'mom said it's okay with her if it's okay with you', but…" he glanced to Marshall who fought a grin.

"I understand," Mitchell groaned as he leaned forward. He ran a thick fingered hand across his face and exhaled hard. "Look, if you want to tag along and provide support, I have nothing against it. But I promised Jack I'd keep my nose out of their business. You have to have his blessing."

Dom felt his face twist as he tried to think of a way to twist the colonel's words. "You think I can tell him that you ordered us to tag along?"

Mitchell snorted. "Absolutely not." He stood and poured another cup of coffee. "*Ask* the man. Plead your case. The worst he can do is say no."

Dom snapped to attention and gave the colonel a quick salute. "Thank you, sir."

"Be safe out there," Mitchell called to the closing door.

He sighed heavily as he sat back down and pulled the folders to him that were copied from Stevens' stack of papers. He rifled through the reports until he came to the armor that the Titans wore.

"Project Gladiator?" He sifted through the papers and pulled up the overview of the battle armor. "Why the hell couldn't we have gotten something like this for our guys?"

The phone on his desk buzzed and Mitchell picked up the receiver. "Mitchell."

"Colonel, you have a call." Lieutenant Gregory sounded a bit confused as he spoke. "The man says that he's your *father-in-law*?" Mitchell gripped the phone harder and felt his jaw tighten. "Do I put it through, sir?"

"Yes. Put him through." Mitchell heard the click and buzz while the call was transferred to a secure line.

"Mister Mitchell?" an unfamiliar and tinny voice asked.

"Colonel Mitchell. I take it this is Walter Simmons."

"You're a very hard man to track down, Colonel."

Mitchell ground his teeth and squeezed his eyes shut. "What do you want?"

"I need to warn you, Colonel. Your people…my *daughter* isn't safe."

*****

Jack finished packing his gear and was preparing to leave when Evan approached him, a broad smile on his face. "You may need these, Chief."

Jack watched as Evan handed him multiple magazines for both a FiveseveN and a P90. Jack held his hands up to stop him. "Doc, those won't do me any good. Silver is useless on these guys and—"

"It's not silver." He handed the magazines to him again and Jack flipped a round out to examine it.

"It looks like a standard silver round."

"It may look like it, but it's a milled bullet from the arrows that Kalen gave us. We finally found an industrial diamond bit that would cut the arrow shafts. I had the boys in the fabrication shop mill you enough rounds to fill these magazines." Evan practically beamed as he spoke.

Jack stared at the round, his mouth hanging open. "You're serious? I have 'angelic bullets'?" His face broke into a wide grin as he stuffed the magazines into his pouch. "Doc, you're a freakin' genius!"

"I aim to please." He gave the man a quick smirk. "You aim, too, please. That's all we have, and the fabricators said that they burned up all of the diamond cutters they had making these. Every shot counts."

"No spraying and praying, gotcha." Jack felt practically giddy. Until Evan delivered, he was afraid he would be facing a demon legion with nothing but an angelic dagger and his dick in his hand. He quickly checked out the pistol and carbine then checked that the rounds cycled freely. "Good job, Doc."

"Just be careful out there, Chief."

"I have his back." Dom stepped beside Jack and clapped a hand on his shoulder. "If you'll have me, that is."

Jack's face fell and he gently shook his head. "Dom, I appreciate it, but—"

"No buts, buddy. We cleared it through Mitchell and Tufo. Both gave us their blessing, but only so long as you'll allow it." Dom watched as Jack opened his mouth to protest and quickly cut him off. "Look, I know we aren't 'supposed' to assist, but you have to admit, having an extra set of eyes on the situation can't hurt. We can provide backup in case something doesn't go as planned. We can hold back and pick off stragglers or something."

Jack sighed and averted his eyes. "Dom, this is supposed to be just—"

Dom held his hand up to stop him again. "We don't have to engage, Phoenix. Me and the boys would just feel a whole hell of a lot better if you had somebody watching your back. Even if that means covering the perimeter."

Jack lowered his eyes and chewed at the inside of his cheek. After what seemed like far too long, he nodded. "Perimeter only. Do not engage unless you have to."

Dom smiled and slapped the man's back. "All we have are these worthless silver rounds. Maybe we can slow them down, right?"

"Possibly."

Allister approached from the shadows and cleared his throat as best that he could. It sounded much like a cat hocking up a hairball. "Chief Jack, we are prepared."

Jack turned and faced his warriors. "Let's rock and roll. We want to catch them with their pants down." Allister gave him a confused look and Jack smirked. "It's just an expression. Means catch them off guard."

"Ah. Perhaps you should have said that."

*****

Laura sat on the front porch and watched as her family slowly began to show up. As each brother arrived, they would hug and exchange pleasantries, but inside Laura felt as though they secretly blamed her for her father's actions. She knew it was because she blamed herself. Only Derek knew what really happened and he didn't act like it was her fault. Why did she?

She knew why; because it was. She fought to break away from the teams and sneak her father a cure. It had taken far too long for her to make a clean break…her sense of duty overriding her devotion to family. She pulled her legs up under her and squeezed her knees to her chest as her eyes scanned the skies.

She felt the chill air begin to bite at her skin and chose to ignore it. She heard the front screen door open but refused to face whichever brother happened to step out there with her.

She felt the warm body sit next to her and she continued to stare upward. It seemed a long time before the voice spoke, and it surprised her when it was Crystal.

"Do you think maybe he's staring at the same sky right now?"

Laura shrugged slightly. "I'm hoping so."

She felt the arm wrap around her then the comforting warmth of the blanket that Crystal placed over her shoulders. "Don't catch a chill." She stood slowly and Laura continued to stare upward. "Try not to stay too long, Laura. You won't do anybody any good if you get sick."

Laura nodded slightly, her eyes still glued to the starry sky. "Do you blame me?" She surprised herself when she asked Crystal the question. She hadn't even been thinking it.

Crystal sat back down beside her and wrapped her arms around her shoulders. "Of course not. Nobody blames you, Laura. You couldn't stop him from…well, nobody could stop that man when he made up his mind."

She turned a blank face to Crystal and stared at her. "Mom could have." She didn't even realize she had said it until the words escaped her. Her eyes went wide and she put her hand over her mouth. "Crystal, I'm sorry. I shouldn't have…"

Crystal gave her a soft smile and simply nodded. "I know. Trust me, I've heard the stories about your mother." She reached up and tenderly tucked a loose strand of hair behind Laura's ear. She turned and stared at the night sky that had Laura so enraptured just moments before. "I think I would have liked your mother."

Laura's face must have registered surprise because Crystal laughed. "Oh, honey, I meant if she were still with us, I think she and I could have become great friends. Of course, your father would still be with her. He absolutely adored her." She smiled again and Laura could tell it was genuine.

"It didn't bother you that...well, I mean..."

"Bother me? Oh, heavens no. That was just one of the many reasons I loved your father so much. His dedication to her and his family was so...refreshing." She leaned into Laura, bumping her slightly. "He tells me that you and she are very much alike."

Laura snorted. "Yeah, I don't think so."

Crystal chuckled with her. "To hear your father tell it, you were a carbon copy of her. Well, except she had red hair. But as for your personalities? You were a chip off your mom's block."

Laura simply stared at Crystal, a newfound respect forming deep within. "You really loved him."

"With everything I had." She continued to stare at the sky, her mind elsewhere.

Laura felt a lump forming in her throat that she couldn't swallow. "I'm so sorry."

Crystal turned and gave her a confused look. "For what?"

"It's because of me that Dad never married you." She fought not to get choked up but she felt her eyes watering despite her best efforts.

Crystal slipped her arm back around her shoulder and pulled her close. "Sweetie, it wasn't just because of you. I think somewhere deep down inside, he felt that he would be betraying your mother's memory if he married me." She pulled back and stared into Laura's eyes. "And you know what? I was okay with that. I took what he was able to share and I cherished every moment I spent with him."

"But, I thought you wanted to marry Dad?"

"Sure I did. But he wasn't ready." She shifted again and turned her eyes back to the sky. "At first, it hurt a little. But I soon realized that I didn't need a license from the state or a preacher to tell me what I already knew in my heart. For the short time I had him, he was mine. And I was his. In our hearts, we *were* married."

Laura sniffed back a tear and leaned her head against Crystal's shoulder. "You're a much stronger woman than I am."

She chuckled again and gently stroked Laura's hair. "No, sweetie, I'm not. You are your mother's daughter. From what I hear, that makes you pretty damned strong."

The two sat silently and continued studying the night sky. After what seemed forever, Crystal leaned forward and stretched. "I'm getting too chilly. How about we go inside and get something warm to drink?"

Laura nodded silently and slowly stood, her joints arguing against the cold. "That sounds like a wonderful idea."

*****

Mark took the command seat in OPCOM and watched as the team made a fast approach on the drop zone. He marked the log and turned to the communications tech. "Verify coms."

"Coms verified, sir. Loud and clear, five-by-five."

"Very well. Enter the time in the log and let's split the monitors between the teams."

The logistics officer turned and gave Major Tufo a confused look. "Sir?"

"First Squad has quite a bit of transit time ahead of them. Second Squad will be backing up Phoenix and his team. Their transit time will be nil." Mark updated the command codes into the chair's command keypad then spun to face the screen.

"Begging the major's pardon, sir, but is Colonel Mitchell aware of—"

Tufo cut off the inquiry before it could be finished. "Of course he's aware, Lieutenant. Second Squad wouldn't be supporting without his blessing. Now, if everybody can focus on the tasks at hand, we have a dual operation to oversee." He spun the chair and punched in the codes for the overhead flat screens. "Tie in coms from Second Squad."

"Aye, sir."

As the monitors flickered and came to life, Tufo slipped the headset on and turned the sound down to a dull buzz. His hearing was sharp enough that he probably could have heard everything with it hanging from the arm of the chair, but he did his best to keep up appearances. "Switch us to red light and let's get the coms on the overheads."

"Done and done, sir."

"Helmet cams on periphery monitors." He didn't look up as he punched in more orders for the drone operators, ordering them to stand by. He looked up to the Logistics Officer. "Isn't the 173rd out of Kinglsey?"

"I'm not sure. I think so, sir."

Mark scratched at his trimmed chin and studied the map on his PDA. "Jack said she was holed up at an abandoned saw mill in Oregon. Little piss ant town in the middle of nowhere…" he trailed off in thought. He suddenly looked up and nodded to the Logistics Officer again. "Notify the 142nd in Portland and the 173rd. See if either has a drone we can commandeer. Use a NORAD Word of the Day."

"Sir?" The logistics officer gave him a questioning shrug.

"They'll be much more likely to *loan* a drone to NORAD for use in U.S. airspace than they would a black operation like us, Lieutenant."

"Aye, sir." The man smiled as he began processing the request. "And the Word of the Day is?"

Mark looked at his PDA and frowned. "Trojan? Who uses a condom as their word of the day? That's just gross."

"Perhaps they meant the people, sir? Or the horse?"

Mark shrugged. "I'm going with the rubber." He shot the lieutenant an evil smirk. "They're all dickheads at NORAD anyway."

"Aye, sir, and I'll be sure to have that stricken from the hard copy, Major."

Mark shrugged. "Like anybody reads them." He sat up straighter in the command chair and motioned to the clock. "Mark the time and tighten your assholes. It's time to make the doughnuts."

*****

Rufus slipped through the door and hovered near where Jack and his crew were still staging. He listened intently for any clues as to where they were going. He knew that his brother was doing his best to glean information as well, but he feared that even if they could pinpoint exactly where Lilith was, they would be too late in getting there. Those damned elves and their portals made travelling far too easy over great distances.

He listened, straining his ears until he heard one of the men say Oregon. His stomach fell as he tried to calculate how long it would take for Viktor to return and for the pair to travel across the continent. He slowly shook his head then swallowed hard.

Rufus stepped back through the doorway and toward the crowd. He motioned to Jack. "A word, if I may?"

Jack paused and dropped his gear on the table. "I'll be right back." He quickly closed the gap between the two and dropped a steely eyed glare on the vampire.

"I didn't mean to eavesdrop, but I overheard one of the men mention Oregon? If this is where Lilith is currently hiding, I would very much like to be a part of the raiding party."

"It's not a raiding party. We're going there to destroy her."

"Yes, of course." Rufus glanced to the side and lowered his voice. "Jack, I have not mentioned this before, but I feel I must be most forthcoming with you."

He crossed his arms and stared down at the man he once trusted, his gaze indicated he never would again. "By all means."

Rufus cleared his throat and tried to choose his words wisely. "After you... left my employ, I met with the council. They were quite clear in their decision. They would only entertain removing the edict if I were to remove the threat of Lilith."

"That's what we're going to do. Lucky for you somebody else gets to put their neck on the line and you still benefit." Jack shot him a smirk and turned to leave.

"*Non*, Jack, you do not understand." Rufus reached out to stop him but held himself short. "The council...they will know. If I am not a part of the force, they *will* know. The edict will stand." He maneuvered himself between Jack and his people. "I know you, *Monsieur*. You are many things, but you would not do anything purposefully when you know it would cost the life of another. Even if you hold nothing but disdain for that person. You simply would not allow yourself to be so callous."

Jack hiked a brow and studied him. "You think you know me that well, do you?"

Rufus gave him a sad smile. "*Oui*. I know you that well."

Jack inhaled sharply and let it out slowly, his eyes pinched shut. "Let me guess, you want to bring dear old dad in law and your deadbeat brother along as well?"

"My brother, *oui*, but Viktor is running an errand for me."

Jack's gaze narrowed. "Where is he? You didn't tell me he was going anywhere."

Rufus held up his hands again to calm the man. "He went to speak with his contacts at the Vatican. In case we cannot stop her, perhaps they can empty the churches. Minimize the damage she can do. That is all."

Jack's Bullshit-O-Meter pegged, but he did his best to give the man the benefit of the doubt. He ground his teeth together and clenched his fists. "Fine. Tag along if you must, but stay out of the way. It's bad enough Second Squad is coming, too. I don't need to babysit anybody else."

"*Merci.*"

"Don't thank me yet." Jack turned to gather his gear. "We have to survive this assault first."

*****

Bigby watched the hangar from the building across the street, his notes jotted down in the pocket notebook of his breast pocket. He tried to ignore the sighs of boredom coming from across the nearly empty office space.

"Tell me something."

With clenched teeth he lowered his binoculars and turned to the werecat. "What?"

"Why are you really doing this? You told Simmons to piss off, so it's not for money. Your army was actually his hired goons, so it isn't loyalty."

Bigby closed his eyes and tried to count before he said something he regretted. "What would you know of loyalty?"

"Quite a bit actually."

"Well, you know nothing of mine. So try shutting your hole before I shut it for you." He lifted his binoculars again and studied the hangar.

"I'm just curious. Indulge me. Nobody's paying you for this job, and you're obviously a mercenary."

"A what?" He lowered his spyglasses and stared at the man. "You called me a mercenary?"

"Well, yeah. You whored yourself out to Simmons once then

double-crossed him. That says quite a bit for your loyalties." Mick smirked at him, a self-satisfied grin forming.

"Listen to me, pup, and listen well. It will do you good to watch your tone with me. First off, I'm nobody's whore. I got into this mess because of loyalty. Loyalty to a good man. A man who saved my life plenty of times."

"Ah, yeah. You mentioned that. The boys across the road killed him, yeah?"

"Yeah, they did."

"And that's why they have to pay? Because your mate turned against them and paid the price? So now you have to as well?"

Bigby took a step toward him then caught himself. He stared at the cat lying on the floor appearing relaxed, a stupid grin painted across his face. "You're not worth it."

He turned back to the window and continued staring at the hangar.

"No, go on. Tell me. Tell me how your mate screwed up so that now you have to go on a killing rampage, because I really don't get it."

Bigby clenched his teeth as he stared at the carpeted floor, his binoculars hanging from his neck. "It wasn't like that." His voice was barely a whisper.

"What wasn't?"

"The bloody vamps got his family. Held them. Threatened Sherry if he didn't…if he didn't do what they ordered."

Mick sat up straighter and cocked his head to hear better. "Go on."

"They wanted him to kill another vampire. A vamp that had gotten hisself in tight with the Yanks. He was the leader of the *Beastia* clan." Bigby turned and Mick saw the pain in his eyes. "They had his mum and his sister. Threatened to rip their innards out and mail them to him if he didn't do it."

Mick got to his feet slowly and studied the man as he spoke. For the first time since meeting Bigby, he saw an emotion other than hatred or rage. "What happened?"

"The Yanks. They got wind of the deal. They ruined Sherry." He tilted his head back and stared through the ceiling. "Oh, they managed to get to his family and put them all in some kind of witness protection in the middle of nowhere. But they killed Sheridan. For all intents and purpose, the man was dead." He turned and glared at Mick. "He stopped taking the bane. Found out that he could shift at will once he did. Then he came and found me."

"Why?"

Bigby snorted. "To get the band back together, of course. Why else. Once an operator, always an operator."

"I mean, to what purpose?"

"Imagine, boy. Monsters hunting monsters? For profit?" Bigby laughed. "Yeah, it was a dream, but he sold me on it." He shrugged as he marched the short distance back to where Mick stood. He picked up a bottle of water and twisted the lid.

"I'm not following."

"Aw, Sherry didn't have to sell me on the idea. I'd have followed him to the gates of Hell. But the other boys? Yeah, some of them needed convincing." He took a long swallow and shook his head. "Some couldn't be convinced."

Mick saw the look on his face and knew without a doubt what became of them. "He killed them."

"Made it look like an accident, but yeah."

"And yet you followed him? They were your mates."

"And he was my commanding officer. Like I said, to the gates of Hell."

Mick leaned against the wall and let him continue talking.

"I couldn't bring myself to stop taking the bane. Yeah, I knew I'd be stronger and faster, but to me, I felt like I'd be a slave to the moon, ya know? So I kept taking it. Not Sherry. He said he needed the added strength to overcome his wound."

"What wound?"

Bigby hitched his jaw toward the hangar. "The one his 'best Yank friend' gave him. Shot him through the foot with a silver round. Ruined the bones of his instep, the bastard."

Mick grimaced. "Damn. Some friend."

"Look, if it's all the same, I'd just as soon not talk about it anymore. Just accept that they have it coming."

*****

Jameson leaned back in the chair and watched as the helmet cam feeds shimmered. The Titans had turned off their active camouflage and were now visible to their potential targets. Pandemonium broke out as targets began to panic and break away from the main groups.

Ingram let out a whoop as the first volley of rounds struck the main body of fangers and their bodies ashed almost instantly. The Titans had flanked the slow moving group and were firing at 45 degree angles into the advancing group. As they broke away and tried to retreat, the lead fangers ran into those in the rear causing even more panic. A tertiary group of Titans closed the gap and began mowing them down as they were bunched into a ball.

Ingram watched as the Predator came online and dropped a silver nitrate bomb into the main mass of bodies. They quickly dissolved into a large fireball of ash.

Jameson propped a foot up on the console and shook his head. "This isn't a test, Robert. This is shooting fish in a barrel."

"I know. It's awesome, isn't it?" Ingram laughed as the Titans continued to engage and decimate the ever shrinking group of vampires.

Small groups of one or two would break away and try to make a run for it only to be run down and find a blade sunk between their shoulders, ashing them before they could hit the ground.

The entire encounter was over and done in a matter of minutes. Jameson watched as the few surviving humans were rounded up and shot, their bodies piled onto the embers of the vampires and doused with motor fuel. He stood from his chair and pulled his jacket straight.

"We'll need more than this before we pit them against a more dangerous enemy."

Ingram spun in his chair and glared at him. "What are you talking about? This was flawless."

"This was no challenge."

"So?" Robert shrugged. "They're too well trained. They're too fast. They're too *efficient* at their jobs. That gives you doubt in their ability to remove the squads?"

"The squads *shoot back*, or have you forgotten?"

"No, I haven't forgotten. But you were the one who thought that this should be the go-no-go test for these boys. Have you forgotten that?"

Jameson stared at the screens again and shook his head. "Gypsies."

Robert paused, his brain not understanding the response. "Say what?"

"These were gypsies, Robert, not warriors. Just…nomads. There was no fight in them."

"What are you saying?"

"I'm saying there was no fight in them. This wasn't a test of anything but how quickly our boys could pull the trigger." He marched to the screen and pointed to the ash piles scattered across the fields. "Not one of them attacked. They all ran."

Robert turned and stared at the ash piles. They were all meters away from the Titans and where they were staged. He pulled his remote to him and rolled back the footage. As he replayed the carnage, it finally sunk in what Jameson had picked up the first time. He sat back in his chair and sighed heavily.

"Do you see it now?"

"Yes." He ran a hand across his face and stretched his neck. "I really thought that..." He turned and faced Jameson. "How are we supposed to give them the experience they need? What can they face that will challenge them enough to prepare them for the squads?"

Jameson leaned against the concrete column in the center of the room and shook his head. "I have an idea, but I don't think either of us would like it."

"Tell me."

Jameson pushed off the column and squared his shoulders. "The only source of monsters I know of that would definitely fight back." He stared Ingram square in the eye. "The Council."

13

"When the hell *aren't* we in danger?" Mitchell barked.

"That may well be true, but this danger is imminent. And, as much as I hate to admit it, it may be my doing." Walter Simmons' voice cracked, "I hired a man to…to kill you. For what you did to my daughter."

Mitchell groaned. "You mean Sheridan and Bigby?"

"Yes, I'm afraid so."

Mitchell tried very hard not to scream into the phone. "You realize that Sheridan has been neutralized?"

"Yes, but Major Bigby has picked up the gauntlet and—"

"*Major* Bigby? I hate to burst your bubble, but Bigby was Sheridan's sergeant. He may know a thing or two, but it sounds like his ego inflated."

"I should have expected as much."

Mitchell interrupted him, trying to get back on point. "Regardless, do you know where he is now?"

"No, Colonel, I do not. I tried to call him off, but he refused. He said that he didn't care what happened to Jennifer. He said that collateral damage happened all the time in war and…and that simply is not acceptable."

"So that's when you decided to pick up the phone." Mitchell punched a button on his intercom and held his hand over the receiver. He ordered the security doubled and an APB and BOLO put out on Bigby. Turning his attention back to Simmons he glared at the wall. "If you don't have any specific intel for me, what good is this call?"

Simmons flustered momentarily then cleared his throat. "I know that you have no reason to trust me, Colonel."

"We agree on something."

"Yes, well…when it comes to my daughter, I'm sure you understand why I might be a bit overprotective. She's the only family I have left."

"And she's my mate now, so that makes her welfare my priority."

"Be that as it may, you'll understand why I wouldn't hesitate to offer my resources to assist you in stopping this madman."

"One man. You think I need your help in stopping one man?"

"Colonel, I think you underestimate the depths that this man would stoop to."

"And I think you underestimate the abilities of my men, sir." Mitchell stood, the veins in his neck standing out as he did his best to refrain from reaching through the phone and choking his 'father in law'. "Forgive me if I don't run and hide from this limey buttplug. My boys and I have held our own against far worse than anything he can throw at us, and we will continue to handle far worse long after his bones have turned to dust. Trust me when I say that I'll give him his due diligence, but I'll not lose sleep over what he *might* do. Once we have a lead on him, we'll be sure to send enough high velocity silver his direction to ensure he doesn't bother anybody else." He gripped the phone tighter and feared it might crush in his hand. "Good day to you, sir."

He did his best to lay the phone gently in the cradle and failed miserably.

*****

Jack watched as the last of his team stepped through the boulder and then turned, staring into the trees leading down the mountain. He estimated they had at least a six-kilometer hike before reaching the mill and he knew it wouldn't be long before they were engaged in a battle that could likely be their last. He turned back and waved his team over to converge on him.

"Remember your staging points and areas of coverage. There's likely to be a shit ton of demons there dressed in human meat suits. As much as I wish we could save them all, we can't allow them to escape. If any get by us, they could just as easily try to follow through with Lilith's plan."

"Chief Jack," Allister stepped forward, his head nearly a foot taller than the soldiers surrounding him, "if you will allow me a few moments before you commence fighting, I can ensure that the demons do not leave the area. At least, non-corporeally."

"Say again? In English this time."

Allister cocked his head to the side and Jack had trouble reading the expression on his face. "They will not be able to leave as a light being. They will be trapped in their host bodies."

"Excellent." Dom elbowed Jack. "Does that mean bullets will kill them?"

Allister shook his feathered head. "No, but you can damage them enough to take them out of the fight. And they won't be able to slip into a new body and rejoin the fight. At least, not until the spell is broken."

Kalen held a hand up to interrupt. "You can trap them with a spell?"

"Of course."

"Can you send them back to the depths from which they came?"

Allister shook his head again. "Only the death of Lilith can do that."

Rufus turned a questioning look to Paul who shrugged. "*Excusez moi.* Did I hear you correctly? Removing Lilith from the battle will send her demons back to Hell?"

"Yes, that is correct." Allister didn't understand why this seemed like new information to the hunters. He truly thought this was common knowledge.

"And the Fallen one?" the Nephilim asked. "He will be banished back as well?"

Allister shuddered at the thought of Samael and his torturous ways. "Yes, all of those who call her 'queen' shall be sent back to whence they came."

Jack glanced around at the team and nodded. "New goal. Lilith goes down first. If we can drop the bitch early, the fewer people who can get hurt. Understood?"

Allister perked up again. "You do realize that she can't be destroyed."

Jack turned a surprised look to him. "But you said—"

"I said her death would send them all back to the depths, but she cannot be destroyed. She has been marked by the hand of God."

"So…what *are* you saying?" Dom asked, unsure there was an answer he'd like.

Allister smiled as best as he could. "Rip her heart from her chest and the body dies. Lilith herself may not be destroyed, but her life-force will exit."

Jack nodded. "Good enough for me." He racked a round into his P90 and stepped from the circle. "Rack 'em and stack 'em boys and girls. Time to make the doughnuts."

*****

Laura sat on the edge of the bed, the phone pressed to her ear. "It's been heartbreaking, Evan. It seems like the more I tried to fix things, the worse they became."

"I wish I had an answer for you. Some magic word that could restore your hope or make you see a silver lining, but...I have nothing."

She gave a half-hearted chuckle and sniffed back tears. "You're such an optimist," she joked.

"Hey, I don't candy-coat with you, you know that." He leaned back in his chair and glanced around the lab. "You know I don't really buy into the whole fate thing, but maybe there's something to it. Maybe this was meant to be."

"What? That I was meant to screw up my whole family and cause them this kind of pain?"

He shook his head at the phone and sighed softly into the speaker. "No, love, maybe it was predestined that you were going to lose your father, but...rather than lose him to death, you lost him to...I dunno. A different path. A different life. A...another chance at being happy. Or something. Hell, I don't know. Like I said, I don't buy into the whole fate thing."

"For somebody that doesn't buy into it, it sure sounds like you've given it some thought."

"I'd be lying if I didn't admit that." He glanced up toward Mitchell's office. "I mean, our CO is 'mated' to his fated mate. Tufo should have died on the hangar floor...hell, he should have died three times on my table. He got infected by both a wolf and me, yet somehow, he defied all the odds and not only survived, but he's thriving." He leaned forward and pinched the bridge of his nose. "I know jarheads are tough, but nobody lives forever."

Laura glanced out the window towards the woods and could almost imagine her father staring back at her through wolf eyes. She smiled at the idea and pressed the phone closer. "Maybe not. And maybe you're right. Maybe it was my destiny or maybe I just screwed up. Who knows, right?"

"There ya go. All you can do is accept that things are the way they are and go on."

She sat silently for a moment then said what she feared the most. "What if I can't?"

"What if you can't what? Go on?" The worry in his voice was evident.

"What if I can't accept what happened and just let it be?"

"What more can you do, love? Your father doesn't want to be found. He doesn't want any part of the cure. You said he crushed the other vial, yes?"

"Evan, I worry. What if he…what if he doesn't transition all the way to the wolf? What if he's stuck as a Halfling and somebody sees him? What if the squads have to—"

"Shh, don't even think like that." He did his best to set her mind at ease. "I ran all of the scenarios through the modeling and it's a ninety-six percent chance that he'll continue mutating until he reaches the wolf stage. The odds of him being stuck as a Halfling are…very small."

"The way my luck has been running, I wouldn't trust a hundred percent odds."

"Well, it sounds to me like you're due a break." He wished he could be there to hold her tight. "And it sounds like you need some sleep. You must be exhausted."

"I am. I just don't know if I'll be able to rest."

"Alcohol works well as a depressant. I'm just making a suggestion."

She snorted into the phone. "Are you prescribing me a shot of whiskey?"

"Or bourbon or scotch or whatever you have on hand."

"Just a shot? I think a fifth might be in order."

"No, ma'am. I want you to sleep, not get drunk. Trust me, the last thing you need is to battle a hangover in the morning."

"Yeah, you're right." She stood and stretched, her eyes scanning the woods again. "One shot then hit the sack." She paused and leaned against the open window sill, the cool breeze whispering past her skin. She held the phone close again and said softly, "I love you Evan. Don't ever change."

"Never. Now take your medicine and get some rest."

He hung up and stared at her picture on his desk. He studied the lines of her jaw, the glimmer in her eyes, the long mahogany hair. "What has happened to the strong woman I knew? She gets around her family and she becomes twelve again."

*****

"Sierra Actual, OPCOM. Coms check." Tufo gripped the arms of the command chair and stared at the screens showing the helmet cams as the team followed Jack's warriors down the mountain.

"You're five-by-five, OPCOM," Dom's voice huffed as he landed from a short jump off a rock outcrop."

"Sierra Actual, be advised, you have air support inbound. ETA approximately one-five minutes. Copy?"

"Copy that, OPCOM. One-five mikes. Is she outfitted with high velocity silver supplements?"

"Negative, Sierra Actual. But the Reaper will have a full complement of Hellfires."

"Hooah! That's what I like to hear, Major."

Tufo watched as the team continued working their way down the mountain. He monitored their heat signatures from the satellite feed against the incoming Reaper. "Widen the field of view. I want to see what they're about to get into."

The tech controlling the satellite feed sent the necessary adjustments to the satellite, and moments later the picture widened, showing a much larger grouping of heat signatures at the base of the mountain. "Holy smokes. Do they know what they're marching into, Major?"

"Unfortunately, yes." He leaned back in his chair and watched as Jack's team slowed their approach and stopped just inside the tree line. "What are you up to, Phoenix?"

He brought up the helmet cam from one of the members and watched as he slowly swiveled from scanning the area to watching the large griffin. They had built a small rock altar, and now a small oil fire was burning. The creature was digging bags out of his satchel and sprinkling them into the fire.

"Major? Any idea what's going on?"

"Beats me, Lieutenant. Whatever it is must be necessary or Jack wouldn't be standing still for it." He switched back to the satellite feeds and highlighted the heat signatures downhill from the group. "Keep your eyes on this group and let me know if any of them break away or head anywhere close to the teams."

"Aye, sir."

Tufo fought the urge to stand and pace the OPCOM as his adrenaline levels rose. He felt the urge to join the fight rise as each moment ticked past and his mouth began to go dry. He instinctively reached for his water bottle and felt something stick to the end of his fingers. He glanced down and beheld a sight that made his heart skip a beat and his heart fall into his stomach.

His nails had elongated and thickened, appearing much like claws, but unlike anything he had ever encountered. His plastic water bottle was skewered and dripping from the sharpened appendages.

Swallowing hard, he glanced around the OPCOM to see if anybody else had noticed. Satisfied that everybody else was too busy with their jobs, he quickly twisted the cap off and swallowed down the remaining liquid.

Tufo turned his hands so that his fingers were inside the arms of the command chair and hidden from view and then tried his best to return his attention to the men on the screen. Occasionally he would steal a glance at them to ensure nothing else had grown out of his fingertips.

Using his pinky he quickly pushed the internal coms button. "Somebody call for Doc. We may need his expertise in here."

"Aye, sir."

Mark exhaled hard and waited for Doctor Peters to arrive. If he was lucky, the fight-or-flight effects would diminish and he would only have to describe it after the fact. He glanced again at his fingertips and shook his head.

"Could I have picked a worse time to lose my shit?" he muttered.

*****

Rufus watched from the rear of the pack as the griffin performed his ritual. He made sure to keep Foster close to his side as they worked their way down the mountain and kept the Gatekeeper in view the entire way. Now, as the group's attention was focused on the majik taking place, Rufus and Foster made their move.

Rufus slipped in beside the Greater Elf and nudged him to get his attention. "I must beg your forgiveness, but I am in need of your assistance."

Kalen gave him a confused stare and noticed that Rufus gave a slight nod to the side. Kalen followed his gaze and saw the other vampire standing behind Brooke, a silver bladed dagger in his hands and hovering close to her spine. She had no idea as her attention was focused entirely on the griffin.

Kalen spun on Rufus who held a finger to his mouth. "Please, we wish no harm. Only an exit."

"What do you mean, undead abomination?" The hatred in his eyes was apparent.

"We need you to open a gateway." Rufus handed him

coordinates. "To here."

Kalen stared at the coordinates and shook his head. "It is daylight there. You'd be dead as soon as you stepped through."

"At these coordinates, the stone is *inside*. It is safe, I assure you."

"You fear dying by Lilith's hand." Kalen squared his shoulders as he glared at the vampire.

"*Non*, but I know that even if I were to wield the blade that carved out her heart myself, the council would not lift the edict they have placed on my head."

"So you run?"

"I go to face them while you and your army defeat her." He lowered his voice even more, "They will be watching this battle, I assure you. My brother will remain and fight as my Second. This satisfies their decree. But I will go and face them while they are distracted."

"And what is to stop me from killing your brother the moment you've left?" The venom dripped from his voice as his eyes bore into the other man's.

Rufus shook his head softly. "You are a man of honor, a warrior, and you value another warrior in a battle such as this. Every warrior…" He glanced at Paul then back to Kalen. "Even one whose only purpose might be as a distraction, is still a plus."

"Or I could simply kill you both where you stand." His hand hovered over the blade strapped to his waist.

Rufus nodded. "You could. And you would have every right. Or you could follow me back over that small rise and open a gateway for me so that I can destroy the Council." He looked to Foster and shook his head. Foster slid the dagger back into the sheath on his own belt and stepped back from Brooke. "I wouldn't have let him harm her. But I needed you to know the importance of this."

Kalen narrowed his eyes on the vampire. "I cannot trust you."

"Then send me away. To here." He handed the coordinates back to him. "If it is daylight here, and I am lying, then I will be dead as soon as I step through. Or you could open a pathway to another location and place me in a meadow with no shade to protect me. The decision is yours."

"You would go blindly?"

"I would have no choice. I need to get to the Council while they are distracted. My man, Viktor, will be arriving there shortly. I cannot ask him to do what I must."

Kalen glanced at the crowd then took a silent step backward. "We must be quick or I will be missed."

"Thank you, *mon ami*."

"I am not your friend. I am only doing this because I fear you would double-cross us in battle if I did not."

*****

Mick played out numerous scenarios in his mind. Attacking and killing Bigby, bringing the bloody corpse to Jenny and she'd swoon, accepting his gift and wrapping her arms around his neck, kissing him, telling him how she had been wrong and proclaiming her undying love for him. He sighed as reality set in and he remembered the last time he'd actually seen her.

She didn't care two whits about him. She was mated to the leader of the human hunters now. She wanted nothing to do with a werecat. Her father wouldn't allow such a mating even if she had wanted it. He would stop at nothing to hunt them both down and end his bloodline with their own deaths.

He felt his eyes watering up and he sniffed back the tears that threatened to streak his cheeks.

"What's your problem?"

Mick looked up at saw Bigby staring at him from across the open office space.

"Allergies." He wiped at his nose and turned away.

"Yeah, right. You're a were. You don't get allergies."

"I'm allergic to dogs and bullshit. And, oh look…the room is full of both." Mick got to his feet and marched toward the door.

"Where do you think you're going?"

"To take a piss. Want to come and hold it for me? The doctor says I shouldn't lift anything heavy. Bad for my carpal tunnel syndrome." He hiked a brow at Bigby who flipped him the bird.

Mick pushed through the door then stuck his head back out. "If you change your mind, wash your hands first."

Mick walked into the third floor lavatory and stared out the window at the same hangar that Bigby had been studying since he stumbled upon the lair. He sighed and pressed his forehead to the glass. He felt the window give slightly in its frame and he pulled back, studying it.

Applying a bit of pressure, he felt the window give a bit more. An idea sprung to life, and he quickly guesstimated the height of the window and assessed the ground below. Concrete sidewalk and hard-packed earth. He took a deep breath and tried to remember the longest jump he had made as a cat and the hardest ground he had landed on. He was certain he could make it.

But then what? How to alert the human hunters without being killed first? How to do it without Bigby dropping him in his tracks before he could clear the hundred and fifty yards to the hangar?

He glanced at the night sky and the moon above. Barely a sliver of silver hung in the air and the night was as dark as pitch. If he was lucky and darted wide, he might could stay outside of Bigby's range.

He felt his body begin to shift before he made the decision to do so and his hands pressed against the edges of the window frame. His sensitive ears picked up every grain of grit as it ground against the metal frame. He felt one side break loose, and he instantly thrust his arms outward, pushing the window as far away from the building as he could.

In a flash, he shifted, mounted the narrow opening, and planted his feet along the concrete edge of the window opening. He heard Bigby stomp across the floor toward the bathroom and just as the door burst open, he pushed off and out from the window with all of his might.

For a brief moment he felt the cool night air as it rustled through the hair covering his body. He felt his thick tail trailing behind him and the world slowed as he sailed through the air like a giant, striped bird.

As the ground came rushing to greet him, he tucked and rolled then gathered his feet under him. He could hear Bigby's cursing from high above him and the slamming of surplus office equipment as the man rushed back to the main floor.

Mick did his best to zigzag across the open terrain toward the hangar. He wanted to be the most impossible target possible for the SAS sniper. His mind raced as he tried to calculate where the man might expect him to be. He'd leap right, then left. Then he'd leap left again, then right, constantly moving, constantly putting as much distance as he could between himself and the man that he knew was trying to paint crosshairs on him. Tufts of dust, rock and debris erupted from the ground around him as Bigby's shots went wild.

He saw men in military uniforms rush from the dual guard shacks and rapidly close ranks, weapons at the ready. Mick had to make a decision…stop and try to explain why he was there and hope they didn't shoot him, or do his best to evade them *and* Bigby.

He chose the lesser of the two evils and leapt toward the guards, sailing over their heads in a long graceful arc. He didn't hear the shot that ripped through his midsection, but he felt the bite of the bullet as it shattered ribs. Shell fragments and bits of bone destroyed the lower portion of his lung, a lobe of liver and several feet of intestine.

Mick fell, sliding to a stop just inside the open door of the hangar, blood pooling around him as he slowly shifted back to his human form. He knew he was going into shock because the mad rush of activity around him dulled to an annoying buzz in his ears and his eyes began to lose focus as he stared toward a lone Humvee.

One of the guards pressed a knee against his legs and pulled his hands behind his back, cuffing him before rolling him back to his stomach. Mick grunted with the pain and spat a mouthful of blood as he tried to cough and clear his chest of the precious body fluid that was choking him to death.

He lifted his head and stared at the guard beside him. "Bigby…across the road. In the office building. He's going to gas the whole lot of you…"

"Say again?" The guard lowered himself and placed his ear closer to Mick's mouth as he gasped, trying to force air into his ruined lung.

"Big…Bigby. Across…the…road. Gas. Wants to…gas you all…" Mick's eyes glazed over as his heart stopped beating and he stared into the great nothingness that only death can bring.

His last coherent thought was, *Please let me save her.*

*****

Jameson folded his trench coat and draped it over his arm. "Robert, as soon as we can figure out the logistics, we'll make arrangements to fly the entire Spartan program overseas and…"

"Sir? Something strange just came over the wires." A man in a white lab coat and holding a clipboard interrupted. "I think you might want to take a look at this."

Jameson glanced at his watch then laid his coat back down. "Make this quick. If I hurry I can still meet my wife for after dinner drinks."

Ingram fell into step behind the older man and the trio re-entered the command center. "Sir, we intercepted a NORAD request for a Reaper drone."

"NORAD? Why the hell would they want a Reaper?" Ingram

reached for the report and scanned it.

The technician in the lab coat shook his head. "That's just it, sir. They didn't. I mean, it is their codes, but it wasn't NORAD. I contacted their command duty officer and he denied any such request."

Jameson pulled the sheet from Ingram's hand and glanced at it. "This drone is domestic. Pull the video feed from it." He handed the sheet back to Ingram who ignored it as the screen came to life.

"What frequency are they on?"

"It's a scrambled military channel, sir. Shouldn't take a moment to decrypt."

"Well do it then." Jameson took his seat again and watched as the drone slowed and began making lazy circles in the sky, its visual record fed to their monitors. "Can we switch to thermal?"

"Yes, sir. Whoever is utilizing this bird will have no idea that we're piggy backing off their feeds." The tech tapped in a few commands and a moment later thermal imaging appeared on the next screen.

"Good heavens. What is that? A protest?" Ingram whispered.

"In Bumfuck, Oregon? I highly doubt it." Jameson scoffed. "I want high resolution images. Focus on this smaller group outside the perimeter."

"Are you thinking what I'm thinking?"

"If you're thinking that it's the Monster Squad and that they've commandeered a domestic drone, then yes." Jameson leaned back and watched as the image enlarged then focused, enlarged and focused and continued to clarify until he could see men in uniform. The camera panned and Jameson nearly choked.

"What in the holy hell is that thing?"

"A sphinx?" the technician guessed.

"Get me hardcopies of every heat signature in this perimeter group, understood?"

"Understood, sir."

Ingram leaned in to Jameson and whispered, "What in the world are these guys doing? Now they've got a sphinx working with them?"

Jameson shook his head. "I have no earthly idea. I know that they had a fanger helping them, but this?" He glared at Ingram. "This is just…wrong."

"Uh, sir?"

"What now?" Jameson barked then swallowed hard as the camera focused on what appeared to be a giant winged man. He spread his wings and leapt high into the air, his bat like wings scooping air until he reached altitude, allowing him to glide. "Jeezus H. Johnson…what was that?"

"A demon?" Ingram fell into the chair beside Jameson and tried to swallow. "Are they in league with the Devil?"

"Sir? We got two more anomalies. This one is burning quite a bit hotter than the others and the one next to him. Ambient temperature." The tech turned and gave him a wide eyed stare. "Could it be a zombie?"

"How the hell should I know?" Jameson barked. "Do I look like I know what the hell is going on down there? Just keep making me hardcopies of each subject."

"You want to send the Titans against a group like this? When we don't even know what kind of resources they have at their disposal?" Ingram choked. "Jesus, Jameson, they're protected from fangers…but zombies? An infection like that would decimate the entire program."

"We don't know what it is, Robert. You'll do well to keep your head about you. It could be a damned fanger for all we know."

"Really? We've seen fangers in action. They had *some* kind of heat signature. Even if it was a residual from their activity or from earlier in the day. This thing is *cold*, whatever it is."

Jameson reached across the short space and grabbed Ingram by the shirt front. "You will keep your cool, and we will watch this play out. Do you understand me?"

Ingram nodded, his head bobbing up and down. "I understand. I don't like it, but I understand."

"We'll see what this Monster Squad is capable of against a couple hundred targets."

"Sir, there's nearly a thousand by the computer's best estimate." The tech turned and handed him the printouts of the hardcopies he had requested.

"Fine. We'll see how they do against a thousand." He sifted through the papers then turned back to the tech. "How do we get faces on these?"

"Sir, they'd have to look straight up. The satellite can only look down, so..."

Jameson sighed. "Of course." He tossed the hardcopies aside and crossed his legs. "Let's settle in, gentlemen. Something tells me this may be a long night."

14

"I have no doubt that he's concerned for my well-being but I can't believe he actually called you." Jennifer paced slowly in Mitchell's office, the glass of scotch tinkling in her hands. "If he's that concerned about the mercenary he contracted, why doesn't he cancel the hit?"

Mitchell sipped his coffee and tried to avoid the aroma of the smoky alcohol in her glass. He also tried to avoid staring at her form as she marched back in forth in front of him.

"He tried. It didn't take."

"A mercenary that doesn't take orders isn't worth much in my book."

"Agreed. But this guy isn't your average soldier of fortune. He's an ex hunter from an overseas team. His boss tangled with us and was removed. He's holding a grudge."

"By removed, you mean you killed him."

Mitchell shrugged. "Not originally. We simply removed him from his team and…look, it doesn't factor into the equation now so there's no sense in rehashing the details."

A knock sounded from Mitchell's door. He barked and it opened, a flustered master sergeant appearing at the edge. "Sir, we have a situation with the prisoner."

"The prisoner? Oh…the CIA guy. With everything else going on, I'd almost forgotten him. What's the problem?"

"He's freaking out down there, Colonel. He keeps screaming that the Titans are coming and that we're all going to die. Personally, I say we drug him to shut him up, but he's got some of the men so agitated that I'm not sure what to do."

Mitchell groaned and ran a thick fingered hand across his face. "Get Doc down there and see if he can sedate him. Not knock him out, just calm him down. I'll be down there after he's got his shit together and—"

A security officer pushed past the master sergeant and ran into the door jamb. "Colonel! We have a problem topside."

"Problem? Why didn't you call on the intercom?" He stood and marched toward the man.

"It wouldn't go through, sir. We tried." The security officer escorted him to the lift with the master sergeant and Jennifer in tow.

"Sitrep." Mitchell held the door until all had filed in and then pressed the button.

"The werecat, sir. He came back and…somebody shot him." The security officer cast a worried look to Jennifer who couldn't contain her shock. "It wasn't one of ours who dropped him sir."

"Then who the hell was it? A base patrol or—"

"We think it was Bigby, sir. The cat said—"

"His name was Mick!" Jennifer interrupted, her face stern.

"Yes, ma'am. *Mick* told the topside guard that Bigby was across the road in the old office building. Said he planned to use gas on us."

"Gas?" Mitchell clenched his jaw so tight that he feared his molars would crack. "Get an engineering team on that intel. Any possible way of implementing that threat, I want it neutralized."

The doors opened and he marched out toward the small crowd gathered around the fallen werecat. One of the security officers had draped a tarp over his body but the blood had begun to run from under the edge. Jennifer closed her eyes and looked away as they closed on his form.

"Who spoke to him?"

The security guard stepped forward and motioned Mitchell to the side. "I did sir. He claimed that Bigby was in the building across the road. I've already sent two teams to investigate."

Mitchell stared at the building and noted the missing window. "Son of a bitch. He was right here all along. And not a single squad member to send after him."

"The man who shot Mick is over there?" Jennifer's face was stone and he could tell by the way her shoulders were set that she was ready to go on the hunt.

"We don't know yet. We've got people checking."

"I want his balls, Matt."

"I want all of him." He cast a glance at the man on the floor, his mind imagining Apollo being struck down without warning. "And he will suffer."

*****

Jack watched patiently as Allister finished his spell and waited for some awe inspiring crescendo. He was disappointed when the griffin simply leaned across the makeshift altar and blew out the candle. He looked up at those around him and whispered, "It is done."

Jack glanced around and shrugged. "That's it? No flash of light or eerie glow or...not even a healthy fart?"

Gnat cracked a grin as he leaned on the handle of his hammer. "I could work one up for ya there, Chief, but we'd have to carry you into battle."

"No thanks, Travelocity. I just really thought there would be something to indicate it worked."

Allister replaced the last of the items into his bag then met Jack's stare. "You mean something that would alert them that they were locked in this plane? I think not."

"Good point." Jack turned to the warriors gathered around and motioned to them. "You know the drill. Take your positions and prepare for the worst. Remember, Lilith is the primary tango. We drop her, the rest are neutralized. Let's move out."

Marshall leaned across to Dom and mumbled, "Why do I get the feeling this op is gonna be FUBAR?"

"Do your job and let them do theirs. Everything will be fine." He reached up and keyed his throat mic. "Sierra Team, switch to channel three. We don't want to walk over their coms with cross chatter."

He received a series of clicks as affirmatives then heard each of his squad members key in on the new channel. He keyed the coms again and directed his team to the obvious staging points. "Sierra Three, Sierra Four, western flank. Sierra Six, Sierra Seven, eastern flank. Five, take overwatch and keep your mags ready. Two, you're with me."

He watched as his team split up and disappeared into the darkening shadows of the woods. He sent up a quick prayer for each of them and gave a quick glance upwards. He actually felt a bit of relief as he barely made out Azrael's black silhouette against the night sky, gliding overhead.

The greater elf trotted past him and caught up with Jack's team. Dom watched as the elf continued to cast furtive glances toward both Sullivan's sister and Jack. He knew something was going on, but he couldn't begin to guess what. He just hoped that whatever was eating the white haired elf wouldn't distract him once the fighting started.

Dom saw the saw mill through the thinning trees and set up with Marshall by his side. The two men staged behind a fallen old growth log and dug in. He watched through the thermals as Jack's team effectively surrounded the large metal building. Dom keyed his mic once more, "Sierra Team, go silent."

Each man attached the suppressor to their weapon and trained on their respective areas. Dom did a quick check with his team and verified the area clear. He switched to Jack's frequency and reported the all clear. "They must be inside Phoenix. We're all clear out here."

"Copy that, Sierra One. We're moving in now."

Dom switched his coms back to his teams' frequency then adjusted his ear bud so that he could listen in on Jack's radio chatter as well.

Jack walked to the front double doors of the warehouse and kicked them open. "Hi home, I'm honey!" He leveled his P90 and began picking off the closest of the demons. He smiled to himself as the possessed practically exploded in balls of yellow light.

His team rushed through the doors and was met by a wave of demons intent on crushing them before they could reach their queen.

*****

Laura tossed and turned, her dreams more disturbing than she could have ever feared. Glowing amber wolf eyes glared at her, blaming her for trapping it for eternity. She saw a Halfling…a deformed version of one, writhing in agony, forever trapped in a crippled body, wracked with pain.

She sat bolt upright, sweat dripping from her body as she tore the blanket off and sat on the edge of the bed. She breathed heavily and tried to calm her racing heart.

Derek flipped on her light and stared at her through squinted eyes. "What's wrong?"

"What? I, uh...had a bad dream."

He flipped the light off and stepped into the room. He pulled the short chain on the bedside lamp and sat beside her. "I heard you yelling. I was afraid that maybe..."

She turned and stared at him. "What?"

He chuckled lightly and patted her leg. "It's stupid, but I thought maybe Dad had come back and..." he trailed off, shrugging. "I know, stupid, huh?"

She shook her head and inhaled deeply, still trying to calm her ruined nerves. "Not really."

"You don't think he'd come back here, do you?"

She shook her head softly. "No. He's where he wants to be." She glanced out her window and watched the wind blow the lower limbs of the pines. "I just hope he's truly happy."

"Yeah, me too." Derek stood and stretched his lower back. "I'm going back to bed." He gave her a wan smile. "Maybe you could try some warm milk?"

"If Jack Daniels can't help me sleep, I doubt Elsie-the-cow can." She patted his arm as he walked by.

She listened for his door to shut and strained her ears to hear if anybody else might be up. She cast a weary eye at the bedside clock and sighed. Had she been back with the squads, she might be up for three or four days in a row. What was it about family that just drained her?

She laid back on the bed and stared at her ceiling. Her mind drifted back to the rusty old hangar that felt more like home than this house did. She smiled as images of Evan flashed through her mind. She could feel herself relaxing as she imagined him holding her, his cool skin against hers, soothing her as she fell asleep.

If she allowed herself to, she could almost imagine that she was floating above herself, with Evan, still in the hangar. She could see how he made her happy, how he loved her, how they seemed to fit like two pieces of the same puzzle. She could see how his quiet intelligence complimented her strong and commanding presence.

Her brow furrowed as she focused on herself. At the hangar, with the troops, she was strong, confident, imposing. Here, amongst her family, she had allowed herself to slip back into the role of 'little' sister. Her older brothers always thinking they had to protect her, to help guide her, mold her. In many ways, they still treated her that way…but why? She knew that they were aware of her accomplishments. Her career choices. How could they simply assume that she still needed their guidance, their gentle urgings to do things a certain way, or accept their judgments?

Her eyes opened as the realization struck her. Because she allowed them to…

She sat up and turned to face the mirror. The image she saw wasn't the Laura Youngblood that was the XO of the Monster Squads…it was Laura Youngblood, teenage daughter of Jim Youngblood. She stood and walked slowly toward the mirror. She stared at the image and her head cocked to the side as she studied the reflection.

Instinctively, her hands reached for her long hair and pulled it back into the pony tail she so often wore at work. She leaned in and looked at the image more closely. In the low light of the room she couldn't see how she had aged. How time and worry and stress had caused the fine lines around her eyes and the corners of her mouth. Laugh lines her mother had called them.

Slowly her mouth curled into a smile. Yes, she thought of Evan and how he could make her laugh without trying. She reached over and flipped on the overhead light and the older more confident woman she once knew stared back at her. Not the scared little girl that had taken over the moment she saw her father lying in the cold sterile hospital bed.

Laura straightened herself and squared her shoulders. She stared at the woman in the mirror and gave herself a stern stare. "What's done is done. There's no going back and changing it. Now pull on your big girl panties and deal with it."

The image in the mirror became more serious and nodded slightly. It was time to take care of things here then get back home where she belonged.

*****

"Major, the Reaper is responding slugglishly."

Tufo leaned across the arm of the command chair and studied the controls of the remote drone operator. "Have you run diagnostics?"

"Affirmative, sir. It says it's all good, but…it's like something is piggy backing our signals."

Dr. Peters stepped into the OPCOM and gave Major Tufo a curious glance. "You called, sir?"

Tufo held up a finger to indicate 'one moment' and Evan gasped. He immediately pulled his hand down and hid it behind the arm of the command chair then glanced back at the drone operator. "Get the techs on it. I want that thing a hundred percent."

"Yes, sir."

Tufo slid out of the chair and pulled Evan to the rear of the OPCOM. "This is why I called you. As soon as the adrenaline started pumping…" He held his hands up and allowed Evan to study the thick pointed claw-like nails that had erupted from his fingertips.

"When?"

"Just a few minutes ago. Please, Doc, tell me it's like that unwanted erection in fifth grade math class."

Evan shot him a totally confused look and Mark gave him a knowing look. "You know…when the teacher wants you to come up and work out a problem on the board but you'd rather take the zero."

Evan shook his head slightly. "I'm afraid I'm still not following you."

Tufo leaned in closer and practically growled in his ear, "Tell me it will go away."

Evan shrugged nervously. "I honestly have no idea." He pulled Mark's hand closer and studied his fingers. "I mean, I'm assuming it's a fight-or-flight response but...I have no idea."

"So, you're saying it might be like a hybrid erection?"

Evan sighed. "No, Major, I'm saying I simply don't know. Maybe you're evolving. Turning into something...else."

"Like hell!" Mark averted his eyes and pulled Evan even further into the depths of the OPCOM as the techs and officers gave him a curious look.

Tufo waved his hands under Doc's nose. "Make it go away."

Evan gave him a droll stare. "Like the unwanted erection? Have you tried cold water?"

"Not funny, Doc."

"I'm not trying to be. And why are you acting like you need to hide this? Everybody that you work with knows that you were infected with both..."

"Because other than *this* I look pretty much normal."

"That's a matter of opinion."

"Don't push my buttons, Doc. I think I could filet you with these." He waved them in his face again. "And, good lord! How am I supposed to pick my nose with these?"

"You heal very rapidly, you know." Evan tried not to smile. He failed.

"You're not helping." Mark turned and wished there was more room in the OPCOM so he could pace or throw furniture or do something else destructive.

"My question is," Evan cleared his throat and tried to keep his composure. "How will you wipe your bottom without shredding your cheeks?"

Mark exhaled hard and fought the urge to run a claw-like nail across the vampire's throat. He was really afraid that Mitchell might get butthurt if he harmed his favorite blood sucker.

"Go away, Doctor. If I wanted lame jokes, I could have told Phoenix about this. Or Laura. Or…hell, any of the operators."

"Major, I'm sorry. All I can tell you at this point is what we already know. Your blood tests from this morning were exactly the same as all of the others. Either this is a response to the battle or you're evolving. Only time will tell."

"What if I grow fangs or a tail or, or, or…"

"Calm yourself, Major." Doctor Peters patted his shoulder and slowly walked him back to the command chair. "Finish your operation here if you must or call in Colonel Mitchell to take over and we can go to the lab and run more tests."

"No more needles." Mark slumped into the chair and glared at the screens. "Go on, Doc. It's about to start here, and I need to be ready."

"Sir, they're about to breach."

"Very well." He regained his composure and squared his shoulders. "Doc, stick around just in case anything else pops up."

"Like a second unwanted erection?"

Heads turned and curious stares came from nearly everyone in the OPCOM. Mark groaned and shook his head. "Strike that comment from the hardcopy."

"Stricken, sir."

"Doc, just sit down, shut up, and keep your eyes open," he groaned as he watched Jack and his team approach the front doors. Tufo sat up straight and stared at the doc. "Erections? Oh, my God. Doc…how the hell will I…I mean with these?"

"Sir! They've breached!"

*****

Rufus sat patiently in the shadows and waited. When the roll up door opened, he looked away and waited while the Mercedes pulled in before he stood and dusted himself off.

The rear door opened as he approached and Viktor stepped out. "It is good to see you again. I was afraid you wouldn't make it."

"*Oui*, I had my own doubts. I fear that bridge is burned now." Rufus slid into the back seat and waited while Viktor slid back in and shut the door. He reached over and pulled the small curtains that covered the windows then tapped on the glass separating them from the driver. "I take it you had no problem picking up the package?"

"No. They met me at the airport. We touched down, they handed me the case, claimed the instructions were inside. We left and came straight here."

Rufus smiled. "Excellent. Did you inspect it?"

"No. I thought it best to leave that for you."

"We shall have to test the device beforehand then." Rufus leaned back in the seat and exhaled deeply. He tried not to think about the task at hand, but his mind kept racing back to it. He glanced to Viktor who stared through a sliver of tinted glass between the drawn curtains.

"Do you think we shall succeed?"

Viktor turned from the windows and gave a slight shake of his head. "I do not know. It is a bold plan, taking on the council with so few."

"Your people need not be involved. You know that."

Viktor nodded and turned his attention back out the window. "I know. But I fear I must insist. Even with the wolves we are so few and I fear that it won't be enough."

"They need only to distract the guards enough to allow us within. Unless they've increased security since our last meeting, we should be good on our own."

Viktor pulled his cell phone and checked his messages. "The wolves are assembled at the staging area." He clicked his phone shut and sat up straighter. "We should be arriving shortly. Within a few short hours, your edict will no longer be an issue."

"We have to ensure that all members are present. Otherwise,

this will be a wasted effort."

*****

"You seem deep in thought," Little John had to yell to be heard over the drone of the engines.

"You might say that," Spalding responded in his ear. "I'm still spun up over Apollo."

"With any luck, we can get back quick and you can hunt for the shooter again."

Spalding shook his head. "Trail's too cold. We're gonna have to wait for him to pop up and make himself known."

"Don't let it distract you, bro. If this thing is as nasty as the major lets on, you're gonna have to be on your toes." He punched Spalding in the arm light heartedly.

Darren nodded. "No worries. My head's on tight. You stay frosty out there, too. These things are quick and nasty."

"I dug through the database. I'm not seeing much more than what the XO sent with us. Are they that rare?"

Darren shrugged. "No idea. All I know is what you've got. They're fast, they're cranky, and they're lethal."

Sullivan leaned back and stared at this PDA. "I hate to say this, but I almost wish I had some of the freaks from Thompson's team with us."

"You mean like your sister?" Darren gave him a sideways glance.

Sullivan opened his mouth to argue then quickly shut it. He nodded slowly. "Yeah, I guess I do."

"Do you think they're better fighters than us, Little John?"

Sullivan shook his head. "No, sir. But I tend to worry about Brooke. Maybe if she were with me, I could keep her safe."

"You do realize that she's your *older* sister, right? She's been doing this since you were…what? Ten?"

"Yeah, yeah, rub it in." Sullivan grimaced. "I can't help it, boss. She still looks like a kid to me."

"The advantages to not aging, I suppose." Darren shook his head. "You know, I see Thorn and I think to myself, 'I've got socks older than this kid' but then I remember that he's centuries old and it just floors me. Can you imagine living that long?"

"Are you kidding? In our line of work?" Sullivan laughed. "I thought our life expectancy was just short of two years?"

Darren shrugged. "I dunno. Something like that." He leaned back and closed his eyes, doing his best to shut the idea out of his head. "Every day you wake up not dead is a gift. Enjoy it."

"Copy that, boss."

*****

Bigby shot around the corner of the office building and made for the maintenance buildings on the opposite side of the block. He hoped that whoever he'd seen coming for him was stupid enough to search the building he'd been set up in first.

He slid in the loose gravel and fell into the ditch beside the road, his head popping up to check for anybody following; his rifle to his shoulder and his eyes scanning the darkness for forms advancing on his position.

"Fooking cats." He switched on his IR and checked for warm bodies. "I knew there was a reason I hated the fuzzy bastards."

Satisfied that the trail was clear, he slipped down the slope and made his way across to the empty maintenance buildings. Thankfully these facilities weren't a twenty-four hour operation. He listened intently at the doors, ensured that no lights were on, then circled the building while looking for any windows that might be open. He found one on the second floor and slung his rifle over his shoulder.

With a three step leap, he jumped and grasped the bottom of the window then hauled himself up and through the open second story opening. He sat crouched in the darkness and listened, ensuring that nobody was inside before dropping to the concrete floor below.

The smell of oil and metal shavings overpowered his senses. He knew this had to be some kind of fabrication shop. He also knew that they'd be open at the crack of dawn, and he'd have to make his getaway long before the first base personnel arrived for work.

Leave it to a cat to screw up his plans.

Big sat alone in the dark and tried to plan his next steps. Could the werecat have somehow warned the hunters of his plans before he expired? He really didn't think so. It looked like a clean shot through the chest. Should have exploded his heart and lungs with that one round.

Still…he couldn't be positive. What if the hairball had somehow spilled the beans? Bigby desperately wanted to kick over something. Perhaps tear something up. Destroy something. But he didn't want to leave any evidence that he had been here either.

He ground his teeth and stifled a scream.

"That fooking cat!" he whispered through gritted teeth. "I knew I should have cut his throat the moment I saw him." Big clenched his fists and shook them in the air. "That fooker had it bad for Simmons' daughter. I knew he'd be trouble."

Bigby stopped and did his best to control his breathing. "Well, I don't have to worry about him alerting anybody to my position any longer." He marched to the rear of the building and sat down at the rear windows. He stared across the emptiness toward the vacant office building. He could see lights reflecting against the numerous windows and he knew that Mitchell's men were combing the building floor by floor.

"Very soon, Colonel. Very soon."

*****

Lilith bellowed with anger as Samael lifted her into his massive arms and made for the rear of the warehouse. "My army!"

"Leave them to fight the battle. We must keep you safe to win the war!" He spun around, using his massive body to shield her from the attackers.

He felt the sting of the angelic metal as it bit his hide, burying itself deep within his flesh. He roared with pain and hot blood spewed from the wounds as he leapt into the air and attempted to take flight.

Just as he got air under him, the gargoyle crashed through the ceiling, his mighty hammer barely missing Samael's skull as he passed by.

Samael tucked and fell from the air, hitting the ground and rolling away from the attackers. He used his arms and wings to envelope Lilith, protecting her from both the impact and the attacker's weapons. When he came to rest at the base of a support post, he unfurled his wings and set her on the ground, her legs still shaky from the landing. "Go, quickly! Get to safety!"

"Not without you, my prince!" She tugged at his arm and tried to drag him with her.

"I will come to you once the enemy is vanquished! Now GO!" He shoved her further back and away from the fight just as the gargoyle swooped low, tackling him, the pair rolling away and into the shadows.

Lilith turned hesitantly and began to run. She chanced a look over her shoulder and saw the Nephilim and a woman in black burst through the lines of her demons. For the first time since her resurrection she knew fear and her speed increased.

She ran for all that she was worth and soon came to the back wall of the warehouse. She groped in the darkness looking for an escape. She knew there had to be an opening here somewhere.

Lilith glanced back over her shoulder and saw the giant Nephilim closing on her and she panicked. She began to claw at the rough metal surface of the wall. She inhaled sharply to scream just as Samael and the gargoyle struck the wall, exploding the metal outward.

Without looking back, she leapt through the opening and into the night. She looked up and saw her beloved Samael grasp the gargoyle by the throat, his arm drawn back to strike him just as the gargoyle brought his angelic hammer up and over in a double handed strike to the top of the Fallen One's head.

Samael staggered, his grip loosening, as he dropped the gargoyle. The light skinned, winged beast wasted no time as he hefted the hammer and swung with all of his might. Another mighty blow to the side of the Fallen One's head sent him reeling. Blood flew from his nose and mouth before he slid to a stop in the moist ground beside Lilith.

He barely lifted his head and whispered to her, "Run…" before his heavily hooded eyes rolled back in his head.

Lilith slipped into the shadow of the building and ran for the woods as fast as her booted feet would carry her. Tufts of dirt erupted around her as she ran and she heard the whizz of bullets as they flew past her. While she doubted that they would actually kill her, she knew that they could stop her, and it would definitely hurt if she were struck.

She dove for the ground and tried to roll down the hill toward the tree line, hoping to avoid whoever it was that was shooting at her. As she came to a stop and stared up at the night sky, two men with rifles stepped from the shadows and pointed their weapons at her. "That's far enough."

She watched one reach up to his throat and press a device. "We have a female tango."

15

"He's in the wind." Mitchell fell into his chair and grimaced. "He was that goddamn close to my base of operation, and I didn't have a fucking clue." He slammed his fist down on the desk and ignored the items that bounced and fell into the floor.

"He'll be back." Jenny stepped behind her mate and rubbed at his shoulders. "And when he does, we'll strike back."

"You got that right." Mitchell closed his eyes at her touch and tried to relax. After a moment he slipped out from her talented hands and stood. "I need to keep my head about me. He could pop back onto the radar at any moment."

"And when he does," she crossed her arms and smiled at him, "you *will* be ready for him. I have no doubts." She stepped to his wet bar and poured herself a drink.

"Too many irons in the fire, Jen. I'm having trouble keeping tabs of everything." He poured himself a coffee and sat back down.

"It's getting to where I'm going to need a damned primer just to know what all the different threats are."

"Isn't that why you have an XO? Someone to help you keep up with all of this?" She sat on the corner of his desk and crossed her shapely legs. He tried not to notice.

"Yeah, but…"

"But, what?"

"But…there's a good damned possibility that he's one of the threats." Mitchell gulped down the lukewarm coffee.

"Because he's infected?" She gave him a sideways look. "Please!"

"Well, it could be true." He sounded like he was pleading even to himself.

"I'm sure there are folks who would like you to believe that. But, Matt, listen to yourself." She stirred her drink with her finger then licked it clean, sending a shiver down him. "So he's got the wolf virus. Did that change you?"

Mitchell shrugged. "Maybe a little."

She gave him a deadpan stare. "Okay, fine. What about the vampire infection? Has he shown any signs of vampirism? Is he stalking people and sucking them dry?"

"No!"

"Then what's to worry about?" She stood and drained her glass, then set the empty on his desk. "It sounds to me like you're trying to invent reasons to not trust the man. Sure, he can be a little brash, but wasn't he always?"

"Well, yeah."

"And wasn't he always rude and uncouth?"

"Of course, he was a Marine," Mitchell chuckled to himself.

She hiked a brow at him then threw her hand up. "So now he's a Marine that heals almost instantly. And won't age. And he doesn't eat people. So I guess I'm not seeing the problem."

Mitchell sighed and rubbed at his eyes. "I guess if you break it down to its most basic and simplistic—"

She spun him around in his chair, cutting him off. "Is there any other way to break it down? Dammit, Matt, don't read any more into it than you have to. The man is your friend and he's your second."

Mitchell sighed heavily and nodded. "You're right, of course you're right." He pulled her closer and kissed her. "I just wish Laura were still here to sort of...I dunno. Balance things out."

"I'm not sure I approve of you wanting another woman in your life." She teased as she nibbled his earlobe. "As long as it's Laura, though, I think I'll let you live."

"You're so forgiving."

*****

Jack's forces pressed through the demon army, slicing, dicing, shooting and hammering their way through the lines. Kalen jumped into the rafters and fired down into the crowd, watching the demons explode into yellow balls of light as each angelic arrow pierced the demons below.

His eye was drawn to one lone demon who stood in the back directing the others. Kalen spotted him pointing the others to trucks and keyed his communications. "I think we have a leader to the rear."

Phoenix shouted over the coms, "Take him out! Now!"

Kalen took aim and let his arrow fly. The demon was struck in the shoulder and spun to the ground. Not a killing blow, but a painful shot that stopped him for the moment.

Raven stood near the center of the warehouse, bodies collected around her in piles. Her blades dripped with the blood of the demons and her chest heaved with each breath she gasped. Her eyes fell on something she hadn't expected. She keyed her own communicator. "Chief Jack, they're strapping on the suicide vests!"

"Where? What's their location?"

"The rear of the warehouse!" The panic in her voice was palpable as she lifted her blades to begin dropping more of the demons.

Jack hesitated for just a moment then ordered his people, "Fall back! Fall back! Out of the building! Now!"

Each warrior turned and made for the double doors as fast as their legs could carry them. Allister scooped up Gnat, tossing him up and onto his back.

Just as the group made the entrance, they heard Jack's voice over the coms again. "OPCOM, bring the flame! Danger close!"

"Copy that, Phoenix. Hellfires away."

Jack and his warriors didn't slow their retreat as the twin rockets appeared in the night sky and swept low over their heads. The concussion from the blast knocked the group to the ground and sent waves of heat over them as a bright orange fireball erupted into the night sky. Shards of metal flew in multiple directions, deadly missiles shredding everything in their wake.

The warriors kept still as debris rained around them and the heat from the fire dissipated. Jack finally rolled to his side and looked to the remains of the warehouse. "Did anybody see what happened to Lilith?"

A voice crackled over the coms, "We have her in custody, Phoenix. She's not going anywhere."

"Any other tangos get loose before the strike?"

"Negative. Line of sight is clear."

Allister came to his feet and ruffled his feathered wings. "We must destroy her now."

"Agreed." Jack rolled to his feet and did a quick head count. "Where's Azrael and Phil?"

The large gargoyle and the Nephilim appeared from the shadows dragging the broken body of the Fallen angel. "We were occupied, Chief Jack. But we have her right hand subdued."

Jack looked to Phil. "Is there a way to ensure he stays out of the picture?"

"Destroy the queen." Phil planted a foot squarely between Samael's shoulder blades and held him to the ground. "He'll be sent back to whence he came."

Jack clenched his jaw and nodded. "Sierra Teams, converge on my location. Deliver the tango."

*****

Laura finished packing her bags and walked to the front of the house. She loaded her things into the Jeep and came back in to make sure she hadn't forgotten anything. As she made one last walk through, Derek stood in her doorway. His eyes were still puffy from sleep and his hair looked as though he had been wrestling with a motorcycle helmet.

"You just gonna leave and not say goodbye?"

She turned and gave him a wan smile. "I need to go."

"Why? Figure you've had enough of family time?"

Laura closed the drawers of her dresser and pulled the bed spread tight on her mattress. "I've caused enough damage here. It's time I get back to where I belong."

"Damage?" Derek leaned against the doorjamb and crossed his arms. "You figure that's all you've done here is cause damage?"

Laura paused and stared toward her bedroom window. "Haven't I?"

"Not the way I see it."

She turned and faced him. "How's that, exactly?"

"You made peace with Crystal. That would have made Dad proud."

"Ah. Yeah, that makes up for everything else." She crossed her arms and studied him.

"Considering Dad was on his death bed when you showed up...yeah." He pushed off the doorjamb and crossed the room. He sat down on her bed and patted the mattress beside him for her to join him.

"I just made that bed."

"So make it again, crybaby. Sit down."

With a huff she sat beside him. The two sat in silence for a moment before Derek wrapped an arm across her shoulder. "Did he ever tell you how proud he was of you?"

"No. Not in so many words."

"He was. He was always bragging about you. The big CIA intelligence officer," Derek chuckled. "Then you quit and went to work as a contractor or some such…he never did figure out exactly what. Well…until you told him. Yet, he knew it had to be important."

"He wasn't disappointed that I quit?"

He shook his head. "Nope. In fact, these last six months when you kept saying you were going to come home, I think he held on because he knew you would as soon as you could."

She inhaled deeply, forcing herself not to allow emotion to take root. "He was that bad?"

"Oh yeah. The doctors thought he was going to die months ago. But not him. Oh, hell no. His little girl was coming back home. So he held on."

"Jesus, Derek, why are you telling me this?" She wiped at her face.

"Because, Laura, you gave him another shot. He chose to…well, he chose to take it to the level he took it to. That isn't on you. That's all him." He turned and stared at her. "Don't you dare blame yourself."

He stood quickly and went to the window. Daylight was just beginning to creep its tendrils over the eastern horizon. "Somewhere out there, he's living his life the way he chose. And he owes that second chance to you."

She stood and stared out the window with him. "That was a

really nice thing to say."

"Whatever." He leaned into her, bumping her. "It's true."

Laura looked at her wrinkled bed. "Fix that." She picked up her makeup bag and turned for the door. "Tell the boys that I'm sorry I can't stay. I have to get back."

"You coming back?"

She paused at the door and shrugged. "I don't know. Maybe one day."

She walked out of the house and climbed into her Jeep. Derek stood in the doorway and watched her drive down the long driveway then turn out onto the main road. "Love you, sis."

*****

"Major, I think we've discovered the problem with the Reaper." The tech was scratching his head as he read the printouts.

"Spill it."

"Sir, it seems that somebody at Langley Air Force Base has been monitoring our video feeds." The tech handed the printouts to Tufo who stared at the sheets of paper.

"Langley? Who the hell would want our..." his voice trailed off and he spun, pulling Doc to him. He lowered his voice to a whisper, "Get the colonel and tell him what the hell happened here. Somebody is eavesdropping on us." He shoved the printouts into the Doc's hands and pushed him toward the door.

Evan nearly tripped as he stepped down off the command platform and left the OPCOM. He rushed to the colonel's office and knocked on the door. When Mitchell barked, he poked his head in. "Sir, we have an issue. Major Tufo said you needed to know as soon as possible."

Mitchell stood and stepped past his new mate. Evan handed him the printouts and Mitchell scanned them. "What am I reading here?"

"From what I've gathered, somebody at Langley was tapping

the video feeds from the drone on the operation, and Major Tufo is quite concerned."

"Langley?" Mitchell glanced up and shook his head then remembered Stevens in holding. "Did you dope up the CIA spook downstairs?"

"I sedated him, if that's what you mean."

"Can he still answer questions?"

"He should be coherent. Just…calmer."

"Come with me." Mitchell pushed the vampire out of his office then paused. He stuck his head back in and gave Jenny a sad smile. "Sorry, sweetheart, another time."

"Go. Be a hero. Maybe I'll knit a sweater or something." She lifted her glass to him and gave him a mock salute as he left.

When Mitchell and Dr. Peters entered the holding cell, the colonel sent the guard away for privacy. He held the printout up for Stevens to see. "Is this your people?"

Stevens sat on his bunk, his eyes swollen from crying. He lifted his head and squinted. "Huh?"

"This!" Mitchell shook the paper. "Is this your people spying on us?"

Stevens approached the door to the cell and reached for the printout. He scanned it rapidly and his hand began to shake. "They're ahead of schedule."

"Ahead of schedule on what?" Mitchell snatched the printout from his hands and folded it, stuffing it into his back pocket.

"Their command bunker." Stevens gripped the bars, his forehead pressed against the cold metal. "It wasn't supposed to be ready for months."

"Command bunker? At Langley?"

"Yes." Stevens squeezed his eyes shut. "It's state of the art."

"Tell me about it."

"There was a brief in the papers I brought you—"

"I said tell me!"

He jumped back and stared at the man. "Yes, sir." He cleared his throat and began reciting what he could remember. "Built to withstand a nuclear blast, the main portion is below ground…not unlike this complex, but newer. And smaller. They may have more soldiers, but…they don't have the needs that your men have."

"Explain."

Stevens saw the anger in the man's eyes and nodded. "The Titans are…well, they're different than your soldiers. For one thing, they're programmable."

"Like machines?"

Stevens shook his head. "Not exactly…but…kind of."

"Speak plainly or so help me…"

"Colonel, it's all explained in the papers I brought you. They're not machines, but they have certain triggers. Not unlike brain washing. But not really brain washing. They use chemicals, hormones…"

"Drugs?"

"Not in the classical sense, no." Stevens sighed and slowly began to pace in his small cell. "The men are stripped of their personalities. Whatever fears they might have had are washed away. Whatever desires they might have had are replaced. They want only to please. And they please by following orders. To the letter. They've been chemically augmented and genetically enhanced to be bigger, faster, stronger, smarter…they *are* the perfect killing machines."

Mitchell crossed his arms and glared at the man. "And you helped create these monsters?"

"What? No! I was a data cruncher. I was basically a hacker working for the government. I just…I got sucked into all of this."

"And you found out about this Titan Project by accident?"

"Spartan. It's the Spartan Project. The warriors are the Titans. And if you see one up close, you'll see why. These guys are huge. Like, seven foot tall huge. I think the average weight for these guys is three hundred and fifty pounds. And they're solid muscle. They're giants."

"Regardless."

"Right. Um, I stumbled upon it, and the guys who created it made me data mine you. Apparently they stumbled upon the fact that monsters exist. They got it into their heads that *all* monsters needed to be wiped out. Including the ones that we created." He cleared his throat. "And by 'we', I mean, of course, you."

"So these self-righteous pricks consider my boys to be monsters because…" Mitchell trailed off, unwilling to state what he already knew.

"Because they were augmented with werewolf virus." Stevens chewed at the inside of his cheek. "Yes, colonel, they know."

"So our own government is coming after us, after they sanctioned our actions?"

Stevens shrugged. "I don't think our government knows about the Spartan Project. This is a Black Op pet project. Totally off the books."

"And run by the NSA and the CIA. Against their own charter and in violation to their Constitutional restraints."

"Pretty much, yeah." Stevens plopped back down on his bench and sighed. "That's why I thought you needed to know. So I printed out the highlights and ran like hell to your doorstep."

"And they know you're here."

"More than likely, yes."

Mitchell scratched at his chin and stared away. "So why haven't they struck yet?" he asked rhetorically.

"My guess is that they aren't sure if the Titans are up to the task. They aren't sure if they're ready."

"And that's why they're spying on our video feeds. To measure us up."

"Again, that would be my guess."

Mitchell smiled. "Maybe it's time we gave them something

worth watching."

*****

Wallace dragged Lilith's prone body to where Jack and his warriors were gathered and dumped her unceremoniously at his feet. "The concussion from the blast knocked her on her fanny. She's been out since."

Jack turned to Allister and lowered his voice, "Is there anything special we should do before—"

"Remove her heart. Quarter the body and separate it," the griffin seemed almost giddy as he spoke. "Quickly, before she recuperates and strikes."

Jack pulled the angelic dagger that Brooke had given him and hefted it in his hand. The small blade suddenly felt much heavier. As he looked down at the bound woman lying at his feet, he suddenly felt as though what he was about to do was somehow wrong. She wasn't able to defend herself...she wasn't attacking anybody. It felt like...like *murder*.

He looked to Allister and shook his head. "I can't just—"

Before he could finish his sentence the griffin struck out with its front claws, slicing open her sternum with its razor sharp talons. Jack practically jumped back as Allister's massive head snapped forward and he plucked the still-beating heart from the woman's gaping chest; the bloody muscle still pumped as he held it in his beak.

"I guess that settles that," Hammer muttered as the griffin stepped back and cocked his head at Jack.

Phil stepped close and lifted his sword. "Stand clear." In quick swipes, he severed limbs from torso and head from neck. His actions left the group standing silent over the carnage. He wiped the blood from his blade then picked up the heart. "We should package these separately."

Dom stepped back slowly and shook his head. "I thought there'd be more...I dunno...*something*, involved. A bright light. A blast wave. Something."

Brooke pulled one of her angelic blades and sunk it deeply into the chest of the Fallen one. "It moved." She gave Jack a steely stare then leaned on the blade, sinking it deeper.

As the blade sliced through Samael's chest, a bright green light erupted, temporarily blinding the crowd. The light slowly dimmed and the warriors all lowered their hands from their faces. The winged angel had departed, leaving the broken body of Damien Franklin in a pool of blood that was soaking into the dry, rocky ground.

Jack swallowed hard and looked to Dom. "Let's get this mess boxed up and out of here."

"Aye, Chief."

Paul Foster stepped forward and raised a hand to get Jack's attention. "If I may? Rufus had a few ideas on how best to reduce the possibility of her ever being brought back."

Jack shrugged, a sick feeling forming in his gut. "I'm all ears."

*****

Each member of Delta Team made landfall and secured their chutes. Using their locator beacons they converged on the landing zone and made ready. Spalding performed a coms check with OPCOM then pulled his topomap of the area.

"This is the last known location of our spotter. The secondary wasn't able to locate him but OPCOM got a single ping off his cell before it either went dead or got shut off. That was over twenty-four hours ago. You've all been briefed on the wendigo and know what it's capable of. Keep your eyes open and your ears alert. These things are supposed to be stealthy sons of bitches. They're sneaky as hell and dangerous."

Lamb clicked off the red lensed torch and nodded to Spanky. "Shoot first scenario?"

"Normally I would say no, but that's probably not a bad plan. Just ensure your target is clear. Know what's beyond your tango. These are some dense woods. If anybody got separated out here and wounded, we might not find them until it was too late."

"Copy that."

Spanky folded the map and stuffed it back into his pouch. "Everybody on your toes tonight. This is our first encounter with one of these."

Sullivan stood first. "I'll take point."

Tracy patted the big man's shoulder. "I'll cover your six."

"Two by two and let's make a clean sweep. Remember, anything that remotely looks like a cave or cover, alert the team. Move out." Spalding slid in just behind Sullivan and placed a hand on his shoulder. "Go time."

The men broke into two man groups and moved silently into the woods. More than once Sullivan reached for his helmet to lower his night vision goggles, but waited. Once they were in place, his natural night vision would be gone. He preferred having his full peripheral vision available; it allowed him to concentrate on his surroundings without necessarily focusing on any one thing in his field of view.

After less than two kilometers of slow moving through rough terrain, Spalding slowed to a halt, his fist hovering in the air. He turned slowly and pressed a finger to his nose indicating that he smelled something, even if he couldn't see it.

Spanky gave a slow nod and slid in next to the large man. He lifted his face and inhaled deeply. The sweet rot of decayed flesh tickled his olfactory and he fought back a gag. He covered his mouth and motioned to the men behind him to spread out but stay within view of each other.

The deepening darkness of the woods and the lack of moonlight had cast the area into an inky blackness that even their enhanced vision had difficulty cutting through. One by one, the click-whir of enhanced night vision activated and each commando found their heads on a swivel as they scanned the area ahead of them.

They slowly made their way through the woods, the sound of rushing water rising in volume, telling them they were closing on one of the many active streams that fed the lake.

"Delta Actual, we've lost all satellite visual on your team," Tufo's voice echoed through the earpieces. "Arial drone dispatched to your area to feed inputs."

Spalding clicked his throat mic and whispered, "Copy that, OPCOM. Advise when on approach."

Spanky felt a hand on his shoulder and he turned just as a scream broke through the silence of the woods. He could hear something large crashing through the underbrush and headed in their direction. He pulled Little John back and yelled to his team, "Defensive positions!"

Each man dropped to their knee or to the ground, their weapons trained on the sound coming from the woods. Spanky keyed his coms once more. "OPCOM, we have incoming."

*****

Kalen worked his way through the debris and approached Brooke from her blind side. He wrapped his arms around her and picked her up from the ground, spinning her around before setting her down and sliding his hands up her back. "You have no idea how relieved I am that you are unharmed."

She stared at him in shock for just a moment before a sly smile crossed her pale features. "So happy not to disappoint you."

"Don't misunderstand, I know that you are an accomplished warrior, but I couldn't help but worry when I saw you plunge headlong into the throng of demons." He pressed his forehead to hers and sighed. "I truly don't know what I would have done without you by my side."

She leaned back and stared at him, he smile widening. "I'm sure you would have figured out something." She instinctively reached up and tucked a long strand of his white hair behind his ear. Her smile widened as she traced the pointed tip with her finger. He looked into her eyes and noted a certain mischievous glimmer that he hadn't noticed before.

"You seem…happy."

Brooke threw her head back and laughed a deep, hearty laugh that caught Kalen by surprise. When she finished she tucked her face close to his ear and whispered, "Who wouldn't be? We've won, haven't we?"

He nodded slowly and leaned back to study her. "Yes, I suppose we have." He released her from his embrace and looked out over the destruction. Many of the bodies still smoked from the blast and bits and pieces of the building were still burning. "Still, this wasn't how I expected the battle to go."

"Well, lover, exactly how did you think it would happen?" She slid in next to him and traced a nail across his sinewy shoulders. "You'd show up and they'd simply surrender?"

Kalen shook his head slowly. "Somehow, I thought the battle would be more…epic."

"Epic?" She laughed again and walked around to face him. "What could be more epic than to vanquish your enemies while none of your warriors are harmed?" She pranced around, her arms wide as she gestured wildly. "From your mightiest to your least, not one single warrior so much as bloodied. From the giant winged one to the lowliest gnome…not one so much as met a blade. Imagine how they will sing of your battles throughout your realm. When we tell them of your skill and bravery, they'll make you King."

She ran a hand over his chest and squeezed his shoulders as she gave him her most sultry stare. "When *we* tell them of…" he trailed off.

"Of course." She kissed the corner of his mouth and ran her fingers through his long white hair. "You'll want somebody with you to corroborate the story, somebody who can regale them with your heroics. Who better than me? Your future queen." She smiled again and kissed him full on the mouth.

Kalen pulled her in tighter and returned her kiss. His hands ran up her back and grasped her by the back of the head, holding her in place as he kissed her roughly. His mind raced and his heart broke as his tongue danced with hers.

"Break it up, you two. We still have work to do." Jack nudged Kalen in the shoulder as he walked by.

Kalen flustered for just a moment and then gave her a lopsided grin. "We shall continue this later." She turned to leave and he slapped her on the ass, catching another smile and raised brow from her before he himself turned and trotted away.

He quickly approached Jack and pulled him aside. "We must talk."

16

Mitchell unlocked the handcuffs, releasing Stevens and pushed him down into the chair at Dr. Peter's workbench. He tossed the cuffs unceremoniously onto the counter and pulled the stack of files to the edge. "You get to explain this crap to our resident expert."

Stevens stared at the printed sheets he had brought to them and gave Mitchell a wide eyed stare. "It's not like I designed this stuff, Colonel. I just copied it and..."

"It wasn't a request," Mitchell growled through gritted teeth. He spun and pointed a finger at the doc. "If he tries to worm his way out of this, eat him."

Evan tried to hide the smile tugging at the corners of his mouth. "If I eat him, who will help me?"

"We'll nab another CIA spook and twist his knickers until he's willing to cooperate."

"Wait...what do you mean, 'eat me'?" Stevens' head bounced between Mitchell and Evan.

"He's our resident vampire."

Evan extended a hand. "Dr. Evan Peters, at your service."

Stevens reached out to shake hands then pulled his arm back suddenly. "Good Lord. Your hands are like ice."

"Comes from being undead, I'm afraid." Evan smiled and settled in across from him at the table. "Shall we begin?"

"Holy...you weren't kidding? He wasn't kidding? You really are a vampire?" Stevens stammered as he stared at the man.

"He wasn't kidding. I really am a vampire." Evan opened a file and spun it around to face Mr. Stevens. "Now, shall we start at the beginning?"

Stevens began to shudder and his eyes darted to Mitchell. "You aren't leaving me here, are you?"

"You're in good hands." He nodded to Doctor Peters. "Keep an eye on him, Doc."

"We'll be fine." The two watched Mitchell step down out of the lab and march toward the stairwell. Evan turned back to the files and pushed them slightly forward. "From the top."

Stevens swallowed hard and eyed him warily. "You wouldn't really eat me, would you?"

Evan laughed and shook his head. "Good heavens, no." He watched as Stevens visibly relaxed, his shoulders slumping slightly. "No, I'd simply drain you of all of your blood and then dump your lifeless corpse into the incinerator."

Stevens' eyes widened as he stared at the man in horror. "You're kidding...right?"

"Let's not test your hypothesis." He pushed the folder closer once more. "Now...shall we begin?"

*****

Jack stood silently, his jaw clenching and unclenching. His eyes darted around the ruined facility as his mind raced. "You're sure?"

Kalen nodded solemnly. "I wish I weren't. But yes."

Allister approached and fluttered his large feathered wings. "We need to depart soon or we'll face the daybreak upon our arrival."

Jack squeezed his eyes shut and pursed his lips. He turned to Allister and motioned him closer. "You and I need to talk. Kalen, gather the troops and have them prepare to return. See if you can find us a portal that's closer than the one we came in through."

"Chief Jack, what shall we—"

"Just find us a portal back. We can't risk Azrael being stone if we have to face her. Again. And I'd much rather do it on familiar ground. Just get the troops ready to return. OPCOM has a clean-up team inbound. They can handle what we leave behind."

Kalen nodded and turned to leave.

"Should I ask?"

Jack turned and faced the griffin, his face stern. "How many more of those spells do you have up your sleeve?"

Allister glanced down to his taloned feet. "I have no sleeves, Chief Jack."

"It's just an expression, my fine feathered friend. Just an expression." Jack wrapped an arm over the griffin's neck as best he could and pulled the bird like head in closer. "Listen up. We have a problem."

Jack led the griffin off to the edge of the debris field, making an effort to appear as though he were discussing the damage to anybody who might observe the pair. He watched as Kalen gathered the troops then went to the edge of the river looking for a boulder large enough for Azrael, Phil, and Allister to travel through. All the while, he explained Kalen's worst fear to the legendary monster.

"So, is there any way to save her?"

"The girl?" Allister cocked his head to the side as he spoke.

"Of course, the girl, who the hell else would I be asking about?" Jack's frustration was evident as he spoke.

Allister thought for a moment then shook his mighty head. "No."

"Come on! There has to be a way." Jack began to pace as he pleaded with him. "I mean…even Kalen says that she *must* still be inside there. She's fighting this. Somehow feeding her false information or…phony memories or *something*. Otherwise she couldn't have tipped him off."

Allister continued to shake his head. "Even if that is so, in order to destroy the beast, the host most be killed." He sighed heavily and hung his head. "I am just so sorry that I didn't foresee this as a possibility. I cast the net that contained them all to this area…but I never thought that she would leave her own vessel for another while her vessel was intact."

"I wouldn't have thought it either or I would have made Brooke stay at the base." Jack ground his teeth as he stared at him. "But there has to be a way. An exorcism or…something."

Allister shook his head. "The longer she possesses her body, the harder it will be for Brooke to maintain any control. It won't be long and Lilith will know that we are aware of her."

"But how do we yank that bitch out without killing Brooke?" Jack had to force himself to keep his voice low.

"That is what I am trying to tell you. We cannot. In order to kill Lilith, we must kill the host while she possesses the body."

Jack spun on him. "And what's to keep her from jumping to another body?"

"She can only possess a soulless body, Chief Jack. An undead body. Two souls cannot possess the same…well, they can, but not…Lilith cannot or she will lose who she is."

"You're not making sense."

"When a person is possessed by a demon or a spirit, it is only a *part* of that spirit that possesses it. Usually, the most evil part since that is the portion with the most strength. Lilith wishes to maintain all of who she is, so she will only possess an undead body. If she attempts to possess a body with a soul, she will be stripped of the grand majority of who she is."

"So we have to…no." Jack's eyes widened. "Doc is back at base. He's a vampire. He's got no soul."

"So when we cast the net, it will have to be a tight one. We will have to bind her to the body she is in."

"And then kill it."

Allister's eyes reflected the sadness that Jack felt when he spoke. "Not just kill her, Chief Jack. We must utterly destroy her."

*****

Mark listened to the coms as Spanky announced an incoming tango and the OPCOM suddenly erupted in activity. He began barking orders over the buzz of activity. "Relay their helmet cams through the approaching drone and get them on the screens! Now!"

"The feed is too weak for satellite, sir. Drone is too far out to act as relay," one tech reported.

"Boosting gain on the RF antennae," another responded.

"Repositioning satellite for optimal transmission."

Tufo stood up in the chair and squeezed the armrests. He felt the metal give under his grip and he could feel his nails elongating as he barked new orders. "Get me those feeds!"

"Coming in now, sir!" The tech pointed to the main screen and a static filled green glow showed what appeared to be a forest scene with a very large person blocking half of the view. "Delta Actual is onscreen!"

"Split the views. I want each helmet cam up and viewable." Tufo slowly sat back in the chair and his palm brushed the crushed armrests. He glanced down and realized what he had done. He lifted his hands and stared at them in the red light of the OPCOM.

His fingers had thickened, his knuckles nearly doubled in size and the sharpened nails that had sprung from each fingertip now curved back like a bird of prey's talons. He flexed each hand, expecting excruciating pain and was surprised when there was none.

"Activity, sir!"

Tufo's attention snapped back to the viewscreen and he watched as a figure burst from the underbrush. He definitely wasn't expecting the view that filled the widescreen. "What in the hell is that?"

*****

Rufus glanced at his watch for the hundredth time and sighed. The wolves were restless and their anxiety was beginning to wear off on him. He could feel his own nervousness begin to build and he had to force himself to calm down. He slipped down from the empty desk he had been sitting on and paced the office slowly.

Viktor stepped inside and nodded to him. "Your test subject is here."

"Excellent." He reached for the case and flipped it open. He pulled the polished stainless steel device from the foam padding and fell into step behind the werewolf.

"My men are securing him now." Viktor pointed to a concrete column to one side of the underground parking structure and Thorn's eyes fell upon the vampire struggling against the chains being wrapped around him as the wolves held him in place.

"You are certain he works for the council?"

Viktor nodded solemnly. "A point he made vehemently and numerous times as my men brought him here."

"And there is no way the council may have followed?"

"Not this time. I fear that their envoy will be quite late arriving wherever it was that he was sent." Viktor motioned toward the young vampire and Thorn settled the device against his shoulder as he stepped forward.

"I will see you all gutted! I'll wear your hides for boots!" The vampire struggled against the chains holding him to the concrete column, spittle running down his chin as he bellowed his threats.

Rufus stood in front of the young man and seemed to measure him. "Do you know who I am?"

"Of course I do. You're a dead man!" The young vampire struggled again, doing his best to free an arm so that he might rip out the other vampire's throat.

Rufus nodded to the wolves on either side and waited until they stepped back. He flipped the power button on the side and felt the device hum in his hands. A slight blue glow emitted from the vents on the side and for a moment he remembered the explosion at his home on the island. *It has been tested and is safe.*

"Your sacrifice may well save numerous innocent lives."

"Fuck the innocent! I eat the innocent for—"

The young vampire never completed his thought. Rufus squeezed the trigger and a sky blue light erupted from the snubbed barrel of the device. It seemed to only flash along the young vampire's skin for a moment, but he suddenly and completely turned to ash, the chains falling to the ground where he once stood.

The device still hummed in Rufus' hand as he continued to stare at the spot where the man had been standing only a moment before. "That was...interesting."

"A UV weapon of some sort?" Viktor stepped beside him and studied the shiny metal device.

Rufus flipped the power off and shook his head. "*Non.* It is a specialized weapon." He turned a sad eye to the werewolf standing next to him. "A most dangerous one, *mon ami.* But at least it works."

"And this weapon will be sufficient to destroy the Council?"

Rufus leaned the device against his shoulder once again and nodded. "*Oui.* We need only have them together."

"Then what are we waiting for? They should be assembling as we speak."

Rufus pulled his phone and flipped through his messages. He nodded solemnly as he closed it. "*Oui.* The demon queen has been destroyed. That alone should grant us access to the Council."

Viktor walked to the Mercedes and held the door open for Rufus. "And if they agree to remove the edict? Will you still destroy them?"

Rufus slid into the rear and laid the weapon next to him in the seat. "If they remove the edict, there will be no need. But we both know that they will not." He pulled his overcoat on and slipped the device under his arm, attaching the sling to his shoulder before pulling the coat around it.

"You knew they would not before you agreed to kill Lilith, didn't you?"

Rufus inhaled deeply while he considered his answer. "I suspected their treachery. Much as they must suspect my own. I'm sure that they are aware that your wolves are in their territory. They probably assume that they are here to secure my escape should they back out on our agreement."

Viktor nodded knowingly. "And the wolves will kill their guards, securing our departure once you have removed the Council."

"*Non*. Once the Council is removed, their power should shift. The guards will either stand down and await their new orders or they'll attempt to avenge their old masters."

Viktor gave him a shocked stare. "One extreme or the other." He shifted in his seat to give his full attention to Thorn. "And who will their new master be?"

Rufus shrugged. "They will either revert to their separate *familias*…or shift to the one who killed their masters."

*****

Spalding peered over Little John's shoulder and did a double take as a human shaped form sprinted from the thicket directly in front of them and leapt over a fallen log. The being moved with an awkward grace that surprised him.

He heard John yell, "Going live!" and the muffled report of his suppressed rifle belched as he opened fire on the advancing creature. Chips of bark exploded from trees and sprays of dirt erupted from the ground around the creature as it zig-zagged its way toward them. Spalding was still trying to capture the bouncing figure in the optics of his sights when it sprung into the air and leapt over them, swinging a large stick as it flew overhead.

Donovan yelled as the stick made contact with the side of his helmet, knocking him to the ground. The entire squad spun and tried to follow the creature as it disappeared in the darkness of the woods.

"Son of a bitch! I lost it," Lamb reported first.

"Same here," Jacobs replied, his rifle scanning the area.

Gus Tracy side-stepped from his position and checked on Donovan. "You okay, buddy?"

Donnie held up his ruined night vision goggles and swiped blood from his temple. "Bastard tried to crack my skull."

Spalding kept his hand on John's shoulder. He leaned closer and whispered in his ear, "Do you have it?"

"Negative. I lost it after it jumped us."

Spanky sunk lower into the spongy peat moss and keyed his coms. "OPCOM, we lost contact with the tango. What's the twenty on the eye in the sky?"

OPCOM's static-filled reply broke up, but he was able to pick up pieces. "Delta *SHH*-tual, *shkrik* is approximately two zero mics *shkrriiict*."

"Dammit." He pulled his earbud and let it dangle while he scanned the area. "Did you catch any of that?"

"Sounds like we have at least twenty minutes." Little John shifted his weight and peered back from where the creature had burst through the woods. "I think we should backtrack and see where that thing came from. Maybe we can find its lair."

Spanky stood slowly and did a full sweep. He made a motion with his hand and waved his squad back into formation. "Donnie, you gonna survive?"

"Roger that, Spank. Might have a bit of a headache, but I'm good to go."

"Copy that. Converge on Little John. We're gonna see if we can track where that thing came from." He tapped John's shoulder and sent him forward. "Fall in. Gus, cover our six. I don't want that thing creeping back on us."

"Roger that."

The column started forward with Sullivan stopping periodically to check for tracks and to read the terrain. The sound of the rushing water still acted as a white noise in the background masking most of the natural forest sounds.

Gus walked backwards the majority of the way. He continually scanned the area to either side of the team as they made their way through the thickets. He froze when leaves fell from the treetop around him. He glanced upward and saw nothing moving in the canopy other than limbs swaying slightly in the breeze. Still, the idea that the creature could be shadowing them from above stuck with him.

He continued to scan left to right, up then down. Left to right, up then down. Gus felt the hair on the back of his neck stand on end. He continued to scan the area and saw nothing. His hand automatically went to his throat and keyed his coms. "Boss, check the canopy. I have a creepy feeling we're being shadowed from above."

Spanky stopped the column and began to scan the treetops. He detected no movement and was about to order the squad to move out again when a blur fell from above, tackling him to the ground and rolling him away from the others.

*****

"Dom, debrief your squad and copy me on the reports. We've

got our own business to take care of down below." Jack slapped the big man on the shoulder. "I appreciate the support out there, buddy."

"Any time, Phoenix." Dom shot him a wink before stepping over to the stowage table and removing his gear.

Jack motioned his team together and nodded toward Allister who was stepping into the freight elevator. "Everybody down below. We need to debrief before we start cutting people loose."

He watched as the team began to meander their way to the stairwell. He instinctively reached out and grabbed Phil by the arm, holding him back. The Nephilim gave him a curious look, but Jack gave a barely perceptible shake of his head, his eyes studying the warriors as they made their way behind the steel door and into the stairwell.

Once he was certain they were out of earshot he pulled the Nephilim aside and took a deep breath. Phil cut him off by speaking first. "You *do* intend to return the angelic weapons as agreed, do you not, Chief Jack?"

Jack stared at him open mouthed for just a moment before shaking his head. "Yes, of course. No, I need to...there's some bad news, and you need to be aware of it." He turned and nodded toward the door. "Lilith survived the attack."

The Nephilim gave him a surprised look. "I don't see how. We have her remains in those crates and..."

"No, her...*essence* survived. She..." he trailed off as he tried to think of how to explain what happened. "She 'took over' Brooke's body."

Phil nodded with understanding. "The vampiress. Yes, that makes sense." He rubbed at his chin as he stared at the doorway. "And now we must kill her again."

"Do you know of any way that we can remove Lilith from Brooke's body? Maybe some angelic device or weapon or...anything?"

Phil shook his head. "I am sorry, Chief Jack. The only thing at the weapons cache is weapons."

Jack sighed and rubbed at his eyes. "There *has* to be a way. There just has to be."

"Why?" The Nephilim gave him a confused stare.

"What do you mean, why?"

"Why must there be a way to save the vampire?" He leaned upon his hammer and studied Jack. "She was fully aware of the risks when she agreed to go to battle."

Jack shook his head. "There's no way she could have known about this. If I had known I would have made her stay here."

"And yet, here we be. Lilith yet lives, and you hesitate to kill her because of who she has possessed." The Nephilim shook his head. "It makes little sense."

"She trusted us. Trusted ME." He jabbed a finger into the Nephilim's chest. "I promised her…"

"What? That you would keep her safe?" The Nephilim swept the finger away and grimaced at the smaller man. "You should not have made such a promise."

Jack sighed and felt the energy drain from him. "It isn't fair. She's just a kid."

"Child or not, she is a warrior. Warriors know the risk they take when they go into battle. Whether cut down by the blade or cut down by the treachery of evil, there are always risks."

Jack felt the Nephilim's large hand gently squeeze his shoulder. "Let us do what must be done."

Jack watched as the Halfling strode purposefully toward the stairs. He took a deep breath and fell into step behind him. As he stepped into the darkened stairwell he wished he could be anywhere in the world but here.

*****

Director Jameson sifted through the stacks of papers and sighed.

"Good grief. We can't even get an identification on half of these...whatever they are." He slammed the files down and reached for the cup of coffee that had been cooling on the table. His eyes lifted and he noticed that the sun was rising outside. He had no intention of staying until daybreak and yet, here he was, sifting through raw data and photographs like an underling.

Ingram leaned across the table and slid the folder Jameson had been reading closer. He ran his finger along the lines of data and shook his head. "This can't be right. The spectral analysis on these weapons...they don't match anything on the periodic table." He lifted his bleary eyes to meet Jameson's. "Are we looking at alien tech here?"

"How in the hell am I supposed to know?" Jameson stood slowly and walked toward the coffee pot. He poured out what was in his cup and replaced it with fresh, hot brew. "There's no telling what these assholes are using."

"I know I'd like to have it for the Titans. Could you imagine how much more deadly they'd be with alien weaponry?" Ingram gave him a weak smile.

"We have no idea what these damned monster hunters have available to them." Jameson plopped down in his seat again and ran a hand across his haggard face. "They've been operational for far too long."

Ingram leaned back in his seat and yawned. "Who sits on their appropriations committee?"

Jameson shrugged. "I don't know. I never got the report from Stevens."

Ingram groaned. "Surely you have another hack who could get that for you."

"And then what? Try to dig up dirt on whichever congressman or senator happens to sit on it? That's a good way to find myself sitting before my own hearing. No, thank you." He leaned forward and sipped at the coffee, his mind racing.

"There has to be a way to find out the inner workings." Ingram stood and stretched before pouring his own cup of coffee. He glanced around the room and noted that only two of the techs still remained, and they were leaning across their consoles. "We've got so many pieces of the puzzle. We just need to figure out how they fit together."

"Do we?" Jameson shoved a pile of loose photos across the table at him. "Do we really? Since when did they get a winged monster on their team? Since when did they have a sentient zombie working for them?" He shoved the rest of the photos harder and they scattered to the floor. "And what the hell are these other…*things*? What is this? A hobbit? A giant? They're obviously part of the squad. See how the operators work as support for them!"

Ingram watched the photos flutter to the carpet and met the older man's eyes. They were wide with anger and worry. He bent and scooped up a handful of the photographs and placed them back on the table.

"Look, Jameson, I'm not about to start second-guessing who these people are. Or even *what* they are." He sifted through the photos and came to the image of the winged monster gliding over the warehouse. His face scrunched as he studied the photograph then he began to sift through the rest. Finally he pulled out the one he was looking for. The winged creature and the giant were dragging a second winged creature across the ground after the building had been destroyed.

"Here." He handed the photo to Jameson. "Maybe they called in a specialist to fight fire with fire?"

Jameson studied the pictures and shook his head. "I don't get it. What am I looking at here?"

"The winged monster flying around in these pictures is the same winged creature that is dragging…" he handed him the other photo, "this winged creature. Maybe they're the same species? Maybe they called in a specialist to help bring down one of their own?"

Jameson studied the photographs, his head shaking as he switched from one to the other. "I'm not reading you."

"Stay with me here." Ingram sat down and took a long drink from his coffee. "We've had all kinds of reports on the Monster Squad for some time now, haven't we?"

"Yes, of course."

"Okay. So what if they were facing…well, whatever the hell this thing is?" Ingram pointed to the winged creature being dragged across the ground. "In order to bring this thing down, they had to call in one of their own to help hunt it down and stop it?"

"But they don't look the same." Jameson flipped from photo to photo. "This one has wings like a bat. Sort of. This one has…"

"So maybe they're the same, but different. I dunno. Like comparing humans from different races. They have different physical attributes, but they're still the same." Ingram stood and pointed to the two creatures. "They're both winged. They're both large. Granted, their skin tones are different. This one has hair, this one doesn't. This one has a tail, this one doesn't, but, who's to say they aren't the same species?"

"And the giant? What is it? A juvenile? Hasn't sprouted its wings yet?" Jameson asked in a snarky tone.

"Possibly. Who knows? Maybe it's a physical defect or they were chopped off in battle?" He tossed the photos down in front of Jameson. "Who gives a flying fuck why, the point is that we've never heard of these asshats before because they aren't actually part of the Monster Squad."

Ingram stood in front of the older man with his arms crossed smugly over his chest. Jameson picked up the photos once more and glanced between them again. "How confident are you in your hypothesis?"

"I'd bet your life on it."

Jameson stared up at the younger man and raised a brow. "Would you bet your own life on it?"

Ingram gave him a slow smile. "Better yet, I'd bet the Titans on it."

Jameson studied him for a moment and then turned back to the photos. "That's a pretty damned expensive wager you're willing to place, Robert."

"That's how confident I am that I'm right."

Jameson continued to study the photos and nodded. "Get a satellite on their base of operation. I want their every movement scrutinized from this moment forward. If these...*things* are part of their forces, I want to know about it before we commit the Titans."

"Agreed."

Jameson tossed the photos onto the table and stood up. "And Robert?"

"Sir?"

"We still have to make plans to deal with the Council." He stepped over to where his coat hung and shrugged it on. "I sent them the test video and requested the first half of the payment. You might want to check your Swiss accounts."

17

Mitchell hung up the phone and stood behind his desk, peering out through the window and toward Doctor Peters' lab below. "Will they be of any use?"

He shook his head. "No, love, they won't. But if they can keep Bigby on the move, he can't act against us." He closed his blinds and turned to face his mate. "It seems that there is always somebody trying to remove us from the playing field, but to have so many at one time? This is new, even for us."

"You're worried?" She stepped closer and cupped his face with her hand.

"I worry for you." He gave her a wan smile. "If we hadn't mated, I'd yell at them all to bring their worst. But now that you could be put at risk?"

"Don't think of me as a china doll. I don't break easily." She gave him a warm smile and kissed his cheek.

"Of that, I'm certain." He took her hand in his own and kissed her palm. "At least now we can take your father off the list of those trying to destroy us." He shrugged slightly. "At least, I think we can."

"Now that we are mated, you most definitely can." She led him back to his chair and gently pushed him back into it. Her hands went to work on his shoulders as she tried to put things into perspective. "But you still have this British soldier who wants to destroy you. You also have another branch of your own government who wants to destroy you. And your people have just returned from removing a 'great threat' to mankind? You must be relieved that at least one of your worries has been dealt with."

Matt shrugged. "There's always some power-hungry numbskull trying to destroy humanity or take over the world or some such. That's just another day at the office for these yahoos." He closed his eyes and allowed himself to relax. "But the other threats could be devastating for us."

"The lone soldier may be a threat, but I think your people can handle him if given the chance."

"That's just it, they have to have a lead on him. Once they pick up his trail, he'll be taken care of." He groaned as her artful hands worked at the knots at the base of his neck. "But these government funded assholes? That's another story altogether."

"And that's why you have the prisoner downstairs talking to your vampire?"

Matt chuckled at the way she said, 'your vampire'. "Doc's a pretty sharp guy. If there's a chink in their armor, he'll exploit it. If these Spartans or Titans or whatever the hell they are have a Kryptonite, he'll find it."

"You sound confident."

"I am."

She leaned in close to his ear and whispered, "Then why worry so much?"

Matt opened his eyes and turned to her. "Because that's my job, sweetheart, I have to worry. All the time. I have to try to think of all the things that my people might have forgotten or overlooked."

"Allow them to do their jobs, my love. Allow them to show you just how good they are." She spun him in his chair and crawled into his lap, stirring feelings that he'd rather not feel in his office. "You have surrounded yourself with the best of the best. Allow them to *be* the best by doing their jobs and you relax and do yours. Sign your papers and approve what they ask of you and stop worrying about what you cannot control."

Matt chuckled again and pulled her close for a quick kiss. "If only I could allow myself to do that."

She sighed and ran her hands through his thick hair. "One of these days, Matthew, I will teach you to relax and trust your people."

"I do trust my people." He gave her a warm smile and squeezed her tightly. "But it's my job to worry. And I do my job very well."

*****

Jack entered the underground conference room and noted the few still milling about. Allister had taken up a strategic position by the freight elevator, essentially blocking the rear exit. Phil had taken up a position at the main entrance, blocking it. Jack nodded to Kalen then moved to the front of the room.

"Everybody, take your seats." He stepped to the white board and pulled the marker from the tray. "First order of business is to turn in our angelic weapons. As we all agreed to before this started, they have to be returned to Phil and there's no time like the present."

Jack lifted the lid on a plastic cargo container and pulled the dagger that Brooke had given him. He dropped it into the container and watched as each warrior stood and walked by, dropping their weapons as they reached the container. He watched Brooke especially close, but felt confident that she removed all of her blades and dropped them into the container. He continued to watch the group as each deposited their wares.

Gnat squeezed the handle on the hammer he held and met Jack's gaze. "It seems a shame to surrender such a finely crafted tool." He cast a glance back to Phil. "Are ye sure they wouldn't miss just one?"

Phil crossed his massive arms and gave the gnome a nasty look. Gnat grimaced and reluctantly dropped it into the container. "It doesn't hurt to ask."

Kalen went last and handed his bow to Jack rather than dropping it into the container. "The drawstring is sensitive. I'd hate to see the crate fill with arrows unintentionally."

Jack gave him a knowing smile and tucked the bow gently along the side. Casting one last quick glance about the room, he placed the lid back on the container and sealed it. Phil nudged the crate to the side with his leg then moved back to stand beside the door.

"Next order of business." Jack turned to Phil and gave a slight nod. The giant stepped toward the table and reached for Brooke just as Kalen grabbed her wrists and held her. Her eyes shot wide with shock and she struggled against the elf's grip.

Phil pulled the whip from his belt and wrapped it around her wrists, binding her. With a spin of his wrist, he flipped her over and pulled her across the table. All of the warriors were on their feet, a murmur of shock and confusion rising in the air as they tried to understand what was happening.

Jack held his hands high and yelled for their attention. "Hold it down! Hold it down! We have an unwanted visitor with us today."

"Let me go, damn you!" Brooke kicked and writhed as Kalen tried to hold her down upon the table. "Let me loose!"

Kalen looked to Azrael. "Help me hold her!"

The gargoyle stepped forward and grasped her ankles, locking her legs to the table. He searched Kalen's face for answers. "What is happening here?"

"Lilith took her." Kalen choked on his words as he spoke them. He let Brooke go and stepped back as tears welled up in his eyes.

"You traitorous little bastard! I'll drain you for this!" Brooke continued to struggle as Azrael tried to hold her in place.

Allister lit the last candle and muttered the end of his incantation. He looked up at Jack and nodded. "It is done. She cannot depart again."

Jack felt his hands shaking as he looked to Brooke who finally showed true fear. He glanced back to Allister. "How long will it last?"

"Until I remove it."

"Then we don't have to be in a huge hurry, right? I mean, maybe we can find another way."

Allister and the Nephilim both yelled, "No!" at the same time, startling the crowd. Phil glanced back to Jack and shook his head. "Do not waste time looking for an answer that cannot come."

Jack clenched his jaw and shook his head. "There has to be another way!"

Kalen fell into the chair next to Brooke and reached for her bound hand. "Please forgive me, my love."

"I'll eat your heart, you traitorous son of a whore!" Brooke spat in his face and snapped her extended fangs at him.

"Enough of this!" Phil squeezed the handle of the whip and a charge shot through it causing Brooke to dance and convulse on the table. Azrael's grip tightened on her ankles as he felt the surge of energy tear through his flesh. He watched as his hands began to turn to stone.

When Phil let go, Brooke passed out, her head lolling to the side. He looked to Azrael and nodded. The gargoyle waited a moment for his skin to shed the fine layer of stone and then released her legs, the thin layer of rock breaking away and dusting her leather pants.

The Nephilim stepped back and looked to Jack. "She is subdued for the moment. I do not know how long it will last." He held the handle of the whip in his hand, just in case.

Jack paced quickly, his mind racing. "There has to be another way. There just has to be." He suddenly stopped and looked toward the ceiling. The other warriors in the room first stared at him, then gazed at the same spot he was staring at.

"Azazel!" Jack yelled as he continued staring. "I know you can hear me!"

Gnat nudged Azrael. "Who's he yelling at?"

The gargoyle shrugged. "Perhaps the angel that appeared to him earlier?"

"Damn it, Azazel! Get Michael! I need his help!" Jack spun in a slow circle as he continued to shout at the ceiling. "This is your fucking fight, not ours!"

Allister stepped forward. "Chief Jack…"

"No!" Jack spun on him, his face red with anger. "No, this was their battle, and we got suckered into it. Now this kid is about to have to pay the ultimate price because they refused to intervene. I won't allow that. Do you hear me, Azazel? I won't allow it! This isn't her fault!" He reached for the pointer on the white board and threw it at the ceiling.

"Damn you, you winged bastard! Answer me!"

The room fell silent as they waited for an answer that wouldn't come. Jack continued to spin in a slow circle, his eyes glued to the ceiling. "I swear to you, Azazel…if you let this happen, I won't rest until I've hunted down every last one of you winged rats and put you out of your misery!"

Azrael cleared his throat. "Um, excuse me, Chief Jack, but do you think it wise to threaten an angelic being?"

Phil shook his head. "No, it is not."

"I don't fucking care!" Jack spun on the Nephilim and stuck a finger in his face. "If your uncles won't help when we really need it, then fuck 'em all! I meant what I said. I'll hunt every last one of them down."

Phil raised a brow and gave him a bored look. "And what do you possibly think you could do to an angel?"

Jack kicked the lid off the crate and pulled one of Brooke's swords. "I'll cut their fucking heads off, that's what."

Phil's eyes widened as he stared at Jack holding the angelic weapon. "You swore an oath that the weapons would be returned once the mission was completed."

Jack gave him a smile that didn't reach his eyes. "And as mission commander, I decide when the mission is complete. If they aren't willing to help save this girl, then the mission isn't complete until every last one of those winged demons are lying in a pool of their own blood."

Phil squared his shoulders and narrowed his eyes. "You wouldn't dare."

"Try me."

*****

Evan had separated the files into three stacks. One contained information pertaining only to the Titan warriors and their capabilities. Another dealt with their support, including the complex at Langley, the equipment at their disposal and the staff required to maintain their operations. The third stack was much smaller and it dealt with what little information Stevens had brought on the two men running the Spartan Project.

Evan continued to search through the short stack of files looking for anything that stood out about the two agency men when Stevens stood and stretched. "Any chance we could get some coffee in here? I'm dragging."

Evan nodded and pushed away from the table, pulling a French press from one of his shelves. He set up a Bunsen burner and placed a beaker of distilled water above it to boil. "I've got Chilean

Espresso or a very fine Costa Rican breakfast blend. Which would you prefer?"

"Whichever is strongest." Stevens rubbed at his eyes and yawned.

"The espresso has the strongest flavor, but the breakfast blend has the most caffeine."

"Breakfast blend it is then." He stood and stretched his back, working the kinks out of it as Evan prepared the press. He watched the vampire work and sat on the edge of the workbench while the water heated. "What are the odds I'll ever get out of jail?"

Evan shrugged. "It took them over three years to let me out."

Stevens stared at him, his mouth agape. "What the hell did you do?"

Evan shook his head. "Existed."

"Excuse me?"

"It wasn't their idea. They actually busted me out and…well, it's a long story." He poured the water into the press and worked the handle on it, pressing the grind to the bottom.

"And yet, you stayed with them. Helped them."

"Like I said, it wasn't their idea to lock me up." He poured the coffee into a mug and handed it to the agent. "Enjoy."

Stevens inhaled the rich aroma and blew across the top of the mug before taking the first sip. "Ooh, good bean."

"You're welcome. Now, if we can get back to work." Evan pushed his wheeled chair back to the table and went back to the files.

Stevens eased over and set the coffee next to where he was working. "You know…the more I look at these, the more I think that there has to be something obvious that I'm just not seeing. These guys may be good, but they aren't gods. There has to be a weakness."

Evan glanced up and nodded. "There is."

Stevens nearly choked on his coffee as he stammered. "There

is? Well, why didn't you say so! What is it?"

Evan shook his head. "I'm not at liberty to say. Not yet anyway."

"Why?" Stevens was on his feet now and sifting through the files. "I've gone through this stuff a dozen times. I can't see any…wait. You don't trust me?"

"I don't know you." Evan closed the dossier and eyed him.

Stevens sat back down and sighed heavily. "You guys wouldn't know anything about the Titans if I hadn't risked my career…my *life* bringing you this information. And you tell me you don't trust me. Great."

He stood and pushed away from the table. "Thanks for the coffee, but I'd rather go back to my cell now." He turned and walked to the door. "Guard!"

"Sit back down, Mr. Stevens," Evan spoke in a calm manner.

"Go stake yourself." Stevens kept his back to the vampire and continued staring through the acrylic walls. "Guard! Take me back to prison."

"I said sit down, Mr. Stevens."

"And I said, go st—" Stevens didn't finish his sentence as Evan grabbed him by the throat and swung him backward toward the chair.

"I deplore violence, but I will make a meal of you if I must."

"So do it." Stevens glared at him while Evan continued to hold him by the neck. "Go ahead. Do it!"

Evan studied the man, clutching to his arm while he held him in the chair. He tilted his head to better stare in his eyes. "Why do you wish to die?"

"I'd rather not. But I'm sick of being treated like I'm the threat! I came here to warn you people, and rather than saying so much as thank you, you toss me in jail, tell me I'm untrustworthy, and threaten to *eat me?*" he spat, struggling to breathe as Evan steadily squeezed, holding him down. "So if you're going to kill me, do it and get it over with!"

Evan released the man and watched him fall back into the chair. He continued to watch him for a moment then stood up straight and straightened his lab coat. "EMP."

Stevens gave him a confused stare while rubbing at his neck. "Excuse me?"

"You asked how to stop them. An EMP." Evan took his seat and opened the dossier on Jameson and Ingram. "Their battle suits are quite advanced, but they're not hardened. An electromagnetic pulse will short circuit them. They'll lose their displays, their communications, their ability to seal off wounded limbs, their networking with other operators. They'll essentially be men in very heavy Kevlar armor."

Stevens stared off, his mouth hanging open. "I can't believe that nobody thought to shield their armor."

"Neither could I. But I went over their schematics numerous times. They're most definitely *not* shielded."

Stevens smiled. He began to chuckle. His chuckling turned into full on laughter. "All of the money they spent on R&D and nobody thought to shield against an EMP? That's rich!"

"They probably didn't think that they'd have the need since they were designed to face monsters. Not much need to protect from an EMP when fighting vampires and werewolves and the like."

Stevens nodded. "I would have to agree." He reached for his coffee and took a long pull from it. "So, is there a way to create an EMP big enough to shut them down without setting off a nuke?"

Evan smirked. "Does a Northern Greater Elf delineate his borders with bioluminescent markings?" He noted the bewilderment on Stevens' face. "I mean, uh…does a bear defecate in the woods?"

"Ah! Yes! Yes, they do!"

"And yes. Yes, I can."

*****

The limo pulled to a stop and Viktor opened the door. He stepped out into the twilight and adjusted his suit. He glanced up the steps at the two vampire guards waiting at the top of the landing. He gave the two men a slight nod but neither responded.

Holding the door open for Rufus, he kept his eyes moving for any others who might be lurking in the shadows. Once Rufus was clear of the car he gently shut the door and stepped in front of the vampire, acting as a shield as the two made their way up to the main doors.

Both guards took a step closer, effectively blocking the entrance and Rufus gripped Viktor's shoulder. He pulled him back gently and stepped forward. "Inform the Council that Rufus Thorn is here to meet with them."

"You aren't cleared for access, Mr. Thorn."

Rufus gave the guard a slight bow and smiled. "If you'll inform the Council that their request has been met. The demon queen has been removed. I believe they'll allow my audience."

One of the guards spoke softly into his sleeve and a moment later he nodded to the other. Both men stepped aside and the smaller of the two opened the door allowing both Viktor and Rufus to enter the building.

Once inside and away from inquisitive ears, Viktor leaned closer and whispered, "Should I be alarmed yet?"

"Not yet, *mon ami.*" Rufus entered the elevator and punched the button for the top floor. As the doors shut he stared straight ahead. "Are your people in position?"

Viktor pulled a small device from his breast pocket and punched a series of buttons. "They are. And they are monitoring me. I need only to give them the word."

Rufus nodded. "Let us hope they won't be needed."

Viktor stiffened as the lights slowly rose closer to the top. "Do you truly think that is a possibility?"

"Anything is possible." He turned and gave a sad smile. "Not probable, but possible."

The doors opened and a very large vampire stood before the pair. "Monsieur Thorn. I am to escort you to the Council."

"Very well."

"Your dog stays here." The large vampire sneered at Viktor who showed no emotion.

"My *Second* comes with me."

The vampire stiffened and stared at the much smaller man. "We were under the impression that your brother was your Second."

"He was. He was released and Viktor has taken his rightful place once more." Rufus held his head high and motioned to the vampire. "Shall we?"

With a low growl, the vampire turned and escorted the pair to the Council Chambers. Just shy of the door he paused. "Wait here. You'll be called when they are ready."

The large vampire disappeared through an alcove and Rufus stood ready. Viktor cleared his throat and whispered, "How long do you think they'll make us wait?"

"Long enough to remind us of who is in charge."

"Great."

*****

"Spanky!" Little John yelled as he tried to focus on where the pair had rolled to. He could see arms and legs grappling as the pair rolled down an embankment, dirt and debris flying as each tried to gain footing to best the other. John stood and took off toward the tumbling pair. "Move! Move! Converge on Spalding!"

He took off down the embankment, sliding through the wet mossy mud until he reached the bottom of the hill. He could see where the two had struggled further down the dry creek bed that led to the rushing water they had been listening to on their approach. He crested a small rise and saw the pair still struggling and rolling toward the river below. "Double time it!"

John took off at a sprint, his night vision bouncing as he tried to avoid low hanging limbs and prickly vines. He ducked low and rolled under a fallen tree, coming up with his rifle at the ready. By the time he focused the reticle, he saw only Spanky coming to his feet, his head spinning in different directions, looking for his attacker.

"Delta One, report!" John barked as he made a slow approach.

"Operational." Spalding slapped mud and leaves from his uniform and pulled his carbine back around from his back. The strap had nearly strangled him during his encounter.

John slowed his approach and scanned the area, Lamb and Jacobs flanking him and taking a higher position to scan for the attacker. Donovan laid a hand on John's back. "I don't see Five."

Spalding's ears perked and he was suddenly up the hill, his carbine leveled. "Delta squad, report."

Donovan nodded to him. "Delta Two, ready."

"Delta Three, five-by-five, boss," Lamb reported from above him.

"Delta Four standing by." Jacobs was on one knee and scanning the hillside with his carbine.

Little John felt the bile rise in his throat when Five didn't report. He looked to Spalding and shook his head. "Delta Six, at the ready."

"Fuck me standing." Spalding reached down and pulled his boonie hat from the muddy moss and slapped it across his leg. "The attack was a diversion."

"There's two of them?"

Spalding shrugged. "At least." He ground his teeth and hit his throat mic. "OPCOM, Delta Actual, we have multiple tangos. They have Delta Five."

"Copy that, Delta Actual. Air support inbound. Switching to

thermal and beginning an expanding search pattern."

"Roger that, OPCOM." Spalding released his mic and turned to Lamb. "You and Ing check for tracks. Look for anything that might indicate where they took Gus. There's no way the big guy went down without a fight."

"Copy that." Ron tapped Jacobs and the two double-timed it back up the hill, their eyes scanning the ground and surrounding foliage for any indication of a struggle.

"What do want us to do, boss?" Donnie asked.

Spalding ground his teeth and glanced down the hill where his attacker had suddenly released him and disappeared in the darkness of the forest.

"We're gonna hunt that other fucker down. Odds are, they're gonna meet up somewhere. I want to be there when they do."

*****

Jameson returned to his office rather than trying to return home for thirty minutes of sleep. He opened his door to a ringing phone and assumed it had to be Ingram. He punched the button and lifted the receiver to his ear. "This couldn't have waited?"

"I've got people gearing up to move into an empty office complex across from the Monster Squad hangar. Since it's basically across the street and has three stories of glass facing their operation, I thought it would be the best place to set up surveillance."

"And?"

"And, as soon as you walked out I got a call from my contact at Tinker. Apparently Mitchell put in a requisition to commandeer that building. He wasn't too happy when he found out that someone else had laid claim and was in preparation to make the building operational again."

"Too bad for him." Jameson fought a yawn and sat down in his chair. "How soon before we have boots on the ground?"

"A few days. They're already making repairs to the building and getting support staff set up. Apparently there was a bit of activity that took place there recently."

"Am I supposed to care?"

"You might." Ingram paused, hoping that Jameson would rise and take the bait. He didn't. He exhaled hard and continued, "Apparently they had a sniper set up there. He took a shot at the hangar. Reports are sketchy at best, but rumor has it that somebody was killed."

"One of the abominations?"

"Nope. Somebody close to them, though. At least, that's the scuttlebutt."

"Again, I'm supposed to care, why?"

"I just found it interesting that somebody else was watching them besides us. And that somebody took a shot at them." Ingram waited for the older man to add to the conversation. When he didn't, he continued. "The enemy of my enemy…"

"Could very well be my enemy, too," Jameson deadpanned. "I'm sorry, Robert, but I simply don't buy into old adages. They tend to get people killed." He spun in his chair and glanced at his map of the Middle East to remind him exactly of why he didn't believe such things.

Ingram sighed and Jameson could hear the phone shift. "All I'm saying is that if there is somebody out there who is trying to put the hurt on these guys, maybe we can use them. We don't have to crawl into bed with them, just…let them rattle the cage a bit and keep them off guard. You know, keep them guessing what the left hand is doing while the right hand swats them."

Jameson shook his head and wished that he had a large cup of coffee to help jump start his brain. "I understand your desire to preoccupy the Monster Squads, but the whole idea was to alert them to the threat of the Titans, remember? Allow them to prepare themselves as best as they could so that they would throw everything they had at our troops at once. Wipe them out in one fell swoop. No survivors. Nobody to try and return to avenge their fallen comrades."

"I know, but…with what we've learned recently, it just seemed prudent to use whatever we could to our advantage."

Jameson smiled although Ingram couldn't benefit from the gesture. "My boy, if our super soldiers can't handle these mutts, then they don't deserve to wear the mantle of 'defender of mankind', now do they?"

"Well, I don't know if I'd go that far. Our troops have the right stuff to protect humanity from monsters. I'm just not sure if they're prepared to face the—"

"They're *monsters*, Robert. Plain and simple. They may believe that they fight for our best interest, but they are still monsters. And the Titans were created to destroy monsters, were they not?"

"Well, yes, but—"

"No buts." Jameson leaned forward, preparing to hang up. "They will face the Council and destroy them. Then they will face the Monster Squad and destroy them. If they aren't up to those tasks, then they simply aren't worthy."

"So, what? We wash the project down the drain?"

"Of course not, dear boy. We simply create a better monster hunter."

18

"What do you mean we can't appropriate that building? I already cleared it with General Litchfield's office. They said that nobody wanted that building because of the condition and—" Mitchell got cut off and clenched his jaw while the woman on the other end of the phone made excuses.

He pinched at the bridge of his nose and did his best not to yell. "Ma'am, I understand that, but we were assured that we could utilize that building as long as we were willing to renovate to current code and standards and we agreed to in order to ensure the security of our operations. General Litch—" He was cut off again, except this time she explained that somebody much higher up, from the Pentagon, had authorized the use of the three-story office complex, and the new tenants were already making renovations.

Mitchell groaned and leaned back in his chair, the fight having left him. "In other words, there's not a damned thing that neither I, nor General Litchfield can do. Somebody with more brass than brains has already made the decision."

"That is correct, Colonel."

Mitchell fought the growl rising in his throat as he thanked her and hung up. "More bad news, I take it."

"You could say that." He turned and filled his coffee cup again, wishing for the umpteenth time that it was scotch. "We lost the building across the way that Bigby set up in."

Jennifer nodded as she tried to find a silver lining. "I suppose if somebody is utilizing the building, the odds are much lower that somebody else can do what Bigby did, correct?"

Mitchell shrugged. "I suppose."

Jennifer fought the smile tugging at the corners of her mouth. "So what is the proper military protocol when you get a new neighbor? Do you take them a cobbler or a pie and welcome them to the neighborhood?"

"You're not funny." Mitchell sipped the coffee and lifted his blinds to study the two men down in the lab.

"I really wish you'd lighten up a bit." She wrapped her arms around his middle and nuzzled his neck.

"When all of this is put to rest, I'll do my best to take a little time off."

Jennifer snorted and hid her face. "I thought you said there was always some sort of threat that needed your attention?"

He gave her a sidelong glance. "Did I?"

"I believe you did."

"Hmm. Well, maybe I should choose my words more wisely in the future."

She stepped between him and the window and gave him a devilish smile. With a sudden jerk of her hands, she pulled open her blouse and exposed herself to him. "Maybe if I can distract you from all of these worries."

Mitchell opened his mouth to comment just as his office door burst open. "We have an operator miss—Oh, my God!" Tufo spun on his heels and headed back out of the office.

"Would it kill you to learn how to *knock!*" Mitchell yelled.

"I didn't see a damned thing!" Tufo yelled from the hallway. "And for the love of Pete, turn up the heat before she catches her death!"

Mitchell ground his teeth while Jennifer laughed and refastened her blouse. "Go. See what's so important."

"I'm gonna kill him."

She placed a hand on his cheek and gave him a loving smile. "We're wolves, my love. Nudity doesn't faze me."

"But it was *him*." Mitchell's eyes narrowed.

"Go!" She pushed him toward the door, tears of laughter forming as he reluctantly left.

Mitchell did his best to stomp menacingly toward the OPCOM. He threw open the door to find Mark sitting at attention in the command chair, his eyes glued straight ahead at the overhead screen.

Mitchell shut the door and stepped to the chair where Mark refused to even blink. "What was so damned important that you felt it necessary to interrupt," he glanced around the room and cleared his throat, "such an important meeting?"

"Gus Tracy has been abducted." Tufo's eyes continued to stare straight ahead. "And let the record reflect that I didn't see a thing."

"Bull cookies." Mitchell glanced to the boards and checked the readouts on the drone. "Anything on the thermals?"

"Negative, Colonel," the drone operator responded. "We're doing an expanding grid, but so far we're not picking up anything larger than a raccoon."

Mitchell glanced to Tufo, his face a mask of confusion. "Are you thinking what I'm thinking?"

"Turn up the heat in your office?"

"No! For the love of…underground tunnels!" Mitchell slammed a fist down on the rail between the command chair and the technicians. "If they nabbed Gus and they're not reading on the thermals, they must be travelling through some kind of tunnel system."

Mark's eyes widened as it suddenly became clear. "That area is supposed to be eat up with caves. Who says there can't be tunnels connecting them?"

Mitchell nodded to the coms officer. "Notify Delta Actual. Tell him to keep his eyes peeled for any kind of underground access. And for God's sake, be careful out there."

*****

"Chief Jack, the Wyldwood asked that I provide guidance while here and I must profess that this course of action is foolhardy at best." Allister took a half step forward, his face unreadable. "Might I suggest that you take a moment to calm yourself and—"

"When I want your opinion, I'll give it to you. Understood?" Jack pointed the angelic blade in Allister's direction, sending the griffin back the half step he had advanced. "That goes for all of you. If you're not part of the solution, then you're part of the problem."

Azrael's brow furrowed as he spoke. "We're either with you or against you? Is that what it's come to, Chief Jack? Because the last I heard, you were our leader."

Gnat stepped from between Azrael's legs and propped his familial war hammer across his shoulder. "Aye. I pledged my allegiance to you, Chief Jack. To live, fight, or die by your command." He glanced across the room to the others. "I stand by that pledge. Even if I believe your threat to be foolhardy as Allister has proclaimed."

"Nobody wants Brooke to live more than I, Chief Jack." Kalen stepped between him and her immobile form. "But I also understand that we must not suffer the demon queen to live. The risk is too great."

Jack felt the sword becoming heavier in his hand and he slowly lowered it. "There has to be another way. There just has to be." He looked to each of his warriors and saw the sorrow in their faces.

Kalen leaned down beside Brooke and gently kissed her forehead. "It is time."

Jack watched his body move forward as if on autopilot. His mind was still searching, doing its best to find another way out of this, but it felt as though he were drugged. As if he could no longer think properly.

He reached the table and stood beside Brooke's still form. He glanced to Kalen who was wiping tears from his eyes. A glint reflected from the Gatekeeper and Jack's hand reached out, grasping the elf by the wrist. "Call her."

"Who?"

"The Wyldwood. Maybe she knows of another way. She has the gift of sight. Maybe she has seen another way."

Phil crossed his arms and muttered, "You are grasping at straws."

"It's worth a shot, dammit." Jack pulled Kalen's arm up until the stone was in his face. "Use it."

Kalen nodded. He stepped away and turned his back on the others. He waved his hand over the stone and waited for the light to shine through. It took longer than he had hoped but eventually Loren's face reflected through the stone. Kalen sighed when he saw her reflection.

"You know what we face, Wyldwood?"

She nodded solemnly. "And I knew you would face it, young warrior." Her eyes reflected the sadness that he felt. "I tried to warn you not to become involved with her."

"Tell me there is a way to save her and still destroy Lilith. Please. I will do as you ask. I will renounce my feelings for her and return home, never to..."

"It cannot be, Kalen. The Brooke you know is already gone." The Wyldwood lowered her face, and when she peered back into the stone, he saw the tears streaking her face. "For two spirits to inhabit one body, one must be destroyed. That is why Lilith cannot possess a body with a soul. The essence of her spirit would be destroyed."

"But Brooke has no soul, Wyldwood. She is vampire. You know this."

Azazel nudged Jack and nodded to the elf. "To whom does he speak?"

Jack whispered back, "Only the wearer of that bracelet thing can see and hear the person speaking through it on the other side."

The Wyldwood nodded. "Yes, Kalen, but she still has her spirit. That is her essence. It is what makes her, *her*. It is her emotions, her feelings, her memories, the very thing that makes Brooke who she is. Once Lilith took over Brooke's body, a large part of her essence was destroyed. The longer Lilith has been within her, the more of it she has destroyed. If you could remove Lilith without destroying Brooke's body, she would be little more than a ghoul. A mindless zombie. A mere shadow of the woman you once loved."

The Wyldwood choked on her next words and it almost made Kalen break down. "You would be granting her a mercy if you ended her life. I am so sorry, Kalen."

Kalen shook as he stared at the reflection in the Gatekeeper. "Why didn't you warn me? I could have stopped her from going. I could have saved her!"

His anger was palpable, and the Wyldwood didn't back away. She allowed her tears to continue flowing as she replied. "It was predestined. All of the visions were the same. Brooke had to be sacrificed to destroy Lilith forever. She had to be in a mortal body. She couldn't be destroyed in her original form."

Kalen screamed and pulled the Gatekeeper from his wrist. He threw it across the room and pounded his fists on the table.

Jack stepped forward and placed a hand on his shoulder. "You don't have to tell us what she said. We can pretty much tell from your reaction."

Kalen hung his head and sobbed. "She knew."

Jack leaned closer. "What?"

"The Wyldwood. She knew this would happen. She said it had to be this way. It was the only way that Lilith could be destroyed completely and forever. She couldn't be killed in her original form." He lifted his reddened eyes and peered into Jack's. "They sacrificed Brooke to meet that end."

Phil stepped forward and reached for the sword that Jack held. "Perhaps your fight is with the elves and not with the angels."

*****

Laura pulled her Jeep into the parking lot at the hangar and killed the engine. She glanced up at the rusty old hangar and smiled. "Be it ever so crumble, there's no place like home."

Stepping down from the four-wheel drive vehicle she left her bags in the back and headed for the doorway. The guards at the guard shack gave her a mock salute when they saw her approach.

"Please tell me you're here to stay."

"If they'll still have me." She gave the sergeant a smile and a pat on the arm as she walked past and through the open roll away door.

The familiar sights and smells assaulted her as soon as she walked in and the first thing she wanted to do was run down the stairs and throw herself at Evan. She turned and stared at the stairwell. Three flights down and a quick left should take her straight to his lab.

"No time like the present."

She hit the door at a jog and took the stairs two at a time. When she pushed through the metal doors that led to the large floor with Evan's lab she could feel her heart racing. With each step, she could feel the muscle in her chest hammering to escape. She saw the clear acrylic walls of his laboratory and her breath caught in her throat.

She mounted the steps and launched herself through the doorway. "Hi, home, I'm honey!"

Evan spun on his chair and his eyes widened at the sight of her. "Laura?"

"I missed you." She ignored the man sitting across from him and closed the gap between them. She wrapped her arms around his neck and pulled him to her for the longest, deepest kiss they had ever shared.

The man sitting at the table cleared his throat and squirmed while she ran her hands through the vampire's hair. Finally he muttered, "If this is how you 'eat' somebody, I'm glad you opted not to eat me. That could get a little weird for me."

She raised one hand and gave the man a one fingered salute.

When the pair finally broke loose, Laura was gasping for air. "God, I missed you."

"Me, too," Evan stammered. "I mean, I missed you, not that I missed me, too." He blushed slightly and did his best to straighten his lab coat again.

Laura glanced to the side and raised a brow at the man sitting across the workbench. "Who's your friend?"

"Oh. Uh, well, technically, he's not my friend, per se. I mean, well, he was a prisoner of sorts. But now he's assisting us in, uh, well…it's a long story."

Stevens stood up, his hand extended. "Robert Stevens. Ex-CIA analyst."

Laura raised a brow. "And you were a prisoner here?" She tentatively reached out and took his hand.

"Like he said, long story." Stevens sat back down. "But, don't mind me. You two feel free to go back to what you were doing." He gave her a crooked smile.

Evan pulled her aside. "Your father. What…happened?"

She shook her head. "He absolutely refused. When Derek tried to hunt him down to give him the other shot, he destroyed the serum."

"So, he's…the wolf?"

"I didn't actually see him. You know, afterward. But yeah, that's my guess."

Evan inhaled sharply and let it out slowly. "And now you're here to…what?"

She shook her head. "I had to get away." She stared into his eyes and felt herself smiling. "I had to come home."

"Home? Here?"

"Home is where the heart is."

*****

Viktor stiffened when the door opened and a vampire of very slight build appeared. He stepped slowly forward and nodded to Rufus. "The Council will see you now."

Rufus nodded back and the pair stepped through the large double doors. Viktor tried not to be impressed with the large conference room with the antique furnishings but the word opulence immediately came to mind.

A long oval table with overstuffed chairs surrounding it sat in the middle of the room and most of the Council members appeared to be busy pouring over paperwork of different kinds.

Rufus and Viktor approached to within a few meters of the head of the table before Rufus stopped and silently stood, waiting to be addressed. Viktor followed suit.

The pair stood silently, observing the Council members as they murmured amongst themselves, quiet discussions that didn't pertain to the guests who stood quietly waiting for their audience. As if on cue, the members all stopped and turned to face the pair.

"We are told you have news."

"*Oui*." Rufus stepped forward, his hand gesturing slightly to keep Viktor behind him. "I am quite certain the Council is already aware that the demon queen has been vanquished. My brother ensured representation for both of our houses during the onslaught and he assured me of her destruction."

"And where is your brother now?"

Viktor noted the older grey haired vampire who sat at the head of the table who now questioned Thorn. The other members appeared to relinquish authority to him in this matter and he seemed almost bored with the topic. From what Rufus had told him earlier of their apprehension of Lilith, he would have expected them to show more relief that she had been dealt with.

"He is on his way to meet me here." Thorn gave a slight bow. "He brings the heart of the demon queen that the Council might ensure she never rises again."

The grey haired vampire nodded absently. "And he will arrive when?"

"He should arrive tomorrow, my liege."

The vampire's face wrinkled in puzzlement. "If he doesn't arrive until tomorrow, then why did you demand an audience with the Council this night?"

Rufus bowed again and did his best to act naïve. "To formalize the lifting of the edict, of course."

Viktor felt the hair on his neck rise when the members all began to chuckle amongst themselves. The grey haired vampire stood from his seat and turned to face Rufus. "Surely you jest. You truly believed that this Council would lift a death edict that was pronounced more than two hundred years ago?"

Rufus raised his head and faced the older vampire. "Yes. I believed this Council to be an honorable body. A noble body. A most trustworthy body. One whose word was their bond."

The chuckling turned to outright laughter by some and Viktor brought his hands together, grasping his wrist with his other hand, right above his watch. His finger tapped nervously along the edge of the casing of the watch. Once Rufus made his move, he would push the button on the side of his watch, signaling his wolves.

The grey haired vampire stepped forward and looked down at Rufus. "You are far too old and far too powerful to be that foolish, Monsieur Thorn. This Council never intended to lift your death edict." He turned and smiled at the other members. "We hoped you would be successful in your endeavors against the she-witch, but even in that effort we thought your odds too astronomical to survive."

"And so you have underestimated me." Rufus unbuttoned his overcoat, letting it fall slightly open. "And I overestimated your honor."

*****

"Underground? Did he say tunnels?" Donovan groaned as the squad worked through the woods, glints of sunlight sliced through the canopy as dawn brought a new day.

"That's what I heard." Spanky scrambled up a mossy hillside and laid low, trying to detect depressions in the spongy material.

"How the hell do we find tunnels? We can't find the bastards who live here, how are we supposed to find the holes they use to—" Little John's words were cut off as he abruptly disappeared, falling through the moist earth.

Spalding and Donovan sprinted to his position and stared down into the hole that Sullivan sat in, dirt and detritus falling around him. Sullivan spat dirt from his mouth and looked up at the pair. "I think I found something." He spat again then scraped his tongue across his teeth. "I think I swallowed a bug."

"Leave it to Little John to fall into the damned thing." Donnie slid down the side of the hole and landed next to the big man. He offered him a hand up then they both stepped into the tunnel as Spanky jumped into the hole.

"Which way, boss?" Little John asked, still spitting dirt from his mouth.

Spanky looked both ways then checked the hard packed earth they stood on. "No prints. Your guess is as good as mine."

Donovan tried to get his bearings then pointed away from the river. "That way is away from the water. My guess is, this is their quick access to drinking water. Their base of operation is probably that way."

Spanky shrugged. "Sounds plausible." He stepped into the tunnel and switched on the LED torch mounted to the end of his carbine. "We'll have to crouch to fit through here."

Little John shivered. "Christ…feels like a tomb. What's to keep it from collapsing on us and burying us alive?"

Donovan patted the big man's shoulder. "The fact that you're down here and not stomping around on our heads, for one."

"Ha-ha."

"Cut the chatter." Spalding took one last look around then nodded to Donovan. "Take point. I'm going to transmit our coordinates to Delta Three and Four and have them relay to OPCOM that we're underground. We'll be radio silent once we start." He narrowed his gaze to drive home his point. "We're at half strength and facing multiple tangos. Everybody stay frosty on this one."

"Roger that."

✻✻✻✻✻

Bigby heard the doors unlock and he let himself slip through the back window, his boots crunching in the gravel below as he touched the ground. He gently pulled the window shut and slipped alongside the building, keeping to the shadows as the sun rose in the east.

He had spent the entirety of the night listening to security and base police cars zipping across the campus, presumably searching for him and knew that as long as he remained in the locked building, the odds were slim he would be discovered. Now that he was in the open, the only thing that would save him would be the flood of daily workers coming in to their jobs. The base would come alive with the civilian contractors and the Air Force employees who performed their nine-to-five jobs and then went home as though they were also civilians.

He slipped quietly between two buildings and climbed a roof access ladder. He gained enough altitude to see that his stolen truck was now gone. The building he had been camped in was crawling with people and although base security had lightened up, there were far too many folks in uniform between himself and the rusty hangar for him to get any closer; at least not during daylight hours.

With a dejected sigh he climbed back down and worked his way across the parking lot and past the rows of industrial buildings. When his nose picked up the smell of food, he turned and followed it. No matter what he decided to do, he'd have to fuel his body before he could attack the Yanks.

Maybe once he put a little more distance between himself and his targets, he could allow himself the luxury of filling his belly and mapping a new plan of attack.

*****

Kalen spun and gave a worried eye to Jack. "Surely not. We cannot declare war on my people."

Jack slowly shook his head, a mental image of Loren forming causing a mix of emotions that he couldn't understand. "No…we can't."

Phil held his hand out, waiting for Jack to surrender the sword. "If you will not enact your revenge on those truly responsible, then surely you would not attack those who are not. Either way, you have no further need for the heavenly weapons."

Jack slowly raised his eyes to meet Phil's gaze. He felt as

though his mind was in shock, trying to register the mixed turn of events. He glanced down at Phil's hand then to his own. He lifted the sword and lowered the point, offering the hilt to Phil. "As promised."

"But, what of Brooke?" Gnat stood next to the young vampiress, his hand stroking her hair.

"She is already gone," Kalen's voice barely a whisper as he spoke. He leaned heavily against the table, his eyes swollen and red. "Her spirit is destroyed…her essence all but gone. The Wyldwood said we would be doing her a mercy by…" His voice cracked and he turned away.

"How do we know?" Gnat hopped onto a chair then jumped up onto the table. "She lied to you before. Maybe she lies now."

Kalen shook his head. "The Wyldwood is incapable of lying. She may omit certain things to ensure events play out as they should, but she does not lie."

Jack stared at Brooke's still form then glanced to Phil. "I can't do this."

Allister stepped forward. "I will."

"I can." Phil stepped forward as well. "You need not be present."

Kalen stiffened, his shoulders squaring. He turned quickly and shook his head adamantly. "No!" He ran his arm across his face, wiping the tears and sticky fluids from his nose away. "If this must be done, it shall be done by one who loved her truly."

"Oh no…" Jack moaned. He staggered back a step and ran a hand across his face. "What am I going to tell her brother? I swore to him that I'd…"

"She died in battle," Kalen stated. He stared defiantly at each of them, his jaw set. "She sacrificed herself to save us all. That's all he needs to know."

A low murmur of agreement spread throughout the room and Kalen turned to face her. He brushed a stray hair from her face and fought the tears threatening to fall from his eyes again. His hand fell automatically to the blade at his belt and he pulled it swiftly.

He cast one last quick glance to Allister. "The heart?"

"Yes. Then her head."

Kalen paled as he nodded. He turned back to Brookes still form and inhaled deeply. "Forgive me, my love."

*****

"We have Stevens' car still in their parking lot."

Director Jameson wasn't surprised that he made it to the monster hunters. "Any eyes on the man himself?" He had half a mind to give the 'shoot on sight' order, but he knew that would tip their hand.

"Not yet. There really isn't a lot of activity outside the hangar." Ingram could be heard shuffling papers over the phone. "They're still working on a couple of the floors and some of the offices, but the surveillance team we have in place is recording them from every angle. We have limited audio, but again, with nothing going on outside, there isn't much to go through."

"Do we want a wet works team standing by?"

Jameson stared at the speaker phone and shook his head. "Are you stupid or just dumb? What good would a wet works team do? These people hunt monsters for a living. Do you really think a wet works team would stand a chance against them?"

"I just thought...you know, if any of them became isolated from the rest of the group."

"And you don't think that would alert them?" Jameson clicked the button on the speaker phone and picked up the receiver. "We stick to the plan, Robert. We keep them rattled, we shake their cage. We get them worried until they pool their resources. Once they've brought all their chickens home to roost and have all of their resources under one roof, we flatten them. Not until then. We can't risk having any of them running around like loose cannons."

"I just thought it might be nice to have something on the ground, close by, in case things got ugly."

"Oh, trust me, if things get ugly, we're going to need something much more effective than a wet works team standing by."

Ingram sighed heavily into the phone. "Should I have them prepare to transport the Titans then?"

"Robert, I'm beginning to think that planning isn't your strong suit." Jameson pulled over his calendar and checked it. "I'm free this afternoon. Meet me for lunch, I think it's time we plan the next stage of this operation."

"Fine, but you're buying." Jameson heard the phone click and he leaned back in his chair as he held the receiver in his hands. "Do be careful, Robert. I'd hate to have to replace you so late in the game."

19

"When did this happen?" Mitchell stared at Tufo's hands.

"Shortly after the op started getting hairy," Tufo kept his voice low, his eyes glancing about the OPCOM. "I'm *really* hoping that it's a temporary thing. Like a fight-or-flight response to the team being in danger."

"Ya think?" The sarcasm wasn't missed.

"Well, if it isn't, I'm gonna have a hell of a time wiping my ass!" Heads turned and curious gazes fixed on the major while he argued with his CO. Mark grimaced and scowled at the techs. "As you were!"

"Don't bark at them. You're the one who—"

"I know what I said." Mark held a hand up in surrender but suddenly hid it again.

"Okay, fine. Go to Doc and see if he can give you something."

Mark shot him a deadpan stare. "Like what, Matt? Fucking nail clippers?"

Mitchell rolled his eyes. "Like a valium or something to calm your nerves. We can't have you going velociraptor on us every time the heat turns up."

"Yeah, ha-ha-ha. Like my system wouldn't burn right through that crap."

"That's why I said 'or *something*'..." Mitchell stood and squared his shoulders. "That's an order, Major."

Tufo gave him a wide eyed stare and ground his teeth. "Yes, sir." He stood from the command chair and announced, "I stand relieved."

"CO has the chair." Mitchell took his place and watched as Mark sulked toward the door. "Just get this under control, Mark. Everything will be back to normal before you know it."

"I hope to god you're right."

Mitchell turned his attention back to the screens. "Where are we on punching coms through that topsoil?"

"So far, it's a no-go, sir. We've dropped the drone 'til she's brushing the treetops and boosted the gain on the coms as much as the amplifiers can handle. So far, nothing."

"Well, keep trying." He leaned back and studied the thermal readouts. "There has to be a way to stay in contact with them."

*****

Rufus stood atop the conference table, the weapon still humming in his hands as the doors to the Council Chambers burst open. Two of Viktor's wolves rushed inside and took cover behind the large pillars on either side of the entry. "Guards are rushing the chamber!"

"Wait!" Rufus yelled. He held a hand up, preventing the wolves from firing upon the vampires as they cleared the doors.

The two vampire guards slid to a stop, their eyes quickly taking in what they already knew. The Vampire Council had been removed. The once venerable body had been reduced to nothing more than smoking ash. Now, only one remained and he stood on the table, apparently commanding both vampire and wolf.

The guards dropped to one knee, their arm across their heart in salute to the new chancellor. "My liege. Your orders?"

"Send word to the rest of the guards. A change in command has taken place. They shall continue their duties as previously ordered. Once their shift is complete, they shall report to me here."

"Your will be done, my liege." Both guards stood and exited. Neither acknowledged the wolves holding weapons on them as they left.

Viktor turned slowly and faced Rufus. "You did this for more power?"

Rufus raised a questioning brow. "Power? You think I faced down the Council for...power?"

Viktor leaned against the table and stared him down. "I do now."

Rufus switched off the weapon and stepped down from the table, slinging the weapon back into the folds of his coat. "Why would you think such a thing, *mon ami*?"

"Don't '*mon ami*' me." Viktor pushed away from the table and stared down at the man he once considered a friend. "You had been perfectly safe for more than two hundred years. The council cared nothing about you or your so-called death edict." He pointed an accusatory finger at him. "You discovered something. Something that told you if you could destroy the council, you could assume their position. Their power...their *strength,* didn't you?"

Rufus gave him a sad smile. "How can you believe such a thing?"

"Fine. Then disband the council. Walk away from the title and the power that comes with it." He crossed his arms defiantly.

Rufus laughed and swatted away the ashes from the seat at the head of the table. "Do you have any idea what would happen to all of the *familias* if I were to do that? It would be chaos. Utter turmoil.

It would be like a third world nation without any form of government."

Viktor snorted with derision. "I knew it. You're power hungry. Ever since you were put in charge of the *beastia* and then convinced Paul to sign over his people so you could fight the Sicarri, you've gotten a taste of *real* power. And now you want more and more and…you can't get enough."

"Absurd." Rufus waved away the thought dismissively. "You know nothing of the ways of vampires."

"Oh truly?" Viktor jerked away two of the chairs and stood next to him, his eyes filled with anger. "You used me and my wolves to secure your way into the council chamber so that you could steal their power. I watched you do it with my own eyes and then you tell me that I don't know what I saw?"

"I tell you that you are misinterpreting what you have seen. That is all." He softened his voice and gave Viktor his best smile. "Please, *mon ami*, sit. Allow me to explain to you—"

"I have heard enough of your explanations." Viktor pushed away from the table and stared down at the smaller man. "You are not the man I once respected."

"I am still that man, Viktor. You say that I held on to Paul's people for power, but it was to ensure the safety of mankind." He looked up at Viktor and smiled. "And I gave him back his people. They're not mine to control any longer."

Viktor raised a brow and shook his head. "You think me a fool? They are *all* yours now, Rufus. Every *familia* is yours…both *beastia* and *humanis*. You control them all. If you suddenly declare that ALL vampires become *beastia*, what happens?"

Rufus inhaled deeply and nodded. "They all become *beastia*. But that is not what I intend to—"

"Intentions be damned!" Viktor slammed his fist on the table. "You have become what you have warned against for centuries. Whether you rule with love and compassion or with an iron fist, you, Rufus Thorn, are now a despot."

*****

"No more jokes about wiping my ass or I'll see how well these things work at picking your nose." Mark held up his taloned hands and wiggled his fingers at Dr. Peters.

The man sitting at the table swallowed hard and went two more shades of pale as he stared at the appendages. Mark nodded to the man with the marshmallow complexion. "Who's your friend?"

"CIA. He's assisting with another problem we may be having." Evan drew another vial of blood and put a drop on a slide.

"The prisoner?" Mark fell into a chair across from him and gave him a cockeyed stare. "The one with the gloom-and-doom warning of killer android soldiers coming to chop us to bits?"

"One and the same," Evan answered absently as he stared at the slide. He placed a drop of reagent on the sample and readjusted the scope. When he stood, he adjusted his lab coat and turned for a locker on the far side of his lab. "I'm thinking this is reactionary."

"Like hives?"

"More like 'fight-or-flight'." Evan withdrew several vials and set up a Bunsen burner.

"Ah-ha! I knew it." Mark tried to snap his fingers and failed miserably. "So, how come it hasn't gone away? I mean…I'm not all fighty or flighty now."

Evan scratched at his chin as he cast him a furtive glance. "I don't know. It could be that you'll remain this way."

"Like hell!" Mark stood so quick that his chair tumbled and the fellow across from him gasped. He glowered at the man and gave him a squinty stare. "Relax, asshole. If I wanted to hurt you, you'd be laying in a puddle of blood."

"That doesn't make me feel any better." He held up a file folder and attempted to hide behind it.

Mark leaned over the table and studied Dr. Peters. "Whatcha doing over there?"

"Cooking up a bit of tea for you. It should help you to relax a bit."

Mark slumped into another chair and gave him a deadpan stare. "Can't you just give me some Valium or doggy downers or elephant tranquilizers or something? I mean, the way my metabolism burns through stuff, shouldn't you be breaking out the big guns?"

Evan ground a dark root into powder and dumped it into a beaker. He shook his head lightly as he spoke, "It's one thing to attack the problem with pharmaceuticals, it's another to learn to control it. Besides, if it is permanent, the tea will do no damage."

"Neither would the elephant tranqs." Mark tried to prop his chin in his palm and found the position nearly impossible. "Doc, you gotta make this *not* permanent."

Evan poured the boiling water over his concoction and allowed it to steep. "I added a bit of a relaxant to the tea. With any luck, once the hormones in your body balance, you'll be back to your same old snarky self."

"God, I hope so." Mark leaned forward and sniffed the brew, his nose wrinkling. "What the hell, Doc? Did you put your dirty socks in that thing?"

"Only one, Major." He turned to grab a mug. "I was afraid that two would make it entirely too strong."

"Ha! I think I'm rubbing off on you, Doc." Mark reached for the beaker and swirled it, the heat not affecting him as he mixed the concoction. "Over the lips and past the gums, watch out gullet, here it comes!" He tilted the beaker back and sucked down the gritty mess.

Evan stood open-mouthed, the mug still in his hand, then simply set it on the workbench. "Normal people would have waited for it to cool."

Mark belched loudly and made a bitter face. "I'm not normal,

Doc. Remember?"

Evan opened his mouth to retort, but left simply shook his head. "Yes, I remember."

"Yeah, that tasted like boiled assholes." Mark put the beaker back and shook his head. "Maybe next time you could lay off the dirty ball sack?"

"Purely for texture, Major." Evan crossed his arms and studied the man. He made a mental note and began counting back from ten in his head. About the time he reached four, Mark shook his head and looked at him cross eyed.

"I pheel phunny...like my tongue ith covered in hair..." He melted into the floor like a puddle of goo.

"And that ends this session on how to drug an asshole." Evan leaned down and scooped up the major. He placed him gently on the examining table and switched off the exam light.

"Is he out?"

"For a bit, yes."

Agent Stevens lowered the file folder and stared at Mark's hands. "What the hell happened to him?"

"Oh, he's always been an ass." Evan took his seat back at the workbench and sifted through the files. "It's just now starting to affect his work."

Stevens stared at the pair but simply nodded.

*****

Lamb paused and crouched low to the ground. He tilted his head sideways and allowed the light to cast shadows across the soft collection of pine needles, dried leaves and peat moss. "You seeing what I see?"

Jacobs dropped to his belly and stared up the low hill. "If you're seeing a trail, I think so." He bounced back to his feet and readied his rifle. "But how do we know these aren't our own tracks?"

Lamb studied the terrain and shook his head. "I don't recognize any of this. I really don't think we came this way."

"Dude, it was dark and we were moving fast chasing that thing. We could have circled through here twice while Spanky was tumbling with it."

Lamb stepped to the side and studied the lower branches of trees and small brush. "I'm not seeing any broken limbs. Whatever came through here did it trying not to leave sign."

Jacobs shrugged. "Hey man, I'm not saying you're wrong. We got nothing better."

The two struck out once more, doing their best to follow what little path there was. They trekked further up the mountain and to the edge of a small clearing where Jacobs suddenly reached out and grabbed his partner by the shoulder, pulling him to a stop.

"What's up?"

Ing pointed to what initially looked like a berry vine crossing their way. His finger swept to the edge of the path and to a stick shoved into the ground at an angle, the vine wrapped around it. The pair followed the 'vine' up the side of a tree and to a trip that released a large log with wooden spikes embedded in it. Once the trap was tripped, the log would be released, gravity swinging it down and low, impaling anything that happened to be along the trail.

"I thought these things were supposed to be stupid?" Lamb whispered.

Jacobs shook his head. "Looks like the intel was wrong." He reached up and clicked his coms open. "OPCOM, this is Delta Four."

"Copy, Delta Four. We're seeing it ourselves," Mitchell's voice crackled through their earpieces. "Urge extreme caution."

Jacobs gave Lamb a 'duh' look and shook his head. Clicking off his coms, he whispered, "I thought we already were." He clicked his coms back on, "Roger that, OPCOM. Any luck contacting Delta Actual?"

"Negative. They're still radio silent. Our best guess is that they are working their way up toward your location."

Lamb stepped over the trip and entered the clearing. Hard packed earth and prairie grasses disguised the tracks. He walked along the edge of the clearing looking for any sign of where the tango had reentered the woods. "I'm not finding anything."

Jacobs nodded. "OPCOM, tango's trail runs cold at the clearing. Any heat signatures that could point us in the right direction?"

"Negative, Four. Other than small wildlife, you and Three are all that's lighting up."

Lamb sighed and leaned against at tree. "Any bright ideas?"

Jacobs nodded. "Possibly." He clicked his coms again. "OPCOM, any of those wildlife signatures close enough and still enough that they appear to be observing our actions?"

Silence met his request and Ing was about to check his radio when his earbud came back to life. "That's affirmative, Four. Fifteen meters south-by-southwest of your current position. Advise extreme caution."

"Copy that, OPCOM." Jacobs clicked off his coms and motioned for Lamb.

"What the hell was that about? Surveillance bunnies?"

"Think about it. If you move about underground, surely you have ways in and out, right?"

"Yeah, I would guess."

"So, a head popping up now and then would appear as what to a drone or satellite looking for heat signatures?"

Lamb smiled. "Small wildlife."

Jacobs nodded and readied his rifle once more. "Fifteen meters south-by-southwest. Ready to take a walk in the woods?"

"Just keep your eyes open for more of those trip wires."

*****

Gaius opened his eyes and his throat caught as he gulped huge lungfuls of air. He rose from the ground and brushed the gravel from his uniform pants. His legs still felt shaky as he steadied himself and he looked around at the unfamiliar surroundings. Another man in a similar uniform jogged up to him and offered him a hand. "Are you okay, Airman?"

"Yes, I am fine. I just got a bit lightheaded for a moment."

"Maybe you should sit down, get a drink or go to medical?"

Gaius held his hand up, stopping the man. "I am fine, I assure you. I only need a moment." The man studied him a bit then went about his business, satisfied that he was okay.

Jumping into a new body so quickly could have that effect. Without properly preparing, the impact could be deadly for the new host. Gaius spotted this man and simply dropped into him, the nearest vessel to his queen. He knew she was near, but he couldn't tell exactly where. Somehow, she was hidden from him.

Only a handful of his demons had survived the slaughter at the warehouse. Once the spell was lifted and they were able to depart the broken bodies of their hosts, they saw the full impact of the damage. Even the great Fallen one had been slain…something they didn't think possible.

He immediately sent word to those who were transporting her devices and ordered their shipments halted. Their decimated forces had to be gathered. As long as they still dwelt upon this plane, they were bound to her. They must save the demon queen from the human hunters and reclaim her prizes.

He sat upon a bench outside a large concrete building and watched as vehicles drove by. Others in uniform came and left. Mothers with children walked past him, their minds on their useless lives and their endless lists of things that must be done. Gaius stood and stared off toward the horizon. He tried to reach out and detect where Lilith was, but she wasn't reaching back. He could sense her, but his mind couldn't touch hers.

He could feel the others drawing closer and he hoped that once their strength was added to his own, he could locate her. Once he pinpointed her, he would storm the very gates of Hell to save her.

"I can feel you, my queen. And we are coming to save you."

*****

Darren halted his squad and clicked off his torch. He squatted lower and peered around a sharp bend in the tunnel. Light could be seen flickering and based on the orange glow, he was certain it wasn't sunlight. He motioned to the others and pointed around the corner.

Easing slowly forward he strained to listen and could only hear the popping and crackling of an open fire. He waved his hand over his mouth indicating no talking and slowly eased his head around the corner. Seeing nothing but another corner, he slipped out from where he was and leveled his weapon. He flattened himself against the opposite wall and eased along the edge until he could peek around the opposite corner.

An open circular room with a large support post in the middle sate empty. A fire pit built into the wall was the source of the light and flame. In the orange gloom he noted a pack next to a small stack of wood and he motioned to Sullivan. Little John checked it and nodded. "It's Tracy's."

Darren checked the other tunnel entering the room and saw the same series of corners. "We're on the right track. Keep moving."

Donovan shifted around and covered their six while the trio exited the other side. He kept one hand against Sullivan's back while covering with the P90. He nearly tripped when he felt the big man suddenly stop. "What's the hold up?"

"Hit a 'T' in the road."

Darren scanned both sides and shook his head. "I've no idea."

Sullivan pointed to the right. "It goes uphill. Further from the water."

Darren knew they were far enough away from the river that continuing uphill now was moot. But he had no other reason to *not* go right. "Right it is."

The trio continued moving until they hit another series of corners and another round room. They found piles of backpacks, hiking boots, folded tents and other assorted camping gear and two very dirty piles of heavy coats that looked curiously like makeshift beds.

Sullivan poked at one of the piles of coats with the barrel of his SCAR. "I have a really creepy feeling about this."

Darren slapped the big man on the shoulder, "Let's move. Now!"

Another series of corners and another 'T'. Another right and a much longer trail up the mountain. As the trio approached the next series of corners, they could hear a muffled voice that sounded very much like someone struggling. There were also grunts and hoots that reminded Spalding of great apes he had heard at the zoo.

He held his fist up to stop the other two and used hand motions to direct their course of action. They would enter, Sullivan up the middle, Donovan clears left, Spalding clears right. Just as he gave the signal to enter, Gus gave a muffled yell and all three rushed the second corner, weapons leveled.

*****

Bigby tossed the last of his trash and stepped away from the fast food area outside the exchange. He stood beside the double glass doors and stared southward toward where the hangar sat. He knew that he would have to find a way to approach that wouldn't be suspect. He'd need a non-descript vehicle that nobody would second guess, even at high alert. He watched as minivans and sports cars rolled past the large building. Pickup trucks and Humvees. Nothing he saw gave him the warm fuzzy feeling that it would go unnoticed.

Even when a base police vehicle stopped and turned onto the main street, he knew that stealing one of those would only help him get caught faster.

From where he stood he couldn't imagine a vehicle that could give him the proper cover and go unnoticed. He was about to give up his search when he noticed a young airman sitting alone on a bench outside. The young black man suddenly stood and stared off to the south, his face looking as if he were in a trance.

When he opened his eyes and continued staring south, Bigby couldn't put his finger on exactly why, but the hair on the back of his neck stood on end. There was something 'off' about the young man. Bigby stood at the door and watched as the young man simply stood near the sidewalk and stared.

"What's your story, mate?" Bigby leaned against the wall near the door and watched the young man. Could he be a member of base security who was out searching for him? Something told him that wasn't the case.

He watched as the young man lifted his hand and pointed his palm toward the south. After a few moments, he dropped it dejectedly. If he was trying to use the Force, he was failing miserably.

Bigby pushed off the wall and stepped outside. "This may be the dumbest thing I've ever done."

He walked slowly toward the young man and slipped in behind him. "You look lost, mate. Need a hand?"

The young man barely glanced at him before shaking his head. "No."

Bigby gave him a smirk. "Waiting for someone then?"

The young man shook his head again. "No."

Bigby nodded. "Trying to find someone?" The young man ignored him. "Someone who doesn't want to be found maybe?"

"This is not your concern, Celt."

"Celt?" Bigby chuckled. "Something tells me that you're a long way from home, boy-o."

*****

Jameson sipped his coffee and waited for Ingram. He knew that the younger man was many things, but he wasn't stupid. He just needed to be reminded *how* to think strategically. He hoped that this lunch meeting would snap him out of whatever funk of stupidity he was in and get him back to thinking like a spy.

He saw the younger man step into the restaurant and wave at him. He slipped into the booth across from him and seemed far too chipper.

"Great news. I talked to the techs, and we can have the Titans flown to Geneva at any time." Ingram quickly unraveled the napkin and placed his flatware out on the table.

"I told you, now is not the proper time." Jameson motioned for the waiter and nodded. "I took the liberty of ordering for us both."

Ingram paused and gave him a puzzled look. "It would have been nice to at least look at the menu."

"Trust me. I've been eating here for years. There's only three things worth eating, and I ordered them for us."

Ingram slumped in his seat and cast a weary eye at the older man. "I suppose you ordered drinks, too?"

"Oh, no. I always have coffee with lunch. Feel free to order whatever you like."

Ingram sat quietly for a while then reached into his breast pocket. He withdrew a thumb drive and slid it across the table. "You were right about the Swiss accounts."

"Of course I was." Jameson picked up the thumb drive and held it up. "And what is this?"

"Backups of everything. The techs made it for you for your own files." Ingram avoided his gaze while he waited for their food to be delivered. "So, clue me in. What're the next steps in this grand plan of yours."

"You saw the deposit. That's only half of what the Council promised us. If we want the other half, we need to take care of the problem they hired us to handle."

Ingram nodded. "True, but I thought you said they weren't ready?"

"You convinced me otherwise." He sipped at his coffee and studied the younger man. "None of our intelligence indicates that they have the assets we saw them utilize at the saw mill. So, I believe you were correct in your assumptions. They were hired guns brought in to handle a specific problem."

"So we're back to the original plan?"

"Unless you think our team can handle the threat at reduced strength."

Ingram shook his head. "I'm not following you."

"Perhaps we send a strike force to deal with the squads and set up a live feed to the Council. Once they make the final payment, and I mean the very moment it hits the accounts, we have a small team standing by to kick in their doors and eradicate them." The smile that spread across his face sent a shiver down Robert's back.

"I suppose that might be possible, but why so soon? I mean, seriously, does half a day make a difference? Do you really think the Council is going anywhere?"

"Think about it, Robert. You've hired someone to remove the only threat to you, but now that person you hired is an even larger threat. You either cut and run or hire somebody else to remove that threat. Do we really want to risk our boys to a bunch of fangers?"

"That's an awful lot of 'what ifs' there." Ingram rubbed at his neck as he thought about the life and death game of chess that Jameson proposed.

The waiter stepped up to the table and placed the soup and salad before each man. Robert ordered a club soda absently as he continued to play out the ramifications of the ploy. Once it was safe to talk again, he lowered his voice, "Do you think the Titans can handle either job at reduced strength?"

Jameson shrugged. "That's why I was asking you."

Ingram shook his head absently. "I don't know. I just…I don't know." He sipped at the soup, not really tasting it. "Is it beyond the scope of the project to have the team perform their initial duty and then wait to provide proof to the Council until we're in place to strike? Wait until the money is transferred and then have them go in, guns blazing?"

Jameson nodded. "Oh, it's possible. But we run the risk of the Council finding out that the deed is done before we report it. They cut and run, and we miss our opportunity."

Ingram continued eating, his mind racing. "We put a tail on them. Satellite surveillance. The whole works."

Jameson grunted. "They've been around for how many centuries and we never knew they existed until they approached us with this job. Do you really think we can track them?"

Ingram smiled. "Part of their remaining hidden was us not knowing they existed. Not only do we know, but we know where they hang their hats. We know where they do their banking. We know their associates. We know their itineraries, their modes of travel, their preferred places to stay, and best of all, their weaknesses."

Jameson smiled as he stabbed a cherry tomato with his fork. "I'm beginning to like the way you think, Robert." He popped the tomato into his mouth and added, "There may be hope for you yet."

20

Mitchell watched the heat signatures of his two operators as they slipped from object to object, zigzagging through the woods. He motioned to the communications officer. "Please tell me we've broken through to the others."

The man shook his head. "I'm sorry, Colonel. Maybe if we had an exact location we could use a compressed pulse microwave beam, but their portables are just too weak to be effective."

"Put that on my 'to do' list." Mitchell punched up the drone feed and displayed it on the main screen. "They're approaching the last known location of the unknown."

Mitchell scooted to the edge of the seat and watched as the two operators both turned and leveled their weapons on the area where the heat signature was last seen. He flipped the switch on his console and Delta Three's helmet cam fed the main screen. A clump of ferns filled the view as the two slowly approached the spot.

Delta Four held a fist in the air and dropped low. Using his knife, he probed the ground until he found a seam close to the fern.

A makeshift wooden lid with detritus covering it was lifted and Delta Three pointed his barrel into the hole before them. Both men covered the area while Jacobs keyed his coms. "Your call, Colonel."

Mitchell groaned and wiped a calloused hand across his face. He hated the idea of losing contact with all of his men, but he knew the odds were high that Spalding would need assistance.

He pinched his eyes shut and ground his teeth as he keyed his own coms. "Do it. But for the love of Pete, be careful."

"Copy that, sir. Going radio silent." Delta Four switched off his coms and Mitchell watched the two men drop into the hole in the mountain, the helmet cam feed turning to static as they disappeared.

"Somebody find a way to keep in contact with them! Yesterday!" He pushed out of his chair and began pacing the small operations center, his eyes burning holes through the feeds relayed back through the drone and the overhead satellite.

*****

Jack tried not to watch as Kalen moved closer to Brooke. The warrior in him insisted that he pay tribute to one of his own. The soon-to-be father in him grimaced as the Elf lifted the knife to Brooke's chest and the overhead light glinted off the polished blade.

Paul stumbled and fell to his knees, his hands shooting outward to steady himself. He suddenly appeared paler than normal and his eyes widened with both shock and fear. He trembled as he sucked in breath and he turned to stare at Jack.

"Don't tell me that bitch jumped ship again?" Jack strode the short distance and grabbed the vampire by the shirt front, lifting him to his feet and shoving him against the wall.

Foster shook his head animatedly. "No, Mr. Thompson," Foster's voice shook as he spoke. He lifted his eyes and met Jack's contemptuous gaze. "Something I fear that is nearly as bad."

"What could be that bad?" Jack growled as he tightened his grip and shoved him again.

"My brother..." Paul trailed off, his eyes focusing in the distance. "He's...done the unthinkable."

"What does he speak of, Chief Jack?" Azrael stepped forward, his jaw set.

"I don't know." Jack stared at Paul who seemed to shiver in shock. "What the hell is going on?"

"Chief Jack?" Kalen stood ready, his knife still hovering over Brooke's still form. "Does Lilith still reside within her or...can she be spared?" He dared not to hope that she had departed, but the words of the Wyldwood echoed in his mind. Even if she could be driven out, only an empty shell could remain. Brooke would be little more than a ghoul.

Allister shook his mighty head. "She is locked within that body. I have seen to it." He moved forward and nodded toward the raven-haired vampire. "Do it now!"

Jack held up his hand. "Wait! I want to know what the hell he's talking about first."

The Nephilim placed a gentle hand on Jack's shoulder. "That is not a wise course. You have made peace with what must be done. Do it now lest time get away from you and she gets the upper hand again."

Jack gave Phil a sideways stare. "If she starts to stir, zap her again." He turned back to Paul and tried to shake him back to the here and now. "What the hell is going on? What did Rufus do?"

Foster turned slowly and shook his head. "He's the ultimate power now. He...cannot be stopped." He went limp in Jack's grip and fell to the floor. "I see it all so clearly now. It was all just a game...a ploy. A power play...a way to rule us all."

"Rufus?" Jack gave the vampire a puzzled stare. "What did he do, dammit!"

Paul lifted his rummy eyes and shuddered. "He has destroyed the Council. He now rules all vampires."

*****

Laura stepped back into her office and dropped the last of her things onto the desk. She stood with her hands on her hips and gazed about the empty room. "I guess I should have waited until Matt gave me the go ahead before I unloaded all my crap."

She ran a finger along one of the shelves still filled with binders full of operating procedures and looked at the fine coating of dust. "I think the cleaning lady stopped coming by in my absence." She smiled to herself and plopped onto the overstuffed couch that had been her bed on far too many occasions. She sighed as the leather covered cushions enveloped her body, and she suddenly felt like she was truly home.

She tried not to think of what she had done. How she had tried so many times to quit because of her father. How she had stolen the serum and rushed home when she found out how far his health had deteriorated. How she broke every rule in the book to give her father, her hero, what she had hoped would be the cure to his disease. How that cure ended up being the death of Jim Youngblood and the birth of…a monster.

Laura shuddered at what she had done and squeezed her eyes tighter. She couldn't allow herself to lay blame. She had already accepted responsibility. She had bounced back and forth with whether she should come clean with Matt once she returned and she still hadn't come up with a viable answer. She opened her eyes and stared at the ceiling. She tried to lose herself in the thousands of tiny holes each ceiling panel held, but her mind kept creeping back to her father turning and walking away from her. She kept seeing him dissolve into the woods, engulfed in the shadows.

She sat up and propped her face in her hands. She refused to allow herself to cry any more. He was gone to her before she left to go home, he was gone to her now. The only difference was, now he lived on. As what, she couldn't be certain, but she knew that he lived. She had to take solace in that fact. Derek no longer blamed her. The rest of the family believed that their father simply walked into the woods to die.

She stood and squared her shoulders. Time to face the music.

She opened the door of her office and surprised a young Corporal. "Where's Colonel Mitchell?"

"OPCOM, ma'am. There's an op underway."

Thanking him quickly, she brushed past him and hurried down the hall.

*****

Bigby stood a fair distance behind the young airman and studied him. "Where you from, mate?"

"Begone, Celt." The airman glared at him and Bigby smiled knowingly.

"Let me guess. You're borrowing this meat suit, and you're here to serve a purpose." He stepped closer and studied the man closer. "What are you? Witch? Spirit? Some sort of vengeful jin?"

The airman turned and glared at him. "What would you know of such things?"

Bigby laughed, making sure he kept an eye on the lean young man before him. "I know quite a bit about such things. Used to hunt them down and kill them in my day." He sobered and gave the man a solemn stare. "So don't trifle with me, boy. If you're here looking for the hunters, we might be able to help each other."

The airman stiffened and gave him a cautious once over. "How do you know of them?"

"Let's just say I have my own score to settle with them." Bigby stepped closer and lowered his voice, "It might be in your best interest if we threw in together. Enemy of my enemy...you know?"

"I'm listening."

"So what are you? What can you bring to the table?"

The young airman gave him a puzzled look. "What table?"

"Abilities, mate. What do you have to offer in this fight? These chaps won't be easy to deal with. Trust me. I know." He glanced to the side and lowered his voice to avoid passersby, "I've lost two small groups of soldiers to them already."

The airman glanced past Bigby and smiled. "I bring them."

Bigby looked behind him and paled. A group of security forces and armed military personnel were marching toward him. "Fuck me." He turned to face them, ready to run if he could or fight if he had to, when he noticed that they were all staring at the black airman beside him.

The group marched forward then halted before the airman. "Commander. We are all that is left." Each man saluted by crossing his arm over his chest, his fist covering his heart.

Bigby turned back to the airman and narrowed his gaze. "What are you?"

The airman's gaze cut through the larger man and Bigby could almost swear his eyes flashed red as he spoke. "Demons of the Fifth Macedonia."

Bigby stiffened, his eyes shifting over the group of soldiers standing at the ready. "Demons?"

"Roman Centurions. To the last." Gaius squared his shoulders and eyed what was left of his army. "Prepare yourselves. This one knows where the hunters are. And therein lies our queen."

*****

"I think you're being just a bit melodramatic, don't you, *mon ami*?" Rufus reclined in the overstuffed chair and wiped at the residual ashes on the table absently. "Despot is a bit strong."

"What would you call it?" Viktor crossed his arms, staring at the vampire.

"I would call it...fortunate." Rufus smiled at his own joke. "I truly couldn't know that the power would shift to me once the Council had been removed."

"But you had strong reason to suspect it was so. Otherwise you wouldn't have bothered to face them." Viktor strode to the other side of the table and pulled back the chairs, stepping aside as the ashes fell to the carpet below. "In the past, your so-called death edict held little concern for you. You knew that you were safe on your island. The Council held little concern for the happenings in the west. You were safe so long as you stayed put."

Rufus felt anger rising within him and he scratched his nails across the finely polished mahogany table top. "And who is to say that I didn't wish to return to my homeland in peace?"

"So you killed them all?" Viktor nearly shouted as he flung a chair across the table, a trail of ashes hanging in the air as the chair clattered to the far wall. "This wasn't the act of someone trying to defend himself. This was a premeditated attack. Expertly played and executed so that you came out on top."

Rufus stood up and squared his shoulders. "So?"

Viktor set his jaw and planted his hands on his hips. "So, you shouldn't have used me and my wolves as pawns in your game."

"You were never at risk." Rufus lowered his voice, his features softening. "It was all a show of strength."

"The ends justify the means." Viktor motioned to the two wolves standing guard near the door. "Prepare the others. We're leaving."

Rufus stepped between him and the door. "*Mon ami*, wait. Do not leave like this."

Viktor stared down at the smaller man and shook his head. "Whatever friendship we once shared is over." He glanced about the empty conference room and motioned with his arms. "The king is dead! Long live the king!"

*****

Spalding scanned the room and saw Gus Tracy tied to the support pole in the center. The creature that stood above him was unlike anything he had ever laid eyes on before. In the glow of the firelight, Darren could swear he was looking at one of the museum wax figures of a caveman come to life. The creature held a large rock above Gus with its powerful arms and was obviously about to crush his head with it.

Sullivan's weapon barked and three rounds erupted from the suppressed barrel. Two struck the creature in the upper right chest and one round grazed it's temple. The creature bellowed as it staggered back and the rock it held in its hands fell, striking Gus.

Spalding lowered his weapon and rushed to assist when a dark blur tackled him from the side. During his sweep, he missed the other creature huddled along the stack of abandoned hiking gear. The two tumbled and his weapon was knocked free in the struggle. Besides the speed and strength of the creature squeezing the life from him, the stench was nearly overpowering.

He heard shouts and grunts mixed with muted groans as he struggled with the creature in the subterranean chamber. His hand slid to his belt and his fingers wrapped around the hilt of his knife. He slid it from the Kydex sheath and plunged it rapidly into the body of the monster riding him. He felt the hilt of the blade meet flesh before he pulled it free and drove it deep into the monster's soft hide again and again until it finally quit struggling.

He felt the creature move from on top of him and he was relieved to see Donovan pulling the heavily muscled humanoid off of him. He was surprised, however, to note that the attacking monster was a female as Donovan laid it down on the earthen floor beside its mate.

Spalding held his side as he stood, nearly certain that he had at least a cracked rib or two based on the pain he felt when he sucked in air. "Get Gus out of those binds."

"Uh, boss?" Sullivan gave him a solemn look. He slowly shook his head.

Spalding ignored the pain in his side as he stepped over the bodies and rounded the large pole in the center of the room. Gus lay on his side, his skull broken open by the large rock.

Spalding fell to his knees and checked the big man for a pulse. When he was certain there was no sign of life he slumped and collapsed next to him. "This isn't right." He shook his head in disgust. "Taken out by a fucking caveman."

*****

Stevens continued to steal glances at the man sleeping on the examining table. His actions didn't go unnoticed. "He won't bite you."

"I wouldn't be so sure." He finally set down the file he had been pretending to read and studied the man more carefully. "What happened to his hands?"

Evan turned and pulled Mark's hand into his own. "It appears nearly normal now." He rolled it over and looked at the palm before placing it back across his midsection and resuming his place at the table. "It would appear I was correct."

"So, he's going to be okay?"

"That's a relative term." Evan closed the file and pulled another one closer. "The man is…" He sighed. He stole a quick glance at the major and shook his head. "He's pigheaded, he's an ass, and he's nearly intolerable. But he's also honorable. He's loyal. He's a tactical genius." He stood and crossed his arms, staring down at the man he both admired and often times wanted to choke to death. "He's interminable. In both good and bad ways. He demands your best and he gives his. Always. He loves a good practical joke and yet he can be so serious."

"How on earth do you work with someone like that?"

Evan snorted. "It's not easy, trust me. The man can push your limits. But at the same time, he has a way about him that makes you want to give your absolute best."

"You respect him."

"In some ways. In others, I want to smother him in his sleep."

It was Stevens' turn to snort. "I've worked with a few like that in my day."

"Trust me, there are no others like him." He paused and shuddered involuntarily. "If there's a god in heaven, there's no more like Major Tufo. The world couldn't take it."

A claxon sounded that made Stevens jump and Evan startled. Stevens gathered the files closer and looked around anxiously. "What the hell is that?"

"If I didn't know any better…I'd think we were under attack."

Mark was sitting up, his eyes wide as he stared through the clear acrylic walls of the lab. "Are we being attacked?"

"I don't know Major. I believe that's the alarm for—" Evan didn't finish his sentence before Major Tufo's skin changed pallor. It went from flesh tone to a dark mottled grey and his fingertips had grown talons once more. Before Evan could register what had happened, Mark was off the exam table, out the door and up the stairs.

"W-what the hell was that?" Stevens stammered.

"I couldn't honestly say."

*****

Dominic was carrying his weapons to the armory to turn in when the first shots ricocheted off the wall of the hangar. At first, the action didn't register with him, and he stared at where the round embedded itself in the wooden crates stacked near the front entrance.

The second and third rounds caught his attention, and he leapt to the side sounding an audible alarm. The guards in the shack pulled the chicken switch and the claxon echoed throughout the hangar moments later.

"Tactical stations!" Dom yelled to his team, wishing he still wore his coms. He maneuvered around the stack of crates and tried to see who was stupid enough to attack the squads head on and on their own turf.

Marshall slid in next to him and brought his weapon to bear. "How many?"

"I can't see to tell." A corner of the wooden crate exploded next to him sending splinters in all directions. "They're not going to let me stick my head out to count either."

Marshall elbowed him and pointed up. "Give me a boost."

Dom stood on hands and knees and Marshall climbed up and onto the stack of crates. He leveled his rifle and peered through the scope. "Holy shit. They're Air Force."

"Why the hell would the Chair Force be attacking us?" Dom slipped to the back corner of the crates and tried to peer around the other side. The angle was off and he was blind.

"Beats me, but damned if they…hey. I think I see that guy from Team One out there. Sheridan's teammate." Marshall no sooner finished speaking before he rolled off the crate, the top erupting in splinters from gunfire. He sat beside Dom and shook his head. "They saw me."

"No shit."

Hammer slid extra magazines across the floor to the pinned down pair. "I count at least fifteen. Full auto weaponry. Mac and Ben are checking our flanks."

"Get the coms!" Dom yelled, pointing to the stand where they checked their gear. "Secure us a frequency and somebody alert the colonel!"

Wallace trotted up beside hammer with a black bag. He held it up and shook it at Dom. Swinging the bag he let it fly. Marshall dug through and pulled out their earbuds and radios. Assorted flashbangs and extra pistol magazines were dumped and divvied up.

Dom hefted a flash bang and smiled. "Time to make the doughnuts." He pulled the pin and tossed the grenade in a gentle arc. From Hammer's vantage, he watched as it sailed out through the front overhead door and bounce out among the intruders.

As soon as the M84 popped, the operators stepped out and began firing at the targets that were still standing. They folded like wet paper and the four hunters stood near the hangar opening, scanning the area for tangos.

Shots rang out from a distance and Wallace cursed as a round pierced his thigh, collapsing him. Dom grabbed the man by the shoulder and dragged him back inside, Hammer and Marshall providing cover fire.

As the four backed into the hangar and relative safety, Marshall had to do a double take, unsure he was seeing what his eyes were telling him. The men they had just shot and killed…stood back up and were retrieving their weapons from the ground. He tapped Hammer and pointed. "Tell me I'm not seeing that."

"Body armor. It has to be." Hammer leveled his weapon again and opened fire, advancing toward the door once more. He continued firing, emptying his magazine into one person's chest, seeing the pink mist erupt with each round and knowing that if there was armor there, it had been shredded by the silver-plated rounds.

Satisfied that at least one of the attackers was out of the game, Hammer began backing into the hangar once more, only to stop when he saw the attacker he downed slowly get up from the ground once more. Blood poured from his chest wound and his arm barely functioned, but he picked up his weapon and began to advance.

"Uh, Houston, we have a problem here."

Dom's earpiece came alive. "Sierra One, we've got tangos approaching from the east. They won't stay down!" Mac's voice registered the surprise and terror of facing an enemy that refused to die when killed.

Dom keyed his throat mic. "Secure those doors. Nothing gets inside! Do you hear me? *Nothing* gets inside! This is our home and we will protect it!"

"Lock and load, ladies!" Gonzales yelled as he ran to assist Mac and Ben on the East entrance.

Dom slid Wallace beside a lathe and propped him up. "How you doing, TD?"

"Been better." He clenched his jaw as he struggled to pull his belt from the loops. "It's bleeding like a bitch."

"Hit an artery?" Dom ripped open his pants and tried to check the wound.

"I don't think so, but dammit it hurts." TD cinched his belt around the wound and tightened it, wincing as the pain surged. "At least it ain't silver, right? Damn, I'd hate to lose my leg over something stupid like that."

"I hear ya, buddy." Dom patted the smaller man's shoulder. "You sit tight. We'll get Doc to take a look at ya."

"They're advancing again!" Hammer's voice shot through Dom's earpiece.

"Gotta get back to work." Dom stepped out from behind the lathe and leveled his weapon. "Get some!" He opened fire, shredding the men in the front wave of the attack.

"They're not going down!" Marshall yelled.

"Frag 'em!" Dom yelled.

He slid behind the relative safety of a Humvee as an M67 flew through the air. It bounced once on the concrete floor then out into the crowd of advancing shooters. The concussion from the blast sent bits of gravel, dirt and debris in all directions and Dom waited a moment before sticking his head back out. He smiled at the destruction he expected to see and was shocked as the men slowly started picking themselves up from the ground to advance their fight once more.

"What the hell are these things? Zombies?"

Hammer stood in silence as he watched the men in Air Force uniforms try to pick themselves up from the ground again after the grenade had decimated their bodies. He shook his head in stunned disbelief as they refused to stop coming. The ones that were too far gone suddenly fell over and gave up the fight. He could almost see a flash of yellow light erupt from their broken bodies as they finally collapsed.

He looked to Dom and shook his head. "I don't think they're zombies."

A dark blur shot past the operators and their secure fighting positions within the hangar. Dom had to do a double take as the black uniformed…'thing' shot out the front doors of the hangar and began to rip the heads off the fighters that continued to advance. He heard a distinct roar that caused the hair on the back of his neck to stand on end, and he watched in stunned silence as the dark skinned hunter bounced from attacker to attacker, slicing, dicing and ripping until none were left standing.

When the creature stopped and turned back toward the hangar, Dom noticed the short trimmed, grey goatee and he gasped, "Major?"

Tufo's face wrinkled into what Dom could only imagine was a smile before he took off around the corner of the hangar and toward the east entrance. Dom stared at where he stood only a moment before then suddenly snapped back to reality. He keyed his coms. "Ben, Mac, you have an unknown approaching from behind the tangos. Do not, I repeat, DO NOT fire on the unknown. Do you copy?"

"Copy, Sierra One," the disbelieving voice replied. Dom turned and took off for the east entrance.

He slid to a stop next to Charmichael. The bodies littering the parking lot was enough to make him do a double take. "I think the other group was a diversion."

Major Tufo appeared at the door, blood dripping from his hands as he tried to calm himself. "That's the last of them."

"What the hell happened to you?" Dom asked.

"It's a fight-or-flight response. Comes from being infected." Mark shrugged. "I think."

Charmichael swallowed hard and gave him a wide-eyed stare. "Major...you look like..."

"Shit?" Mark asked.

"No. Urban camo. Grey camo. You could like totally disappear at night." He pointed to his hands and Mark lifted them to his eyes.

"Huh, that's new."

"More tangos!" Hammer's voice echoed through the earpieces. "Son of a..."

*****

Jameson's phone rang just as he reentered his office. He sighed heavily and tossed his overcoat aside. Reaching for the phone, he noted that it was Robert's number and rolled his eyes. Would the man ever learn?

"Yes, Robert, what is it now?"

"Check your video feeds now! Somebody attacked them!"

Jameson punched the button to put the call on speaker and sat behind his desk. He entered the security code to unlock his computer and pulled up the video feeds that had Ingram so excited.

"What is it I'm looking for?"

"Roll it back to about twenty minutes ago. Oh, my God...there are more coming after them now."

"So they're still under attack? Interesting..." Jameson scrolled the time back and watched as military personnel spread out and advanced on the hangar. "Why are base personnel attacking them, Robert? What did you do?"

"Nothing, I swear! Whoever this is, it has nothing to do with us!"

Jameson watched as both sides exchanged fire. The hunters stepped out and shot down some of the Air Force personnel then the personnel got back up and fired back. At least they were smart enough to wear body armor.

He scrolled through a few more exchanges then something caught his eye and he scrolled back through. "Robert, go to time stamp 1348. Who...or *what* is that?"

"The black individual that attacks them by himself? I don't know, but if you play it back slowly, you'll see that he's shot at least four times. And...zoom in at 1354. I swear that looks like the bullet is being pushed out of his back. There's hardly any blood and no wounds."

Jameson sat back and studied the fuzzy image before him. "What is this thing, Robert?"

"Beats me. We have nothing on it from our intel."

Jameson rubbed at his chin as he stared at the image. "Another hired gun to assist with...something?"

"Look at his clothing. He's wearing one of their uniforms." Ingram's voice dropped and became solemn, "I think...I think maybe he's one of them, sir."

"Is this what they're capable of?"

"I honestly don't know." Ingram cleared his throat and Jameson heard the phone shift. "If they all have this healing ability and ferocity, perhaps we should...*rethink* our plan."

Jameson slowed the video and watched as the dark figure bounced from soldier to soldier, slashing and tearing, rending heads from bodies with ease. "Perhaps you're right, Robert. Let's continue to observe these...things before we make a final decision."

21

Mitchell stopped pacing and spun on the intruder who opened the door of the OPCOM. His jaw went slack when he saw Laura step inside and he felt as if his prodigal child had returned to him. She shut the door silently and turned to greet him. "Laura Youngblood reporting for duty, sir. Well, if you'll still have me." She gave him a mock salute.

Colonel Mitchell threw decorum out the window and pulled her into a quick bear hug. "I can't believe I'm saying this, but I missed ya, lady."

"Good to see you too, sir." Laura cast a quick glance around the operations center and nodded toward the screens. "May I ask what's happening?"

"We think it's a wendigo. The team has gone underground and we've lost communications with them."

Laura glanced at the other screens and pointed to the video feed from the drone. "You have a drone in the air?"

"Of course."

"Then why not shoot an MI Probe into the ground and bounce your RF feed from that?"

Mitchell looked at her as if she had suddenly grown a second head. "Do what?"

Laura turned to the communications technician. "Does that drone have an MI probe on it?"

"I…I don't know what an MI probe is, ma'am."

"A magneto-inductive probe. They used to call it a 'rock phone' when it was being developed." She slid over the rail and stared at the controls on his screen. "What's that icon on your screen?"

"I…I don't…" The tech slid aside and let her at his controls.

"The magneto-inductive probe is fired into the ground and basically uses the soil, rock or vegetation that it's in as a conductive coil to transmit RF signals back and forth from their radios to the drone." She looked to the drone operator and hooked her chin toward the screen. "Find us a clearing close to where the squad is operating."

"Approaching target area, ma'am."

She lined up the target area and loosed the probe. "And there you have it. Give it a go, Colonel."

Mitchell shook his head. "What did I ever do without you?" He suddenly soured and glared at his communications tech. "And you obviously need proper training." He reached for the button on his command chair to open the coms when the alarm claxon sounded.

He looked to Laura with surprise. "Find out what's going on. I have to stay on this."

"Roger that, sir." She jumped back over the rail and ran out the door.

*****

Jack stood in the stairwell and watched as the last of the battle topside took place. With no weapons, he felt there was little he could do. From his vantage point, he couldn't readily see who dared to attack the squads on their home turf, but he knew that whoever it was had surprised enough people that there were casualties.

He trotted to the east door just as Dom broke away and started running through the hangar. "What's going on?"

"A bunch of Air Force regulars and Security Forces went batshit crazy and opened fire on us."

"Why?" Jack stood back, his mind reeling.

"No fucking clue!" Dom stopped at the gear table and pulled his pack from the wall. "Hammer says the second wave is on their way. These fuckers don't go down easy, man. I guess they're making these Air Force guys tougher than they used to."

Jack stepped closer and grabbed Dom's arm. "What do you mean, they don't go down easy?"

"Like zombie tough. Guts hanging out and they just keep comin' at ya. Like that fuckin' pink rabbit with the drum, man."

Jack stepped back and turned toward the stairwell. He looked to Kalen and Gnat who stood near the opening. He was certain…some of Lilith's demon army survived their attack and they were here now. Coming for their queen.

He turned and ran for the stairwell. "Kill her now! Do it! Do it now!"

Kalen's face registered his confusion, but he didn't get the opportunity to question his leader. An explosion rocked the inside of the hangar, a deafening crash sending Jack tumbling with a cloud of debris and dirt.

He and Gnat fell backward and down the stairwell, tumbling hard on the concrete steps to the first landing. Kalen felt himself being pushed to the side, and Gnat emerged from under him, his leather helmet askew. "What was that?"

"An explosion." Kalen pulled himself to his feet and began climbing back up the steps. "We must help Chief Jack."

"He told us to kill her." Gnat pulled at Kalen's leg, trying to stop him.

"He might be hurt." Kalen glanced down the stairwell toward their lair. "I am sure the others can keep her still until we ensure he is safe."

He stepped back out into the hangar and saw the other human hunters at each large doorway, shooting out toward groups of people. Kalen ducked low and ran from obstacle to obstacle looking for where Jack may have landed.

Gnat waved his arms from close to the back wall. "Here!"

Kalen looked and saw Jack's boots lying next to where Gnat stood and ran to his side. Blood was smeared across his face, but he still breathed. He reached down and lifted the larger man, sliding him across his lean shoulders. "Go, Gnat!"

The pair ran for the stairwell and Kalen had to turn sideways to keep from beating Jack's already bloody head against the concrete walls.

As they reached the first landing and were clear of the fighting, he slowed a bit and felt the adrenaline start to leave him. Suddenly Jack became much heavier. Gnat pushed open the door to the lower level conference room and Kalen stepped inside. Everyone had questions but he had no answers.

*****

Mark paused at the east door and looked around for a better weapon. He couldn't effectively grip a rifle and with his talons at full extension, he wasn't sure he could grip a blade. Maybe a large pipe?

"Major, they said they're attacking the north entrance again." Chad McKenzie slammed another magazine home and racked a round. "You sticking around here with us or going to help Dom?"

Mark growled low without thinking about it. "I think it's time to finish this." He tried to smile, but it looked eerily like a snarl.

Chad gave him a nervous smile in return and watched as the man took off along the outside of the hangar again. He ran wide and flanked the attackers this time, approaching from their rear. He tore into their ranks with renewed vigor, shredding and rending body parts from torsos, leaving a bloody trail as he went.

Without thinking about what he was doing, he ripped the arm from one rather large Security Forces member and used it as a meaty club against the others. Dom and Hammer advanced out the door, cutting down those in the front who didn't realize their compatriots in the rear were being removed from the fight.

Dom and Hammer both slowed their fight as they noticed what they weren't sure they had seen before. A bright yellow light flashed from each of the attackers just before they fell to the ground, dead.

"Something is definitely not right here." Dom shouldered his weapon and stared outward toward the horizon.

"If I didn't know any better, I'd think they were body hopping. What the hell can do that?"

"Your guess is as good as mine, bud."

Mark tossed the arm aside and wiped his bloody hands off on what was left of his uniform shirt. "They stink of sulfur."

"Sulfur?" Dom repeated. "Fuck me."

Hammer groaned, "Demons."

*****

Kalen wiped gently at Jack's forehead with a rag as the others argued.

"We should assist in the battle," Azrael insisted.

"No!" Allister stomped his clawed foot. "I can smell them from here. It is her demon army. We must destroy her now!"

Gnat stood next to Brooke's still form, his hammer at the ready. "We'll not do a thing until the elf is ready."

"Who gave him say over when and how things are done?"

Foster screeched. "If those are her demons up there, they won't stop until they have her!"

Kalen dropped the rag and stood, his shoulders squared. "She is my lover. I will decide."

The Nephilim stepped forward and handed Kalen his blade. "The time is nigh, Woodlander. Do what must be done."

Kalen stared at the blade in his hand and it suddenly felt heavy in his hand. The steel much colder than he had ever remembered. He stood beside Brooke and stroked her hair once more.

Jack lifted his head and had to blink rapidly to focus on the group. "You must. People are dying up there," his voice dry and raspy.

Kalen turned and stared at him for just a moment, his breath catching as he realized that the man was awake. He nodded slowly and pulled the knife from the sheath.

He stood over Brooke's still form and unzipped the top of her leather blouse. He remembered kissing her between those breasts as he pressed the point of the steel blade to her flesh.

Brooke suddenly opened her eyes and gasped, "Please don't, Kalen. I love you so much."

Kalen pulled the blade back and stared into her eyes. "You're not her…not anymore."

"I'm still me. I'm still in here. She's letting me talk to you right now. There is a way to get her out and let me live, Kalen. She knows how."

Kalen shook his head. "No, you're trying to trick me."

"Do it, Woodlander," he Nephilim stepped closer, his voice low and urging.

"Please, Kalen, don't do this. I want so much to be with you…" Brooke's voice trailed off and he saw the tears running down the sides of her face. His hand shook as he lifted the blade again.

"I must, my love. I have no other choice."

He pressed the blade to her chest once more then turned his

eyes to hers, expecting her face to contort to anger or hatred. What he saw surprised him.

He saw love.

"I'll always love you, Kalen." She swallowed hard and nodded to him. "Do it. If there's an 'other side' for vampires, I'll wait for you there."

Kalen's hands shook as he leaned down and kissed her one last time. "I love you, Brooke."

"I love y—"

*****

Bigby watched as his team of Roman Centurions advanced, got cut down and then recycled to fresh bodies. Oh, how he envied them and their ability to simply jump into a new body when they had ruined the one they were in.

As they pressed closer and closer to the hangar, he finally got his brave on and slipped between the numerous cars parked in the lot. He slid along the gravel and eventually made his way to the side of the building. He watched as the Romans wearing American GI meat suits shot their way closer and he inched toward the main door. He pulled a grenade from his belt and hefted it in his hand. One of his Roman soldiers had already tossed a grenade in earlier, but it only caused a short lull in the fighting. He intended to bounce this one right inside the door and cut down as many of the men holding their positions as possible.

He put the pin in his teeth and was about to jerk the pin out when he noticed that his Roman compatriots suddenly left the battle, their meat suits flashing a bright yellow light. Those who were wounded fell to the ground in pain. The mortally wounded died instantly and those yet untouched collapsed in shock.

Bigby stared at the grenade in his hand and debated making his move anyway when he was unceremoniously lifted from the ground and thrown toward the open door. He bounced hard on his shoulder and came up empty handed. The grenade rolled to the side, the pin still in place.

He slapped the rifle barrel away from the closest hunter and broke the man's nose with a right hook then spun him around and used him as a human shield against the others.

Reaching down to his thigh, he pulled his knife, held it to Ben Charmichael's throat, and pulled the man backward as he walked deeper into the hangar. "I want Mitchell! Get me Mitchell or I cut his fooking throat!"

The other man at the door kept his rifle trained on the pair and Bigby nearly shit himself when he saw what it was that had actually thrown him. He had never laid eyes on a monster like this one before. Grey mottled skin, talons at the end of its hands, hair covering most of its face, it reminded him somewhat of the original wolfman from the old black and white movies. Well, except for the white muzzle.

Bigby continued walking backward, dragging Ben with him, the knife against his throat as he worked his way to the back corner and the elevators. "Get me Mitchell, dammit!"

If he couldn't kill all of the American hunters, he could at least cut the head off the snake. It also brought him a certain bit of satisfaction that Walter Simmons would be made to suffer when his rich bitch daughter dropped dead alongside her mate. He actually smiled as he reached behind him and pressed wildly for the elevator button.

"Nobody tries to follow us, you got it? Tell Mitchell that we're taking this all the way down and he's to meet us there. Just him. If I see anybody else, I kill this man on the spot! You hear me?"

The door began to open and sounded with a ding. Bigby barely glanced behind him before backing into the open lift. He stepped into the elevator as a pair of hands reached out and gripped his head, twisting quickly, snapping his neck.

He slumped to the ground with Ben holding the arm with the knife away from his neck. He stepped back from the body and turned around. He gave Jennifer a lopsided grin and a nod. "I guess I owe you one, ma'am."

"Nope. I owed him one for killing Mick." She kicked Bigby in the kidneys before stepping over his body and out of the elevator. "May he rot in hell for all the pain he's caused."

*****

Spalding's coms came to life in his ear and he pressed a finger to his earbud. "Come in, Delta One. This is OPCOM calling Delta Actual, do you read, over?"

"Read you loud and clear, OPCOM."

The relief in Colonel Mitchell's voice was apparent as he came back across the radio. "Thank God. Sitrep, Actual."

Spanky paused and took a deep breath. "Two tangos neutralized, OPCOM. We lost Delta Five."

"Say again, Actual. Has Five still not been located?"

"Negative, Colonel. Gus Tracy was lost in action, sir. We're bringing him home." Spanky paused a moment then added, "Request clean up teams. Doc's gonna want to look at these tangos."

There was a long pause before OPCOM responded. "Roger that, Actual. Clean up teams are dispatched to your location." The channel stayed open a moment longer and Spalding waited...he knew the colonel wanted to say something more, but what can you say? Every man goes into this job knowing that each day could be his last and praying that it isn't.

Sullivan and Donovan carried Gus Tracy's body out in the body bag that each man carried in his pack. Lamb and Jacobs lead the way to the trap door near the clearing and helped lift Gus out and placed him in the clearing.

Sullivan disarmed the tripwire trap before the clean up teams arrived and Delta Team sat quietly in the clearing waiting for the helicopters to break the silence.

Donovan was the first to speak. "Do you think there could be more of them?"

Spalding gave him a surprised look. "Why would you ask that?"

"There was a male and a female. They had to come from somewhere. And that's a pretty elaborate tunnel system down there."

Spalding shrugged. "Who knows, those tunnels could be thousands of years old. Those things looked like cavemen. Maybe they're Neanderthals. I have no clue. If they are, then, those tunnels could be tens of thousands of years old."

"And, we're supposed to believe that the population ended up being just two?" Donovan asked.

Spalding shrugged again. "Not my job code to care."

Sullivan looked to the sky. "Choppers inbound."

Spalding stood and dusted his pants off. "Let's get Gus ready to go home."

*****

Viktor had gathered his wolves and left unceremoniously. Rufus knew better than to try to smooth things over with him now. Things were too raw with the man. Perhaps in time he could rekindle the friendship, but he feared that things would never truly be the same. He watched the large man leave the building and he felt something akin to an ache in his chest. He dismissed it right away. Time had a way of making things right and he knew that once Viktor saw that he was mistaken about his intentions, the two could begin again. It would take patience. Unfortunately, Rufus was not very good at waiting.

He now sat at the table, his security forces surrounding him. "I know that you're not exactly fond of wolves, but I need your assistance. My most trusted associates have decided to cut their ties with me and I find myself in need of those who cannot be swayed by other vampires. Or sunlight.

"My liege, perhaps if you told us what you were needing?" his head of security stated, bowing deeply.

Rufus leaned back in the chair, his hands steepled together. "I need a crew of wolves who can go to the Americas and…dig something up."

"Chancellor?"

"A certain, *artifact* that needs to be dealt with." Rufus smiled and it didn't reach his eyes.

"And where would this artifact be, my liege?"

"Buried under tons of concrete. In the deserts of Nevada…"

*****

Jameson continued to watch the video that was transmitted to him and studied the dark figure who seemed impervious to gunfire, shredded humans with his bare hands and moved faster than any person should be allowed to move.

"What's your take?"

He paused the video and leaned back in his chair. "I'm not convinced that they're all capable of this. This may well be one single…*person*."

Ingram nodded. "Or they knew that, with this kind of ability, only one operator would be needed outside, so they only sent one."

Jameson sighed and slid the file across the desk to him then clicked off the video player on his computer. "It's settled then. We put our plans on hiatus. We watch them for a while and see what more we can learn about them before we commit to the plan."

Ingram picked up the file and nodded. "Agreed." He stood to leave Jameson's office then paused. "Have we heard anything more from the Council?"

Jameson nodded. "Actually, there's been a power shift." He leaned over and pulled open a drawer on his desk. He pulled a folder and slid it across his desk. "There *is* no more Council, per se. There's only one person running the show now."

"Oh really?" Ingram opened the file folder and looked at the grainy photograph. "Where'd you get this?"

"A spy in Geneva. He just sent that over. Looks like a cell phone picture."

"So instead of a group of assholes, it's just one asshole. Great." Ingram closed the file and laid it on the desk. "Do we have anything on him yet?"

"Just a name. Thorn."

"I'll put my people on it and see what we can dig up on him." Ingram stood to leave. "Let me know if you find out anything else from your spy."

Jameson watched him leave and picked up the folder. He opened it and studied the young man in the grainy picture. "Friend or foe, Mr. Thorn? Friend or foe?"

EPILOGUE

Kalen finished packing his meager belongings and closed the door to his room. He paused outside of Brooke's room and pressed his forehead to the steel door. He placed his hand against it and tried to feel her inside. Some flicker of her essence…a shadow of her once having been there.

All he felt was cold steel under his palm.

He pushed off the door and walked down the hallway. Jack rounded the corner and intercepted him. "Hey, kid, got a minute?"

Kalen turned and tried to give him his full attention. "Yes, Chief Jack?"

Jack pulled a cloth bundle out and unwrapped it. "I wanted to ask you about this."

Kalen's eyes widened when he saw the polished stone. "Where did you get this, Chief Jack?"

"Loren gave it to me after our first encounter and the big fight with all of the vampires in the desert." He hefted the rock and held it near Kalen's Gatekeeper. "Are they the same kind of rock?"

"Yes, they are. This is a very large and very rare Gatekeeper." He held his hand over his own stone and lowered his voice, "I cannot believe that she would give this to you, Chief Jack."

Jack held his hand up. "I didn't steal it, I promise." He wrapped it back up and slipped it into the leather satchel. "I didn't even know what it was until she called me on it. Even then, I honestly just thought that it was…I dunno, like an Elf cell phone."

Kalen shook his head, obviously confused. "I do not…"

"A communication…thing."

"It is also a Gatekeeper."

"So, I could open doorways through stone with it?"

Kalen nodded. "If you practice."

"Practice? Like…are there phone numbers or?"

337

"I do not…you simply have to concentrate on *where* you want to go."

"Concentrate?"

"Very much. Yes." Kalen placed a hand on his shoulder. "Good luck, Chief Jack."

"Are you taking Azrael home today?" Jack fell into step beside the young warrior.

"Yes. Allister has been returned to his mountain and Gnat is with Bartholomew. Gideon awaits Azrael's return this evening. Then I will return home."

Jack cleared his throat. "You know, you don't have to go back."

Kalen paused and shook his head. "No, I must."

"It isn't worth it, kid. Yeah, they used you, but—"

"I am returning home to take my place as Gatekeeper, Chief Jack. That is all." Kalen's eyes reflected a sadness that Jack couldn't comprehend. He studied the young warrior who now appeared much, much older.

"Okay, Kalen. But, if you ever change your mind, you can always come and visit me and the pack. They've relocated to a small town in Washington State. We could use someone like you there."

"I will be fine, Chief Jack. Thank you."

Jack watched as the golden skinned warrior walked away and he felt as though he were losing a friend. Again.

*****

Mark sat on the examination table and groaned. "Please tell me it isn't the asshole-and-ballsack tea again?"

"I left the dirty sock out this time." Evan poured the mixture into a mug and handed it to him.

"But, Doc, look at me. I'm back to normal now. Skin is the normal shade of peachy tan, fingernails look like fingernails, the only facial hair is the stuff I don't shave off…give me a break.

You've been making me drink this stuff every day since I wolfed out."

Evan nodded. "We need to build up your system."

Mark groaned again and held the cup in his hands. He scrunched his face as the odor rose to his nostrils. "I think you're just doing this to get back at me."

"I am a professional, Major. I would not stoop to such levels. Now, drink up." Evan tipped the cup toward his mouth.

"Ugh..." Mark held his breath and did his best to swallow the mixture with one swallow. "Gah! At least it doesn't knock me out anymore."

"True. And we'll keep refining it until you can have a fight-or-flight response and not 'wolf out' as you call it."

Mark grunted. "Hey, that whole wolfing out thing came in handy when it happened."

"True. But until we can figure out a way for you to control it, we need to keep it at bay."

Mark hopped off the table and set the mug on the counter. "Great. So, same time tomorrow?"

"Of course." Evan reached for the cup and gave Mark a smirk. "And tomorrow I'll be sure to use a dirty sock."

"You're all heart, Doc."

*****

Sullivan stood over Brooke's remains and did his best to maintain himself. Spalding placed a reassuring hand on the big man's shoulder. "All I can think to say is, I'm sorry. I know that doesn't help."

"I keep thinking how I had just got her back. She was like she was when she left. I mean, when she was taken." He sniffed back the tears that threatened. "And I keep thinking to how I wanted to put her down if I ever encountered her and..." his voice caught in his throat.

"I know. I know." Spalding squeezed his shoulder.

The technician entered the makeshift morgue and nodded to Spalding. "It's time."

"Just give us a minute." He turned and lowered his voice, "They need to take her now, bud."

Sullivan nodded and patted the body bag. He tried not to think of his initial shock and anger when they returned and he was first told of his sister's demise. They had told him that she died in battle at first, but then he found out the details and he wanted to punch something…destroy something…to scream, to yell, to vent his anger and frustration on something, anything. Instead, he collapsed in the floor and cried just like he had done when she was first taken.

He watched as they wheeled her into the other room and Spalding stood by his side as they loaded her onto the conveyor and fed her body to the crematorium. When the flames rose he felt the heat through the closed door and he suddenly felt utterly alone.

Spalding must have sensed that feeling. He placed a reassuring hand on the man's back. "You still got us, brother. I know it's not the same, but we're family."

Little John nodded and turned away. He had to pay his respects to Gus before they 'processed' him.

*****

Mitchell sat quietly in his office while Laura paced slowly. She told her story and avoided his gaze the entire time. When she finished, she stopped and hadn't realized that she had been crying. She stood, staring at the floor and wiped at her cheeks. "I'm sorry, sir."

"For what part?"

"All of it. For not telling you why I was leaving. For stealing the serum. For lying to you…for crying about the whole damned thing." She stood up straight and squared her shoulders. "I'm ready."

"For what?"

"To face whatever punishment you think is appropriate for my actions." She stared straight ahead and felt her legs shake as her mind raced at the endless possibilities.

Mitchell exhaled loudly and stood from his chair. He walked to the mini bar and poured himself a tall glass of scotch. He glanced over his shoulder and decided to pour a second one. "At ease already."

Matt set the scotch in front of her and sat back down. "That's a hell of a story."

She picked the scotch up with trembling hands and took a large swallow. "I debated on keeping it to myself, but it was eating at me."

"And the whole cock-and-bull story about the stuff we do here crossing the line and you needed to get away?"

She shrugged. "Well, okay, that part was true too."

Mitchell took a long pull of the scotch and enjoyed the burn as it went down. "Oh, man, I missed this stuff." He pointed to the mini bar. "That's the missus' idea. She likes a stiff one every now and then."

Laura gave him a cockeyed stare and Mitchell stammered. "I meant a stiff *drink*."

"I knew what you meant, Colonel." She set the glass down and studied him. "What do you intend to do about me?"

Mitchell drained his glass and set it next to hers. "I guess it's a good goddamn thing you never breathed a word of it to me, Ms. Youngblood. Otherwise, I'd be obliged to throw you to the wolves, so to speak. But, since you didn't, and you never will...and yes, that IS an order, then I guess we won't have to worry about it, will we?" Mitchell stood and refilled his scotch. "However, and let me be absolutely clear about this...don't cross any more lines like this again."

Matt kept his back to her as he put the stopper back in the decanter. "I would like to think that my civilian rep would feel that she could come to me with *any* problem. That she felt like she could trust me with anything." He turned and gave her a look that she couldn't quite read. For the briefest of moments, she felt as though his feelings were hurt that she hadn't trusted him. "That she would know I would do anything to help. Including breaking the rules. Again."

She studied him and felt herself smiling at him. "Understood, sir."

"Good. Now, finish your scotch and then you get your skinny little ass back out there and get back to work." He lifted his glass to her.

She lifted her glass in salute. "Never let a good scotch go to waste, sir."

*****

Chad McKenzie sat alone in the Close Quarters Trainer and stared upward at the acrylic windows. He could see the different personnel going about their day, performing their duties and menial tasks. He turned back to the silhouette target he had pinned on the target board and leveled his weapon.

Dry firing at the target, he imagined the bullets entering and exiting the target, blood spraying, brains splattering as the silver jacketed rounds ripped through flesh and bone. He lowered his weapon and smiled.

"Don't worry, Sully, your day is coming. You won't be in misery for much longer." He advanced on the target, dry firing as he stepped closer. When he reached the target, he dropped his weapon and pulled his tantō-bladed knife. He stabbed at the paper image of Little John until only shredded pieces of the black and white image were left.

"I said it before, and I'll say it again. Ain't nobody gonna kill you but me."

From the desk of Heath Stallcup

A personal note:

Thank you so much for investing your time in reading my story. If you enjoyed it, please take a moment and leave a review. I realize that it may be an inconvenience, but reviews mean the world to authors…

Also, I love hearing from my readers. You can reach me at my blog: http://heathstallcup.com/ or via email at heathstallcup@gmail.com

Feel free to check out my Facebook page for information on upcoming releases: https://www.facebook.com/heathstallcup find me on Twitter at @HeathStallcup, Goodreads or via my Author Page at Amazon.

My stories so far:

The Monster Squad Series

The first saga:

Humanity has spent its time enjoying a peace that can only be had through blissful ignorance. For centuries, stories of things that go "bump" in the night have been passed down and shared. When creatures of the night proved to be real, the best of America's

military came together to form an elite band of rapid response teams. Their mission: to keep the civilian populace safe from those threats and hide all evidence of their existence.

This time, they face the largest threat ever to rise against mankind as it prepares its own twisted Apocalypse. The only thing standing in its way is the Monster Squad. Man and monster will fight side by side in an epic battle to the death to try to defeat an evil so great, it could only have been created by the hand of God Himself.

The second saga:

An ancient evil is awakened by a naïve pawn. Planned centuries in advance by fallen angels, the reign of Lilith is put into motion. With a legion of demons at her command, she plans to enact her revenge upon the world's largest religious group before thrusting herself center stage and taking her seat upon the throne as Queen of the World.

With threats coming at them from every angle, the Monster Squad turns to an ex-member to form a new team—a team made up of the most unlikely warriors to hunt down and face the Demon Queen.

However, when it comes time to remove the Queen in this grand game of chess, will they be able to sacrifice their own game pieces to do it?

Caldera

For years, the biggest threat Yellowstone was thought to offer was in the form of its semi-dormant super volcano. Little did anyone realize the threat was real and slowly working its way to the surface, but not in the form of magma. Lying deep within the bowels of the earth itself, an ancient virus waited.

Recently credited with wiping out the Neanderthals, the virus is released within the park and quickly spreads. A desperate plea for assistance reaches the military, but are they coming to help those battling for their lives or to wipe out every living thing in an effort to prevent a second mass extinction? Can humanity survive the raging cannibals that erupt from within?

Whispers

How does a sheriff's department from a small North Texas community stop a brutal murderer who is already dead and buried?

When grave robbers disturb the tomb of Sheriff James 'Two Guns' Tolbert searching for Old West relics, a vengeful spirit is unleashed, hell bent for blood. Over a hundred years in the making, a vengeful spirit hunts for its killers. If those responsible couldn't be made to pay, then their progeny would.

Even when aided by a Texas Ranger and UCLA Paranormal Investigators, can modern-day law enforcement stop a spirit destined to fulfill an oath made in death? An oath fueled by passion from a love cut down before its time?

Forneus Corson

Nothing comes easy and nothing is ever truly free. When Steve Wilson stumbles upon the best-kept secret of history's most successful writers, he can't help but take advantage of it. Little did he know it would come back to haunt him in ways he'd never have dreamt... even in his worst nightmares.

With his life turned upside down, his name discredited, his friends persecuted, the authorities chasing him for something he didn't do, Steve finds himself on the run with nothing but his wits and his best friend by his side. When a man finds himself hitting rock bottom, he thinks there's little else he can do but go up... unless he's facing an evil willing to dig the hole deeper. An evil in the business of pitting men against odds so great, they risk losing their very souls in the attempt to escape...

For a refreshing change of pace, check out this exciting new Young Adult Zombie thriller from JJ Beal.

Lions & Tigers & Zombies, Oh My!

The cold war has heated up again. This time the battle will be fought in every street of America.

Trapped in a major city, hours from their small town country home, a team of young girls find themselves cut off from everyone they know and left to fend for themselves as the world spins out of control.

With nothing but their wits, their softball equipment, and their friendship to hold them together, they face incredible odds as they fight their way across the state. Physical, emotional and psychological challenges meet them at every turn as they struggle to find the family they can't be sure survived. How much more can they endure before reaching the breaking point?

ABOUT THE AUTHOR

Heath Stallcup was born in Salinas, California and relocated to Tupelo, Oklahoma in his tween years. He joined the US Navy and was stationed in Charleston, SC and Bangor, WA shortly after junior college. After his second tour he attended East Central University where he obtained BS degrees in Biology and Chemistry. Heath then served ten years with the State of Oklahoma as a Compliance and Enforcement Officer while moonlighting nights and weekends with his local Sheriff's Office. He still lives in the small township of Tupelo, Oklahoma with his wife and three of his seven children. He steals time to write between household duties, going to ballgames, being a grandfather to five and being the pet of numerous animals that have taken over his home. Visit him at heathstallcup.com or Facebook.com for news of his upcoming releases.

Customers also Purchased:

Shawn Chesser
Surviving The Zombie Apocalypse Series

T.W. Brown
The Dead Series

John O'Brien
New World Series

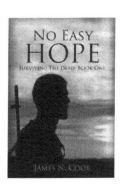

James N. Cook
Surviving The Dead Series

Mark Tufo
Zombie Fallout Series

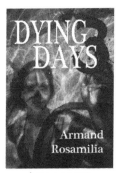

Armand Rosamillia
Dying Days Series

Made in the USA
San Bernardino, CA
03 January 2017